MW00327244

GONE FISHING

The Sinker

Aileen,
I Hope you
enjoy the ending!
Love
Herr
Desrosiers
11/13/19

Jane Herr Desrosiers

Copyright © 2019 Jane Herr Desrosiers
All rights reserved
First Edition

Fulton Books, Inc.
Meadville, PA

First originally published by Fulton Books 2019

ISBN 978-1-63338-874-1 (Paperback)
ISBN 978-1-63338-875-8 (Digital)

Printed in the United States of America

The Novels of Jane Herr Desrosiers
The Piney Bluffs Trilogy
Gone Fishing: The Hook
Gone Fishing: The Line
Gone Fishing: The Sinker

Books are available on Amazon, Nook, Kindle,
Apple iTunes Store, or Google Play
Barnes & Noble
Bank Square Books, Mystic, Connecticut
Savoy Bookshop and Café, Westerly, Rhode Island

Follow me
Facebook: Jane Herr Desrosiers
http://www.janeherrdesrosiers.com
My blog: See Jane, See Jane Write
E-mail: janeherr51@att.net
Instagram: janeherr51

I DEDICATE THIS BOOK TO MY mother and father. They both have long since passed from this earth. My mom, Stephanie Natorski Herr, was a strong and loving woman who nurtured my body and soul and encouraged me at every step of my life. My dad, George Wilson Herr, was an avid reader and a loving curmudgeon. He taught me the love of fishing, even though I was a girl. For those of you who knew them, I know you will catch many glimpses of their kindness, sense of family, wit, and crustiness within these pages. I'm sure my dad would have enjoyed these books. G'night, Daddy. G'night, Mommy.

Nothing we do, however virtuous, can be accomplished alone; therefore we must be saved by love. No virtuous act is quite as virtuous from the standpoint of our friend or foe as it is from our standpoint. Therefore, we must be saved by the final form of love which is forgiveness.

—Reinhold Niebuhr, 1892-1971

CONTENTS

Chapter 1 9

Chapter 2 17

Chapter 3 21

Chapter 4 27

Chapter 5 35

Chapter 6 39

Chapter 7 48

Chapter 8 54

Chapter 9 60

Chapter 10 71

Chapter 11 80

Chapter 12 86

Chapter 13 91

Chapter 14 99

Chapter 15 106

Chapter 16 110

Chapter 17 120

Chapter 18 128

Chapter 19 134

Chapter 20 143

Chapter 21 149

Chapter 22 155

Chapter 23 166

Chapter 24 171

Chapter 25 175
Chapter 26 182
Chapter 27 187
Chapter 28 194
Chapter 29 203
Chapter 30 212
Chapter 31 218
Chapter 32 226
Chapter 33 234
Chapter 34 240
Chapter 35 246
Chapter 36 251
Chapter 37 260
Chapter 38 268
Chapter 39 275
Chapter 40 281

Epilogue 289
A Taste of Piney Bluffs 295

CHAPTER 1

I WAS ANGRY. REALLY ANGRY. I looked at the birth certificate again. The birth certificate of Sophie Anne Blake. Blake? My *sister* Sophie. I had finally found a relative on my mother's side of the family. The entire path to her discovery was mind-blowing. Daddy had never known anything about Momma having a child before they met; that was inconceivable in itself, given the fact that the doctors had told Momma that she might die giving birth to me, which she did shortly after I was born. Sophie's self-confessed father, Joseph Howe, had spent his lifetime living a lie. A lie that had kept an innocent man, Andre St. Pierre, in prison for nearly fifty years. This intricate charade had been orchestrated by Joseph's father, all in the name of carrying on the family tradition at West Point. And now, I had learned both things: Andre St. Pierre was an innocent man, and I had a sister I had never known about.

And now this? The name of the father wasn't Joseph? Henry Blake? How could Henry Blake be the father? Henry Blake was the town clerk of Oxford. I'd had several conversations with him over the past several months, once I had discovered Momma's house. And he'd sent this birth certificate to me. This made no sense. Joseph had professed his love for my mother, a love that ended when his devious father had sent her away to have their child. But Henry was the father?

I slammed the paper onto the counter and turned to Charlie. He had read the birth certificate first.

"Do you believe this?" I asked. I was trying to remain calm as our son EC toddled around the kitchen. Moments before, he'd begun his maiden voyage into the walking world. Walking, which had brought both of us to tears of joy. But now the tears were hot and stung my cheeks as I read and reread this certificate.

"How can this be? Who do I believe at this point? Is there anyone in my life who has told the truth about my mother?" I pleaded to him.

"Ethel, now, let's think this through," Charlie said as he stepped close to hold me.

"What's there to think about? It's here in print. Certified by the Maine Department of Vital Records. I have a sister, and Joseph is not the father of my sister. Henry is. I don't understand." I began to cry into his shoulder. The softness of his flannel shirt was comforting as he let me cry myself out for a few minutes. I sighed and tried to lose myself in the safety of his arms. My husband respected me for my independent ways and had been by my side as we had uncovered the truth for Andre. But now he knew that independence be damned, I needed to be held and protected.

"Come on, Ethel. There's nothing we can do right now. Tomorrow's Christmas Eve, and there'll be time enough to sort all this out in a week or two. You've got a few days off from the paper, so let's enjoy the holidays. Look, we received our Christmas miracle with EC walking." He tilted my head upward and kissed my lips as softly as a feather. He was my rock, my partner in crime, and the best thing that had ever happened to me.

"But it's just not right!" I said as I held the certificate in my hand. "All I want is the truth. Why is that so damn hard to get?"

"You'll get it, I know you will, but it won't be today. Now stop." Charlie held me and stroked my hair.

"You're right. As always," I said and closed my eyes for one more snuggle on his shoulder. And then I felt a tug at my jeans and little arms wrapping around my leg.

"Mommy," EC said and looked up at me with more love than I could have imagined possible.

"Oh, baby," I said and picked him up. He patted my cheeks and then leaned in to give me a fish-lips kiss. "You are the sweetest. Just like your daddy." A couple more tears fell from my eyes. EC patted my wet cheeks again and giggled.

"See, Mommy, your boys will take care of everything," Charlie said and put his arms around both of us.

"I guess you will. Now let's put the rest of this stuff away." I consented to leaving the topic of the birth certificate alone for now and returned to putting the groceries away.

"Say, why don't we go to Andy's for supper and celebrate our track star?" Charlie said as he put the last of the squash and the bags of cranberries into the fridge.

"Great idea. Let me give Daddy a call, and he can meet us. He'll be so happy," I said as I picked up the receiver of the kitchen wall phone. As I waited for Daddy to answer, I watched as my boy toddled over to Mutt and Jeff. His arms reached out to hug them around their furry necks. They were golden retriever brothers, and they let EC hang all over them, saying his baby version of *good boys*. Finally, Daddy picked up.

"Yup, your nickel, start talking," Daddy deadpanned.

"Oh, Daddy," I said, scolding him with those two words.

"Hey. What's my girl up to?" His mood changed. "Get down from there."

"Who's on what?" I asked.

"Oh, that damned cat is trying to walk along the mantelpiece and keeps knocking over my Christmas cards. Get, I said." I could imagine Daddy with a rolled-up newspaper slapping the chair to get Mr. Striper's attention. I could also envision Mr. Striper, a big yellow tabby, giving Daddy the look of "Who, me?" and continuing as only a cat would do.

"Well, if you're not too cranky, want to meet us at the Diner for supper? We have a surprise for you," I teased him.

"Surprise. I don't need no damn surprise. But I would like a nice burger, or maybe Andy's got some meatloaf left. Little bit of gravy on my mashed potatoes, and I could die a happy man," he said as he dreamed out loud about his menu options.

"Now, Daddy, no one's dying today. Just meet us there, okay?" I answered him.

"See you soon." And with that, he hung up.

11

On the drive into town, I noticed the new house that was going up. It was a big cape with an attached garage. Like ours, it had the river adding to its appeal. They'd made a lot of progress this fall, as the snows had held off for a bit.

"Do you know who they are?" I asked Charlie as we passed it.

"Yes and no. I met the builder. Guy from Massachusetts. He and his brother are in the business. Doing a good job too. He gave me the name of the couple, but it's slipped my mind. He's retired military, and she's a writer. Sounds like they'll be good neighbors," he reported.

"Hmm, if she's a writer, that would great for the Emporium," I answered.

The Emporium was going to be the new business venture for the Browning brothers, Russell and Robert. Owners of a publishing house in New York City and would-be fishermen, they'd found their way to Piney Bluffs several years ago and had fallen in love with the town and the people. Charlie was building their brain child, The Book Emporium, that would connect to Miss Ruthie's bakery. The brothers loved all of Ruthie's baked goods and had even helped Miss Ruthie to write and publish her first cookbook. They promised the opportunities were going to be twofold and threefold, as they were considering bringing writer's workshops and author readings to the great state of Maine.

Pulling into a spot in front of the Diner, I saw that Daddy was already inside and talking to Andy. He looked up at the sound of the car and came out to get EC.

"Hey, there's my guy. How are you today?" And Daddy scooped EC from his car seat and carried his adoring fan into the Diner.

"Hi, Andy. What's for supper?" I asked as we got in and took a booth.

"Ethel, Charlie, good to see you. Let's see, your dad commandeered the last piece of meatloaf," he said and nodded toward Daddy. "I've got some nice cod, just came in today. I can broil it the way you like it, lemon and butter. Judy made some coleslaw to go with it. And Ruthie sent over a few loaves of French bread. Now, how does that sound?" He stood with his hands on the counter, waiting for us to say yes.

"I'm sold," I said and looked at Charlie.

"Make that two, and how about a hot dog for the little guy?" Charlie replied.

"You got it," Andy said and went straight to work on our order.

"Not too many folks out tonight," I said. We were the only folks in the Diner, save for George, the oilman, who was finishing up his pie. I looked out the window at the quiet streets surrounding the green. The Diner had been decorated with Christmas garlands and twinkling lights. Each window had a different theme. Ours had little tractors, which was captivating EC at the moment.

"Yeah, lots of people have house parties or last-minute shopping. That's okay. Nice to wind down a bit. You're all coming to the Inn tomorrow night?" Andy asked as he went from the front to the back as he prepared our meal.

"We'll be there," I answered. "I'll give Jackie a call today and ask what I can bring."

"Don't bother. You know Mrs. F. She'll have it all under control," Andy said more into the grill and oven than to us.

"Hi, Ethel, Charlie, Eddy. I hear you got your meal order in. So what are y'all having to drink?" Judy asked. Judy had been a waitress at the Diner since she graduated from high school several years ago. She lived with and took care of her mom, who had multiple sclerosis. Judy had a snappy wit and good advice on today's specials. She removed her pencil from her braid, which she'd decorated with artificial poinsettias, and had it poised to take down the rest of the order.

"Junior's having a chocolate milk. You got his cup, Ethel," Daddy said, making sure EC was first to be taken care of. I handed over his sippy cup to her. EC watched carefully as the cup left his eyesight and got into the hands of a stranger. "I'll have a coffee. And you two?"

"I'd love a glass of wine, but I'll settle for tea," I joked.

"Me too," said Judy. "I told Andy he needs to work on getting his liquor license."

"Water's good for me," Charlie answered.

13

"No need for booze in here. No sense giving family competition!" Andy yelled out from the back. Andy's son, Andy Jr., was married to my best friend, Jackie. And Jackie's parents owned the Trout Brook Inn. Specializing in gourmet meals and cocktails, the Inn had an amazing reputation. "Besides, I'd need a bigger inventory of glasses for Judy to break. I don't think I could afford that. Hell, I can barely afford what she breaks now."

"I heard that!" Judy replied good-naturedly as she readied our drinks and brought them over. "Food will be out in a bit. You folks relax. Here's some crackers for the little guy." And Judy produced a packet of oyster crackers for EC to busy himself with.

"So what's this surprise?" Daddy finally asked after a few sips of coffee.

"Oh, that's right. Let me get EC." And daddy moved out of the seat while I took EC out of his booster. I sat back down and put EC's feet on the ground. I held his hands to steady him and said, "Go see Grampa." With a little wobble, he put one foot in front of the other and he walked over to Daddy. EC put his hands out, and Daddy grabbed him up in his arms. Daddy's eyes glistened.

"This right here is the best damn Christmas present I've ever had! Andy, Judy, George, look at my grandson. He's walking!" he said in a voice that was choking back the tears. And they all came to see our little guy. "God, I love this boy." And Daddy hugged EC for a moment until he squirmed to get down. "You'll have your hands full now." And he watched as EC walked over to George and tugged on his oil-stained pants. Andy and Judy came over to the counter to watch too.

"Hey, little guy. Well, look at you, walking. He's doing a good job, Ethel." George had turned in his stool to watch him walk away.

"He just started walking today. We're celebrating, George." I swelled with pride.

"I remember when mine were that big. Boy, doesn't take long. Well, you all have a Merry Christmas. I got one more call out on the other side of the lake. And then that's it. I'm taking tomorrow off to do my Christmas shopping." And he put on his cap and gave EC's head a little tousle.

"Merry Christmas to you too, George," we all said.

"He just started today?" Daddy asked, watching as EC toddled around the Diner, holding on to a stool here and there to steady himself.

"Yup. I turned around and there he was, standing and smiling," Charlie answered. I held back the tears that I knew, if they came out, would never stop.

The door jingled open, and in walked Caleb.

"I must be paying you too much as an assistant editor if you're eating out," Caleb remarked as he came in and took a seat at the counter. It was then that he noticed EC walking around. "Oh, good Lord. What have we here!" He looked at me with a big smile and shook his head in amazement.

"How about that?" I said.

"When?" Caleb asked as he continued to watch EC toddling and exploring the booths and tables.

"Oh, about an hour or so ago," Charlie answered, looking at his watch to check the time.

"See, I knew there was nothing wrong," Caleb stated. "Wait till Sadie hears this. She'll be tickled pink." While Caleb was my boss and editor for *The Daily Bugle*, he was like family and had lived my anxieties and fears for the past months when EC had failed to walk. A childless couple, he and Sadie were EC's unofficial uncle and aunt and were very supportive of us.

"What are you having tonight, Caleb?" Judy was standing at the counter with her pencil, ready to take his order.

"Is there any kind of dessert left? Sadie's been experimenting with the flavors of the season, as she puts it, and it hasn't been good. I need something to get the taste of peppermint sage brownies out of my mouth," Caleb replied and grimaced. Sadie's reputation for cooking was well-known. Sometimes her combinations were like putting together oranges and newspapers—nothing good came from it.

"My, peppermint and sage, interesting," Judy commented. "Let's see, I've got a slice of triple-layer chocolate frosted cake, which I can make into à la mode with vanilla ice cream. Or I have—"

"Go no further. Sold!" Caleb said. "A coffee to go along with that and I'm fine."

"You got it." Judy nodded and started plating his cake and ice cream.

"And here's dinner for the rest of you," Andy said as he brought out our plates.

"Hmmm. This meatloaf is the best, and the gravy. I've got to hand it to you, Andy," Daddy said as he tasted his first forkful.

"That's what I like to hear. Makes me a happy man. Anything else?" he said as our meals were now set in front of us.

"I think we're good. This cod is so good, Andy," I said as I took a bite of the flaky white fish. I watched as EC took his hot dog out of the bun and held it in his hand like a lollipop. Thank goodness he didn't like mustard or relish yet! I could just envision the messes to come. But the smile on his face let me know that for now, he was as happy as could be.

We talked back and forth with Caleb, Andy, and Judy as we ate. This was what Piney Bluffs was all about. A community of people who cared and respected one another. We'd been blessed with a beautiful environment. Fishing in our pristine lake and rivers was what brought people here and made them return. Every once in a while, they stayed forever, like Caleb and Sadie, or Charlie. They added their special talents to bring a richer way of life to all of us here in our little piece of heaven.

CHAPTER 2

"NO, NO, NO, EC!" AND I ran to grab him as he pulled the candy cane from the big stuffed Santa's hand. We hadn't been at the Inn for more than ten minutes, and he'd already been into the woodland animal display, saying "Woof, woof" and tried to grab the red frosted-sugar cookies from the edge of the dessert table. And now this. "I'm so sorry, Mrs. F."

"Not to worry. It's so wonderful to see him walking all around," she said. She straightened the display and put the "woof woofs" back in their places. The Inn was beautifully decorated with a themed Christmas tree in each of the areas. We were gathered in the lounge, and the tree had different birds and animal ornaments. Garlands had been made from the tiniest of vines and held little white lights, giving the tree a starlit appearance. The larger stuffed animals were standing near the tree and were outfitted with either plaid vests or satin bows. A nearly life-size Santa sat in a corner chair, as if waiting to hear the wishes of the next young child. Just the thing to attract a toddler.

"I thought so, too, for the first day. Now I'm not so sure." I raced to grab the candy cane from his hand.

"Well, my friend, welcome to your new exercise program. Sprinting, bending, stretching, and weight lifting." Jackie laughed as she placed the lobster puffs on the table.

"Where's my guy?" Daddy said as he entered the room.

"Grampa." EC squirmed out of my arms and was off toddling his way to Daddy.

"Oh, thank goodness," I said and collapsed into a side chair.

"Ethel, hold the door for Charlie and Andy. They've got the wood for the fireplace," Andy Sr. asked. "Damn back. Good thing

I've got a few days to recuperate." *No rest for the wicked,* I thought and hurried to help.

"What happened, Andy?" I asked.

"I was trying to get a jump on things for the day after Christmas. I was loading up the flour and sugar. Those fifty-pound sacks are beginning to take a lot more out of me. Anyway, the flour sack started to slip off my shoulder, and I went to grab it before it hit the floor. There was a little snow on my boot, and that was all she wrote. A slip and a twist and down I went, flour sack on top of me. I was doing the twist and the limbo all at the same time. Chubby Checker got nothing on me with my twist. Trouble is, I didn't twist back as well as him!" Andy finished his story, and we all chuckled

"Chubby Checker, my foot!" Marge chimed in. Marge, wife of Andy Sr., was quick with her jibes at her husband. She shook her head. "He needs to go see a chiropractor. All those years hanging over that grill, why, the man can't stand up straight anymore."

"Oh, I'm fine. Just a little rest, maybe a little bourbon on the rocks, and I'll be good as new. To your health, my dear," Andy said and raised his glass of bourbon to his wife.

"Marge, I've got the number for you. Dr. Jeffrey Silverstein, he has a practice over in North Conway. He stays here a few times a year and can't say enough good things about Piney Bluffs. He's always telling me to come over and see him. He said he'll give a discount to anyone from here. It's worth the trip," Mrs. F said as she finished arranging the last items on the buffet.

"I'll take that number. He's too stubborn to admit that he's out of alignment," Marge answered.

"Can EC come and play with us?" little Jack asked me. He had come to my side and was carrying a bright-yellow Tonka dump truck. He and his brother Andy had set up their trains and trucks near the tree. What a welcome diversion!

"Yes, of course, he can," I answered. Jackie's boys were so good with EC. I watched as Jack took EC by the hand and led him over to their play area.

"I think it's about time to have our toast," Jackie's dad, Jack, said as he wheeled in the wooden beverage cart with the gleaming silver punch bowl. The ornate bowl and cups had been Mr. F's parents' and always made our Christmas toasts seem extra special. He started to ladle out the creamy goodness as Jackie helped hand them out. "Anyone have something to get us started?" he asked.

"I do," Daddy said and cleared his throat. "To the good friends gathered here tonight. May we always have full cups and full lives." We took our first sip. "Wow! Jack, this eggnog certainly has a good kick."

"I made it the way I always do," Jack replied. "One and one, a half-gallon and a pint. I'm not saying that I could have gotten things mixed up."

"Hear, hear, and I think it's absolutely the right ratio," Andy Sr. answered in agreement. "Now me. Here's to these good-looking ladies. I hope you continue to have pity on all of us gents and love us the best you can." Marge was now seated next to him and gave him a jab in the ribs. "Marge, watch it, or I won't be able to wrap your Christmas present!"

"Dad! I think the only gent that falls into that category is you!" Andy Jr. raised his glass. "To my lovely wife and family, blessings for another year of happiness." He held Jackie's hand and pulled her in for a kiss.

"These lobster puffs are tasty," I said as I crunched into the flaky delicacy. "What kind of cheese do you use?"

"A combination of cream cheese and Gruyère," Mrs. F said. "And a couple of other secret ingredients." She raised her eyebrows and smiled.

"Mom," Jackie chided her. "She cooks shallots down to nothing and then puts in some Old Bay."

"Well, I've got the secret now." I laughed, and with another bite the puff was gone.

"Jack and I wish that times like this will always be our tradition," Mrs. F said, changing the subject. She put her arm around her husband's waist and leaned into him.

"Yes, we do," Jack agreed. "Refills, anyone?" And we all held our cups out. We mingled and tasted the venison skewers and cups of fish chowder.

"I have one," Charlie said to continue our toasts. "To my beautiful and talented wife, and to my son. The best Christmas present a man could ever have." Our eyes met as we drank the silky liquid.

"Ethel, how about you?" Jackie asked. My friend was ready, with her cup raised. Her eyes searched mine as I hesitated for a moment. I looked around at the scene in front of me. It was as if Currier and Ives had met Norman Rockwell. Here was the homespun New England flavor of Christmas Eve. The clothing we wore was the rich textures of wools and corduroy with the colors of red and green plaids splashed in. The three boys playing with their toys in front of the tree. The food arranged on silver platters and chafing dishes, steaming, waiting to be devoured. The fireplace washed the room with a rich hue somewhere between gold and spun sugar. Everyone's cheeks held a healthy glow, eyes bright with the joy of the season. Here was my family. Whether by blood, marriage, or community, these were the best parts of my life. This was what that Christmas feeling was all about.

"Yes, I do have a toast. Love and smooth sledding for us all!" I said, paying homage to beginning of Momma's book, *Sophie's Sled.* I knew that only Charlie and Daddy might catch the reference. I thought about Momma and how she would have completed the circle of love that surrounded us tonight. While the recent events had cracked the pedestal that Daddy and I had put her on, I was certain that there was a reasonable explanation to all this. And yes, I had promised Charlie to take a break from any further search into the whereabouts of my half sister. But both he and I knew that it wouldn't be long before I was back at it. I wished beyond anything that by this time next year, there would be more people to add to the family. For that, I was almost sure.

CHAPTER 3

"Hey, sleepyhead, Merry Christmas." Charlie's voice was soft as he kissed my ear and pulled me into him.

"Is that you, Santa?" I murmured. I laced my hands into his and snuggled closer. "What time is it?" I looked toward the window and saw only a gray morning sky.

"Well, if we're having grilled cheese sandwiches for Christmas dinner, then time doesn't matter and we can pull the covers up, and I'll show you what your present is. If, on the other hand, you hope to serve a turkey dinner at one o'clock, then it's time to get your sweet butt out of bed, missy." And his hand slid down my back and massaged my left buttock.

"Oh, Santa," I said in a hushed tone. "Maybe we can postpone dinner until two?" Charlie's hand continued to explore and feel its way over my lower abdomen. I could feel that I wouldn't have to coax him into lingering a bit longer.

"How about one fifteen?" I rolled over to face him. His brown hair was tousled; his face held that special smile that was only for me. And with that, we celebrated Christmas morning with the fire of love, longing, and passion that burned as intensely today as it had the moment we'd met.

"Do you think they'd like stuffing with grilled cheese?" I said jokingly as I lay with my head on his chest, my fingers trailing over the muscles of his torso.

"You keep that up, and we'll be giving them candy canes and hot chocolate. Up you go, Julia Child. Let's show them what you've got." And so began our Christmas morning. Charlie went to get EC up, and I headed down to the kitchen. The dogs greeted me with their usual happy dances, and I let them out for their morning perimeter check.

I started to sauté the celery and onions in my cast-iron skillet with some butter and little bit of bacon fat. Aunt Eleanor told me the fat gave the stuffing a meaty flavor without adding the meat. The smell of just those few things made me ravenous. Or was it Santa's present? I chuckled to myself and put some cinnamon bread into the toaster. Charlie brought EC down and fixed his cereal and juice and got the coffee ready. The dogs scratched to come in, and our family was complete on this cozy Christmas morning.

"Merry Christmas!" I handed Mutt and Jeff new bones that they proudly held in their furry muzzles as they pranced over to their beds. "And Merry Christmas, EC." My boy cocked his head to one side as if to ask, "What's that?"

"We need to enjoy these first few years before he begins to under-stand what Christmas is really all about," Charlie said, shaking his head. "My brother said his boys' lists grow larger and larger each year."

"Jackie says so too. Maybe we won't tell him. Ever," I said, and we both laughed at that and I went back to the toaster.

"What are you still smiling about, Mrs. O'Connor?" Charlie asked. He came over and circled his arms around my waist as I but-tered my toast.

"I'll never tell." I turned to face him and gave him a bite of toast.

"Mommy," EC said. And there was our boy with his cereal bowl on his head, giggling away, eating his cereal off the tray of his high chair. Charlie and I couldn't help ourselves as we busted out into laughter.

"Oh, EC. What have you done? Thank goodness you like to eat your cereal dry." I went to pick him up from his chair. I brushed the cereal from his hair and fed him a few more pieces from the tray. The dogs took care of the cereal that made its way to the floor. While I had him in my arms, I brought him over to the Christmas tree and started to tell him about the ornaments. "And here's your first one from Auntie Jackie. And this one is for Mommy from Auntie." Jackie and I always exchanged ornaments on Christmas Eve. Last night, she'd given me a miniature deer slayer hat, like the one Sherlock

Holmes had worn. She said she might get me a real one if I insisted on going around solving mysteries the way I'd done in the past few years. EC started to squirm, having had enough of the historical ornament tour, and so I set him down.

Charlie was crumbing the stuffing bread into a big bowl that I'd found in Momma's kitchen. It was dark-blue pottery with just the tiniest of a chip on the edge. I added some Bell's seasoning to my mixture on the stove, adjusted the salt and pepper, and poured it over the bread. I put the turkey in the pan and began to stuff it. A little butter under the skin, some salt and pepper on top, an aluminum foil tent, and into the oven at seven o'clock. Consulting one of my grandmother's cookbooks, I noted that the time was thirty minutes per pound. We should be about right for a dinner time of one, but maybe it might be two, if the stuffing slowed it down. My Gammie would be so proud of me, fixing a dinner for family and friends. I was about five when she passed away. I remember that I called her Gammie because I couldn't say the letter *r* for the longest time

As I closed the cookbook, one of the bookmarks fluttered to the floor and almost went out of sight under the refrigerator. I put my foot out to stop it and saw that it was actually the backflap of an old envelope. There was a return address: Dr. A. Heard, 10 Willow Lane, Westmoreland Depot, New Hampshire. Funny, I wondered. Whom had the letter been addressed to? And who was Dr. Heard? Must have been one of my grandmother's friends, or was it something more? I checked the other bookmark. This one was an old postcard. The kind that was like a pastel-colored black-and-white. It was a street scene with a stone church and read, "West Chesterfield, New Hampshire." It was addressed to my grandmother. The writing had become very faint, but I could make out the words "Made it, all are well." The handwriting was not my mother's, for that I was sure. I'd seen her handwritten journals and college papers. No, this was someone else. Hmm. Who were the "all" that the sender referred to? The postmark was long since faded, so no help there. Why didn't I have time for this? I was sure if I thought about it, something would come to mind. Well, no time now. I removed them and placed them near my books in the living room.

"What's that?" Charlie asked as he got the vegetables out of the back room.

"Not sure, but there must be a reason Gammie kept them. Both are old. One's an envelope with a return address from a doctor in New Hampshire, and the other is an old postcard from West Chesterfield, New Hampshire. Interesting message," I answered and began to get out the pots.

"Well, they must be something if you're putting them over there with your things," he said. He knew me all too well. I'd made a spot by my chair where I put Momma's journal, her letter, and all things that I'd discovered about her over the past few years. I remembered that Momma graduated from Keene State in New Hampshire. Maybe she'd gotten sick? Yes, that was probably it. A letter from the doctor to my grandmother. But the postcard, now that was puzzling. Had Momma gone on a trip? But it wasn't her handwriting, so how could it be from Momma? So who was it from, and why was it saved?

"I'll figure it out later. Much later. Now, let's get moving there, mister. You're a little slow on your peeling." And so I dismissed the aged pieces of paper for the time being.

We worked together peeling and chopping the potatoes, carrots, and butternut squash. I rinsed some fresh cranberries and an orange to make cranberry sauce. A few moments in the blender with a little bit of sugar, and it was ready. I went through my checklist. Ruthie was bringing rolls and dessert, Russell and Robert were bringing a cheesecake, and I was sure that Ginny would show up with something to add to the feast. Charlie and I put another leaf in our table and covered it with the red-and-green checked tablecloth that Aunt Eleanor made several holidays ago.

"Ethel, how come we don't have your dad's brothers and their families over for a holiday dinner? They live so close," Charlie asked. We now began to set the table with white stoneware. The radio was tuned to an FM station in Portland, and Bing Crosby's "White Christmas" filled the air.

"I don't know. We were always at Aunt Ellie's when I was a kid. But then, it kind of stopped one year," I said as I folded the red linen napkins for each place. "A couple of times, we went over to the

Inn with Jackie and her family. Uncle Ellsworth got his nose out of joint about that. And then you came along and we started our life, bringing Daddy along with it. I mean, it's not like I don't talk to my aunts and uncles, for God's sake. Daddy lives next door to Ellsworth and Eubie, so they're always chatting." And my voice trailed off as I realized how I hadn't thought of how important Daddy's side of the family truly was to me.

They'd always been there as the people who helped Daddy to raise me. My aunts taught me to cook, sew, shop, and keep a house. My uncles helped Daddy in teaching me to fish, fix a leaky faucet, and have a drink when no one was watching. They'd made an all-around unfortunate situation for a widower and his child; seemed like the most normal thing in the world. I wiped the tears from my eyes as I continued to set the table. Charlie looked up and saw me. He came over and put his arms around me.

"Hey, now, I didn't want the waterworks to start. Come on, honey." And I let my tears soak his T-shirt.

"I'm such a brat. Here I've been so focused on Momma and my life that I've completely forgotten how important all of Daddy's family is to me. I have six cousins that I barely know anymore. They may be a little colorful and quirky, but they're our family too," I said as I sniffed back my runny nose. The nostalgia of the holiday made me feel guilty about Daddy's side of the family.

"That's okay. I'm sure they don't give it a second thought," he said, trying to console me.

"But I should think of them and include them in things. That would make Daddy happy too, I think," I said and started to ponder how I could do better at bringing my family together. "I know. This Memorial Day, we'll have big family picnic. The Koontz O'Connor family picnic. How does that sound?"

"I think that's a great idea. And don't worry, the O'Connors got quirky and colorful too! My mom will help get in touch with all on the O'Connor side. She'll love that. Feel better about this now?" He picked up my chin and looked into my eyes.

"Yes. Yes, I do." I gave him a big squeeze and then checked the clock. "Okay, vegetables are on and the table is set. Coffee or shower?"

"I'll shower first. You sit and relax while you can." And with that, he blew me a kiss and headed up the stairs.

Alone with my coffee, I cozied up on the couch and let the morning rush stop for a moment. My thoughts wandered while I watched the pure joy of EC. His second Christmas, and the innocence of a child's life was still with him, keeping him unaware of what was really happening. He hadn't paid much attention to the ornaments and the stockings and all the extra Christmassy things that decorated the house. I would love to know what was going on in that beautiful little head of his. He was just beginning to understand all those fairy-tale times and characters of a child's life. Santa Claus, the Easter Bunny, the tooth fairy, and more would soon wrap him in their enchantment for several years with true, exquisite delight. And then, little by little, the magic would slip away as he discovered the truth of all things. Which one would be the first? And how would he find out? I wanted to scoop him up and never let him know the harsh truths about the world.

Was innocence what confused my mother? At her age when the drowning took place, she'd left the Easter Bunny far behind by that time, but the magic of true love was most likely the next level of magic that had entered her life. How was she trapped by Joseph? How she must've felt when her Prince Charming had dissolved like Cinderella's coach turning back into a pumpkin. Looking back on what I'd recently uncovered about Momma, I realized I'd held her like my own special fairy-tale character. Everything about her was supposed to be wonderful. For my entire life, there was never a time that she could've done anything wrong. But that myth ended, taking with it the soft-pink gossamer layer of a sprite. In its place was the soiled, ragged edge of darkness. Had it always lurked there, waiting in the shadows for its chance to spoil all that it could? How had it crept in and left her with the only option, of giving her baby away? How?

CHAPTER 4

DADDY WAS THE FIRST TO arrive. As he got out of his Chevy, I saw he was carrying a big yellow truck in his arms. He had the biggest smile on his face.

"Ho, ho, ho!" Daddy tried to sound like Santa as he came through the door.

"Merry Christmas, Daddy," I said and gave him a hug. The sound of Daddy's voice brought EC into the kitchen.

"Grampa!" EC came toddling over.

"There's my guy!" Daddy held the truck out to him. EC's eyes widened as he took the truck. He plopped down, then and there, and began with his "Brrmmmm, brrmmm," driving his new truck all around the floor.

"Well, I guess he likes it," Daddy said, and he put his finger up to his cheek.

"Something in your eye?" I asked, knowing what a softie my dad was.

"Never mind about that. Now, what can I do to help?" he said.

"I'm about set. I've got a couple of timers going so that I don't forget anything. Hopefully when they go off, I remember what they were for." And Daddy laughed and shook his head.

"You're too young to be forgetting things, missy." And he gave me a kiss on the forehead.

"I can use a hand setting up the bar, Eddy. And I use that term loosely," Charlie said. "I should've put one in when I built this place. But I think I can make this closet work, run some pipes up for a sink, some shelves, and we're all set. What do you think?" Daddy joined Charlie by the closet that we used for dry goods and the vacuum cleaner and mops. For now, they brought in a narrow high table that we used out on the porch. A Christmas tablecloth, bottles and glasses, a bucket of ice, and a few minutes later, instant bar.

"This would be a good spot," Daddy agreed as he sized up the area.

"Excuse me, but don't I get a say as to what goes into this house? That's my pantry, in case you didn't notice. Where, pray tell, are we going to put all that stuff?" I asked, gesturing to the interior of the closet.

"I can make you a pocket pantry. I saw one the other day when I went into Portland. All the new homes have them now. It slides right into the wall. You almost don't even know it's there," Charlie answered, happy with himself for finding a solution.

"All right, if you say so. Oh, gee, here come Caleb and Sadie. And there's another car, and another. Well, it looks like everyone's showing up at once," I said. Charlie's mom and dad, Miss Ruthie, Caleb, Sadie, Robert, Russell, Ginny, and Andre all greeted one another as they made their way to the house. Everyone was carrying either presents or food, and some had both. They were a wonderful sight of hugs and handshakes. I went to the door, and as I opened it, choruses of "Merry Christmas" came from each of them. Mutt and Jeff woofed their welcomes as they sniffed hands and enjoyed the head pats from our visitors.

"*Joyeux Noel*, Ethel," Andre crooned and gave me a hug and a kiss on the cheek. As I hugged him, I felt some strength returning to his aging frame, if only a bit. He looked happy and stood straighter.

"*Merci*, Andre," I replied back to him. He held out a bag, and I knew what it contained. Andre loved to carve small birds. When he was incarcerated, the prison staff had taken all that he'd carved. They'd sold them in the Maine Prison Store, which was famous for its handcrafted items. Those birds were such a symbol to me in that Andre could fly free now. Gone were the shackles and the cold gray prison. He went over to the Christmas tree and tucked the bag underneath.

EC was happy to see Peggy, Charlie's mom, who came and scooped him up. But in a second, he squirmed to get back down and toddled over to his new truck. The last time she'd seen him was in the fall.

"He's such a big boy! And look! He's walking!" Tears filled her eyes, and she looked at me. "Let's see if your new skates fit." She grabbed the package that she'd brought for EC and let him tear into it. He wasn't sure why he was being able to make a mess, but he was enjoying himself. When at last he got to the box and opened it, he looked up at me as if to ask, "What's this?" Inside was a pair of black double-runner skates. He pulled one out and looked inside of it and, as usual, tried to put it on his head.

"No, honey. Here, let Grandma help you." He sat patiently as Peggy put the skates on his little feet. He tried to stand up and immediately plopped back down. Not understanding why he couldn't stand, he started to cry. "Oh no, don't cry. I'll take them off." And the big crocodile tears stopped and smiles returned once Peggy removed the skates.

"Just wait until he sees what they're really for. He'll love it!" I said as Peggy came over to me.

"When John told me that he wasn't walking, well, it almost broke my heart," Peggy said and pursed her lips and shook her head.

"Oh, I know. We were ready for the next level of testing, and I prayed that he wouldn't have to go through that. Thankfully, our prayers were answered," I said, and Daddy came over to her with a drink in his hand.

"John said you like a little seven and seven. How's this, Peg?" Daddy said and handed her the drink, and she took a sip.

"That's the way I like it," she said, smiling back at Daddy. "You make a good drink, Eddy."

And then I felt a hand on my shoulder. It was Russell, and he was holding a box containing a beautiful cheesecake with bright-red cherries spilling over the creamy yellow cake.

"Russell, this cheesecake looks scrumptious. Thank you and Robert for bringing it," I said.

"Tell her, brother," Robert urged.

"Stop, she doesn't need to know," Russell hissed at his brother.

"What don't I need to know?" I asked, looking from one to the other.

"There were some chocolate-dipped almond crescents that you like. But there was an accident," Russell said.

"An accident? Oh no, I hope no one was hurt." I looked them over to see if there were any signs of injuries.

"Russell." Robert was being very stern.

"Not that kind of accident. I accidentally ate one, and then another, and do you know how long a ride it is to here from the city?" Russell looked at me and then down to his feet like a child who'd been caught with his hand in the cookie jar.

"That's okay, my waistline forgives you." I laughed and put my arm around his chubby shoulder, letting him know all was forgiven. "My, but you two look like Christmas." While they were city boys and dressed in three-piece suits daily, they never shied away from what they felt was New England fashion. The brothers were wearing plaid wool shirts with cuffs turned just so. Their vests—one wore red, and the other green—were so soft I was sure they were cashmere. Black corduroy pants and their comfy Bean boots completed today's outfits.

"We were so happy to find that Pendleton still makes the MacGregor plaid. That was mom's family name, you know. That's where this carrot fuzz and white skin comes from," Russell explained and indicated their bright-red hair and painfully white skin.

"Russell, Robert, I have your Manhattans." Daddy held up two glasses.

"We'll be right there, Eddy." They went over to join the men at the makeshift bar. Caleb and Daddy were assessing the bar inventory and shaking their heads. Charlie was right: we did need a real bar. But for now, the table would do.

As I looked around, everyone was mingling with their favorite drink in hand. Ruthie, Peggy, and Ginny busied themselves arranging rolls and desserts and strategizing where all the food would go on the dinner table.

Andre had gone over to sit on the floor near the tree with EC and the dogs. Dressed in a green turtleneck and wearing a red knit cap, Andre looked like a wise old elf. It was incredible to see the two of them communicate. Andre was so gentle with EC, and EC laughed at Andre's heavy French accent. Andre took his paper bag from under the tree and pulled out one of the birds and held it out for EC. EC's face lit up as he took the bird. He loved small objects and tried to put it in his pants pocket, but it didn't fit. So for a moment, he was content to hold it in his hand, checking to see if anything moved. After he'd lost interest in that, he looked into the bag and up at Andre. Andre nodded yes, and EC's diminutive hand went into the bag. He squealed with delight as he pulled out another bird, a different one this time. Now, having one for each hand, there was no one happier than EC. In a matter of moments, all the birds were out and the two of them were "flying" and nesting the birds in and around the Christmas tree. It made my heart swell with love to know that if I hadn't followed my instincts, this wonderful soul would still be sitting in that horrid prison cell, serving time for a murder he'd never committed.

A ding from one of my timers brought me out of my reverie and into the reality of Christmas dinner. I checked the oven and saw that it was time for the turkey to come out.

"Charlie, a little help, please," I said, summoning him. He came and hefted the pan up onto the counter. "Thanks, love."

"Anything else?" he asked.

"Let me scoop out the stuffing, and then you can carve it." And I grabbed a spoon and the bowl and started. Charlie got the carving set and platter and stood by.

"Ethel, okay to plate the veggies and potatoes?" Ginny asked.

"Sure, and then the only thing left is the gravy," I answered.

"I got this." And Ruthie found my whisk and started to add the flour. "Oh, there's lots of juice. This will be some good gravy."

"Can I look over your shoulder? Caleb never likes my gravy, or anything else for that matter. Maybe I can learn a new trick," Sadie said as she took position next to Ruthie to learn from the master.

"Sure, honey. You whisk, and I'll add the rest." The two of them looked like a couple of witches, hunched over the large roasting pan, as the gravy bubbled and the steam rose.

In about ten minutes, we were ready to sit down. Everyone found a seat around the table. When we'd built the house, I'd asked Charlie for a big table. He and his dad had built a beautiful maple table that could take two leaves. They'd initially made eight chairs, but looking at the group today, I made a mental note to ask for four more or a bench. I noticed that Ginny found her seat next to Daddy. The two of them were talking quietly, and I saw Ginny hold up her hand to her mouth to stifle a laugh. She'd put her other hand on Daddy's to emphasize her laughter. To my surprise, Daddy didn't shrug it off but put his own hand out and patted hers. And that was that, didn't last five seconds, but it was a beginning. Everyone else found a spot at the table, and EC, of course, was between Charlie and me in his high chair. Andre was the last to sit, having gone back to the tree to retrieve his birds.

"*Joyeux Noel*, from me to you. With many thanks." And he walked around the table, handing a bird to each person. Some were no bigger than three inches tall and had the minutest of details. He'd used different types of wood instead of stain to provide the tones and qualities. And all were sanded to a soft patina. Everyone was quite taken with them, offering their thank-you to him. Andre smiled at their responses. Happy to be happy.

"I'd like to say grace, if I may," said Robert quietly.

"Of course, Robert, that would be lovely," I answered. And we all bowed our heads.

"Dear Lord, thank you for gathering these loving people to this table today. Help us and guide us to continue to be the best servants for you. And, Lord, please don't forget that Russell ate all the cookies that were supposed to be a present for Ethel. Amen," he ended, we all said amen, and then we laughed amid Russell's protests that it was an accident.

Over the next hour, we ate, drank, and ate some more. The stuffing turned out exactly as Aunt Eleanor said it would be, flavorful with a meaty hint. And the fresh turkey was tender and moist. Ruthie and Sadie's gravy was golden and flowed like a flavorful lava over the mashed potato mountains on our plates. Ruthie had brought potato rolls that were just made for gathering the last pools of that gravy.

The cheesecake, apple compote, pumpkin pie with shortbread crust, and red and green frosted sugar cookies were the quintessential sweet ending to our meal. Charlie added more wood to the fire, and as we left the table, each person gradually adjourned to the living room to find a comfy spot. As we sat with our coffees and after-dinner drinks, we reminisced about Christmases past. We listened to one another and smiled and laughed at all our stories. Andre had been silent for a while, politely listening, and then he began to speak his mind in his French accent.

"My life was very, very hard in Canada for my family. But every year at Christmas, my mother and father made us the very best with their own hands. My mother was the seamstress in our village, and she would take the scraps that were left from her customers and make us a new winter coat. She would even put our names inside. My father, he carved like me. He would make all kinds of animals for us. The best part was when it snowed and all was quiet and peaceful. But my new favorite Christmas is the one I am having tonight with my new family. Never could I have thought about a night as grand as this. *Merci! Salute!*" And as he raised his glass to us, a tear ran down his wrinkled cheek. He put his hand up and blew a kiss to us as well.

"Hear, hear," Daddy said as we all raised our glasses at these touching words. Our faces rosy and our eyes with a glimmer from tears of joy.

"Look, it's snowing!" John, Charlie's dad, said. "Grab yours jackets and let's go out." With the excitement of children, we made our way out onto the porch and into the chill of the night to see the first snowfall of the year. We stood in silence, listening as the snow landed on dried leaves. A few went out from the cover to catch a snowflake. What was it about the first snow that made people stop and wonder at this lovely gift from Mother Nature?

I thought about how all these people had come into my life. Family was a given, but that was fewer than half of those who were here today. Had it really been a coincidence when I took that particular bus home that day and met Charlie? Or taking a chance on the job at *The Daily Bugle* with Caleb and Sadie? Or purely accidental to stop and give the *Fishing Weekly* to two unlikely fishermen of Russell and Robert? Or was it a fluke wanting to find Momma's home and meeting Ginny, who I hoped would help end Daddy's loneliness? Or mere luck when I followed my instincts to break the silence that I'd found in Momma's journal that would free Andre? Was there something else, something more to all this?

This morning the piece of envelope had fallen like a snowflake onto the floor, almost disappearing, melting, if you would, before it caught my attention. It was as if something or someone was saying, "Don't quit, there's more." Who or what was guiding me to a conclusion? Was it Momma? I knew there were more questions to ask, but as to who would give me the answers, well, that would be my challenge. The story was going to end, that I could feel, but how would be anyone's guess.

CHAPTER 5

AFTER EVERYONE LEFT AROUND SEVEN o'clock, we put EC to bed. Not that it'd been difficult—he was exhausted. He'd been so excited with all the new people and playing with his new truck and especially his birds. Charlie carried him up on his shoulder to EC's objections of "Truck, Daddy, truck!"

"He certainly had everyone's attention, didn't he?" Charlie said as he laid EC down in his crib. Before everyone left, we'd changed him into his pajamas so he could say his "Good nights," and now EC's eyes were heavy as his little fingers circled my thumb.

"Good night, my little elf," I said and bent to kiss him. "I love you to the moon and back."

"Daddy loves you too," Charlie said. No sooner were the words out of his mouth than EC's eyes were closed and he started with a little baby snore.

"Listen, that little snore sounds like his daddy's." I poked Charlie in the ribs.

"Hey, I only do that when I'm really tired," he objected as he steered me out of the room. I looked back, and with help from the waning full moon, there was just enough light to see our little guy, peaceful.

Back downstairs, we finished straightening up, taking out the table leaf and returning the extra chairs to their spots. The dogs lay on their beds near the fireplace, exhausted and full, no doubt from the little tidbits that they'd been handed throughout the day. Russell in particular loved Mutt, calling him his kindred spirit in food, and loved the kisses that Mutt rewarded him with.

"I think that about does it for tonight," Charlie said. "How about a nightcap?"

"Sure, maybe a little crème de menthe to settle my stomach," I said and plopped on the couch. "I must be getting old or something, but I'm pooped."

"Well, it's not very often that we have a dozen people in the house that we're feeding and entertaining. I think it was a great day. The food was wonderful, and I have the best Christmas present in the world sitting right here." Charlie sat next to me and handed me my drink.

"Well, aren't you sweet? But you're not expecting a present?" I asked as I sipped the minty liquor.

"Not at all. Remember, we said we didn't know what was going to happen with EC. And so we didn't want to spend any extra, just in case his medical bills were something we couldn't handle," he reminded me.

"I remember," I answered. "But I think I have a special present for you."

"I got a very special present this morning, if I recall. What could be better than that? What have you got up your sleeve, Mrs. O'Connor?" He looked over the top of his bourbon with his smiling eyes.

"It's not what's up my sleeve, but it's what's under my shirt." I guided his hand to my belly.

"What? Are you sure?" His mouth gaped open and turned into the biggest grin.

"I'm pretty sure. I'm at least a month late, what with the holidays and all the business with Andre and Joseph. I kind of lost track of myself. That, and I'm really hungry, tired, and burping," I said, smiling back at him.

"Oh my, this is great! I can't wait to tell everyone!" He gave me a kiss and sat back with this look of satisfaction.

"I know, I wanted to tell you this morning, but then everything went so fast. And I didn't want to announce it before I told you. I have an appointment with Dr. Simon next week to make sure." And I unbuttoned my pants. "Whew, there, that's better." And Charlie laughed.

"Are you sure you didn't eat too much cheesecake?" he added.

"I only had one little piece—well, maybe a bite of a few other things," I confessed. "And now we can start to fix up the other room." There were three bedrooms upstairs. Ours, EC's, and the other that was waiting for my decision. My office was downstairs, but somehow, I was always drawn to the light from the window in that third room.

"You're going to lose your reading room," Charlie chided.

"That's okay. That will be my upper office," I said defensively.

"And then there's the office by the fireplace, and then there's you real office," he added.

"Now, we share that 'real' office, so let's not be throwing stones. You have just as many blueprints in the wood bucket over there as I have pieces that I'm editing," I threw back at him.

"Okay, truce." He held up his hand. "Waving the white flag, my dear."

"You know when you're beaten, that's all." I smirked.

"What do you think it will be?" he asked. "It would be nice to have a girl."

"And EC would be the perfect big brother, wouldn't he?" I added, then sighed.

"What?" Charlie asked, wondering about my sigh.

"It's just I wish Momma, good, bad, or indifferent, were here. Like today, all those great people who filled our home and our hearts with so much love," I started.

"Now, wait. Have you ever considered that if not for your mother's passing, all those people, even me, might not have been here today?" Charlie was always so good at making me take a step back and showing me another perspective about a situation. "We would've met at that wedding, that's for certain, but with your mother's encouragement, you probably would've gone off to Boston or Providence after graduation. And your dad wouldn't have minded as much, because your mom would've been here."

"You're right, you know that," I relented.

"And think of all the things you've accomplished. Collaborating with Caleb on the *Fishing Weekly*, that got Russell and Robert involved. And now they're building the Book Emporium in town.

Putting Norman and Joseph away where they should be, for the horrible things they did to people. And helping to bring Piney Bluffs into the spotlight. All those things might not have happened," he finished.

"All right, I get it. I feel like Jimmy Stewart in *It's a Wonderful Life*," I responded.

"Sorry, honey. It's just that I've never know one woman who has the drive to accomplish things that everyone else gives up on or hasn't the faintest idea of how to start," he added.

"Well, then, this one woman needs to figure out how to find her half sister before this baby comes," I said.

"I knew that was in the back of your mind," Charlie said.

"It's always there, ever since I found out," I said quietly.

"But you have to be careful and you have to promise: this is the end of being the one-woman detective agency," he said emphatically.

"I think it's more like one-woman, one-man detective agency. Don't you?" And I laughed as he rolled his eyes.

"If you weren't pregnant, I'd tickle you until you cried 'Uncle!'" He lunged at me. "The heck with it, I'm going to tickle you anyways!" His hands were around my middle, and he started at my ribs and I was all done. To stop the torment, I put my arms around his neck and pulled him in for a kiss. "Careful. We don't want to mess up our little girl."

"She'll just come out laughing, that's all," I answered. And we ended our night watching the flames burn to glowing embers, our hands entwined, and making plans for the next addition to the O'Connor Koontz clan.

CHAPTER 6

THE WEEK BETWEEN CHRISTMAS AND New Year's was a slow one for news. That and the fact that it had snowed on and off for almost a week, not much was happening in town. Since Christmas, we'd gotten a foot and a half, giving Piney Bluffs almost a daily dose of a refresher to its white frosting. Everywhere you looked was the perfect shot for a New England postcard. With more snow predicted, a lot of folks were canceling their New Year's Eve parties and staying home to watch Dick Clark and the famous ball drop in Time's Square. So we decided to publish a paper every other day. It was Tuesday, and the snow was starting to fall again.

We'd been working on a column of resolutions for the New Year's Eve edition. Jimmy, our high school intern, was going around interviewing people. Caleb showed him how to use his Canon to take shots of the various folks he'd talked to. He'd even gotten into the darkroom to try his hand at developing.

"I really wish this snow would stop. It's beautiful and all, but really. Thank goodness I have a Jeep, because I have an appointment tomorrow that I have to get to." I got up to stretch and to look out the big window. I sipped my coffee and stifled a little burp. My coffee was starting to disagree with me. Yup. Another sign that I was most certainly pregnant.

"Oh, did someone forget to tell me about an appointment without a forty-eight-hour notice? You keep this up, and I'll have HR put this in your file." Caleb turned around in his chair. He got up to take the *New York Times* and bring it back to his desk. He snapped it open. "Chess and football, not much news to end the year. And Reagan's pitting Poland and Russia against each other."

"Sorry, I forgot to tell you. With the holidays and all, it slipped my mind. I have an appointment with Dr. Simon," I said and let the name sink in.

"Dr. Simon. Why does that name sound familiar? Oh my!" The realization did its job; his eyes grew wide, and he put his paper down. "Are you sure? Really?"

"Pretty sure. That's what the appointment's about. To make certain and to find out when my maternity leave begins." I laughed.

"Let's see, that probably brings us to August, give or take. Hmm…it's after opening day and before Beulah's tournament, so I think we can arrange a couple of weeks of leave for you." Caleb smiled at me. "Your family's growing, and I'm going to be an uncle again. How about that? Do you remember back to that first day when I asked you if you'd ever had a vision?"

"I do. And my vision had nothing to do with all this." I pointed to my belly and shook my head. "Or maybe it did. I said I wanted to give a voice to those who didn't have one. And if I remember, I also wanted to increase the awareness of our natural resources. And while I was sure I wasn't going to accomplish any of that by staying here, it seems I've managed to do just that."

"You have a lot to be proud of. Your daddy says so too," he said.

"Oh, I know. Although I think this last piece of the puzzle about Momma has really hurt him. But I think this needed to happen. I just hope that he can finally turn the page in his book and start a new chapter with Ginny," I said and went back to my desk.

"From what I saw at Christmas dinner, I don't think you have to hope too much," Caleb said as he filled his pipe and lit it. Soon, a soft plume of smoke and the aroma of the cherry tobacco was in the air.

"They were cute together, weren't they? He's already wearing the hat she knit for him for Christmas." Ginny knitted hats for the men and scarves for the ladies when she'd come for dinner. "And he still hasn't smoked since sometime in October. He's very proud of that."

"Oh, how thoughtless of me. I should put my pipe out, for your and the baby's sake." Caleb got so flustered he spilled tobacco all over the *Times*.

"No, you don't have to do that," I said and went over to help him clean up before we had to call the fire department. "It's not like you smoke all day long. Besides, I enjoy the aroma. It's rather relaxing."

"Well, relaxing or not, I'm going to try to quit. There, that's my New Year's resolution," he finished, proud of himself. "What about you, Ethel? What's yours?"

"Hmmm, that's a good question. I could say that I'd let things be and not try to find Sophie, but I'd be fooling myself and everyone else." I put my coffee cup down and wished it were tea.

"Ethel, that's a given. You need something that's a goal, something that you're willing to give up for a better world." Caleb started to go through his drawers, cleaning out his pipe-smoking paraphernalia.

"For a better world? I guess swearing off cookies from Ruthie's is out of the question?" I kidded with him.

"Maybe a better you, but sales would drop and Ruthie might need to close." He laughed. "All right, what else is going on? I've known you long enough to know that there's something eating away at you."

"I found something. It was almost like it was a Christmas present from my grandmother. I was using her cookbook, and when I went to put it away, the pages fluttered and the flap of an old envelope and a postcard fell to the floor," I said. "The envelope was an address of a doctor in New Hampshire, and the postcard was not more than seven words."

"And that means what?" Caleb asked, waiting for my deduction.

"Good question. Could mean something or nothing," I replied. "It was just the way the flap fell out of the cookbook. If I hadn't been paying attention, it would've disappeared under the refrigerator forever. Or until I cleaned or got a new one. Like I said, it would have been there for a long time. But something made me look up that instant, right before it disappeared."

"While I don't believe in such things, it does seem like there's something that's leading you through all this," Caleb said.

"I feel that way, too, most times," I commented.

"But if you hadn't done the things you've done, look at what wouldn't have happened," he said.

"I know. Charlie and I had this same conversation the other day," I agreed.

"So let's get back to your resolution." Caleb waited while I thought.

"Well, I'd really like to finish Momma's story, *Sophie's Sled*," I said. "I think that would be a good end for all this, even if I never find Sophie."

"Sounds good. You and Ruthie will be the town's first authors to have their books in the new Emporium," Caleb agreed.

"The Emporium's going to be a great spot. Robert and Russell are coming back in a couple of weeks to start the interior-design phase. Charlie's just about finished with the rough in." I got up to make some tea.

"Why don't you take some time, what with this snow and all? Go home, see if you can finish the story," Caleb suggested. He sat, waiting for me to come back in and give him my answer.

"I don't know if I'm ready. I've sat and looked at the pictures and the pages, but there's something missing. It's almost like I can't finish it until I know what Sophie looks like." I blew on my tea to cool it.

"What will that do for you? It's just a children's story about a little girl and a sled. That should be easy enough," Caleb said.

"But is it really?" I asked. "I'm not so sure. And I know everyone thinks that I read too much into these things, but I have to tell you, I think it's not that simple." And I took a sip. *Umm, lemon.* Ginny had given me a selection of gourmet teas for Christmas. All that Pappy carried at the General Store was Lipton or Salada. I was going to have to show him these different kinds.

"Well, why don't you go home, anyway?" Caleb urged. "This snow's still coming, and I don't want you out and about when it's not necessary."

"I'm not made of glass. I'm just pregnant, again, maybe," I said.

"Go on, scoot," he said and got my coat from the peg. "Now, let me help you." He held my coat, waiting.

"But…," I started to say as I put my arm into the sleeve.

"No buts. Go home. Write. For you this time. You'll figure this out. I know you. Now, happy New Year." And with that, he gave me a hug, handed me my bag, and motioned for me to go.

"Happy New Year to you and Sadie, too," I said, and out the door I went. The snow was falling harder now, smaller flakes stinging my face. The temperature was dropping, and the sky was graying as afternoon arrived. EC was home with Charlie, so I had a little time to myself. My stomach did a little flip and a growl. I knew exactly what would fix that. I saw Ruthie through the window of the bakery, and she waved me in. Can't fight fate, and so I walked across the street and into a world of cinnamon and deliciousness. The bakery was empty, save for the two of us and Sugar, Miss Ruthie's cat.

"Good Lord, girl, what are you doing out of the office? No news here, unless you want to report that I'm out of muffins. I know that would probably make Caleb sad enough to write an obituary for the lowly muffin." Ruthie laughed and came from behind the counter. I went over and took a seat at her table. The top was cluttered with newspapers and a couple of old cookbooks. A fresh cup of coffee sent up a little steam next to a notepad where she'd written a list.

"Not looking for news. Caleb sent me home because of the snow and lack of newsworthiness in town. He wants me to go home and finish writing Momma's story." I sat down and waited for Ruthie to join me.

"Well, sounds like you don't want to do what you've been told," she noted. "Not that that's news to any of us."

"It's not that. Like I told Caleb, I don't think it's as easy as saying, 'Sophie has a sled and she goes sliding with her friend Annie.' Nothing about all this has been what it appears to be," I said and changed the subject. "Have you got any almond crescents?"

"I have one left, and a coffee too?" Ruthie went back and rolled open the glass case and got ready to plate the last of my favorite cookies.

"No coffee, thanks, but I'd love a cup of tea," I answered. "Do you have any flavored teas?"

"Sorry, just plain tea. Oh, I also made some molasses ones today. I'll get you one of those too," she offered.

"Maybe the molasses, that might help my stomach," I replied.

"Tummy not too good, eh? Well, most likely it's too much good holiday food. Wait. Tea, not coffee. Stomach unsettled. You're not… are you?" Ruthie came over to the table and set the plate in front of me. She stood with hands on her hips. Her eyes narrowed as she looked me up and down.

"I think so. I've got an appointment tomorrow to make sure," I answered and grinned from ear to ear. Ruthie had been one of my surrogate mothers when I was growing up. She gave me my first job as a "glaze application specialist," as she called it. She thought it would look good on my résumé. She'd been there to hug me when I cried and listen to my hopes and dreams as I grew.

"Oh, honey! I'm so happy for you and Charlie! And EC's going to be a big brother—how exciting!" She went to get my tea and brought it over to the table. She took a seat next to me and put her hands over her mouth and then said, "Is it a secret? I just can't wait to tell everyone."

"Caleb knows because I have an appointment, and you know. Daddy doesn't know yet, so I'd appreciate it if you kept it quiet until I confirm it tomorrow," I answered.

"I'm just so tickled about this. Oh, I hope it's a girl!" She took a sip of her coffee.

"I do too. It would be nice, one of each. So what's with the old cookbooks? Running out of things to make?" I asked.

"Russell and Robert wanted me to find the first recipe that I ever tried. You know, to go back and see where I started. I can tell you it's been a hoot looking at some of these old books." She turned a page to show me. "Now, look at this one. It was my mother's. These old cookbooks had everything a new wife needed to know. Look, here's a chapter on 'Food and Body Weight.' We can skip right past that part. Now this one's for you: 'What to Do if You Are Expecting to Have a Baby'! Keep in mind, this was originally written in 1941, but updated in 1951, the year after you were born, if I remember."

"That's right, good memory," I said. "What does it say?"

"Let's see, 'Include one quart of milk each day, citrus fruit, dark leafy vegetable, an egg, wheat germ, fish liver oil.' My, my, but it doesn't say anything about molasses cookies or chocolate-dipped almond crescents." And she pulled my plate away from me.

"Hey, there must be something in there about nuts. Isn't there? Nuts are protein. How about the eggs that are in here? And spices, they're good for you too," I said, defending my pastry.

"Oh, Ethel, how could I deny you a cookie?" Ruthie patted my hand. "Look, here it is. I think this was my first recipe. Baking powder biscuits. Look at the notes in the margin. My mother must have known I'd be a baker. See here, how she has the recipe tripled."

"Ruthie, your mom didn't know you were a baker?" I asked, realizing that I'd never delved too much into her family history. I knew her father had been a good old country doctor, but there had never been any mention about her mother.

"No, child, she didn't. You see, she passed when I was in high school. She was pregnant, and well, complications happened and we lost both of them. The baby was a boy, my brother. I'd already picked out names for the babies. Back then, we didn't know what she was going to have. His name was going to be Russell. Russell Patrick O'Hara. My father never quite got over that. He'd tried his best to save them with what he knew. But back in those days, we were so far from a hospital, never mind any type of specialist like there is today." And she raised her coffee to her lips but put it down, as her hands went to wipe the tears from her eyes.

"Oh, Ruthie. I'm so sorry. I didn't know." I put my arm around her soft shoulders to console her.

"I guess I never did tell you all this, did I?" She dried her hands on her apron and gave me a little smile.

"No, you didn't, and shame on me for never caring enough to know," I said. "Please tell me more. I'd really love to know."

"Oh, it's not your fault. It was a lifetime ago." She took a sip and continued with the rest of her story. "After my mom passed, we moved from Portland to Biddeford. I got a job in a bakery after school. When I graduated from high school, I stayed on with them and worked at a restaurant on the weekends, baking their pies and cakes. My blueberry pies were the specialty of the house, I'd like you to know. Then Dad wanted to move again. Said he wanted to be where it was quieter. So off we went to Sebago. He liked it there, had a nice little practice in the house. And I found a job as the cook at a small breakfast place. One day, I took a drive around the area and found Piney Bluffs. And this place. Oh, it wasn't much to look at then, but it had good bones, as they say. It'd been somebody's home, but I could see the potential for the bakery. My dad had some money saved, and I did too. With that, I started out small with used equipment and ovens. Then as time went by, I was able to buy better mixers and everything else. And here we are."

"Wow, that's quite a journey. But wasn't there ever anyone special in your life?" I asked, hoping her story wasn't finished.

"Well, now, that's where life got interesting." She looked at me with a sad smile. "I went with a fellow, a Navy man, he was. James Ryan Boyle. What a handsome cuss, smart too. He asked me to marry him, right before his last go at sea on the *Pollux*. I said yes, and he promised me the best wedding an ensign's pay could bring. The ship ran aground in a fierce storm, another ship tried to help. All told, over two hundred good men were lost."

"And no one after him?" I wanted her to go on. I'd never heard Ruthie talk about herself in this way.

"Oh, there were one or two, but never anyone quite like my James. I got busy with this place, and then my dad was sick. The years go by. You make your peace with what life has laid out for you. This town has become my family, Ethel. Even though it wasn't the family that I thought I was going to have, this is real. Sometimes you have to accept what you have and be happy with it. I can't imagine my life being any better than this," she finished and looked down at her hands and then up at me. "Now, that's enough about an old woman."

"Ruthie, thanks so much for, well, everything." I leaned over to kiss her puffy cheek.

"You go on home now, before this storm gets worse. And you let me know first thing when I can start spreading the news about our newest family member." She got up and went to the cases. She filled a bag with cookies. "Here, these are for EC and Charlie, well, and maybe you too, but not too many!" she scolded as she handed me the bag and gave me a hug.

"I'll let you know as soon as we get back into town," I said and walked out into the snow. As I walked over to my car, I saw that Jimmy was cleaning it off.

"Hi, Jimmy, thanks!" I opened my door to put my things inside and started to scoop snow from the windows.

"Nope, you get inside and start her up. Caleb told me to get this cleaned off for you." And he gave me a smile from under his snow-covered hood. "Happy New Year, Ethel."

"Happy New Year to you, Jimmy," I said. I got into my car and waited while he finished. When he was done, he gave a tap on my window and a wave goodbye.

Ruthie was right: Piney Bluffs was family. Stand-by-your-side-and-help-you-till-the-end kind of family. As I drove home, I thought about Sophie. Life had given her a family too. And who was I to come barging into her life after thirty-plus years? Was knowing about Momma or me going to make it any better? Up until now, the stories I pursued ended well for everyone except those who'd been the scoundrels. Perhaps this time there was no villain. Maybe, just this once, all the bad people were lying on the bottom of life, like a sinker.

CHAPTER 7

"I WAS WORRIED ABOUT YOU. CALEB called to say 'Congratulations' and to ask if you'd gotten home all right." Charlie met me at the door with a reprimanding hug. I stamped my feet to get the snow off my boots and hung up my coat.

"Oh, I stopped to chat with Ruthie and get some goodies for my men," I said and held out the bag. "The roads are really bad. It's coming down hard."

"You should've called. I would've come to get you. But in this case, you're forgiven," he said and put my things on the counter, opened the bag, and started to nibble on a cookie. "I just put EC down for a nap. And there's water on for tea. I thought you might like some."

"Mr. O'Connor, can you tell me how a girl got so lucky?" I asked and went to stand by the fireplace. The cold was going right through me. I moved a chair closer to the fireplace, took my blanket from the couch, and sat down. Mutt and Jeff came and sat on the bottom of the blanket, sealing off any cold air and waiting for their mom to give them praise. While I petted Mutt, Jeff rested his head on my knee, waiting for his turn.

"Well, it was either I sat with you or with that old lady with the dead animal around her neck," Charlie said while munching his second cookie.

"What are you talking about? Do you mean to tell me that you remember back to that day on the bus when we first met?" I was amazed. The kettle started to whistle. Charlie poured my cup and brought it to me.

"Military training, hard to break. Survey your surroundings, know your exits, and never forget a face." He shrugged his shoulders. "I watched your face when I got on the bus. You looked up and smiled, and that made my decision. Everyone does when they enter a room or a situation. And I'm happy to say I made the right one." He laughed and gave me a kiss. He went to sit on the couch.

"Caleb gave me a few days off. He wants me to finish *Sophie's Sled*," I said as I sipped my tea.

"Why don't you look like that's what you want to do," Charlie asked.

"There's more to this book, I'm sure," I answered and shivered a bit.

"Well, I think you should go put your sweats on and get warm. Then you can decide what you want to do." And I agreed as he gave me a hand to get up and go change. The dogs trotted alongside of us as we went upstairs.

"I sure hope I have a girl. Right now, I'm outnumbered four to one," I said as I went into EC's room with my all-male entourage.

"Look at it this way: if we have another boy, we could always have a basketball team. But that's only if we can teach the dogs to stand on their hind legs," Charlie whispered, and I stifled a laugh as I bent to pull the blanket up around EC's shoulders. Peaceful and innocent—how I wish he could stay that way. I tiptoed out of his room, shooed Charlie and the dogs back downstairs, and went into our bedroom. I changed quickly, putting on my sweats and heavy socks, still chilly. I sat for a moment on the edge of my bed and sank back into my down quilt. Maybe just a few minutes for a little nap, I thought. Yes, that was all I needed, and then I would write.

"Mommm," I heard EC say. Ah, at least I'd gotten a moment to lie down. I padded over to his bedroom in my stocking feet.

"What is it, my boy? Huh?" His eyes were closed, and his face was serene. A little dream, I guessed. I left him and went downstairs. Charlie motioned for me to go to the office and not hesitate at the fireplace. To my surprise, he'd brought a fresh cup of tea and some cookies to my desk. I took a sip and went to look at the drawings again.

This was the third time in as many months that I'd looked at Momma's story. After a while, I sat down and typed *"Sophie's Sled,* by Stephanie Koontz and Ethel Koontz O'Connor." There. Well, at least it was a beginning. That paper had been in the bale of my typewriter for those many months, and now, finally nine words were on the page.

Momma had written on three of the ten pages of illustrations:

> *It was a beautiful day to slide. Some of the children rolled in the snow. But Sophie had a sled. A new red sled. She shared it with her friend Annie. First, Annie would slide, and then Sophie would slide. They took turns.*

And that was that.

I loved looking at the sketches. They were beautiful and were drawn in pastels and charcoal. My mother had been an amazing artist. There were glassine sheets in between the pages to protect the now-fading colors. How I wanted to finish this story. But what was it? I finally realized I couldn't write the story until I actually tried to understand what she'd gone through.

Last year, when I'd first discovered that Momma's house was standing, I was overcome with emotions. I was angry at Daddy for hiding this from me for all this time. I was so elated because I found out more about my mother than I'd ever known in my life. Momma only lived for a few days after I was born. The only images I had of her were the four worn pictures. Although there were no other pictures, her house had let me see another dimension of her, as it held both good and bad details of her life.

After finding her journal and papers, I dismissed the pages of *Sophie's Sled* as just a children's book. My focus was with Momma's journal and unraveling the secrets that it held.

Knowing now that Sophie was the name of my half sister, the child that Momma was forced to give up, raised the level of importance for these pictures and humble words. I now understood why

Sophie's face lacked features. Momma must have never known her. Her first child. Like she'd never known me. How tragic this all was.

There was another girl in the story. Her name was Annie. I supposed that she had named her after Aunt Anne, my grandmother's sister, who'd lived with Momma and her parents in Oxford. Anne died from pneumonia soon after the family had moved there from Canada.

The first pictures were of many small children toddling about in snowsuits, not yet old enough to use a sled. The next pictures showed a large Victorian house with a hilly backyard. At the bottom of the hill were symmetrical indentations of pathways that seemed like old English gardens lined with small evergreen shrubs. At the center of the pathways was a weeping willow. She'd drawn the willow as if a breeze was blowing its long supple branches. Under the willow was a snow-covered form, a bench, I thought, that might be used in the summer and would offer a place in the shade. One of the pictures was a view from up above, as if Sophie was looking out a window. The grounds were covered in snow, and it appeared my mother tried to draw it showing that it was a moonlit night. The tree casting long shadows, the sky a dark blue with stars. At the end of the pictures, Sophie had grown older, from a little girl to a teenager. But she still had the sled as she walked away.

It seemed this was telling the story of Sophie growing up. What had my mother envisioned for her? She'd left a letter for me, knowing that Daddy would take care of me. I still remember her words.

To my dear daughter Ethel,

I don't know when you'll be reading this letter. I told your daddy to wait until the time was right. So I can only imagine you must be at a time in your life for a decision that only you can make. I know a lot about that. My decision for you was made many months ago. Some people told me I was selfish. I wanted to have a baby, wanted to have you. The doctors told me no, that it wouldn't end well for me. But I had to take that chance. I told them it wouldn't happen to me. But as we both know, that was not true.

Your daddy was a good man, and we were so very much in love. I want to tell you how sorry I am for what I have done to the both of you. I know that his life and yours haven't been easy. I only hope the two of you have made your way the best that you can with family and friends. There are so many things that I will never be able to know. Have you graduated from high school or college? Have you ever been in love? Are you married? Do you have children? Are you happy?

As you lie here in my arms, I am so happy to hold you and kiss you. Your dark-brown eyes look into mine, and for this moment, nothing can come between us. I know in my heart of hearts that this was the right thing to do.

My wish and dream for you is to be the kind of woman that will make you proud of you. Life changes every day, and you will never be sure of your decisions until the end.

So, my dear sweet Ethel, whatever time in your life has come to pass, let your heart help you. I wish I could have been with you.

Love forever,
Momma

The last two sentences had always been in my mind. *Life changes every day, and I had to let my heart help me.*

I sat for a moment and tried to imagine Momma sitting next to me at the desk, looking at her pictures.

"Did you follow my words, Ethel?" she asked.

"I have, Momma, I really have," I answered her. "But what about Sophie? Did you write her a letter too?"

"I wrote this story so you can find her," Momma answered.

"But, Momma, I need to know," I said.

The next thing I knew, I felt the cool desk on my face. I must have fallen asleep during my daydream about Momma.

After that, I read and reread those few pages of Momma's story, simple words. There was so much more to this. I needed to talk to Henry Blake. But with my doctor's appointment tomorrow and the holiday, well, my visit to Oxford would have to wait. I imagined that he was waiting too. How could he have spoken with me, knowing this story about my mother and Joseph having a child and never saying a word? How was it that his name had come to be on the birth certificate? Joseph's father and his money had struck again, I assumed, but in which way? What had money done for Henry? He was in a wheelchair, struck down in his prime by an instance of boys being boys. I'd always felt that Henry wanted to tell me something more, and while I'd thought it might have been about the day of the drowning, it was now clear there was a much-bigger story to tell. And it was only a matter of time until he would tell me.

CHAPTER 8

D R. SIMON'S OFFICE HADN'T CHANGED much in two years. Snapshots of the babies that he'd delivered covered the bulletin board near the check-in window. Smiling, happy, cherubic faces full of life and wonder. Light from a large picture window shone brightly into the room. The remaining walls held pictures of families walking, biking, or cuddled up reading with their small children. There were still piles of parents' magazines that had been thumbed through by scores of nervous would-be parents on the waiting room table. The wooden puzzle cube with its brightly colored balls and triangles remained in the children's corner with the miniature table and chairs. And the aqua plastic chairs were still uncomfortable. Today, there was only one other woman who was waiting with Charlie and me. She looked older, tired, and like her due day should've been three weeks ago. Her red hair was fading as more gray strands were taking over her pixie haircut. She wore a black cloth smock over stretchy gray pants. Her down parka was still on, and her boots were well-worn and missing laces. She was looking at her datebook, counting and turning pages.

"How're you doing today?" I inquired, hoping that some friendly conversation would bring a smile to her tired face.

"I'll be better once this kid comes. I've to get the boat ready in another month or so. Season starts soon," she replied, closed her book, and reached over to shake my hand. "Kate Malloy, owner and operator of Malloy's Fisheries. And you? Your first?"

"Ethel O'Connor, and my husband, Charlie. And this will be our second." I took her hand, noticing the calluses. Charlie gave her a wave from his seat.

"This is the fourth. And the last Malloy," she said as she patted her swollen belly.

"Was four you limit?" I asked.

"No. My husband passed away three months ago," she said as she looked back at me with blank eyes. No emotion, no joy.

"I'm so terribly sorry. How unfeeling of me," I apologized to this woman.

"No need, really. It was shame, damn accident. When they were hauling the boat. The block broke loose, and he was buried under scaffolding. He never knew what hit him, poor cuss." She shook her head and pursed her lips.

"Again, I'm so sorry," I said, not knowing what to say.

"Me too," she replied. "He was a decent guy, smart as hell. He was an accountant, imagine that? But he always wanted to fish. He'd done it alongside his grandfather, rest his soul too. And so here I am, four kids under the age of twelve and a life that depends on the sea." She shook her head and smiled. "But I got some good help down at the boatyard. Lots of guys liked my Bobby. We'll be fine. Thank God for the life insurance. Never thought I'd use it this soon." The door opened to the waiting room, and Dr. Simon smiled at the three of us.

"Kate, come on in." He came across the waiting room to give her a hand up. "How are you doing?" The door closed behind him, leaving Charlie and me to stare at each other in amazement.

"I don't know what to say. Can you imagine what that poor woman is going through?" I said. "I think it's bad when EC's a little fussy when I pick him up after work."

"Yup, you sure don't know how good life is until you talk to other folks," Charlie noted. "Good thing we've got life insurance too. I'm going to talk to Dave Leffler, now that we've got another one coming."

"Oh, I hate to think about things like that," I said and squeezed his arm. The door opened, and this time it was Susanne, the nurse.

"Hi, Ethel. Why don't you come with me? And, Charlie, have a seat until the doctor's done with the exam. Okay?" she said and ushered me down the hallway to the exam room. "How've you been?" she asked as we entered the room.

"If it weren't for being tired and my coffee not agreeing with me, I wouldn't have thought that I was pregnant," I said.

"When was your last period?" Susanne asked, opening my chart to note that. Then she got out a specimen cup and a drape from the cabinet.

"November—no, I think it was October, right before Halloween. Holy cow, that means…" I started counting. "EC could have a very special birthday present."

"Yes, he could. Wouldn't that be the best for a big brother?" she commented. "Now, a sample in the cup, please. Our fashion-forward gown as always, with the opening in the back."

"There has got to be a better way to make this thing," I said, showing my distaste for the paper drape.

"I know," she said. "Maybe we could send it to some fashion institute and see what they'd come back with." She laughed.

"It'd probably come back with some type of fringe or a hat," I answered.

"Doc will be with you soon," Susanne said. "Just leave the cup in the bathroom and knock on the other door. I'll be in to get it and test it."

"I feel so bad for Kate. We were talking to her in the waiting room," I said. "I couldn't imagine if something happened to Charlie."

"It's so tragic. But she's a little trooper. Not going to let anything get in her way of putting the boat in and getting it set for fishing. Her dad was a fisherman too. It's the only way she knows how to make a living," Susanne commented, smiled, and closed the door.

Left alone, I undressed, folded my clothes, and laid them on the chair. I took the cup and went into the bathroom and peed. I left it on the sink and knocked on the other door for Susanne to come and test the sample. I took a seat on the exam table and looked around the room while I waited. The pictures on the exam room walls were those of mothers and babies. Eyes closed and serene smiles were captured in black-and-white. Probably right before the little darling opened its mouth and started crying.

Was I ready for another child? I hadn't really thought about it until this very moment. EC had been a blessing, and the fact that I hadn't died after delivering him, well, that was a major accomplishment. I'd been so fearful that something like what had happened to Momma would happen to me. Dr. Simon assured me at every appointment that nothing was wrong. And indeed, nothing was. EC came out with the perfect number of fingers and toes.

The door opened, and in walked Dr. Simon with the same calm, reassuring manner as always.

"Hi, Ethel. So good to see you. Let's see, Susanne tells me that you think you're pregnant, maybe two months?" the doctor asked.

"Yes, I think that's about right," I answered. "I was so busy with everything that it's just skipped my mind."

"Ah, the holidays. They'll do that to you," he remarked.

"Well, it was a bit more than that. You see, I found some more information about my mother," I added.

"Really. What did you find?" Dr. Simon asked and stopped for a moment to listen.

And so I began the CliffsNotes version of discovering Momma's house, the murder, finding Andre, Joseph, and ending with the fact that I had a half sister.

"Wow. I don't know what to say after all that." He looked bewildered. "And it's not the whole cover-up. I'm more concerned that your mother had another child before you and there were no ill effects that anyone was aware of."

"I know. Do you think that's good or bad for me having a second child?" I realized how he might be thinking. My pregnancy for EC went fine. But now with another child on the way, what was the probability that this might be the same situation that had caused Momma to die?

"I can't—no, I won't guess either way. We'll do the same tests as before, and I'm sure you'll be fine. If, as you were told, your mother was sent away to have the baby, then there's no telling what qualifications the person had who delivered her. No way to know if that delivery caused something inside to cause an abnormality. You'll not worry about that here, as you know. The first sign of anything out of my expertise, and you'll go right to Brigham and Women's. But that should be the furthest thing from our minds right now. Now, let's relax for a bit and let me have a look." I lay back as he began his exam. The door opened, and Susanne entered.

"No doubt about it, Ethel. I hope you still have a crib," she remarked and started to help Dr. Simon. Blood pressure, vitals, questions, answers, external and internal exam were all done with kindness and gentle hands. After the exam, Dr. Simon helped me sit up.

"And from what I see here today, you are about three months along. We'll know better at your next visit when we do the ultrasound. Now, let's have you get dressed, and I'll see you and Charlie in my office," he reported, and both he and Susanne left the room.

I dressed quickly. Darn jeans were getting tight already—I left the snap undone. Phooey, no more cookies from Ruthie's for me. I left the room and went to get Charlie from the waiting room. Dr. Simon had kept the door open and called for us to come in and have a seat.

"Hi, Charlie. Good to see you again. Ethel, you are in perfect health. A little tired, but that's to be expected for being two to three months along. Next appointment in a month, we'll do an ultrasound. Here's a script for some prenatal vitamins. Now, what kind of questions do you have?" He passed the script to me and then waited for us.

"I want to know that Ethel's going to be all right," Charlie admitted and sat and waited for an answer.

"As I told Ethel, there's no way of knowing how her mother's first child was delivered and by who. We'll do all of the same tests that we did before, and if anything is amiss, then I'll make the appropriate referral," Dr. Simon said. I could tell he was thinking about what I'd found out but was holding back with any supposition, which I thought was prudent. "Right now, concentrate on staying healthy and happy. That goes a long way to keep the baby in tip-top shape too. Anything else?" Dr. Simon waited.

"I'm good," I answered. "Charlie?"

"No, all set. As long as Ethel and the baby are healthy, then I'm happy," Charlie replied. We got up and shook his hand and went to make my next appointment.

"Let's see…that brings us to Friday, January 30. Any conflicts with that day?" Susanne looked up.

"Nothing at the moment. Let's hope this snow doesn't keep up, or we'll see you in the spring," I joked and took the card and put it in my purse. She laughed too, said goodbye, and we were out into the sunny day. The sun glinted off the snowbanks, and everywhere you heard the warning beeps of snowplows backing up.

"Well, Mr. O'Connor, are you ready for this?" I asked. We were walking through the parking lot.

"I am if you are. We didn't build that extra bedroom for company, you know." He smiled, and we held hands as we walked.

"I hope it's a girl, then we'll have one of each," I said. "And EC will be her big brother. You'll have to teach him."

"Don't you worry. I got this, Mrs. O'Connor," he reassured me.

"I have no doubt in my mind," I answered and leaned into him as we walked.

The ride home was full of conversations about names and personalities and baseball and fairies. School and college to careers and food. We laughed, I cried, and we both hoped our share of struggles was over. Hopefully.

CHAPTER 9

W E GOT BACK INTO TOWN about four and picked up EC at Minnie's. We went straight to Daddy's to tell him the good news and maybe go out for a bite to eat to celebrate both New Year's and the new baby. EC got excited when he saw that we were pulling up in front of Grampa's house. We got to the door, knocked, and walked in. Mr. Striper came to greet us, running up the stairs and poking his head through the spindle and putting his paw out to beckon the petting. Giving him a quick ear scratch, I followed the strains of Guy Lombardo coming from the living room. Daddy always liked the big-band era of music. He must be enjoying this, I thought.

"Hey, Daddy. Happy New Year! And boy, do we have good news for you!" I announced as I walked into the living room. Charlie put EC down and was guiding him as they slowly walked after me. As I reached the living room, I saw Daddy lying facedown in front of the television. "Daddy? Daddy!" I screamed. "Charlie, help!" Charlie came running as I knelt beside my father.

"Eddy! Hey, Eddy, can you hear me?" Charlie gently turned him over and put his fingers to his neck to feel for a pulse. "Ethel, call 911 and Doc McAllister." I ran to the kitchen wall phone and dialed.

"Come quick. Eddy Koontz, my father, he's unconscious. Address is 16 Main Street in Piney Bluffs." I hung up and called Doc and gave him the same message. He said he'd be right over. I looked, and Charlie had propped Daddy's head up with a pillow and was checking him.

"Eddy! Hey, Eddy, wake up! He's breathing, so that's good, but he's just not coming to," Charlie said. EC started to cry. I'd completely forgotten about him. He was standing and looking at Daddy.

"Oh, my poor baby, it's okay. Grampa's taking a little nap." I picked up EC and hugged him, setting him in the sunroom with some of his toys. I hurried back to Daddy's side. "Daddy? Daddy?" I held his head and patted his cheeks, hoping he would wake up. *You can't leave me now, you just can't.* I held back tears as I continued to pat his cheeks and talk to him. It seemed like a lifetime of waiting, just watching him lie there. *Daddy, wake up. Please.* Finally, there was a knock on the door, and I heard it open. The steps came quickly into the living room. It was Doc, who arrived first. It had always been a comfort that he was a close neighbor.

"Ethel, what's going on?" Doc immediately knelt next to Daddy.

"Oh, Doc, we came in and found him facedown on the floor. Can you help him? What's the matter with him?" I said, and I couldn't hold back my tears any longer. They fell from my eyes and onto Daddy's shirt, the drops sinking into the soft flannel and leaving dark, wet stains. Charlie stayed next to me.

Doc opened his bag and took out his stethoscope. "He's breathing, that's good. His color's a little gray. Eddy! Eddy!" Doc called out loudly. Seconds seemed like hours as Doc methodically checked him. Then Daddy's eyes fluttered open. "Eddy, what happened?"

"What? What's everybody doing here? What am doing on the floor? Ow!" Daddy put his hand up to the back of his head. I heard the sirens, signaling the ambulance was near.

"What did you do, Daddy?" I was so happy he was alive and talking. "Did you fall?"

"I was listening to the early New Year's Eve program. I got up to make a drink, and then you were all standing here." He looked up at us. "Damn cat must've tripped me." He scowled at Mr. Striper, who'd hopped up into Daddy's chair and was now settling in to begin a little catnap.

"Do you remember what time that was?" Doc asked. The front door opened. The sound of creaking metal and heavy footsteps made their way toward us. EMTs Billy Wadsworth and Pete Petroski came into the living room, pulling the stretcher along with them.

"No. What time is it now?" Daddy asked, a little bewildered. "I never had anything like this happen before." Doc and Charlie had gotten him up and seated him at the kitchen table.

"It's almost five. Hi, Billy, Pete. Looks like Eddy fell and hit his head. Let's get him over to Memorial and get him checked out," Doc explained. Billy opened his medic bag and readied himself to take Daddy's vitals.

"Eddy, I'm going to check you out too. Do you know how long you were lying there?" Pete asked as Billy did an exam of Daddy's head.

"Ow, hey, watch it." Daddy winced with pain. "I swear it was just a moment ago." Seeing that Daddy was sitting, Mr. Striper wasted no time and jumped up on Daddy's lap. Usually, Daddy would've pushed him off his lap, but he let the cat settle in. He sat quietly, petting the cat for a moment, while Billy finished up.

"I think a little trip to Memorial is a good idea, Doc. Okay, Eddy, let's get you into the ambulance and we'll take a quick ride," Pete said. "Need some help getting up the gurney?"

"I'd have to be dead to be on that damn thing. That and have everybody in town gawking at me. I can walk." And there was the ornery man that I loved. "Hell, why don't I just go with Ethel and Charlie? I'm fine now. I don't really see the need to make all this fuss."

"Eddy, you're going in the rig with the boys. Just to make sure." Doc put his hand on Daddy's shoulder. "And you're going on the gurney, so move along."

"Oh, sweet Jesus," Daddy crabbed.

"Daddy, come on," I urged. "It's for your own good."

"Oh, all right, but I know some nosy body's going to have it all over town before you boys close the doors." And with that, Billie helped Daddy onto the stretcher. The sight of him being strapped in made me shudder. How I hoped that he was all right.

"We'll follow you," I said, turning off lights as we left the house. We got EC into his seat and watched as they loaded Daddy into the ambulance. He sat up and waved to us just as the doors were closing. I blew him a kiss and started to cry.

"Hey, now, he's going to be fine," Charlie said and reached out to hold my hand.

"I hope so. Why did he fall? What could've happened?" I asked and wiped the tears from my cheeks.

"Hard to tell. That's why he's going to the hospital. I bet your dad hasn't been to the doctors in quite a while," he said.

"I bet you're right. He's always been fine. Outside of the smoking. And he stopped that. He's not overweight, and he eats right," I replied. My eyes were glued to the rear door of the ambulance as we followed it down the road. I checked the back seat, and EC had fallen asleep. "Poor EC. I wonder what he thought."

"He most likely felt our fear. What with the loud voices and everybody moving fast, he knew something was going on. Luckily, he's too young and probably won't remember any of this," Charlie said to reassure me.

"I hope so." And we settled into the ride. The ambulance put on the sirens, so we were moving along. Memorial was about a half hour ride, but at this rate, I knew we'd be there sooner.

Once we arrived at the hospital, the emergency room staff took over and we began the waiting game. As I was asking for information about the hours of the hospital cafeteria, I heard my name called.

"Ethel, Charlie, is he all right? Eubie heard it on the scanner and called us. The ambulance left before we could get our coats on and get to the house." And there stood Aunt Eleanor and Uncle Ellsworth.

"Oh, Aunt Ellie. They just took him in. He fell at home, but he's not sure when," I answered and then went to her arms. When I was growing up, she'd always been my shoulder to cry on, and now the sight of her brought me back to that little girl who needed to shed some tears.

"Doc McAllister came and checked him out but couldn't find anything other than the bump on his head from when he fell," Charlie said. He shook hands with Uncle Ellsworth.

"There, there, child. He'll be fine. He's a tough old bird, like his brothers," she consoled me as she patted my back. Aunt Ellie's wool coat and scarf smelled like a combination of mothballs, cedar, and balsam.

"I just saw him this afternoon. He came over for a little nip and then said he was going home to watch the ball drop," Uncle Ellsworth said and stood with his cap in his hands, looking like he might cry too. He was a year older than Daddy, with the similar strong features. When they were young, most people thought they were twins.

"How was he then? Did he say anything about not feeling well?" I asked my uncle.

"You know your dad, always on top of the world. Complaining that with all this snow, we're not going to get much ice fishing in for a while." Uncle Ellsworth had taken a seat next to Aunt Ellie.

"Mommm." EC was pulling at my jeans.

"What is it, honey? Let's say hi to Aunt Ellie and Uncle Ellsworth." I sat down on the other side of Aunt Ellie, with EC toddling to stand by my knee.

"My, my, how this child is growing! Let me get a look at you." Aunt Ellie held her hands out to EC. Tentative for a second, he put his little hand into her pudgy one, and up he went. His hands immediately went up for her glasses. I watched the good-natured exchange of no-nos for a bit.

"We asked about getting something to eat in the cafeteria. Are you two hungry?" I asked.

"No. Your aunt made a venison roast. Eubie and Earl went hunting the other day. Got a nice big buck. Eddy ate with us but only picked at his food. Said he wasn't very hungry. He didn't stay to have a little after-dinner drink like he usually does, either. Said he wanted to get home. I wished he'd stayed a little longer," Uncle Ellsworth said.

"You three run along and get something. We'll hold down the fort," Aunt Ellie said and patted my hand. "We'll come find you if there's any news."

"All right. I'll let them know that you're family too, so they can talk to you if they have to," I said.

64

Charlie picked up EC, and we followed the signs to the cafeteria. There wasn't much to choose from. The hot dishes were the typical, nondescript, tasteless-looking hospital food, so we decided on sandwiches. We got some fruit and two small boxes of cereal for EC. We also got a couple of candy bars in case we were in for longer than we'd anticipated. We sat at a table away from the few staff members who were taking their supper break. And there was our gourmet New Year's Eve celebration.

"I sure wish I were eating venison roast instead of this," Charlie said as he opened the packet of mayonnaise for his turkey sandwich. "Maybe if I put the two halves together, it'll seem better."

"This ham sandwich isn't anything to talk about either. It's amazing how thin tomatoes can be sliced. Tomorrow we'll have a nice dinner. Daddy will like that," I said, determined that everything would be fine tomorrow and I would fix a nice meal for all of us. A few bites of our sandwiches and sips of soda, and we were finished. We took EC's cereal and fruit with us and returned to the waiting room.

"Any news?" I asked Aunt Ellie as I put our things down.

"Nope. I've been real good too. I didn't go up, but I did wave at the nurse. How long does it take?" Aunt Ellie never whined, so I knew she was worried by the tone of her voice.

The five of us were alone in the waiting area, save for a volunteer who'd been trying to get the television to work. Uncle Ellsworth tried to help him, but to no avail. EC was practicing walking up and down the halls. He quickly discovered the automatic door, and Charlie had to be sterner than usual with him about not using it. This, of course, brought crocodile tears and the need for Mommy. He finally fell asleep on the couch as the time painfully and slowly passed. I tried to be patient and only made three trips to the desk to see if they'd forgotten we were there. After my last trip up, I sat down with an audible sigh.

"What's taking so long?" I asked to no one in particular.

"Doesn't look like there's too many folks around tonight. That must be it," Aunt Ellie said, trying to explain things.

"I know, but if he just fell and he's okay, then what's going on?" I said in a tone like that of a fretful child who hadn't gotten her way. I looked over at Charlie, Uncle Ellsworth, and EC. They were talking with the volunteer, and by the hand motions, I could tell the subject had turned to fishing. The sight of them talking easy made me smile. "I bet Daddy would like to be in on that conversation."

"As sure as the sun's coming up tomorrow, he would," Aunt Ellie agreed.

"How's everybody doing, Aunt Ellie? I'm sorry that I haven't been over to talk in a while," I inquired and apologized all at the same time.

"Oh, everybody's doing well, except those that aren't. Your uncles are getting older like your daddy, but no stopping them. They've all retired now and either tinker in the garage with somebody's car or figure out where they'll go fishing when the weather breaks." She chuckled. "Aunt Edna and Aunt Earlene have switched from selling Avon to Mary Kay. They think they're going to make salesladies of the year and drive into Piney Bluffs in that signature pink Cadillac. Now, wouldn't they be something?" We both laughed at the thought of my two bleached-blond aunts and their pink Cadillac. "I tried to help them out, so I got a whole drawer full of stuff that I guess I'll have to learn how to use someday. Your aunt Alice isn't so good. Her happy hour gets a little earlier every day. Good thing your cousin Eunice stayed in Maine after she graduated. Poor Eubie spends most of his time with Ellsworth, working on cars, and then goes home to fix Alice something to eat, not that she wants anything. On a happier note, though, the rest of your cousins have almost all left the nest, with their feet set on good, solid ground."

"I always felt bad, not so much for Aunt Alice, but for Eunice. She was always staying over with me whenever she could. Then Daddy would take us fishing and maybe stop at the Diner for a dish of ice cream, if we'd been good," I said, remembering the good and sad times all at once.

"Alice is the only one who can change Alice, and she never saw that as her job. I'm not preachy by any means, but God does help those who help themselves." She let out a sigh, as she was now done with the family updates. "But enough of that. Let's talk about something more pleasant."

"Well, I do have some good news. But I want to wait until I can tell Daddy and you all at the same time," I said and gave her an upturned smile and tilt of my head.

"Oh! I know, I know! Oh, child, I am just so happy for you!" She put her arm around my shoulders to bring me in for a hug.

"Mum's the word until we see Daddy." And I put my finger up to shush her. "But Charlie and I were talking, and we want to have a big family picnic on Memorial Day. Get everyone from our side and his side and everybody bring a dish. What do you think about that?" I looked into those wise gray eyes and hoped for the acceptance of my idea.

"Well, I think that's a fine idea, Ethel. I can't remember when the last time that we were all together was." Her smile broadened across her face. "Let's see now. May, strawberries will be in season, so we can make buttermilk shortcake and some homemade jam for corn bread. Did I ever give you that recipe?"

"No, I don't think so," I said, and then I heard someone call out my name and saw a woman walk toward us in the waiting area.

"Ethel O'Connor? Hi, I'm Dr. Sandy Moser. You're Eddy's family?" she inquired and came to sit with us. She was a tall thin woman with her brown hair up in a tight bun. She wore green scrubs and a short white coat and looked at us over her bright-red half-glasses.

"Yes, I'm his daughter, Ethel. This is my husband, Charlie, and my son, EC. My daddy's brother, Ellsworth, and his wife, Ellie. How's my father? Is he going to be okay? What happened?" My questions came tumbling out.

"He's doing fine. The first x-rays are all normal, but I'd like to keep him overnight at least, so I can run some other tests tomorrow, when we have a full staff back in the morning. He's in great shape and was very happy to tell me that he'd quit smoking." Her calming voice helped quell some of my anxiety.

"If he's fine, then what happened?" I was anxious to know what the cause was.

"I think he might have gotten up too quickly. He said he hadn't really eaten much of anything today. We'll chalk this one up to low blood sugar. Sometimes when folks live by themselves, especially during the holidays, they tend to forget about getting their three squares. And they might get a little melancholy. I don't think you have anything to worry about, but once he's discharged, he should follow up with your local doctor in about a week or so," she finished.

"Thank you so much, Doctor," I answered. "My mom passed when I was born, and he's been fine all these years, but since I left, he's been alone."

"He told me. He's quite the character, I must say. He did say he has a lady friend, but nothing serious, as he put it," she said and smiled.

"He's a character, that's for sure. And I am surprised he talked about Ginny. They certainly have taken a shine to each other," I agreed.

"You can come in and see him. I'm sure he'll be happy to see all of you. He wasn't too happy to learn that he wasn't going home," Dr. Moser said and led us to Daddy. EC toddled along, holding my hand. When he saw Daddy, he let out a big squeal and went running toward him. Aunt Ellie and Uncle Ellsworth came in, and we stood and waited. Daddy looked surprised to see them.

"There's my guy," Daddy said and got off the stretcher to pick up EC. He gave him a hug and closed his eyes. "This right here is why I get up in the morning." He looked at Dr. Moser.

"Well, then, I'll make sure I prescribe that you see him as often as needed when you're discharged," she said.

"There's going to be another reason to get up," I said as I smiled at Daddy.

"What? What do you mean?" He looked at all of us and scratched his head. And then it hit him. "Are you sure?"

"That was why we stopped by to see you. We went to see Dr. Simon today, and if my dates are right, it looks like EC will be getting a little sister or brother for his birthday," I answered and went to give him a hug.

"Another one? Oh, happy day!" Uncle Ellsworth shook Charlie's hand.

"Congratulations to you all," Dr. Moser said. "Now, Eddy, you stay out of trouble tonight. They'll be down shortly to take you to your room. And don't be too shy about Ginny. Happy New Year to you all." She gave Daddy a handshake, and then she was off to her next patient.

"For the love of Pete, I'm going to be a grampa again!" Daddy smiled and clapped Charlie on the back. "Congratulations. But what are you two doing here?" He was now addressing his brother and sister-in-law.

"Eubie heard the call come out over the scanner and called us. But the boys had already taken you in the rig by the time we got ready to leave," Aunt Ellie said. "How are you? You feel okay?"

"No need for you all coming out like this." Daddy shook his head at Aunt Ellie.

"Hell of a knot you got going on there, brother." Uncle Ellsworth had come over to see the knot on the back of Daddy's head.

"Careful there, damn thing hurts like hell." Daddy pushed his brother's hand away.

"Besides, I wanted to know whether or not you were dead. You got a lot of fishing gear that needs to be divvied up. I wanted to get the jump on Eubie and Earl." Uncle Ellsworth laughed.

"Don't you be writing my obituary just yet. I got a lot of time left to beat you and anybody else at fishing." Daddy smiled at all of us. "Don't know why I can't go home. I feel just fine. No need of this." And he picked up the edges of his johnny.

"Daddy, now, the doctor knows best. One night in the hospital won't hurt," I said and held his hand.

"Eddy Koontz?" A chipper orderly had walked in with a wheel-chair. "Ready to take you to your room now. Let's see, you're going to 106B. Window view of the woods. How does that sound? Do you need help?"

"Window view, huh? I'm fine. I can get off this thing just fine," Daddy said and got down from the stretcher, holding his johnny behind his back, and took his seat. "You all go home, and Happy

New Year." We said our goodbyes; he waved at us and was wheeled away.

"We're going to run along home. I'll check in on the cat, Ethel, so don't worry about him. You let us know if anything changes," Aunt Ellie said and came to put her arm around my shoulders. "He'll be fine. Don't you worry."

"Thanks, Aunt Ellie." I squeezed my eyes tight to hold back another round of tears. "I know."

"I'll see you tomorrow. G'night, Daddy!" I called out after him.

"G'night, Ethel," I heard him say as the orderly turned the corner with him.

CHAPTER 10

NEW YEAR'S DAY. *GOOD MORNING, 1981.* I was up about five and slipped out of bed, leaving Charlie sleeping peacefully. With Daddy on my mind, I hadn't slept much. The need for more tests worried me, but my realistic side told me that he was in the best place he could be. I'd call around eight to see how his night had been. I pulled my fluffy robe around me to chase the chill. I put on a pot of coffee. That should help, I thought. Nope, still cold. A fire would do the trick, so I put some logs on the fireplace, and after an elaborate tenting of kindling, I was able to coax the wood to ignite. I pulled a chair close to the hearth and sat for a while, staring into the soothing magic of the red-and-yellow flames. The dogs came over to investigate what I'd been doing. Mutt lay down and put his paw on my leg and laid his head down. It was if he were saying, "Things will be all right." Jeff was a bit more arduous with his affection and started to lick my face. He sat back satisfied, his job done. I sat for a while, quiet, thinking and not thinking. Then Jeff gave me a little nudge with his nose, signaling it was time.

"Okay, you two, how about a little run?" I let the dogs out. They loved to run in the snow and made a circuit of pathways around the house, to the trees, the river, and back again. I watched as they played with each other, their golden fur now snow-covered from one last tussle before coming in. I let them in, they slurped some water, and then they retired to their beds to lick the snow from their paws.

I poured a cup of coffee, but when the first whiff went from my nose to my palate, I poured it back into the pot. I'd make some tea later. Restless, I walked down the hallway to the office. In the soft hues of twilight, I looked at the drawings of *Sophie's Sled.* Were they just that, only drawings of what Momma might have wished for her daughter? A happy life with a friend named Annie? Was there a clue? Was there something that I was missing? I looked at the face of Annie. Who was she? Was she my aunt, as I'd first thought? I turned on the light and looked closer to see if a word or initials had been written anywhere on the drawings. Nothing. The only words were written on the sled, "Flexible Flyer." And that was that. Focusing on the sled reminded me that we needed to get a sled for EC. I imagined him like the toddlers in the picture, rolling in the snow and sledding. I heard footsteps, and there was Charlie, hair mussed from sleep.

"What are you doing up so early?" he asked and walked over and put his arms around me.

"Couldn't sleep, thinking about Daddy," I said and nestled into his arms. He'd put on a flannel shirt, and the softness of it was comforting to me.

"I'd say that was natural, but what are you doing in here? Thinking of writing?" He kissed the top of my head.

"No writing, but I can't shake the idea that these pages are showing me something. I just don't know what it is yet," I answered and turned out of his arms to hold up one of the pictures.

"You'll find her, I know you will," he said.

"This has to be someplace that Momma knew. Although, it doesn't look like anything that I've seen in the times that I've been to Oxford." I put the picture down. "Ready for a nice breakfast?" I asked him.

"You know it. What's on the menu?" he said and poured himself a cup of coffee and took a seat at the breakfast bar.

"Well, let's see. EC loves his pancakes and sausage. And maybe a quiche for us. I'll start the quiche now, and then we can wake EC." I turned on the oven and started to prepare the quiche. "All I have is cheese and turkey. Is that okay with you?"

"Anything you make is wonderful, unless you want me to take over," Charlie said, pointed to himself, and smiled. Charlie was masterful at the grill but had a long way to go when he took his game inside.

"That's okay, dear. You go relax. I'll call Dad…" And I stopped in midsentence. It was automatic to think to invite him for breakfast. "Phooey."

"Why don't you call the hospital now and get it over with?" Charlie said.

"Do you think it's too early? It's only six thirty," I said. I'd finished the quiche and popped it into the oven.

"Ethel, it's a hospital. Someone should be on his floor to answer the phone," he replied. "And they've probably been checking him most of the night, anyway."

"You're right. I'll call now." I took out the phone book and found Memorial's number.

"Memorial, how may I direct your call?" an efficient voice answered.

"I'd like to speak to a nurse. My father's in room 106B," I said.

"One moment." A click and then a ring.

"Med One, this is Lisa, how can I help you?" Another efficient-sounding voice was at work today.

"Hi, Lisa. I'm inquiring about my father, Eddy Koontz. He was admitted last night. I'm his daughter, Ethel. Can you tell me how he's he doing?" I waited.

"Let's see. They're just giving report, but I can tell you he seems to have had a good night. I've seen him up, walking around. He's stopped by the desk to chat. He's a friendly guy. He keeps asking when he can go home. They've got some blood work ordered. That's about all I can tell you. You can give a call back in about a half hour. His nurse will know more by then." And now she waited.

"That sounds good. Can you tell him I called? What time are visiting hours?" I said.

"I'll tell him. He should be happy to hear you called. Visiting hours start at ten. Anything else?" The efficient person now needed to wrap up.

"No, thank you very much," I said, and that was it.

"How's he doing?" Charlie asked.

"Up and walking around and wants to know when he can come home." I turned back to the stove and began to cook the sausage. "I just hope there's nothing more than low blood sugar. The part that the doctor said about him being melancholy, well, I've never thought about Daddy sitting around, feeling sorry for himself."

"Aw, I don't think he's feeling sorry for himself. But I do think he might raise an extra glass to your mom and chat with her from time to time." Charlie's thoughts were probably true.

"I have to talk with him about a lot of things when he comes home. I want to make sure he's okay," I said and turned the sausage over. "And if I find Sophie, well, that's going to remove another star from Momma's crown."

"That will be hard for him. To look at Sophie and realize the secrets your mother kept from him. He's not going to like it." He shook his head at me.

"I know. A lot has happened over the past year, but if and when it happens, he'll have to face it. Now, why don't you go find the poster child for the terrible twos and I'll make some pancakes?" I relented.

And so the first morning of the new year began. *What do you have in store for us?* I wondered. I wished for understanding and forgiveness when it came to Daddy. And my hope was that somehow, this year, I would finally have the piece of Momma and the rest of the family that I needed.

The hospital was busy this morning. Staff bustled this way and that, in and out of patients' rooms. The hallway tiles gleamed bright white and gray. EC's shoes sounded like soft claps as he tottered his way along between us. Almost at Daddy's room, I could hear his voice.

"I hope I'm not staying for lunch. Breakfast was no prize, you know," he was telling someone.

"Well, Mr. Koontz, to be on the safe side, the doctor wants you to limit your salt intake." A female voice was defending her point of view about the food.

"You mean limit the taste. Have you ever tasted this food, Ms. Johnson?" Daddy was not seeing the reasoning behind her nutritional intentions.

"What's this? Complaining about food?" I asked as we came around the corner to his bed. "Hi, I'm Ethel. I hear you're trying to let my father know what's best for him?"

"Hello, I'm June Johnson, assistant dietician here at Memorial. And yes, your father and I were discussing the value in limiting his salt intake and other things for maintaining a healthy diet." Ms. Johnson was petite and, with her trim figure, appeared to be testament to healthy eating. She was trying her best to be good-natured with my curmudgeonly father.

"Healthy-schmealthy. I'll be much better when I'm out of here. Come see Grampa." And Daddy swung his legs over the side of the bed to grab ahold of EC. EC climbed up in bed with Daddy, and after a hug, Daddy started to show him how to play with the bed controls.

"I don't know when they'll let you go, Daddy. You have to wait for the doctor to come in," I said, and we put our coats on the vinyl chairs.

"Well, I'll let you visit with your family, Mr. Koontz. But remember, try to think about the different foods you eat. I'll leave this pamphlet with you. Nice to meet all of you." She nodded and left us.

"Can you get me something from the cafeteria?" Daddy pleaded. He picked up the pamphlet, shook his head, and started to look for the wastepaper basket.

"Daddy, you've only had one meal. How bad could it have been?" I asked and started to fluff his pillow. Feeling the plastic under the pillowcase, I realized it wasn't going to fluff.

"I wouldn't have fed that stuff to the dogs. Damn toast was dry. Scrambled eggs were in name only. I don't think an egg ever went near that scoop of yellow goo." He shook his head. "And don't even get me started on the coffee."

"So I suppose you'd like to go home." And there stood Dr. Moser with a chart in her hands. She must have been standing within earshot. "I don't like the coffee here very much myself."

"Good morning, Doctor," Daddy said and blushed a bit, having been caught in his complaint. "Yes, ma'am, I would."

"Well, good, then. Your lab tests all came back normal. The x-ray of your skull showed no sign of fractures. Just keep on doing what you're doing, watch your salt intake, and don't forget to follow up with Dr. McAllister. I made some copies of your blood and radiology reports for him." She handed Daddy an envelope. "And don't forget, get at least five days a week of this little guy." She pointed to EC, who was reaching for her stethoscope.

"I was so worried. This is good to hear," I said as I inwardly let out a sigh of relief.

"Thanks, Doc, that's great news," Daddy said and reached out to shake her hand.

"Outside of this one blip, you're a very healthy man for your age. Good luck with your lady friend too. Take care, all of you," she said and shook Daddy's hand. At the mention of Ginny, Daddy wrinkled his nose.

"You're sure there's nothing more? Of course, I'm happy that he's okay. Is there anyone other than our local doctor that he should check in with?" I was thrilled with the news, but I wanted to make sure that my daddy was really okay.

"Ethel, this very smart doctor has said I'm fine. Now let's go. I need a decent cup of coffee and a real breakfast," Daddy said and headed toward the closet for his clothes.

"He really is going to be okay. Just don't forget to miss a meal," she answered with a smile.

"Don't you worry, I got plenty of good food all around me. I'm not too shabby of a cook, even if I do say so myself." Daddy was dressing in record time and was buckling his belt as Dr. Moser waved goodbye.

"Oh, Daddy," I said and linked arms with him as we all left his room. *Phew*, I thought. *Thank you to whoever's up there for helping him dodge a bullet.*

The trip back to Piney Bluffs found not a single place open for breakfast on New Year's Day. There was one gas station that advertised coffee, but Daddy decided he could make his own pot once he got home. When we opened the door to Daddy's house, the smell of coffee and bacon filled the air.

"Whoever you are, you can take whatever you want, but leave the coffee and bacon," Daddy said as we made our way to the kitchen. And there stood Aunt Ellie at the stove. Crispy home fries in one pan, bacon going in another, and the coffeepot full, just waiting to have its first cup poured. Uncle Ellsworth was sitting at the table, reading *Field and Stream* and smiling when he saw his brother.

"You got nothing I want, Eddy, except for Mr. Striper here." She stood with her hands on her hips next to one of the kitchen chairs. The cat was sitting in the chair, waiting patiently for what I was sure wasn't his first morsel of bacon.

"Damn mooching cat," Daddy said and walked over to scratch him behind the ears. "Thanks, Ellie. I tell you, that hospital food is awful!"

"Good to see you, brother." Uncle Ellsworth gave Daddy a handshake, and they had just a moment as two old guys looked into each other's eyes. They set their jaws and nodded at each other.

"Morning, Aunt Ellie, Uncle Ellsworth," I said and gave her a hug. "Thanks." Charlie had taken the coats to put them over the hall railing. EC went to "help" his daddy. When they came back into the kitchen, EC went over and tugged on Aunt Ellie's apron.

"Hi, Charlie. And good morning to you, EC." She bent over, picked him up, and gave him a kiss. "How about a nice piece of bacon? I got some cooling right here." She gave him a piece, which he grabbed with his pudgy hand, and then he asked to get down. Mr. Striper lost no time in going to EC's side, in hopes for more bacon, or at least a lick of EC's hand. "I wasn't sure if you'd be coming home or not, but I saw Ethel's car go by, and I figured I'd take my chances. So I told Ellsworth we were going to fix you all a nice brunch or breakfast. Now, let's sit down and I'll start some eggs. Who wants what?"

I got up and started to make toast and fill juice glasses. For the next hour, we sat and enjoyed, as Daddy put it, a meal that was almost as good as Andy's. Daddy's eyes showed how happy he was to be seated at his table, surrounded by his family. I was sure that last night, in the silence of his hospital bed, he'd had some time to think about a lot of things. What would have happened if we hadn't come when we did? I could only imagine if he'd hit his head worse than he did. I'd never thought of Daddy as vulnerable. But then again, I'd never thought of my mother as anything but perfect. How things change. As we started to clean up, the phone rang. I went to answer it.

"Hello, happy New Year," I said into the receiver.

"Happy New Year to you, too, Ethel. Is your dad there?" It was the familiar voice of Ginny.

"He sure is. Hold on a second. Daddy, somebody wants to talk to you." I held out the receiver to him and smiled at him.

"Who the heck could be calling me? I got just about everyone I know right here in front of me. And what are you smiling about?" he asked me and took the phone. "Hello? Oh, hi, Ginny. Happy New Year to you too. No, you're not interrupting anything. We're just sitting around, having a little late breakfast, but we're finishing up."

Aunt Ellie and I tried not to appear that we were eavesdropping; however, with the size of Daddy's kitchen and location of the wall phone, well, we heard every word. It sounded like Ginny was asking Daddy to come visit her. My aunt and I exchanged smiles as we nudged each other at the sink. Uncle Ellsworth and Charlie took EC into the sunroom to turn on the football game.

"Sure, that sounds fine. Five o'clock tomorrow, then. I'll be there. Thanks! You too." And with that, he hung up. Aunt Ellie and I turned to look at him.

"Well?" I asked and waited. Aunt Ellie was drying her hands on a towel and waited as well.

"What? Ginny asked me over for dinner tomorrow night. That's it." Daddy scrunched up his face at me and Aunt Ellie. "Let's see about the Rose Bowl. Hey, Charlie, is Michigan winning? Washington doesn't have a chance, if you ask me." And that was that. Nothing further to say.

"Has Daddy said anything to you and Uncle Ellsworth about Ginny?" I asked once I knew Daddy was out of earshot.

"He has. First time since your mom passed that he's talked about anyone," she replied.

"She's really a sweet woman, and she likes to fish," I added.

"That's what he told us too. I'm happy for him. It's about time. And with all the other business that's happened, well, I think he knows what he should do. He needs to listen to his heart again." Aunt Ellie patted my hand and brought the dish towel up to dry her eye.

"I hope he does, Aunt Ellie," I agreed. "I hope he does."

CHAPTER 11

Monday morning, and finally back to work. *Finally* was maybe not the right word to use. We'd enjoyed the extended time off for the holiday, but I liked the structure of work and our morning routine that went along with it. Even EC had been a little off after a few days. I think he missed all of his buddies at Miss Minnie's. While the dogs were happy to sit by his side, they were in no way equipped to help push his trucks around the living room or build towers with his blocks. We'd gotten him a flying saucer for Christmas and tried to harness the dogs to pull him around. However, we soon understood that retrievers were not mushers. That was until we discovered that if we threw a snowball, the dogs would chase it, pulling EC screaming with delight behind them.

The good news was that it hadn't snowed in a few days, but the winter air had become frigid. EC was bundled up in his new snowsuit and ready to go. Looking at him in the rearview mirror, I realized I could see more of him now. Growing up way too fast. Soon there would be two faces in that mirror. *And who would you be?* I patted my tummy as it did a little growl. *Hungry, my little one? I know. We'll have something soon.*

We arrived at Minnie's, and it was a quick change: snowsuit and boots off, shoes on, and he was off. The clinging-to-my-leg period of goodbyes had vanished. I gave Minnie a wave as she, like Mother Goose, was gathering the children around her for their morning story. As I rounded the corner into town, I saw that the lights were already on inside *The Bugle*. Thick frost framed the windows in a Currier and Ives fashion, with Caleb in the center, at work at his typewriter.

"I was wondering if you'd gotten another job or won the lottery," Caleb said as I came through the door.

"No, I turned it down. Who could give up all this? And you?" I replied back to him as I put my things away.

"Good. I'd hate to have to bring someone else in at this point in my life. You were a tough pony to break, I'll tell you that much," he said as he continued to take shots at me.

"Was I now? Let me see, where did I put that number for the *Herald*?" I rummaged through my purse.

"Okay, truce. Good to see you, Ethel. Coffee's on," Caleb said and finally stopped his banter.

"And good to be back. But no to the coffee. Remember my heartburn? Well, it's back with this pregnancy, too," I said and went to put water on for tea.

"Oh, my goodness, I completely forgot. How did you make out at the doctor?" Caleb asked apologetically. "Are you feeling all right?"

"I'm fine, perfectly perfect. However, the doctor was very interested to know that my mother had another child before me," I answered.

"And...?" He waited.

"And nothing, really. There's nothing to base anything on. Doesn't that sound conclusive? Without any knowledge of how or where my mother delivered my sister, well, like I said, there's nothing to know. I'll need to keep my appointments and watch for anything out of the ordinary, just like last time," I said as I sat back at my desk, dunking my tea bag in my cup.

"As long as you're going to be fine, that's the main thing. How about your writing? Did you get anything done?" he inquired.

"No. Although I did write the first line, but that's it. Honestly, Caleb, I don't think I'll be able to write this story until I find Sophie. There's just something in my gut that tells me that," I responded.

"So what's your next step, then?" he asked.

"I have to go talk to Henry. I mean, he's the one who dropped the bombshell with the birth certificate showing his name as father," I answered. "And then there's the vague information that Joseph gave me about his father sending Momma away to have the baby. Who knows where that would even be?"

"Why not call him? Wouldn't that be better?" Caleb pursued.

"No, it wouldn't, not with Henry. In the conversations with him, when I was trying to find out more about Momma, well, he holds back. It's almost like talking to Daddy. You have to draw the information out of him. He'll tell you, but it will be when you've cracked opened the door to that particular thing," I said.

"Ah, your journalist skills at their finest," he commented.

"Exactly," I concurred.

"You can go anytime, you know that," Caleb offered.

"I know. I was hoping for the weather to break a little," I said.

"If you're waiting for that, then you'll be sitting here until March." He laughed.

"You're right, maybe I'll go up on Friday. I can stop in and see Ginny and Andre too," I finally decided.

"Okay, that's settled. And how's Eddy? I heard he had a little fall?" Caleb continued to catch up.

"Ah, small towns. But yes, he did fall. We were on our way back from the doctor to tell him the good news about the baby. We walked in, and there he was, out cold on the floor. I was so scared. I didn't know what'd happened. Still don't, really. He spent the night at Memorial. He wasn't pleased about that, let me tell you, hospital food and all. X-rays and blood work were normal. Low blood sugar is all the doctor could pin it on," I explained.

"Well, that's good," Caleb said. "Anything else?"

"Daddy had a dinner date at Ginny's house on Friday," I said.

"Eddy is smitten. I knew it. I told Sadie that right after Christmas dinner. The way he was so attentive to what she was saying, and how they looked at each other. Now, that should keep a smile on his face." Caleb was happy to comment on this.

"I know. I called him Saturday to ask how it went. He was very noncommittal, saying it was fine, it was dinner, and that was that. I asked if he'd brought her anything, and he said he'd stopped at Ruthie's earlier in the day and brought some cookies for dessert," I related.

"Anything else come of that?" he asked.

"If you ask Daddy, I'm sure there's nothing he'd say. Ginny, however, would be happy to tell me. I think I'll give her a call tonight to say happy New Year and then let her know I'll be stopping by on Friday," I replied. "And how about you and Sadie? Did you celebrate the new year?"

"Yes, we did, in fine fashion, if I must say so. We treated ourselves and went over to the Inn. Alice put together a great menu. She started us with a shrimp cocktail—oh, they were spectacular, so succulent. Beef tenderloins with blue cheese béarnaise, mushroom casserole with just the right amount of cheese and bread crumb topping, bright sautéed green beans and snow peas, all on a snowy pillow of their secret creamy mashed potatoes. Oh, out of this world. And for dessert, little pots of chocolate, like adult pudding." He sat there almost dreamy-eyed as he described the meal. I thought back to our hospital meal of turkey and ham sandwiches and was extremely envious.

"Watch out, or we'll be needing you to do a food column with those luscious descriptions. Gosh, that made me hungry!" I opened my drawer to see if there was anything to munch on. I'd brought a piece of quiche and an apple for lunch, but I'd completely forgotten about my breakfast.

"That might not be a bad thing. Like in the big cities, they have the mystery diner. Someone who visits great restaurants and then writes accolades or scathing reports on the food. No one knows when he'll strike. Hmmm, you may be on to something, Ethel," he joked.

"So once you've reviewed the Inn, Ruthie's, Andy's Diner, and maybe the Gas-N-Go for their hot dogs, then where?" I smiled and shook my head at this idea.

"Well, I could do a regional gourmet review. Yes, call it something like, let's see…I've got it, New England Noshes, by Ned Nesselrode." And he put his hands out as if he were writing his alliterative title on a banner.

"That's just dandy, Ned, but do you have a cookie or anything in your drawer? I'm ravenous. In trying to get EC ready for Minnie's, I forgot to pack myself something for breakfast," I lamented. I'd gotten up and went into the back room, searching through the cupboards. Nothing.

"Sorry, there's nothing here," he said as he looked in all the pigeonholes in his desk. He held up a piece of gum. I shook my head no. "Just to show you what kind of boss I am, how about I go over to Ruthie's and get us something for breakfast?"

"Oh, that would be wonderful. Let's see, what do I want? A muffin. No, maybe a scone. No, wait, almond crescent. Oh, I don't know." I was torn between all the wonderful things that I remembered to be in Ruthie's cases. Caleb was chuckling as he put on his coat.

"I'll get an assortment. That way, you won't have to go through executive decisions so early in the morning." And with that, he was out the door.

I stood by the window and watched him hurry across to Ruthie's. The bakery was full of customers this early Monday morning. Every table was full. I turned to look over at Andy's. The counter at the Diner was packed with patrons as well. I was sure they were telling and retelling one another about their holiday weekend and the resolutions that they'd already broken. Everyone was back to the routines of their daily lives. Routines were so routine, but comforting. I laughed to myself.

I saw Charlie pull up in front of the Emporium. He stomped through the snowed-in walkways and onto the porch. He looked over toward *The Bugle* and, seeing me in the window, gave me a wave and blew me a kiss, which I returned. I watched as he fumbled for his keys. *Other pocket, honey,* I called to him telepathically. Finding it, he unlocked the door and flipped on the lights. The rough-cut wood made the light seem so much brighter. Russell and Robert had decided to keep the ceilings open with exposed beams for a rustic look. Charlie had finished with the insulation before Christmas and was waiting for the brothers to decide on the walls and shelving units. Charlie ordered several catalogs for their selections. They were coming up next week to make the final choices on that and the furniture.

I saw movement out of the corner of my eye, and Caleb was back, carrying a box and a bag. I went to open the door for him.

"Holy cow, is it cold out there! I think we're going to have to defrost these just from the walk back here." He went to the back room while I closed the door.

The blast of cold air gave me a quick shiver, and I grabbed the edges of my down vest around me and zipped it up to my neck. Hmm, getting a little snug already, I thought as I pulled it down over my hips.

"I was going to get you another tea, but I figured it would be ice-cold by the time I got back. Ruthie sent you over a couple of bags of some new kinds of teas she's getting in from a company in Connecticut, Bigelow Tea. The flavor is Constant Comment. Interesting, don't you think?"

"This tea smells amazing. I'm making a cup right now," I said as I inhaled the aroma from the tea packet. "There's fruit and spice. And what's in the box?" I said as I lifted the lid.

"Ruthie made you a special ham-and-cheese croissant with sliced apples. I told her you were famished, and she went right to work. Got myself one as well." Caleb put the croissants onto plates. "Oh, good. She wrapped them in foil, so they're still warm."

"What kind cheese did she use?" I asked as I took the steaming teakettle from the stove. "Oh, this tea is heavenly." I dunked the bag, releasing its aroma.

"Fresh Havarti from McCreery's, and she put on just a touch of spicy mustard." He brought the sandwiches back to our desks, and we dived in.

"Hmmm, this is wonderful. I'm not sure if it's because I'm hungry or this is just that good," I murmured through my first bite.

"No, it's *that* good. See how the creaminess of the cheese oozes and fills the gentle, buttery folds of the croissant? Then there's the tartness of the apple to surprise you. And finally, the mustard gives that slight kick to the ham and pulls all the flavors together." Caleb was continuing with his gourmet chatter.

"Okay, Ned," I joked with him. "But what about Sadie's culinary experiences? How are you going to describe all your lovely wife's gastronomical adventures?"

"Carefully, very carefully," he answered.

CHAPTER 12

I T WAS THURSDAY, AND I was stopping at Daddy's after work. I knew he'd gone to his appointment with Doc McAllister in the morning, and I wanted to see how he'd made out. I'm sure he'd pooh-poohed anything that Doc would recommend, but there was something more that we, or should I say that I, needed to talk to him about. We really hadn't talked much about Momma and my half sister since the day of the fishing derby and Joseph's confession. While I was sure he'd wrestled with it in his own way, we needed to have this conversation. If in fact I found Sophie, I wanted to know how he felt and what it would mean to our family. Charlie and I decided that he would pick EC up today so my conversation with Daddy could take place without any distractions.

The wind whipped the Jeep's door closed as I got out in front of the house. Damned cold weather. I pulled my coat closer around my neck and tugged at my hat to cover my ears. When I got to the front step, I realized that I hadn't been in the house since New Year's Eve, when we found him on the floor. I knew it was silly, but I steeled myself against another such sight as I opened the door.

"Daddy, hi, it's me," I said as I came through the door. Mr. Striper must have heard my car, as he was already at his spot on the stairs, waiting to have his chin scratched when I walked in. "Hey, there, sweetie. How's Daddy doing today, huh?"

"If you want to know how I am, then you should ask me instead of that damned cat," Daddy called out to me. He was standing at the stove, cooking sausage and getting ready to make pancakes. He didn't look up as I went over to him and kissed his cheek. Some sausages, plump and juicy-looking, were already on the plate, and I snatched one.

"This is yummy, Daddy. But how come you're making so much?" I saw that he was cooking about two dozen sausages and had a couple of cast-iron skillets ready with the lard slowly melting in the bottoms.

"I told your aunt Ellie and uncle Ellsworth to come over tonight. She's been cooking and sending something over every day since I got out of the hospital, so I thought I'd return the favor." He put the last of the sausage links into the pan to cook. "You're welcome to stay too. Hey, where's Junior?" A twinge of guilt came over me. Even though it had only been a couple of days since he'd been home, I'd called every day, but I hadn't seen him, or even thought to bring him any food. He'd told me that he was fine and could fend for himself. Oh, phooey, some daughter I was.

"Charlie picked him up early today, so they're home, waiting for me," I said and tried to figure out where to begin.

"Well, come on, sit down. When you come alone, there's always something on your mind." He turned the burner down to low, wiped his hands on his towel, and we both sat at the table. Just when I thought he'd never paid attention, he surprised me at how well he knew me.

"What did Doc have to say today?" I started. I looked at Daddy. He seemed the same, maybe a little tired around the eyes, but not much had changed.

"He said I've got a hard head and don't forget to eat," he replied as he drummed his fingers on the table. "Next question."

"Gee, Daddy, don't be such a grump," I said and wrinkled my forehead, trying to understand why he was cranky.

"I'm not grumpy. I know something else is bothering you, so out with it." He looked me in the eyes.

"Daddy, I'm going to try to find Sophie," I began.

"I know that. I'd think something was wrong with you if you didn't," he stated. While he wasn't saying no to anything, he wasn't really making this any easier.

"I want to know how this is going to make you feel," I began. "When she comes to meet us, I'm sure it will be a shock and surprise to her."

"Ethel, there's a lot of what-ifs going to happen before whom-ever you find is able to sit down at Sunday dinner with us. Shock and surprise is nothing. The person you find might not want what you're offering," he said, his crankiness gone. I could tell by the way he spoke that he'd been thinking about this too.

"I know, Daddy. I just hope that I can find her, and then…," I said and looked off.

"And then it will be up to her to either slam the door in your face or let you in. It's really going to be her call," he said with more wisdom than I gave him credit for. "She'll have a family who most likely haven't told her anything about how she came to be. Never mind that they themselves might not know about your momma. Remember, you told me that the birth certificate could be a trumped-up thing as well."

"Oh, Daddy. I'm so sorry for doing all this," I said as I wiped the tears from the corners of my eyes.

"Now, now, crying's not going to help this. What happened before I met your momma was a part of her life that she wasn't proud of. People never tell you their whole story, Ethel. You should know that by now. Do you think I told her about all the things that happened while I was in the war? No, sir, I didn't. There were lots of things we did that we weren't proud of either. But we had to do it to survive. Bad things like what your momma or I had to live through will eat you up if you let them. But you have to go on." He took a sip of coffee, and we were both quiet for a moment.

"I'm going to talk to Henry tomorrow," I finally said.

"Well, that seems like the best place to start," Daddy agreed. "Talk about having something inside of you all this time and not telling a soul."

"I know. I can only imagine what he's going to say." I shook my head and let out a sigh.

"You're going to find her, for better or worse. But keep in mind that while you've been chasing after a family that might be, you've got a pretty good lot of us right under your nose," he reminded me and patted my hand.

"I know, Daddy. You, Charlie, EC, and whoever this one is and not to mention all my aunts and uncles and cousins, why, they are the most loving family that anyone could ask for. Maybe that's what makes me want to find her so badly. I want her to know us, all of us." I rubbed my belly and thought about who this child was going to be.

"You always did want the best for everyone. That's just the way you are. So do you have a name yet?" he said, changing the subject.

"No, we don't know what the sex is yet, so we haven't even given it a thought," I answered, somewhat bewildered by his question.

"Well, I think we should give it a name. Maybe a little nickname, until you know for sure. Let's see...I know, how about Minnow?" Daddy smiled.

"Daddy! That was the name of our last cat! You're not going to give my child a cat's name!" We both laughed.

"I think it's a fine one. Could be for either a boy or a girl. Yup, that's it for me. Now I've got a Junior and a Minnow." And he smiled, very satisfied with himself.

A knock on the door and a "Halloo" signaled that Aunt Ellie and Uncle Ellsworth were here. I heard them stomping their feet and putting their coats on the railing as they came along the hallway.

"Well, Ethel, it's so good to see you, honey. How are you feeling?" Aunt Ellie came over to me, and I got up to give her a hug.

"I'm fine, Aunt Ellie. And how are you? Daddy tells me you're keeping his pants from falling down with your good cooking." She returned the hug with a little pat of reassurance.

"Oh, he's an ornery cuss, if you let him get hungry. Got to feed him a little to keep him smiling," she said, proud of herself.

"I was the one with the better temperament," remarked Uncle Ellsworth, sticking his thumbs under his suspenders. I gave him a hug too.

"Hell, you were," Daddy joked. "I can just as easily give this food to the cat, you keep this kind of talk up."

"Now, if you two can't be civil, I'm taking Aunt Ellie to my house and getting her away from this," I said and laughed at the good-natured chatter.

"Where's Charlie and the little guy? Aren't you eating with us?" Aunt Ellie seemed disappointed.

"Not this time, Aunt Ellie. But we will soon. I know, why don't you all come out to our house, say, next Saturday? A family pot-luck—how does that sound? Would you like that?" I looked at the three faces and saw the smiles broaden.

"That sounds great. Be good to get everybody out and see how they're doing. None of us are getting any younger, you know." She nodded toward Uncle Ellsworth.

"Hey, it wasn't I who ended up in the hospital," my uncle responded and pointed his finger at Daddy.

"Real sport you are," Daddy said and got up to turn the sausages. "Here, Mr. Striper, come and get it." While Daddy was fooling, Mr. Striper knew his name and immediately jumped right up into the chair at the table. His tawny striped head all but rested on the table as he waited for sausage. We all laughed.

"Okay, all of you, now be good. I've got two boys that are probably wondering where I am. Love you all." I hugged each one. I left them as they continued to lovingly jaw at one another about this and that.

I thought about what Daddy said about family as I drove home. I'd been searching for something about my mother ever since I could remember. In the past couple of years, I'd been able to take charge of that quest. For better or worse, I'd found information both surprising and questionable about the people I knew and loved. This hunt for Sophie would be the end of Momma's story. And as Daddy had put it, right under my nose was some of the best family that anyone could ask for. I just wanted to add one more to my family. Just one more.

CHAPTER 13

IT STARTED TO SNOW THURSDAY night, just before we'd gone to bed. It would be nice, I thought, to have a fresh cover of white. In the past few days, the snow had begun to look less than pristine, but when we got up on Friday morning, we found it must have snowed all night long, as there was now at least ten inches on top of the hard pack of the other day. So much for my thoughts of a little fresh coat! As I looked out the window, I thought about changing my mind and not going to see Henry today. But I convinced myself that the sooner I talked to him, then the sooner I could get on with wherever this was going to take me.

I got EC ready, and we went downstairs to have breakfast and get ready for the day. Charlie had already been up and had plowed the driveway. He came in with rosy cheeks and chilly hands that he childishly slid down my neck.

"Hey, there! That's cold!" I scolded him. He grinned at me.

"You sure you don't want me to drive you up there?" he asked, now turning from a mischievous child into my chivalrous husband.

"I can handle this, hon. Being three months pregnant hasn't impaired my driving skills yet, anyway," I answered. "Besides, don't you have stuff to get ready for Russell and Robert?"

"Yes, but they'd understand," he replied.

"No, I won't hear of it. You stay and get ready. I've got four-wheel drive. I'll be fine." And with that, the conversation of my safety ended. We ate a quick breakfast of oatmeal, bananas, and maple syrup. EC recently discovered a liking for oatmeal and was very happy when it appeared in his little blue bowl. All done with breakfast, Charlie bundled up EC, and my two men were out the door to begin their day. I looked out the kitchen window as Charlie carried our little guy in his arms. EC's conversation was really only appreciated by Charlie and me, and maybe Daddy. I could see Charlie laughing as he buckled EC into his seat. I took another sip of tea, the last bite of banana, and I was out the door too.

The drive up was slick in spots as I crossed state roads and town roads, but for the most part, the snow blew away as I drove along. Finally arriving at the Oxford town hall, I was happy to see that the parking lot had been plowed. It was empty, save for one car near the back ramp. A teenager was shoveling the sidewalk as I walked up to the door. He stopped and politely held the door for me as I entered.

"Not too many folks in today, ma'am, what with all this snow. It's been something, hasn't it?" he said. He looked like he was happy to have a break from his shoveling and rested his arm on the handle.

"Yes, it has. Is Henry here today?" I asked, momentarily chiding myself for not calling ahead.

"Aw, Henry's always here. Says he doesn't want to disappoint anyone," the young man replied and opened the door.

"Thanks," I said. I smiled and let the door close behind me. Doesn't want to disappoint anyone? I guess I mustn't be on that list. The offices were quiet. No clacking typewriters, and no phones ringing. The light was on in the selectman's office, but that was it for any other signs of life. I walked the corridor to Henry's office. I took a deep breath and opened the door. His head down, intent on the documents in front of him. As before, his desk was piled with books and papers crossed this way and that.

"Have a seat. I'll be with you in a minute," he said without looking up. I took a seat on the one wooden chair that constituted the waiting room. I picked up the same two-year-old *Farmers' Almanac* that had been there since the first day I'd walked into this office about six months ago.

"Next time I come, I'll bring you a new magazine. I've almost got this one memorized," I replied with a bite to my tone. Whether it was my tone or the fact that he recognized my voice, he looked up immediately.

"Ethel." He looked up. In an instant, his face went through a myriad of emotions, with relief coming last. He turned his wheelchair to face me.

"Hello, Henry," I answered and waited.

"Please come over and sit. Listen, I can explain," he started. He ran his hands through his thick gray hair and appeared to be in thought, considering where he should begin.

"I hope so," I said and got up to take the chair near his desk. For almost a month since receiving Sophie's birth certificate, I'd gone through countless emotions as well. I'd been lied to, and I was angry. This man had sat silently, knowing the information I'd been searching for.

"I loved your mother," he began. "And she loved me too."

"Really?" I stopped him. "Then why did she have Joseph's baby?"

"You have to understand, there was nothing…," he started and stopped.

"Nothing? Nothing what? Nothing you could do? Tell me!" I demanded, my voice showing the anger that had been growing.

"He never treated her the way that I would have. I would have…," he stammered.

"You would have what? What is it?" I asked, trying to calm myself.

"Joseph. I hated him with every ounce of me. His father was such a big shot, didn't want to have anything to do with this town. Joe, or I should say *Joseph*, caught on to the gist of that real quick," he responded. Emotions were still raw for him even after so many years.

"That's still not answering my question," I demanded. "Why didn't you tell me the first day I walked in here? Why? Did you think this was such a grand secret that no one was going to find out?"

"I had no idea how far you would go, or what you'd find. I mean, no one in all this time has ever come looking for answers. No one outside of Joseph's family ever knew about the baby, except for Stephanie and me. I put this whole thing so far down inside of me that nothing was ever going to bring it back to life. But then you started with your questions about this and that and began poking around." He suddenly looked very old and gray. His eyes stared off at a point behind me.

"And you never told the truth about Joseph's lying about Andre? How could you have let that poor old man sit in prison for a crime you knew he didn't commit? Or was that too far down to remember?" I moved forward in my chair, leaning into his desk.

"I never knew that Joseph had lied. I didn't know anything about that, you have to believe me." He was adamant. "I only found out that Andre didn't do it after you got Joseph to confess. If I'd have known, I wouldn't have hesitated for one second to turn Joseph in."

"I don't have to believe anything about you at this point. And your story about overhearing a conversation, the one about how someone didn't trust Joseph? You made that up, didn't you?" I pressured him.

"Yes, that was a lie," he admitted. "I knew somehow Joseph had been part of the drowning. But I could never prove it. And nobody cared. People were sad, that's all. They wanted to forget, put it behind them, and get back to normal."

"So the drowning happens, and then my mother gets pregnant, has Joseph's child, and your name is on the birth certificate. Why? I want to know why." My voice cracked as I edged myself to his desk, my clenched fists on top.

"Old man Howe needed a fall guy for his *heir to the throne.* Couldn't have any trace of impropriety on your record when you're going to West Point. No, sir. So they looked for a sap who would keep his mouth shut, and they threw him a bone." His cheeks flushed, and he shook his head slowly as he relived his embarrassment.

"How big was that bone?" I asked.

"Seemed like a lot back then. You have to understand, when you're twenty and your folks don't have anything and someone offers you more money than you've ever seen in your life, just to put your name on a piece of paper, well, you jump at the chance," he answered.

"How much? This can be useful information," I pressed him. "If Joseph is still waiting for a court-martial, this amount could show just how far this family was willing to go to protect his name."

94

"That money was going to be for me and Stephanie when I got out of the service. Then I was going to come back here and marry her and go find that baby. And that would be doing the right thing. Not that Howe's family ever knew what honesty and right was all about," he added.

"How much?" I asked again. I saw him weighing his answer.

"Well, at this point, I'm not protecting anyone anymore. It was ten thousand dollars, cash," he admitted.

"I see," I said and nodded at the amount. Joseph's father had certainly been a very dangerous and devious man. He hadn't let anything stand in the way of Joseph going to West Point.

"That's not much now, but my whole future was ahead of me, and that was going to help me from struggling. I had my eye on a little house just outside of town." His voice was full of anguish.

"But then there was the accident," I said.

"Stupidity. Summer before my second year in college. I went swimming in that same damned lake as the drowning. Jumped in, hit my head, and broke my neck. Howe's father found out and sent me some more money for my troubles, just to make sure I stayed quiet." Henry was back in time when all this had occurred. He was silent for a while.

"And my mother? Where was she when all this happened?" I could only imagine my mother being heartbroken, yet again. Having to hide in shame and give her baby away. And then to find a good man in Henry and have her life torn apart once more. I thought about how I would have felt, pregnant and the one that was supposed to love me turning his back on me. God, how I loved Charlie.

"She'd just gotten back from having the baby. Howe had left by that time. He never saw her again after she went away. That bastard. She couldn't believe that Joseph wasn't man enough to put his name on the birth certificate. She told me I was her real hero." He looked down at his hands, trying to find his words. "We started going together that summer, before she went to school. I told her about my plans for ROTC and how, after I got out, we'd get married and go find her baby. I would be the real father to that little girl. They'd never have to worry." There was sadness in his eyes as he continued.

95

"You never asked her about the baby or if she knew where it was?" I was trying to will this man to give me a clue, anything that would help find Sophie.

"No, I never got the chance. After the accident, the doctors told me I'd never walk again. I told her to go on with her life and forget about this cripple. This was all I was ever going to be. Gone was my future in the service. No house, no kids running around in a yard. She'd end up hating me, and I'd end up resenting her. No, it wasn't going to be any good. So she went to college. She'd come and see me when she came home, but it was different. We both knew it was over before it had begun. She met your dad that summer when she got a job at some inn. She told me all about him." Henry looked up at me with the years of sadness etched on his face. And then he looked away, heaving a sigh.

"She did?" I was trying hard to understand this entire saga about passion, love, and how it had all turned to emptiness.

"I'd become more of a friend to her. She was happy, really happy, when she met your father. I told her she deserved a good man and a good life." He was tearing up now. I waited a moment while he turned away from me to wipe his eyes. "She came to say goodbye right before she got married. I never saw her again after that. I ended up answering phones in the selectman's office and living with my parents. Wasn't anywhere else I could go. My mother had to take care of me until I had this whole handicapped thing figured out. After a few years, I started helping out the town clerk, Beatrice. She passed away a few years after that, and here I've been."

"But what about the baby, my half sister? What happened to Sophie?" I asked urgently. "Surely, if you had plans to marry my mother and have a family, then you must have known where Sophie was."

"I never really knew. Stephanie was taken away by Howe's father. He told your grandparents about some contest that she'd won. And that since she was such a bright young lady, he was going to get her into an early-admission program at Keene State that was going to take her away for about a couple of months. Her parents were so proud they never asked any questions, they never knew. They just let her go. He took her out of school and brought her to some place in New Hampshire." He was deflated. "She came back after the program, worked at a summer job, and began college in the fall like it was the most normal thing to do."

"But you two were going to be married. She never told you?" How I wanted this man to remember something.

"No, Stephanie never told me where. But I know she went back there. I think it was before she left school. She told me she would know where to find Sophie when the time was right." As he ended, he put his hand out on top of mine. "I truly am sorry, but I really don't know any more."

"But the birth certificate. Why does it say Portland?" I pushed for more information.

"There really isn't any good explanation that I can figure, except that Howe's father wanted the trail of anything connected to his family to lead very far away. Your sister was born someplace in New Hampshire, wherever it was that Howe's father took her," Henry answered.

"Isn't there anything else that you can remember? Anything at all?" I pleaded.

"I wish there were something. I really do. New Hampshire was the only thing she told me. Maybe it was near where she went to school?" He looked truly sorry. "You have to know how everyone in this town appreciates what you've done for Andre. A man's reputation is all he has at the end of the day, and for you to clear that up for him, someone you didn't even know, speaks to your integrity," he answered.

"Thank you, that's kind of you to say," I said and stood up to leave.

"What will you do now?" he asked.

"I'm going to try to find Sophie," I stated.

"I sure hope you find her. And I hope she'll know what you've gone through to get to her and set her story straight." He looked at me and smiled. "While I never met her, I was so happy to think that I was going to be her dad. Maybe you could tell her that?"

"Sure. I only hope that if I do find her, she wants to know this story," I said. Henry gave me a nod as if to say, "Good luck," and I closed the door behind me.

Back in my car, I went over all that I'd uncovered today. One was already a given. Joseph's father had stopped at nothing to get his son into West Point. Money had been no object, as he'd doled it out to those he had used along the way. Next was that Henry had finally told me all he knew. During my previous visits with him, I could sense that he'd been holding back. And now he was free of those demons that haunted him. The last thing he mentioned was that New Hampshire was where Joseph's father had taken Momma to have her baby. I'd had a hunch before about the importance of that envelope flag from my grandmother's cookbook. But now I was sure that it was the one clue that would show me where my mother had gone and where Sophie had her beginning. Westmoreland Depot. *Thanks, Gammie.*

CHAPTER 14

S INCE I WAS IN OXFORD, I decided to pay Ginny and Andre a visit. The side streets hadn't been plowed, and the snow was starting to pack down where cars had tried to go through. But my four-wheel drive lived up to its name, and after I fishtailed around a corner, I silently thanked Charlie for insisting that we have this Jeep. Turning onto Sunrise Street, I saw someone hard at work shoveling Ginny's walk. As I got closer, I saw that it was Andre. I stopped the car in between their homes and got out.

"Andre! What are you doing?" I scolded him. When he saw me, a big smile came to his face. He pushed his knit hat up, and some of his white cotton-candy hair escaped, billowing about his face.

"Oh, Ethel!" he called to me. His French accent always made my name sound like *Ettel*. I loved that. He motioned for me to wait while he shoveled a spot so I wouldn't have to jump over the mounds of snow. I stood patiently by my car. Ginny's door opened, and she came out to her porch.

"What is he doing? Isn't there a neighborhood kid who can do this?" I yelled up to her.

"I've told him that. He insists that he can do it. And when he's done, he's hardly winded. At eighty-three, I don't know how he does it," she said and shook her head. He'd quickly cleared a spot for me and took my hand to guide me through.

"And a gentleman as well," I added and gave him a hug. He shouldered his shovel, gave me a tip of his cap, and walked back to his house, whistling a little ditty.

"I guess I don't have to worry about how he's doing, now, do I?" I said and shook my head, looking at that jaunty little soul.

"No, you don't. Now, come on in. What are you doing in Oxford, anyway?" Ginny asked as I followed her into the house. I had never entered her home through the front door; the other times, we'd walked through her gardens and sat in the sunroom. There was a small foyer at the bottom of the carpeted stairs. A white-marble-topped table was placed up against the wall and held a basket that collected the mail. There was a living room to the left with a cream-colored sofa and two overstuffed chairs clad in a fading violet-blue-and-white print. The walls were a continuation of her gallery of photographs. Most were of her flowers, but here and there were a few of woodsy streams. A fire was going in the small fireplace, and it felt very inviting on this snowy morning. To the right of the foyer was her dining room. The oval maple table had six chairs waiting for company. The table was set with brass candlesticks and a miniature fern on a small white pedestal. In both rooms, the walls had been painted a very light shade of violet. I hung my coat on a sturdy hall tree that looked handmade. I wondered if this was another example of my grandfather's handiwork.

"I came up to see Henry," I explained, and she nodded her understanding. Since I had met Ginny, she and those close to me had become familiar with my search for Momma's family. At Christmas, I'd told them about the birth certificate.

"Well, let's have some tea and you can tell me what happened," she said, and I followed her into the kitchen. The kettle was already boiling, so it didn't take long before we both had steaming cups of tea. I chose peppermint. Somehow my oatmeal hadn't settled well this morning, and I hoped the minty brew would work its magic. We went into the living room, where we each took a seat in the comfy print chairs and let the first sip of tea settle in.

"This room is so lovely," I commented.

"Oh, it's so old now, but thanks. Abe and I loved these chairs. We used to sit, just like you and I are doing now, and talk about the day," she said and stared into her tea. "Now, what happened with Henry?"

"The poor man really is another casualty in this horrible saga. Henry got paid by Joseph's father to have his name on the birth certificate instead of Joseph's," I started.

"No! Really? What a scoundrel that man was!" she remarked, wrinkling her face in disgust.

"Yes, he was. And poor Henry, it seems, truly loved my mother and had made plans for a future with her. After he got out of the service, he was coming back and they were going to get married. Then they would find Sophie. But there was the swimming accident that left him paralyzed and confined to his wheelchair. And so there was another heartbreak for my mother. It makes me so sad to think of her trying to love and be loved. Every time she was about to wrap her arms around that love, something would break that hold, and there she was, alone." I put my tea on a side table and searched in my pocket for a Kleenex as I wiped my tears with the back of my hand.

"Here, dear. Here's my hankie." Ginny got up and gave me a white linen handkerchief with a violet lace around the edges.

"Oh, I can't. It's too pretty." I looked up at her with tears streaming down my face.

"Ethel, use it, please. There's no harm in wiping tears on old lace." Her smile and tender touch were such a comfort to me. I dried my eyes and dabbed at my nose.

"Let's change the subject for a minute," I said and snuffled in my runny nose and gave her a smile. "How was your dinner date with my dad? He hasn't said much, except that he brought something from Ruthie's."

"He's quite the man. We had a grand time. He didn't know what to do with himself when he first got here, so I showed him to the glasses and my meager bar essentials and he made us a couple of cocktails. He was fine after that. He helped carve the roast and mash the potatoes. We talked and talked back and forth about our lives and about you. He's worried about you, but he didn't tell me why. Is everything all right?" Her eyes lit up as she told me about Daddy but then showed concern for me as she asked the question.

"He didn't tell you that I'm pregnant again?" I asked in disbelief.

"No, he didn't! Why, that little devil! Now it makes sense. How far along?" she answered.

"About four months now, but I'm fine. However, this new piece of information that my mother had another baby is not sitting well.

He was so afraid for me when I had EC. After EC was born, he was sure that I was out of the woods. But now, knowing that Momma died after having me, her second child, well, he's got himself in a bit of a tizzy again," I said. Each time I relayed this information about how Momma died after her second child, it started to take that mere suggestion and turn it just ever so slightly into a hint of reality. I pushed the thought away.

"I can see now why he's so worried," she agreed. "I am too. Are you sure? Have they done the right tests? Oh, Ethel, you have to make sure." Ginny was truly worried, and the look on her face told me so.

"Yes, please, don't worry. Dr. Simon has done every genetic test he can up to this point. And he'll do more as I progress," I said to reassure her.

"I don't know what Eddy would do if something happened to you," she fretted as she looked back at me.

"Daddy tries to hide his fears and anything bad. I bet he didn't even tell you that he spent New Year's Eve in the hospital," I asked, knowing almost for sure that he hadn't.

"What? No! He never said a thing. What happened? No wonder he didn't answer his phone that night. I tried to give him a call right before the ball dropped. That was after I'd had a glass of liquid courage. I like a bit of port before bed." She was concerned but so cute in explaining her nightcap routine.

"He got up from his chair, was a bit light-headed, fell, and hit his head. At least that's what the doctors think. We stopped to see him after going to the obstetrician so we could tell him the good news, and that was when we found him. Out cold. I was so scared. The ambulance brought him over to Memorial. They x-rayed and tested, but nothing conclusive showed up. And then he came home the next morning," I summed it all up as best I could.

"Well, I'm going to have to scold him tonight," she said, seeming a little perturbed.

"Tonight?" I asked.

"Yes. He told me he'd take me up to Norway. I told him about this little place that serves fish and chips on Friday nights. The food is so good and fresh. He's coming by about four for cocktails." She blushed a bit as she tucked a piece of her salt-and-pepper hair behind her ear.

"I'm so happy for you and for my father. If there were ever two people who deserve some happiness, it's you and my dad," I said. My heart was so happy right now. I was sure I had the Cheshire cat grin all over my face.

"That's sweet of you to say. We're finding our way, so we'll see where we go." Ginny had a little smile too, but it was clear that this topic was between her and Daddy. It was now her turn to get me back to my day's purpose. "But what else happened with Henry? Did he have a clue about Sophie's whereabouts?"

"The only thing he was able to tell me was that my mother was taken to someplace in New Hampshire to have the baby. He did say she would know where to find Sophie when it was time," I added. "And then that next summer, she met my father and started the next chapter of her life."

"That truly is so sad. But that's not much to go on, is it?" she said.

"Well, I have a little clue. It somehow didn't seem like much at that time, but now I'm almost certain it's important," I offered.

"What's that?" she asked.

"The very first day I met you and you let me into my grand-mother's house, I grabbed two cookbooks from her kitchen. The French one had two bookmarks. One was the back of an envelope from a doctor in New Hampshire. And the other was a postcard. I didn't think much about them then. But the more I think about it now, the more I know that this doctor will somehow fit into this puzzle," I divulged.

"Where was the postcard from?" Ginny asked.

"It was from another town in New Hampshire. I haven't checked the map yet, but I think it's too coincidental for them not to mean something," I concluded.

"What was the name of the town?" she said as she asked another question.

"Chesterfield. Do you know it?" I asked. I looked at her as she set her cup of tea on her side table.

"Oh my, I haven't heard that name in a long time," she said.

"Really?" I asked. "What's there and where is it?"

"It's a little town on the western border of New Hampshire, right before you get to Vermont. Abe and I were going to go there to see this abandoned castle and its stairway. Some famous New York socialite moved up there. What was her name? Oh, it was Madame Cherry or something like that. Anyway, she was quite scandalous as the story goes and threw wild, decadent parties, lasting entire weekends. All types of people came to see her. They say the parties would rival those at Hugh Hefner's Playboy Mansion, if you get my drift. It was rumored she drove around town in a fancy car, wearing her fur coat and nothing underneath. Can you imagine?" She was having fun recalling this story.

"Somehow I can't imagine small-town New Hampshire folks taking to a naked woman in a fur coat. But then…" And I stopped as my mind raced. I thought about those decadent parties and the wide-eyed innocents who surely had attended and wound up in misfortune. Hmmm.

"What are you thinking about?" Ginny asked.

"Well, I bet there might have been an adventurous girl or two who would have taken in all that this madame and her friends could provide. And if they found themselves in, say, a bit of trouble, wouldn't you think a small-town doctor might have been the answer?" I proposed.

"It sounds like a possibility, but this happened a long time ago. You're talking the late twenties, and your sister was born in 1941? And now it's 1981? That's a span of almost sixty years. Who knows if this doctor is still around?" she reasoned.

"I know it seems like a stretch. Say, do you have an atlas? I want to see just where this place is," I said, looking hopefully at Ginny.

"As it turns out, I do. I get my new Rand McNally atlas every year. Wait here, I'll go get it," she said, almost as excited as I felt. Moments later, she returned with her 1981 atlas in hand.

"Great, okay, let's see. The index is in the back," I said out loud as I searched for the town. Then I flipped the pages to the map of New Hampshire. Finding the numbered and lettered coordinates, I tapped my finger on the map. "Here it is. And what do you know? Look how close it is to Keene State. Just a few towns over."

"What town was the doctor in?" she asked as we scanned the map.

"Westmoreland Depot," I said. "And look where it is. Right in a line."

"My, it seems to be quite the coincidence, don't you think?" Ginny admitted.

"Yes, I do. And now I just need to make sure my hunch is correct," I said as I continued to stare at the map.

I was more confident than ever that this mere ten-mile stretch of road had been the longest in my mother's journey from motherhood to becoming a college coed. And I was going to make that same journey to find the truth, and possibly Sophie. This had to be the right place. It just had to be.

CHAPTER 15

I HEARD THE PHONE RINGING AS I walked up to the porch. I fumbled with my key ring and finally got the right key into the lock.

"Hold on!" I yelled to no one. With EC in my arms and the dogs swirling around my legs, I scrambled to get to the phone.

"Hello?" I said. EC was squirming, so I put him down, and off he went.

"Ethel? You sound out of breath. Are you okay?" It was Jackie.

"Oh, I'm fine. I was outside and ran in when I heard the phone. We really need to get a new answering machine," I replied, trying to catch my breath. "What's up, Jacks?"

"Listen, Russell and Robert just got into town this afternoon, and they're having early cocktails and a casual dinner for those involved with the Emporium. Mom's throwing something together for us. There's not many folks in for the weekend, and she doesn't expect too many for dinner tonight either. Come by about four o'clock. I've got our big table by the windows. And don't worry about EC. I have my on-call babysitter, Samantha, who'll watch him and my boys. How does that sound?" She reeled off the information with the plans for my evening.

"It sounds terrific. This will be a great treat. I'll let Charlie know as soon as he walks in the door," I answered.

"He already knows. He and the boys were here when the decision was made. He's finishing up his beer and said to tell you he'll be home in a jiffy," she added.

"Well, how about that? This sounds like a fun night. I'll see you later." And I hung up. As I turned, I saw three sets of eyes on me. The dogs were sitting patiently but glancing sideways at their empty bowls. EC was checking to see if I was watching as he went to the bookcase and started to pull out a book.

"Okay, boys, let's feed you first, and then I'll see about this book-stealing bandit over here." The dogs were happy to have food, and EC laughed as I lunged at him to try to steal back his book. I sat down on the floor, and he curled up in my lap as I opened the book. By the time Charlie came through the door, the dogs had joined us on the floor as I read Green Eggs and Ham. EC's vocabulary was getting better and better every day, and he mimicked the rhyming sounds of Dr. Seuss.

"Isn't this about the best sight anyone could see when they walk into their home?" he said. He took off his coat, kicked off his boots, and joined us on the floor. EC pulled the book from my hands and brought it over to Charlie. He backed into Charlie's lap, with his tiny hands gripping the book.

"Daddy, book," EC said and settled in with Charlie for his daddy to finish the story. I watched as Charlie read and EC pointed to the pictures. Yes, indeed, this was one of the best sights.

"I hear we're going out?" I stated.

"Yup. I've been with Robert and Russell since nine this morning. We got most of their wish list attended to, but they want some input from folks. You know, things they might not have thought about." Charlie paused from reciting "I do not like them here or there," while EC was trying to turn the pages.

"Who else is coming?" I wondered out loud.

"Caleb and Sadie, Ruthie, Andy Sr., us, Jackie and Andy Jr., and Mr. and Mrs. F. That's it," he answered.

"The elders of Piney Bluffs assemble," I replied in my best witchlike voice as I tented my fingers. "Remember, I told you there'd be ceremonies like this to test your loyalty." I let out an evil little cackle, which made EC turn and look at me, more surprised than afraid of the new sound that his mommy had just made.

"That's okay, EC. Mommy's just practicing for Halloween," Charlie said and kissed the top of his head. EC walked over and gave me one of his neck hugs, which was usually reserved for Mutt and Jeff. It seemed like it was his own way of saying it was okay.

"Well, we'd better get moving. It's already three o'clock," I said, untangling his little arms, and rolled to one side to get up. Only a few months along, and my body seemed to have remembered the back-saving moves from when I was pregnant with EC.

"Are you okay, honey?" Charlie got up and put an arm around my waist to help me up.

"I'm fine. Just have to move a little different again." I shook my head and headed up the stairs, unbuttoning my pants as I climbed.

I looked in the mirror and turned sideways and back, assessing the growth of the newest member of the O'Connor family. I tried to suck in my stomach. *No use. You are there, my little darling. And definitely no jeans tonight. Now, where was that corduroy jumper?* I flipped through hanger after hanger and finally found it. Phooey, it had some kind of stain on the front. Now what? I finally found a long charcoal-gray skirt that I'd worn for Christmas Eve. I pulled it over my head and watched as it settled over me. Not bad. Still some room for a little more growth, although it was edging more toward an empire-style waist than one that usually rode on my hips. Turtleneck, funky-embroidered vest that I'd gotten at the North Tunbridge Craft Fair, and my little belly was camouflaged for another night. I surveyed the rest of the closet. Not much left that I'd worn when I'd been pregnant for EC. On the next visit to the doctor, I definitely had to stop at the mall.

I heard Charlie getting EC ready in the other room and went to check on them.

"You're going to be a big brother pretty soon," Charlie was telling him. *Big brother indeed,* I thought. How life was going to change.

"Hello, Earth to Mommy." Charlie was standing in front of me with EC in his arms. EC had been waving, trying to get my attention.

"Oh, dear. Sorry, I was just thinking," I said and gave a little sigh. "Why don't I take EC downstairs and let you get ready?" Charlie put EC down and pulled me into his arms for a hug.

"That's my Ethel, always thinking," he said and kissed my forehead. EC had already made his way to the top of the stairs.

"EC! No, no! Wait for Mommy." I quickly went over to him. He looked up at me as if to say, "What's the fuss?" The stairs had braided treads on each step, but still, if he fell, there were sure to be some tears and bumps. He had just started to learn how to go up and down the stairs. It was a slow task, however, as he treated each of the eight stairs as a rung of a ladder with a built-in chair for resting in between. I went in front of him, encouraging each step. By the time he was done, Charlie had already taken a quick shower, changed, and was coming down the stairs after us.

"Look at our boy coming down the stairs," Charlie said and picked EC up and swung him around. "You ready to go and play with the big boys?" EC loved to play with Andy Jr. and Jack. While they were older, the boys were kind and played to EC's level. He looked at his daddy and smiled.

"Okay, then, off we go," I said and held out EC's coat. I had already pulled my parka around me the best that I could. I was happy it had snaps, but they were holding on for dear life. "Uh-oh, this is really snug. I was hoping I could make it through the winter without getting a new coat for this pregnancy."

"Maybe you could get one that wraps around, like a trench coat," Charlie offered.

"A tent coat would be more like it," I said, and we both laughed as we headed out the door. "Wow, it's snowing again. This is the perfect snow for sliding." Sliding. There it was again, the sled, always in the back of my mind. For tonight, I would put that thought aside. Much the same way you would prop a sled up against the shed. The snow dripping from the runners, preparing to take you on its next adventure down a hill. My hill was the climb to reach Sophie, wherever that hill was. And as always, this was promised to be another adventure.

CHAPTER 16

THE SHORT TRIP TO THE Inn was anything but. The snow buffeted our sturdy Jeep this way and that. We went from one whiteout to another all the way into town. Charlie stopped a couple of times to get his bearings. The forecast called for another couple of inches, but this was more like a blizzard.

"Maybe we should've packed a bag and left the dogs some extra food," I said as I kept my eyes riveted to the windshield. Familiar landmarks were gone, replaced by blurs of white.

"No kidding, this is some of the worst I've seen in a long time. But we'll take our time," Charlie answered.

"The sun will be out tomorrow—at least that's what the weatherman said." I tried to sound positive.

"Yeah, right. Only job in the world where you can be wrong a majority of time and still continue to have a job," Charlie said. Finally, we arrived and saw the welcoming glow of the Inn's lanterns. Charlie grabbed EC, and we made our way to the front door. EC, oblivious to the trip we'd made to get here, was trying to catch the snowflakes on his mittens and kept putting them in Charlie's face.

"Come in, come in. Will you look at that snow? I just cleared that walk not ten minutes ago," Mrs. F said as she opened the door and now stood with her hands on her trim hips and shook her head at the snow. Casually elegant, she was dressed in navy wool slacks with a luxurious cream sweater that looked like cashmere. A pair of navy leather flats completed her look. I pulled my vest a little closer over my belly. I sighed and hoped one day to have that effortless, elegant look.

"It's been a doozey of a couple of weeks for sure," Charlie answered.

"Oh, look at you! You look like you're in full bloom," Mrs. F said. We stamped the snow from our boots. "Give me your coats, and I'll put them away."

"Thanks. Although my bloom seems to be fading fast today," I said as I gave her a hug, and she helped me out of my coat. Charlie helped EC off with his and then took the coats from her. EC saw Jack and ran off to play with the boys.

"I got these, Mrs. F," Charlie said as he took our coats from her. "You don't have to wait on us."

"Thank you, Charlie. Come on in. Everyone's here except Caleb and Sadie," she said, and she put her arm around me as we walked in. "You feeling all right? What did the doctor have to say?"

"I'm good, really. Even when I told him about Momma giving birth to another child prior to me, he wasn't concerned. So I'll take my lead from him and not worry either," I said as I tried to make light of lots of possibilities.

"And your dad said you've got information about your half sister. You're going to try to find her, aren't you?" She turned to face me with that look of concern in her eye.

"You know I have to. I realize there's some of Momma's family that are cousins and live in Canada, and they wouldn't be too hard to find. But they will have to wait for another time. For me to have a sister that may be as close as New Hampshire and not try to find her, why, I couldn't live with myself," I said emphatically.

"You've always been the one to care so deeply and search for the truth. I hope you find her. But be careful. Eddy worries about you. We all do," she said and gave me a squeeze.

"I'll be fine. What could happen?" I said and patted her hand to reassure her.

"Oh, I've heard that one before. A couple of times, if I'm not mistaken," she said and shook her head at me.

"Heard what before? What's she doing now that she shouldn't?" Ruthie was looking out the window and turned when she heard me.

"Remember, there's a new little someone coming along, so let's not have you running off on another one of your adventures."

"Oh, Ruthie. I'm a grown woman, for heaven's sake. I can take care of myself. Besides, I know if I need help, I don't have to look too far," I answered her.

"We only want to keep you safe." And she came over and patted my back like the caring woman she was. She wore a heavy Irish fisherman knit cardigan over a red turtleneck. Her green corduroy slacks were stuffed into her snow boots. She looked like one of her Christmas cookie characters that had come to life.

"Thank you. You're all so special to me. Don't worry," I said to them.

"Ethel, look at you!" And there was Russell coming to see me. "And congratulations to you both. I can't tell you how happy we are for you. And look at EC walking. You don't know how brother and I were so worried about the little guy." He took a moment to wipe his eye. "Must be some dust, or maybe an allergy." I gave him a kiss and wiped the "dust" that had fallen to his cheek.

"That's so sweet of you, and don't you two look sporty tonight," I complimented them. They were dressed in similar black, white, and gray tones. Charcoal worsted slacks with a knife crease down the front. I had taken sewing lessons from Jolene at her Sewing Box when I was a teenager, and I knew how to spot a quality fabric. Russell had a black sweater and white broadcloth shirt underneath, while Robert wore a black-and-white houndstooth check sport coat over his white turtleneck.

"Oh, these old things," Robert said, making light of their wardrobe but definitely pleased that I'd noticed.

"And here is our hero, master craftsman, general contractor, and two-time father-to-be!" Russell waved his hand toward Charlie.

"Easy, Russell, he's not that good. I still have one door that's been out of whack ever since he built my addition." Andy Jr. and his father were sitting at the bar. Andy Jr. walked over with a beer for Charlie. "But I figured, what the hell, give the new guy a break." They clinked the long necks of the bottles and nodded toward each other. Both of them had that ruggedly attractive look. The lines that were starting to appear on their faces only gave more depth to their handsomeness.

"You two, I swear," Jackie commented as she came over with a plate of cheese puffs with lobster filling. They had just come from the oven, and the flaky pastry had hints of a creamy pink sauce oozing around their edges.

"I thought your mom was throwing something together?" I commented as I picked one and carefully bit into the delicate pillow. "Ooh, hot!" I said as I put it back on my plate.

"You never could wait, my friend. And you know Mom. Her throwing something together could still win a Michelin award." She laughed.

"How's the back doing, Andy?" I asked Andy Sr. He'd gotten up from his seat and was walking a wee bit bent to one side.

"I have to say it's getting better. Marge's got me seeing this chiropractor, and he's twisting and snapping everything back into place," he replied and laughed. "I should be ready for a dance contest any day now."

"Mommy," I heard EC's voice call to me. I looked, and he'd stopped playing with the boys when he saw Auntie Jackie come out with food. His palate had not yet reached the sophisticated level of lobster puffs, and he scrunched his face when I gave him a taste.

"Hey, Jacks, what do we have for kid-friendly snacks?" I asked Jackie.

"Already there, my friend. I've got a tray of apple slices with peanut butter and pretzels and cheese. My boys aren't into lobster yet either, and with the price of lobster, that's a good thing," she said, and Jackie went back in and out of the kitchen in short order.

"Here we are," she said and held the tray out for the boys to grab. I got an apple slice with peanut butter and a piece of cheese for EC, and he toddled away, a treat in each hand.

"Hello, are we late?" called out Caleb as he and Sadie came in from the entry, stomping their feet.

"It's still snowing! Can you believe it? Gosh, I hope you have some rooms, Alice. We may be staying over!" Sadie exclaimed. She came around, giving hugs and kisses. She combed her fingers through her pixie-cut red hair as it routinely went in place.

"Never to worry. We have plenty of rooms. We only have Russell and Robert and one couple in tonight. And the couple has already had their early supper. I sent them off to their room with nightcaps and chocolates. So we have the place to ourselves," Mrs. F said. "Jack, what's on tap for our guests?"

"Well, I've made my special hot toddy. I know you ladies will like it." Jack filled in as bartender when Lloyd had the night off. And because of the storm, Jack and Alice had sent all the staff home early. He ladled up the toddies, and Sadie and Ruthie took their glasses, murmuring their enjoyment of the spicy, hot liquid.

"Can you untoddy one for me, Jack?" I asked.

"Sure can, my dear. Give me a minute." And Jackie's dad went about making a new batch for me.

"Ethel, try these," Jackie said. She had come back out of the kitchen again with two more trays. One held toast points with thinly sliced beef tenderloin with a creamy horseradish sauce. The other was grilled chicken wrapped in bacon with what looked like a sprinkle of blue cheese that had been lightly broiled on top. I placed a few of each on my plate. Ah, the wonderful aroma of bacon.

"These look really good. I remember when your mom told us how to make this sauce. Some mayo, sour cream, horseradish, bread crumbs, and the secret ingredient, applesauce," I recounted and then took a bite. "Oh my. Next to having a baby, eating is the best thing about being pregnant."

"How far along did the doctor say you are?" Ruthie asked. She had come up to the table to join me.

"Four months, about. We'll know more precisely in a few weeks, when we go back for the ultrasound," I answered. "I'm thinking June."

"It will be another lovely child. I'm certain of that." Sadie was now standing with us. "I don't know how Alice does it. I mean, I couldn't find a thing in my kitchen for Caleb and me to eat tonight, let alone entertain a bunch like this." She was referring to Mrs. F and her ability to "throw something together."

"Be glad that we're invited." Ruthie chuckled.

"You're right about that," Sadie agreed. And the two happily munched away on the tasty appetizers.

"And there's my star reporter. How was today's search?" Caleb came over and gave me hug.

"Search for what?" Russell chimed in. He had a bourbon in his hand and was quite curious about the details of our mysterious topic. "Why don't you come right over here and tell me what new adventure you've gotten yourself into is?" He was sitting at the table and pulled out a chair for me.

"Thanks, Russell. I do need to sit," I replied and took the seat next to him.

"I hope you're right there with her, Charlie," Robert added.

"She hasn't asked for reinforcements yet." Charlie smiled. "But I'm sure it won't be long."

"This time I really won't need the cavalry to come charging in. I'm sure of it," I said with certainty. "This will be more like searching for that needle in the haystack."

"We've heard that before." Jackie had rejoined the group and took a seat next to Andy.

"So tell us," Russell urged.

"But we're really here about the Emporium, aren't we?" I was trying to get us back on track.

"Oh, we'll have plenty of time to talk about the Emporium. Why, we're only on hors d'oeuvres, for heaven's sake!" Robert stated. "And I understand that Alice had Rocky create one of his seven-layer lasagnas for supper." He grinned from ear to ear and closed his eyes a bit, as if dreaming of eating the scrumptious, cheese-laden pasta.

"Okay, but just the CliffsNotes version," I said as I began. Those around the table had learned about Sophie when Joseph made his confession, but they knew little more than that she existed. "Today I went to see Henry Blake, who, as I told you, sent me a copy of Sophie's birth certificate that shows his name as the father and not Joseph. He explained to me that after Andre's trial, Joseph's father paid him a visit. He offered Henry ten thousand dollars to put his name in place of Joseph's on the certificate. All so Joseph could attend

West Point without any blemish on his record. And Joseph's father had changed Joseph's name to make it almost impossible to trace anything back to him about Andre and the supposed murder. God only knows whom he paid for that favor and how much it cost for that to happen."

"That cad!" Russell commented. "I must say, that was quite a tidy sum, especially in those days."

"Indeed, it was. Imagine a young man who had his entire life before him to have more money than he'd ever seen before and all he had to do was give his name. Henry told me he truly loved my mother and wanted to make a home for her and Sophie after he returned from the war. But the summer before enlisting, he was diving at the lake, hit his head, and that was the end of his young man's dream. He's been paralyzed ever since," I continued.

"What a tragedy for them," Sadie said. "Your mother had such an awful battle for happiness at every turn in her life."

"That she did. Although they remained friends, after Henry's accident, he told her to move on and forget about him. She went off to college and eventually met my dad when she was working here at the Inn in the summer. She and Daddy fell in love, and he went off to war, and when he came back, she was waiting," I concluded.

"But wait, what about Sophie? When and where did that happen?" Ruthie asked. Everyone was waiting for that answer.

"The *when* was in Momma's senior year of high school. Joseph's father had convinced my grandparents that my mother had won a contest and needed to go to college for an early admission program. And they wouldn't have to worry as she'd won a full scholarship to Keene State in New Hampshire," I said as I began the second part of the story. "The 'scholarship,' as Joseph's father had put it, was Momma's price for keeping silent about everything."

"Your grandparents must have been so thrilled for her," Mrs. F said. "And never to have realized that they were duped by the likes of that man."

"But even still, for them to have a grandchild and never know her. That is truly hateful," Ruthie added.

"I can't even begin to understand how that monster worked," I answered.

"Keene State is the big clue as to the *where*. Henry told me that Joseph's father had taken Momma to a home for unwed mothers someplace in New Hampshire. She never told him where but said she would know where to find Sophie when it was time for them to become a family."

"New Hampshire's a pretty big state," Jackie said. "And there was nothing in all of your mother's things that would indicate a possible location?"

"Nothing in her things. But quite by accident, I did happen upon an envelope and a postcard in my grandmother's cookbook. I never thought much about them at that time. The envelope had the address of a doctor in Westmoreland Depot, the next town over from Keene State. Even though I knew Momma had gone to school there, I had dismissed it. I figured it was something to my grandmother about my mother being sick. But now I feel otherwise." I related the details to the group, who were now silent and waiting for my next words.

"And what did the postcard say? Where was it from?" Sadie asked.

"Very few words: 'Made it, all are well.' It was from Chesterfield, New Hampshire. But I found out that town was the next one over from Westmoreland Depot. I'm not sure if it's all a coincidence, but I'm going to see what these places will tell me. And that is that," I finished and pushed my plate away from me.

"That can't be where this story ends!" Russell was beside himself with wonderment. "Oh, Ethel, you have got to write this story. It will be a terrific mystery—people would eat it right up! Wouldn't they, brother?"

"Yes, indeed. I can see the cover now. A woman standing at the edge of the water. She's looking for answers to her life questions." Robert held his hand up to demonstrate the cover.

"Hold that thought for a bit. Right now, we have some lasagna and salad to eat up." Mrs. F had wheeled in a cart with the lasagna, bread, and salad. Jackie got up to help serve. We got EC settled next to us in a high chair, while Jackie's boy sat next to their grandpa.

"Where's your dad tonight, Ethel?" Ruthie asked.

"He has a date with Ginny. They're going up to Norway for fish and chips," I said with a little smile.

"They seem to be getting along pretty well," Sadie commented.

"Old guy deserves a little happiness and a good meal," Andy Sr. added.

"Who are you calling old?" Jack asked. "Last time I looked, wasn't much difference between the three of us."

"Oh, you know what I meant. It's Eddy's time," Andy said and set his jaw with a nod.

"This is simply wonderful, Alice! The bread has a great crunch with a savory, herb-filled interior. And the salad is crisp, with the right amount of olive oil and lemon. The sauce on the lasagna is seasoned perfectly, the garlic, basil and oregano—so fragrant. The cheeses, I think there's a few different ones, aren't there, Alice? They are a velvety goo holding the pasta and sausages in its arms." And Caleb was off again on his gourmet descriptions.

"Goo? I'd hope that my sauces could be more appropriately described than mere goo." Mrs. F pretended she was dreadfully hurt by the comment.

"Alice, I'm so sorry. Let's see now, if only I had my thesaurus. Ethel, help me out on this." And Caleb pondered for a moment as Mrs. F waited, tapping a single finger on the tabletop.

"Sorry, Caleb, you're on your own with this," I said.

"All right, I've got it. The cheeses are a velvety robe holding the pasta in its arms. How's that?" Caleb looked at Alice for approval.

"Much better. I may have you help with the new menu descriptions," she said. "But let's make sure *goo* does not show up in any of them!" We all laughed and settled into the hearty supper.

Over the next couple of hours, we discussed the Emporium. We decided on a children's story hour on Saturdays, monthly book club with books from the *New York Times* best seller list, and book signings by famous or local authors. The brothers were certain they could attract famous authors who needed the tranquility of Piney Bluffs as a retreat. And they were adamant about comfy leather chairs from L. L. Bean with ottomans to match. They also wanted a couple of cats that would grow up with the store. Andy Sr. suggested a dog, but the dog would need to go home with someone each night, so it was back to the cats. They could be friends with Sugar, Miss Ruthie's cat in the bakery and at night keep the mice population at bay. The best part was that Miss Ruthie's cookbook would be ready to have it officially launched on the opening day of the Emporium.

In consideration of authors from near and far, Russell wanted to develop a series of retreats for writers. With the accommodations available at the Inn and then the Spa, it was a pleasing, natural environment for people to escape to and to hone their craft.

Staffing was the next consideration. We thought it would be a good place for high school students to get some work experience, but who would manage it? Caleb and I had often talked about Sadie as the right woman for the job. I waited to suggest it, but then Robert spoke.

"Sadie, Russell and I were wondering if you would like to manage the Emporium?" Robert asked, hoping for a confirmation. "With your intelligence and people skills, we think you'd be the right woman for the job."

"Oh my, why, that's such a wonderful offer! I accept!" she said without hesitation. You could see how delighted she was.

"Outstanding! There, now, all we have to wait for are the furnishings and the books. And by gosh, we've got ourselves the Piney Bluffs Book Emporium!" Robert confirmed and held his glass high. "To the Emporium!" And we all followed with glasses raised and chorused, "To the Emporium!" I looked over at EC, who had raised his cup along with us. He was smiling back at Charlie and me. A new opportunity was happening in Piney Bluffs. Most would say, "It's just a bookstore." But I looked at it in terms of fishing. The line is thrown out, with a bobber on the surface of the water. The bobber by itself is what you see, but the ripples it sends out will attract more than just those looking for the bobber. So too the Emporium would be the bobber, but the ripple of opportunities that could happen because of it would be amazing!

CHAPTER 17

"OH, DARN, THE SNOW HAS stopped," said Sadie, truly disappointed as she looked out the window. "So much for our big sleepover." Caleb was helping her on with her coat. She pouted like a child who didn't want to go to school.

"That's okay. I wouldn't have had enough to feed you all breakfast, anyway." Mrs. F laughed as she helped the little ones on with their coats. Charlie and Andy Jr. had gone out, cleaned off the cars, and had them warming up, defrosters on.

"Everyone, be careful. It doesn't look like the State's been by with the plows in a while. The snow may have stopped, but this wind is going to throw some good-size drifts in your way," Andy Jr. warned.

"I was only kidding about breakfast. Really, you're all welcome to stay. I don't want any of you ending up in a ditch," Mrs. F said lightheartedly but had a worried look on her face.

"We'll be fine, Mom," Jackie said and kissed her parents' goodbye. "Come on, Senior." They were dropping Andy's dad off on their way home. You could see his back was still bothering him as he was listing to one side. "Careful not to slip."

"Never mind me. You look out for the kids. I've gone through worse snow than this. Why, I remember the blizzard of '78. Margie and I lived in the diner for nearly a week, feeding anybody who could get through." Andy Sr. tried to straighten up as he walked out the door.

"Here, Ethel, let's put that hood up for you. I don't want you to catch a cold." Russell pulled my hood up around my head. "You really should have another coat, dear. I know, I'll order one for you. There's a great shop in the city. They'll fix you right up with something that can take you through the next few months and into spring." The brothers were so kind the way they doted on me.

"Thanks! You're so sweet, but this jacket will do," I said as he fretted over me.

"Can't you all stay? It would be wonderful to talk about our winter adventure tomorrow morning over a nice cup of coffee," Robert said.

"I think I'm going to stay put right here. Besides, I'll be closer to the bakery tomorrow morning than if I go home tonight. I got some customers who get a tad cranky if they don't have their breakfast treats when they want them," Ruthie said as she nodded toward Caleb.

"That would be me, and I don't get cranky. But I'll be over, so you'd best keep your promise," Caleb said as he and Sadie stepped out into the night and got into their truck. We all left, horns honking our goodbyes as we headed in our separate directions.

Our drive took us through the center of town. Andy had been right: no plow had come through here in a while. The sharp edges of everything had been softened into glistening white mounds. The moon peeked in and out of the cloud cover, creating eerily long shadows of every house and tree. As we passed Daddy's house, I saw it was dark and his pickup was gone.

"Well, I'm going to have to speak to him about his curfew," I joked with Charlie.

"Ethel, give the man a break. The snow's pretty bad. If we had to drive anyplace but home, we'd have stayed over too. Let's just hope he's at Ginny's and wasn't pigheaded about driving home," Charlie said, defending Daddy.

"I'm sure he did the right thing and stayed. Heck, he could've gone next door and kept Andre company," I added. "It's just that they're so right for each other. And when I think about everything that's happened, I think Daddy knows the time is right for him to begin the next part of his life."

"I just hope we can continue with the next part of our life," Charlie said as he gripped the wheel.

We had left town, and the helpful beacons from the streetlights were gone. The constant wind swirled the snow across the windshield as we rode in silence. The Jeep's lights gave little help, as the edges of the road all but disappeared. I turned to check on EC, and he was asleep.

"The blissful sleep of a child," I said and tucked his scarf around his head to keep it from bobbing against the window.

And then it happened. Without warning, the car went into a slide. On one side of the road, the small pond loomed in front of us. On the other side of the road was a stand of maple and pine trees.

"Hang on, honey," Charlie said. "This thing has a mind of its own. I can't get out of the spin." And he struggled to keep the Jeep on the road. The rotation as we spun slammed us back and forth inside. EC woke up and started to cry.

"Charlie, no, no, watch out for the tree!" I screamed. "EC!"

"Ethel!" Charlie yelled.

And then silence.

"Come on, Ethel, come play with me. Don't you know me? I'm Sophie," the girl said, and she took my hand. She was older than me. Her hood was pulled up around her head. Strands of light-brown hair escaped from the edges of her hood. I couldn't see her face. "Let's go over here. There's a great hill to slide down. And I've got a new sled. Isn't she a beauty? Momma gave it to me."

"Momma gave you a sled?" I was surprised. Momma had never given me a sled.

"Yes! It's a Flexible Flyer, and it's for us to share. Now, come on with me," Sophie urged, pulling my hand.

"I don't think I can. I'm not supposed to be here. I have to go," I said and let go of her hand. I was six and didn't want to get into trouble.

"Come back tomorrow, then, okay?" Sophie said and walked away, pulling the shiny sled behind her. She turned toward me, but not enough for me to see her face. She waved at me with her mittened hand.

"I don't think Daddy will let me," I answered, but I stood and watched her climb to the top of the hill. She lay down on the sled, and it took her as fast as I'd ever seen anyone slide before.

"Tomorrow, come back tomorrow!" her voice called out to me. Both she and the sled drifted away with the wintry wind.

It was the smell I noticed first. What was that? Cleaning fluids, maybe? I tried to move my legs and feet, but my body was wrapped tightly. What the heck was going on? My eyes fluttered open as I tried to focus. I wanted to rub my eyes, but there was something around my wrists. I looked around as my eyes started to focus on my surroundings.

"Nurse! Call the doctor! She's coming to!" A voice was frantic. "Oh, Ethel, honey. You've come back to me. Thank you, God, oh, thank you!"

My head spun as I closed my eyes. And peaceful sleep came again.

"Ethel, honey, wake up." I'd never heard that voice before.

"Who is it?" I heard myself ask the question.

"Ethel, it's Momma," the voice said again. I tried to open my eyes, but they wouldn't open.

"Momma, what happened? Where am I? Where are you? I can't see you." I was desperate to see the mouth that was saying my name.

Just once, I wanted to see her. To see those soft brown eyes. I could feel tears on my face. Were they hers or mine? I couldn't move my hands to reach out to her.

"Ethel, honey, it's not time for you to see me. You have lots of great things to do. You have decisions to make. And you'll find that the answer's right in front of you." And the voice started to fade away. I could feel a light touch on my face and a small squeeze of my hand.

"No! Come back! You have to come back. I need you, I need your help! I have to find her. You have to help me! Please! Momma!" My throat ached as I screamed.

And now I felt another hand in mine. This touch was different. I'd felt that hand before. It was Charlie's. My eyes opened and closed. I shook my head, trying to focus.

"Oh, Ethel, my Ethel, you're back!" Charlie's voice was hushed, holding back sobs.

"Charlie, Charlie! Did you see her? It was Momma! And Sophie was there too," I cried out but winced from the pain in my throat. It was as if razor blades were cutting me each time I spoke.

I looked from side to side. Charlie was next to me, sitting in a metal chair. I looked down and realized I was in a hospital bed. *Focus, Ethel.* It looked like I was in a hospital room.

"Charlie, what am I doing here? What's happened? Where's EC?" I felt I'd gone mad. Why couldn't I use my hands.

"Easy, honey, you'll be fine. Do you remember the accident?" Charlie's eyes searched my face.

"Accident? What accident? What are you talking about? Where's EC?" I was nearly hysterical, trying to understand.

"Remember? We were at the Inn and had dinner with Russell and Robert. We were talking about the Emporium with everyone. And on the way home, we got into an accident." He was holding my hand and kissing it.

"I remember dinner last night, but there wasn't an accident. Now, tell me what's going on. And did you see Momma? She was right here!" I was wild to try to find the truth.

Two women in hospital uniforms with stethoscopes around their necks walked into the room. Their faces were all smiles when they saw me. Behind them, I saw Daddy as he tried to look over their shoulders. He looked worried.

"Ethel, the accident wasn't last night," Charlie said hesitantly and looked around for help with his answer.

"Welcome back, Ethel. I'm Dr. Sandra Lossing. I'm a neurologist. And this is your nurse, Robin Wilder. You're in the neurology unit at Maine Medical. You've given us all quite a scare," the one woman said, making the introductions. She looked like she could have been related to Ms. Ruthie. She was probably in her forties but had a round body with a smiling face. Her black hair was mostly tucked into a surgical cap. Robin, the nurse, was younger and was tall and thin and wore bright-blue scrubs. Her nurse's cap perched on top of brown ponytail. She started to take my blood pressure.

"Oh, Ethel, you're awake. Doctor, is she going to be all right? What about the baby?" Daddy tried to put a smile on his face.

"Wait a minute. How long ago was the accident?" I asked, beginning to realize that this might be serious.

"Your accident was nearly two months ago, Ethel. You sustained a very bad concussion. You were lucky in the broken-bones department. Only a few broken fingers on your right hand. And they have healed quite nicely while your head was recovering. I called in an obstetrician, who's been checking in with you every other day or so, and he said the baby's heartbeat is strong. The baby's a little smaller than it probably should be, but that's because you've only had fluids. Now that you're awake, we'll make a quick change to your diet. Soft foods first, and then you can have a BLT. Charlie said that's one of your favorites." Dr. Lossing went through the immediate questions and answers. "Now, let's get these restraints off." She and Robin started to unbuckle the soft, padded cuffs.

"Two months?" I couldn't believe it. I looked at the expectant faces in the room. I also realized that there were dozens of cards and balloons and flowers on every conceivable spot in the room. Tears started to stream down my cheeks. I went to use my right hand to wipe them and found it had a thick padding.

"The bones have healed, but we needed to pin them. We took out the hardware a few days ago. That dressing can come off tomorrow. We've been doing passive range of motion with your limbs to keep some tone in those muscles. But you'll need some physical therapy to get those arms and legs moving. The tests we did show all your muscles and nerves are 100 percent intact. You'll probably be out of here in a couple of weeks at best. Anything you want to ask?" Sandra said as she covered most of the immediate things that I could have worried about. She pulled the covers back from my legs and was doing pinprick tests on my feet. I winced with the insertion of each pin. This reminded me of EC and when he'd had the same testing when he couldn't walk.

"Where's EC? How is he? What did you tell him? How have you managed, Charlie?" I looked into the happy eyes of my husband. His eyes were wet with tears.

"He's fine, honey. He didn't have a scratch on him. I've told him that you'd been hurt when we had the accident and that you'd be home pretty soon. I thought it best not to bring him here. But he's had lots of playmates. Everyone's been wonderful, helping me with him." He related in a couple of sentences what I knew must have been a tremendous undertaking.

"We'll leave you all to visit, now that you're back with us. But get ready, you've got quite a job ahead of you," Sandra stated and patted Charlie and Daddy on the shoulders as she and Robin left the three of us.

"I don't know what to say," I said as I looked from Charlie to Daddy.

"There's nothing to say. You're back with us, and that's dandy with me," Daddy said and wiped his eyes. "And don't you worry about Junior. We've been hitting it off real good. Got him so he likes my grilled cheese sandwiches just like you did. He's not so hot with the tomato soup yet, but I'll get him there." I could tell he was very proud of how he'd helped.

"Oh, Daddy, those were so good! I could go for one of those right now." I smiled at my father, who beamed back at me.

"Well, I'll get back home now and let everyone know the good news. I'll see you tomorrow." He bent and kissed the top of my head and held my cushioned hand. He waved when he reached the doorway and quietly walked away.

"I saw Sophie and talked to her, and I talked to Momma too," I admitted softly to Charlie.

"I heard you calling Momma right before you came to. The doctor told us that might happen. People and things come from our subconscious as our brain heals. One day you were really fidgety and whimpering but using a child's voice," he replied.

"I saw them both. Sophie told me Momma had given her a sled for the both of us to share. And Momma said the answers were right in front of me. Oh, Charlie, I know I've never put any faith into dreams or anything like that, but I feel this is a sign to let me know that I'm so close," I admitted.

"I've never said no to you, Ethel, about anything. But you've got to put this business about Sophie to one side for now. You've got to get your strength back, for EC and the baby, and for us. Because I don't think I could ever go through another night without you." Charlie took me in his arms and wept.

As I stroked his wavy brown hair, I thrilled to the sense of it and how it felt between my fingers. Our bodies heaved with sobs. Charlie took my face in his hands and looked into my eyes and smiled through his tears. I had lost two months of my life. Two months of EC changing and growing. Two months of life together with this wonderful, loving man. I was not going to take anything for granted. And whether they were true or not, I remembered Momma's words: "The answers are right in front of you." I just hoped I asked the right questions.

CHAPTER 18

CHARLIE STAYED FOR A WHILE and had supper with me. Supper—
well, that was what they called it. I knew now why Daddy complained when he'd been in the hospital on New Year's Eve. At least he'd had normal food. Everything on my plate was creamy, beige, and in a mound. They all tasted similar but were listed as mashed potatoes, pureed cauliflower, and ground turkey with gravy. The soup wasn't much better. The chicken broth tasted like the chicken had been in the next room when the soup was made. And anything else that was supposed to have been in my bowl left the building along with Elvis. There was vanilla pudding, which was the most palatable item on the entire tray. And that was that.

Charlie, on the other hand, had gone to the cafeteria and brought back two BLTs, chocolate chip cookies, a vanilla milkshake, and a chocolate ice cream Hoodsie cup. The aroma of the bacon was better that any smelling salts that could have been used to rouse me. Now here was what my tummy was thinking of. My pregnant body had been awakened from a long sleep, and it was ready to get going.

"Hey, there, I got those for me, not you," Charlie joked with me and slapped at my hand as I grabbed for a half of a BLT. I knew full well that he'd gotten that meal with me in mind. "Maybe if you're good, I'll give you a bite."

"I may bite you if you don't share!" I said back to him and started to take a bite. One of the nurses—her badge said Phyllis—came into the room when Charlie returned. She looked to be in her fifties or better and was nearly as tall as Charlie. She wore vibrant-patterned scrubs that seemed to reflect her personality. Her short black hair was cropped close around her perfectly shaped head.

"Now, child, I know his meal looks really good, but I need to warn you to take it slow. That soft food is what your body needs right now to remind itself how to eat. Your stomach has shrunk a bit too. If you've got any intentions on one of those BLTs, you'll not be a happy camper in about an hour or two. The milkshake and the ice cream are okay, but only a little bit. We don't want your first day back among the living to be a miserable one." And Phyllis rearranged my beige tray and placed it back in front of me.

"You're just no fun at all, you know that, Phyllis?" I said and put the sandwich back on Charlie's plate. I was pouting like a little kid who'd been told to finish her spinach before she could have dessert.

"Don't I know that? That's why I took this job. The ad read, and I quote, 'Big black nurse wanted: Must be stricter than hell and, above all, cannot have a sense of humor.' Sounded like a dream job to me." She smiled at the two of us. "Now, don't have too much of that good food, really. And buzz if you need me." She shook her head as she left.

I did as I was told and ate only a bite or two of Charlie's feast. I actually found myself feeling quite full. And tired. Although I couldn't understand why, if I'd been asleep for nearly eight weeks. I looked around the room, and my eyes settled on a calendar for March.

"Is it really March?" I asked in disbelief.

"It is. March 13 to be exact. I'm glad you'll be able to make the St. Paddy's Day dinner tomorrow, Mrs. O'Connor. It says on your menu, the usual beige mounds will be colored green." Charlie laughed but could see how all this was affecting me.

"Damn, I feel like Rip Van Winkle," I said and sighed.

"I think that was something like twenty years, honey. Now I'm going to go home. You look tired. I'll be back tomorrow. It's Saturday, so I'll bring EC with me. I'm going to pack your sweats and sneakers so you can start tearing up these hallways. Anything else you think you need?" Charlie said and stood up to leave.

"Can't you stay any longer? I feel like there's so much I missed, so much I need to ask you." I looked up and extended my hand to him. I started to feel alone.

"Ethel, I've been here every day since the accident, just praying that you'd come back to me. And it's killing me that I can't stay, but Minnie's doing me a favor and keeping EC at her house. I told her I'd pick him up by seven tonight. I'll be here tomorrow for the entire day. We can be together, as a family, and we'll talk all day." He took my hand and kissed it. "Is there anything you need?"

"Besides you? Nothing right now. Maybe my brush?" I answered as I put my hand up to my head. My hair felt stringy. I needed a shower. "And my herbal shampoo and conditioner." I smiled at him.

"You got it. Remember, you are beautiful to me, no matter what," he said and gave me one last hug and kiss before he was out the door.

"I love you!" I called out to him and stretched my neck to watch him as he walked away.

Alone now, I put my hand up to see what was underneath that big mitt. My index and middle fingers must have been the ones that broke—they were more discolored than the rest. I tried to wiggle my finger against the stiff padding, with little success. I started to examine the rest of my body. My baby belly was more noticeable now, and I placed my hands all over to see if I could feel any movement. Was there something, or was it just indigestion? I examined where Phyllis had removed the IV lines. The residue left behind from the tape made the crook of my elbows itchy. I needed a shower. I know she'd told me to ring for help if I needed to get up, but with the catheter out and the baby resting on my bladder, I really needed to pee. I started to stand up, but with my right hand in the thick padding, I couldn't grip onto anything.

"Phyllis!" I yelled out and heard her come running. By the time she got to me, I had softly bumped my way into a heap on the floor. How was it that I thought I was going to walk to the bathroom? Hell, I couldn't even stand up by myself.

"Oh, Lordy. You are going to be my problem child, aren't you?" Phyllis said and gently helped me up and sat me back on the bed. She politely scolded me and put the buzzer in my hand. She left the room and returned moments later with a walker. I looked at it in disgust.

"Here's your new best friend," she said as she placed it near the side of my bed. It had tennis balls on the two back legs. My name was written on an adhesive tape label. All I could think of was some of the seniors in town whom I saw coming and going at the Diner. No, no, this wasn't for me.

"I'm not using a walker," I said defiantly. "Just help me into the bathroom, please. I'll be all right."

"Oh, pardon me, Ms. Van Winkle," Phyllis sassed me. "I must have missed that 'independently owned and operated' sign on your butt. Remember, you got somebody else in there to worry about if you take a worse fall than what you just did." She pointed to my belly and wagged her finger at me.

"I know, but I won't fall again. I'll be fine. That was my first step, but I got this now," I said and squared my shoulders. "Can you help me without that thing? Please?"

"Okay, come on. Let's see what you can do," she said and helped me stand. When I was steady, she put her arm around me, and off we shuffled the ten feet or so to the bathroom.

Once in there, I glanced in the mirror. I was surprised at what I saw. My eyes were dull and sunken, with dark circles around them that were the color of ash. My hair was plastered to my head. I looked gaunt and sad.

"Holy jeez! Look at me. What a mess!" I said, and tears again filled my eyes.

"Ethel, honey, you've been in coma for almost two months. Your body had to slow things down so that you and your baby could survive. But you're young and strong, and like Dr. Lossing said, two weeks tops, and you'll be out of here. So don't pay any attention to what you're seeing now. I've left a toothbrush for you and a facecloth. I figured you'd like to get some fresh water on your face. Tomorrow, we'll get you in the shower nice and early. Then when you see Charlie and your little boy, you'll be good as new. Now, let's get you set down and hold on to these railings. Here's the buzzer. You know what to do with that now?" She had given me that gentle kick in the butt that I'd needed. When I was finished, I buzzed for her, and she was happy I had complied. A few minutes later, with teeth brushed and face washed, I felt much better.

"So how was that trip?" Phyllis asked, knowing full well how tired I was.

"I hate to admit it, but you're right," I acknowledged. "I'm bushed."

"Your mom must have had some time with you," she said as she pulled the covers up and straightened my pillows.

"My mom passed away when I was born. It was just Daddy and me," I said softly.

"Oh, honey, I'm so sorry. I didn't mean to..." I could see she felt awful.

"That's okay. It's a subject that I've dealt with my entire life. It's just the way it is." Then changing the subject, I asked, "Phyllis, do people in comas like me ever tell you that they've heard or seen things in dreams?"

"Lots do, yes. Why, whom did you see?" she asked as she stood by my bed.

"My mother and my half sister," I answered. "Actually, I only heard my mother."

"But I thought you said your mother passed?" she asked and looked quizzically at me.

"She did. And I've never seen my half sister either. In fact, I just found out I have a sister about six months ago. And the only picture I have of her is a story that my mother wrote that I discovered quite by accident," I related.

"Well, I've been talking to you on and off for two months while you've been lying here, so how about you tell me the real story about yourself?" Her brown eyes were kind and nonjudgmental as she took a seat on the edge of my bed. I began to tell her about Momma and Sophie. When I was finished, she was quiet for a moment.

"Lord almighty, girl, you do have a way of getting to the bottom of things, don't you?" she remarked.

"It does seem that way. That's why I'm so frustrated with this. I felt I was so close to finding Sophie," I said, gesturing to my body.

"Well, I've always believed that things happen for a reason. And I have a few relatives who believe in talking to those who have crossed over. It seems to me that these two months in the coma have given you a cooling-off period of a sort. While you thought you were going in one direction, maybe now you might see that another is better," she answered. "Do you remember anything that will make you think differently?"

"I remember that Sophie said that Momma gave her the sled to share with me. And Momma said that I had decisions to make and the answer was right in front of me," I said to her, but in a way, I was saying them out loud to see if they made any sense at all.

"Uh-huh. And what do you think about that?" Phyllis asked.

"I think that sharing the sled has got to have some deeper meaning. And then, what my mother said about the answer being right in front of me, why, I've got to get out of here. I've got to get back home and find the real meaning of those things in the box that belonged to her," I theorized and then yawned, although in my mind I was trying to "look" at the contents of the box.

"I think you have had enough for one day. Let's take your vitals, and then I can let you sleep. I'm happy to finally know you, Ethel," Phyllis said as she put the blood pressure cuff on and went about the ritual of taking and recording my vital information. By the time she was done, I was almost asleep. She wordlessly patted my shoulder and left my room. I could hardly wait for Charlie and EC tomorrow. Yes, tomorrow was going to be a new beginning.

CHAPTER 19

"Ethel? Mrs. O'Connor? Time to wake up. I'm Robin, one of the nurses you met yesterday." A firm yet quiet voice was entering my sleep. I felt a hand on my wrist. That was right. I was in the hospital.

"Morning," I murmured and opened my eyes. I focused and saw her smiling. It was that "I'm the nurse and aren't we all happy today?" smile. "What time is it?"

"Six forty-five on the button. I'm going to take the rest of your vitals, and by that time, your breakfast tray should be here." She smiled again.

"Obviously, you haven't seen my meal trays. Nothing to smile about." And I realized how much I sounded like Daddy.

"Breakfast is usually better. There may even be toast," she said hopefully. "I can also make you a milkshake. That usually makes everything more palatable."

"A nice, hot cup of tea and a muffin would be great. Ooh, wow! It's the baby. I felt a kick." I looked up at her, and this time it was a genuine smile on her face.

"Oh, Ethel, that's so good to hear. Do you know what you're having?" she asked.

"Charlie and I were going at the end of the month, uh, I mean January. Oh, wow, my doctor. Dr. Simon. Has anyone told him about me being here?" Things were starting to click now.

"Yes, Charlie called and let him know. Dr. Simon was in a week ago to see how you were. He spoke with the head of OB/GYN here and explained your and your mother's history. We'll call and let him know that you are awake. But we can do the ultrasound here if you'd like," she answered.

"That would be great, but I want to wait for Charlie. When could that be scheduled?" I was hoping for sooner rather than later.

"I think we could get someone up here today. I'll check. Now, want to try walking to the bathroom?" She pulled the walker from the front of the bed. *Oh, great. That thing.* "Let me help you up and see if you can maneuver it."

"If there's anything that's going to motivate me to get moving, it's that thing. I can't stand the thought of it," I said and swung my legs around and stood up. "Not too bad. Better than my first flight yesterday. That was a doozy."

"I read that. You and Phyllis had quite the evening. How are you feeling after your trip to the floor?" Robin asked. She'd lost that nursey attitude and was not dwelling on my indiscretion or orneriness.

"I feel okay, not even light-headed," I said. "But this bandage is a pain. I can't get a grip on anything."

"That's coming off this morning. You'll do better when you can use both hands. All right, let me get you in there. Walk with me." And with one of her arms around me, off we went and got into the bathroom with my little shuffle. In a few minutes, she was back and my meal tray was on my table. I sat back down, and she removed the silver lid to the plate.

"Oh, boy, cream of wheat and a half of banana," I remarked. "You were right, the breakfast tray is soooo much better." I was being a little bitchy.

"At least it's a real banana. I'll make you some toast too. Now dig in." She opened the milk carton, took the top off the cereal, peeled the banana, and out she went.

I poured in some milk. I wanted some sugar, but my fingers were not cooperating. I finally tore the packets open with my teeth and then mixed it into the cream of wheat. The warmth and sweetness were a good combination, and I surprised myself by finishing all of it. There was a tea bag and a cup of lukewarm water. *Oh, well, make the best of it, Ethel. The sooner you get your strength, the sooner you get out of here.* Robin came back with some toast and peanut butter and jelly.

"Well, look who's hungry. Or am I going to find the cereal in the wastebasket?" She waited for a sassy remark.

"I have to admit, it was good. Now, that peanut butter and jelly and toast looks like a gourmet meal," I said as she set it down on my tray. "Could I please have hot water? This is a little cool," I asked contritely. It wasn't her fault that I was here and had to eat and do the things I had to do.

"You got it. You keep this up and you'll be out of here this week," she said. From her lips to God's ears, I hoped.

"Can I shower after I eat? Can someone please help me?" I asked. I had become aware that I smelled like old ladies who only get their hair done once a week. Again, between the walker and my body aroma, I was motivated to get going.

"Sure. Evelina is our aide, and she can get you all set up. Finish your toast and I'll be back with the hot water." Out she went but stopped short. "Oh, and Dr. Chuttley is doing rounds now. He's your hand surgeon. He'll be in shortly to take that bandage off."

I smiled and lifted my bandaged hand to wave. I used my snugged-up fingers to hold my toast while I spread the peanut butter for my decadent feast. While I was left-handed, I used my right to hold my knife. As I tried to handle this operation, the piece of toast flipped off the plate and onto my lap.

"Dammit!" I muttered to myself. I started to fish around under the bed tray for my errant piece of toast.

"Let's see if I can help. I'm Dr. Chuttley." I looked up and saw a pudgy man of about fifty. He had on green scrubs and a white coat. He had a smile on his broad shiny face that showed almost-perfect teeth through a bushy blond mustache. He took my knife and spread the peanut butter and jelly onto the toast. "I could never understand how they expect patients with any type of hand injury to maneuver these packets. Hell, most times I can't even get the things open." With my toast prepared, I took a bite. It was truly heaven.

"Thank you, Doctor. I'm happy to meet you. And thanks for this," I said and held up my hand.

136

"And I am happy to finally meet you. Now, let's see if you'll thank me when this dressing comes off," he replied and took out his bandage scissors. He cut along the side of my wrist, and the dressing came off. My fingers looked awful, especially the two that had been pinned. They were scrawny and scarred, and the skin was peeling. I must have made quite a face. "I know they look a bit gruesome, but they look nice and straight."

"Wow, I was so worried that I wouldn't be able move them," I said as I moved my hand all about.

"Good, nice range of motion," he remarked as he took my hand and started to move each finger separately. "If anything hurts, let me know."

"Nothing. The two feel a little stiff, but I'm good," I said hopefully and looked at him.

"Okay, now grip my hand, really squeeze hard. Good. Make a fist. Good. Pull your fingers back. Terrific. Now, let's do the same thing with your left hand, so I can compare," he commented as he put my hands through their paces. "Wonderful! You've lost some strength, but that's to be expected. But with some exercises, you'll be back good as new. Any questions?" he asked and rubbed my right hand to remove some of the dead skin.

"I guess the only question I have for anyone is why. Why don't I remember anything about the accident?" I asked as I looked at him expectantly.

"The brain has a way to protect itself and you. The memory of terrible traumas lies deep down in the subconscious. Some never reappear, and others can come without warning. Say, you're driving in the same area where the accident occurred. Your brain makes a choice without you even knowing it. It can bring it back all at once, or it can dole it out in small increments. But don't spend too much time worrying about that. Time now to focus on your recovery," he thoughtfully explained. "We're happy that you've come back and can start to gain your strength and go home."

"Thank you, Doctor, and thanks for helping me with my toast." I smiled up at him.

"You're welcome, Ethel." And he patted my shoulder with his pudgy hand and left. I picked up my knife in my right hand and was happy to see that it remembered how to spread peanut butter and jelly. I closed my eyes and imagined that I was sitting there in the bakery with one of Miss Ruthie's famous surprise muffins brimming with fruit and nuts and sipping a piping hot cup of tea.

The rest of the morning sped by. After breakfast, it was time for my long-awaited shower. This time, with two hands, and under Evelina's guidance, I used the walker. I sat on a bench in the shower stall and let the warm water flow over my body. I scrubbed everything, needing to feel the rough facecloth on my skin as the pall of two months flowed down the drain. I rubbed my right hand to remove the dry, snakelike flakes, leaving behind fresh pink skin. The water flowed around the sides of my belly. Our first shower in two months. *I hope you like it,* I thought to Minnow. Wow! I remembered that Daddy had given my unborn its first nickname. When I was finished, I felt almost human. My hair dried and didn't look stringy. I dressed in several layers of cotton tops and a pair of baggy pants and hoped that Charlie was indeed bringing me real clothes.

Back in my room, I began to read the cards and notes that had been sent over the past couple of months. Beautiful pictures and words from my aunts and uncles, everyone in town, and elsewhere. I found one from Mike O'Brien at the *Herald*. In typical Mike fashion, he wrote, "Cut the crap, get your butt out of bed, or Caleb's going to have a new assistant editor. Love, Mike." I laughed. There was one from EC's day care, with all the tiny handprints on a sheet of bright-yellow construction paper with "Get well soon" scrawled by one of the older kids. Ginny had sent a small photo book with pictures of her beautiful gardens and a note of hope for my recovery. One after another, sometimes two and three from the same person, I read and reread them.

The amount of love and support was overwhelming, and I began to cry. As I sat there, I felt another kick. It was as if Minnow were saying, "Come on, let's get going and stop that crying." I wiped my tears and smiled as I wrapped my arms around my belly and leaned over for a hug. I heard footsteps in the hallway, and into my room ran EC, with Charlie behind him.

"Mommy!" he screeched to me as he tried to get up onto the bed. I pulled him into a big hug and rocked and cuddled him. I didn't want to let go. He pulled back and put his tiny hands on my face and gave me a big fish-lips kiss. I laughed through my tears of joy at this simple act of love from my son.

"Look at you, EC! What a big boy!" I was amazed at how much he had changed. At twenty months, he was changing from a baby to a little boy. *Oh, thank you, God, for bringing me back.* "And look at your shirt! 'Kiss me, I'm Irish'! Well, I'm going to do that." And I held him and smothered my little boy with kisses and hugs. Charlie stood in the doorway and smiled at the sight of the two of us. "Now, let me see, how big is your hand? Oh, so big!" I took EC's hand and held it with mine. He chatted away with "Mommy, this" and "Mommy, that." I couldn't take my eyes off him, examining every bit of my beautiful boy.

"Top of the morning, Mrs. O'Connor," Charlie said as he wiped tears away from his cheeks.

"Top of the morning, yourself, my handsome Irish husband," I replied and put my face up so he could kiss me. His lips were warm and tender. He sat down on the bed, and all three of us had a group hug.

"This is a beautiful scene," said Dr. Lossing from the doorway. "How are you doing this morning, Ethel?" she asked, looking down at my chart, reading the findings of the last twelve hours.

"I'm feeling good. Got my bandage off my hand, took a shower, ate, and now I'm ready to go home," I said as I summed up my morning activities, with my goal punctuating the end.

"That's great, but we'll save home for another week or so. We need to make sure that as you get up and go about physical therapy, your body is firing on all cylinders," she said as she made notes in my chart.

"And I see that an ultrasound has been requested. The tech should be in sometime soon. So you'll know whether or not you need to build an addition or bunk beds." She smiled at us. "Now, let's take a look at your range of motion and nerve sensitivity." At that, Charlie took EC from my arms and took a seat in the chair.

Dr. Lossing began to check my reflexes with various small instruments similar to ones that Dr. Chung had used on EC when he failed to walk. He asked me to stand up, which I was now getting better at, and held my hands to test my strength. I took a step or two toward her, and then the exam was done. She made more notes in my chart.

"Very good. Very good, indeed. Your age and your general fitness level have helped. We'll have you down to physical therapy today to start getting you going. Now, do you have any clothes other than these johnnies?" She smiled as she gave EC's head a tousle. "Are you going to help Mommy walk?" EC grinned at her.

"Got her things right here, Doc. She'll be zooming along before we know it." Charlie held up my little suitcase.

"Wonderful! Now, here's a little something for your hands." She took out a tennis ball. Tennis ball? Really? First, the walker, and now this? I had never thought so much about disliking a sport than I did at this very moment. "Use this in each hand to squeeze. It will get some tone back in your entire arm. And then you can roll it around on the bottom of your foot too."

"Thanks," I said and took the bright-yellow ball from her. I squeezed it with my right hand and saw it really did make all the muscles work.

"I'll check back in with you tomorrow." She was out of the room with her brisk step.

"Bye," I said, although I wasn't sure if she was even still within earshot.

"Now, can I please have some real clothes?" I asked Charlie, and he set my suitcase on the bed.

"I wasn't sure how much or what you needed," he said, and I found numerous pairs of underwear and socks. Expecting to find my old gray sweatshirt and pants, I found there was a new set. They were a pretty shade of pale salmon. And some new, soft T-shirts to go under the hooded sweatshirt. They were embroidered with the initials "PL Spa."

"Did you go shopping over at Piney Lodge?" I remarked as I held them up.

"Jackie did. When I called to tell her the good news last night, she said she wasn't going to have her friend hanging around in old stuff. She went over to the spa at Piney Lodge this morning and brought them over," he said with a sheepish grin.

"Oh, my dear, sweet friend," I said as I touched them and held them to my face. They were the most luxurious sweats I'd ever felt.

"She's the best. You wouldn't believe what she's done for us. I think we ate with her, Andy, and the boys five out of seven nights. And your dad, he insisted that he take EC three out of five days instead of going to Minnie's. He's had a ball with him. Everyone's been waiting and worrying with me about you. You'll have quite the reception when we get you back home," he said. I watched him, and today the worried look of yesterday was gone. He gazed into my eyes, and my soul was happy.

"Mrs. O'Connor? I'm Julia from Radiology. And I'm here to do your ultrasound." A petite woman in gray scrubs entered the room, rolling the ultrasound machine with her. "Let's see, would your family like to stay? It's okay with me." And she went about plugging in the machine and setting it up near my bedside.

"Hello, and yes, of course, they can stay. Can my son be on the bed with me?" I was so happy that as a family we would learn who Minnow was going to be.

"Sure, let's have him sit down at the foot of the bed. I wouldn't want him to get into this gel." Her caring eyes smiled at EC. Within a few moments, the machine and I were ready.

"What names have you picked out?" she asked as she moved the probe over my gelled abdomen.

"Outside of my dad nicknaming this child Minnow, we haven't had the chance to…well, since I've been out…" And I couldn't go any further. I'd lost so much time. I tried to hold back my tears, but they spilled from eyes. Charlie squeezed my hand, and I looked at him. I shook my head. The emotions of being in the accident, in a coma for two months, and now finding out what we would need to name our second child made me almost reel with all the impossibilities that had brought me here.

"In that case, you'll only have to concentrate on girl names, from the looks of it." And she turned the screen for us to see. "She's a little small, but everything seems to be in the right place. See, there are her hands. I think she's waving at you, little guy." And she pointed at the screen, and EC clapped his hands. I don't think he really knew what he was looking at, but it was exactly what we needed. Charlie leaned over and kissed me.

"Mrs. O'Connor, looks like we've got ourselves a little girl. I only hope she's half as pretty as her mom." I shook my head as I looked back at him.

"Oh my, a little girl. We'll have to switch gears, Daddy. I don't know nothin' about birthin' no girls!" I laughed, stealing a line from *Gone with the Wind*. "I've really got my work cut out for me now."

Being here in this hospital room with the news about our little-girl-to-be, well, I couldn't have been happier. More family—how wonderful! As I remember Caleb saying to me once, no one ever gets here today by planning for this exact moment. My life to this point had been nothing like I had planned the day I graduated from college. But as I looked from my husband to my little boy, and to the screen showing my unborn little girl, I wouldn't have had it any other way. And while I knew I had some work to do on myself, I made a silent promise that I was not going to forget about Sophie.

I'll find her, Momma, I will.

CHAPTER 20

F OR THE NEXT WEEK AND a half, I put my determination to the
test and consumed myself with therapy workouts. By the third
day, I'd said goodbye to my walker and its tennis balls. And when
I wasn't in the physical therapy department, I was walking the hallways to get my legs back. Some of the staff would start humming
the *Rocky* theme whenever they saw me in the hallway and give me
a thumbs-up. In bed, I used my tennis ball to help strengthen my
hands and arms. Phyllis had brought me some vitamin E cream to
use on my fingers. I was amazed at how it was helping to heal the
scars. The doctors were in continually checking on my progress. As
well, the nursing and ancillary staff were supportive and encouraging
at every step I took.

While I wanted to get home in the worst way, I also couldn't
wait until I could get back to the contents of the box and the papers
I'd found in Momma's house. Had I overlooked something? What
was left in the box that Daddy and I hadn't been over time and again?
And her journal and other papers? Was there something I'd missed?
I knew I would have to let those things wait for a while, after having
both Momma and Sophie appear in my dreams right before I came
back from my coma. Well, I knew it was another indication that I
needed to finish what I'd started.

I'd come back from my morning physical therapy session and
decided to take a nap before lunch. I was almost dozing when I heard
a knock on the doorjamb.

"Ethel?" Dr. Simon stood at the door. The smile on his face
showed how happy he was to see me. He was in street clothes but
wore a short white coat over his shirt and tie.

"Oh, Dr. Simon, come in," I said and sat up.

"Were you sleeping?" he asked and pulled up a chair.

"No. I just finished therapy and was resting before I went for a walk. So what's the verdict on my little girl?" I asked, getting right to the point.

"Ethel, you are quite a phenomenal woman, I have to tell you that. When I came to see you several weeks ago, I have to admit, I was worried. I've never had a patient in your state. And while your body slowed itself down to protect you, your baby continued to persevere. Always a strong heartbeat and lots of movement. You are my miracle patient," he said, and I could tell he was noticeably moved by the way he set his jaw to ward off tears.

"I don't know if I'm a miracle or not, but I know it certainly is good to be awake and moving and getting ready to get out of here and have this baby," I responded.

"You're always ready to lead the charge, aren't you? Okay, let's have a listen," he said and leaned over with his stethoscope. After a bit, he pressed here and there all around my abdomen. "Great heartbeat, everything feels normal. The ultrasound shows a beautiful little girl is waiting to come and see her bright, new world. So about five months down and probably less than four to go. Do you have any pain? Any bleeding? How active is she?"

"No pain, no bleeding, and she is a busy girl in there. I'll say that," I answered. "I think she's going to come out running."

"Good to hear. From the notes, it looks like your discharge will be soon. Physical therapists are scheduled for two to three home visits a week. A case nurse will also be there to assess your progress. No driving and no heavy lifting. When you get out, call the office and we'll schedule an appointment to see how you're progressing. Any questions?" He had given me the report I wanted to hear, but yes, I had one more question.

"With the accident, is there any way to know if something happened to her?" I asked very quietly and bit my lip.

"Ethel, all the tests that have been done since the accident on both you and her have been normal. There are no signs of any ill effects. While the coma put her back a little bit in weight, I'm sure she'll pick that up before she's born. You having an extra helping of proteins and vegetables each day will help her," he said, reassuring me.

"I'll eat much better once I get out of here. I know they can only do so much, but jeez. I've been having Charlie bring me things from home. I just want to go home and sleep in my own bed, hold my boy, pet my dogs, and say hello to everyone who's been so wonderful this entire time." I sighed and looked up at him.

"You won't have to wait much longer. Now, have a nap before your next gourmet meal arrives." He chuckled and patted my knee and left.

"Thanks, Doctor. Gourmet, my foot," I said to no one as I closed my eyes. My legs ached. Today I'd been on the bicycle, and I could swear if that thing were a regular bike, why, I'd have been halfway to Florida. My therapists always pushed me to the next level. They reminded me that if it wasn't physical, it wasn't therapy. Every day I looked to break another milestone. I was at 75 percent, which most people would have been satisfied with. But thinking about running after EC, and now with Minnow coming along, I knew I needed to be better.

I put my hands in the pockets of my hoodie and felt the softness of the material. Charlie had gone back to the Piney Lodge Spa to get me two more outfits like the one Jackie had given me. Thinking about Charlie, I couldn't wait to see him tonight. Charlie was here every day with EC, and we'd share supper. EC was still dumbfounded as to why Mommy couldn't come home and always cried when they left without me. Seeing his tears broke my heart and made me more determined than ever to get my strength back and go home. Daddy came out every other day or so, and he'd bring me a treat from Ms. Ruthie's. She'd always send along a note to "get well soon," or "Gosh darn, I miss you." Most folks sent their best wishes for me with Charlie or Daddy and said they couldn't wait until I came home. Caleb called on the phone every few days to run things by me, so I wouldn't feel out of the loop. His reassuring tone let me know how much he missed me and how everything was going to be all right.

"Did I hear someone say gourmet meal?" And there stood Daddy and Ginny in the doorway. The two of them looked so right together.

Their eyes were bright, and the smiles were genuine. Ginny had on a celery-hued barn coat from Beans over trim fitting jeans with a white cable-knit sweater. Daddy looked a little spiffier than usual, with jeans and black goose down vest over a long-sleeved T-shirt that was the color of a light-blue sky. Must be Ginny's influence. *Gosh, do I have a lot to catch up on!* I thought as I looked at the two of them.

"Daddy! Ginny! It's so good to see you." And I got up to give hugs.

"Good to see you, girl," Daddy said as he held his arm around me.

"No, no, you sit, poor thing. Save your strength," Ginny said and fussed to get me to sit back in bed. She handed me a little wrapped package. "Here, I thought you might like this."

"I'm fine. I have great strength. Want to see me crush this tennis ball?" I remarked. "Why, Ginny, that's so nice of you!" And I opened the gift. It was a glass jar with a black top. It looked like a type of cream. I opened it, and immediately the air was perfumed with lavender. I dipped my fingers in and felt the creaminess of it as I applied it to my hands. I saw her face change as she looked at my right hand with its scars.

"It's okay, I'm lucky. These are the only scars from the accident." I raised my hand to my nose and stopped. "Ginny, this is heavenly. Wait. Did you make this from your own lavender?"

"Yes, I did. Oh, I'm so glad you like it. I went to a craft class up in Bar Harbor with my girlfriends. One thing led to another, and I've made a few batches. It keeps me busy." She blushed and pushed her salt-and-pepper hair behind her ear.

"And here, Ruthie sent along your favorite cookie." Daddy gave me a brown paper bag. I knew before I looked inside that it was my favorite almond crescent cookie dipped in chocolate. I took it out and bit off the chocolate-covered end. The outside had a little crunch from the shaved almonds covering it, and the chocolate was rich and creamy. This time, Ruthie had written a note on the bag: "Keep up the good work and come home soon." Daddy smiled as I enjoyed my treat. "So, sport, when you getting out here?" he asked.

"They keep telling me I'm ahead of schedule, so I'm hoping that it will be any day," I answered and continued to munch on my cookie. "I know I can't wait to get outside. Once in a while, I can get them to take me outside, but this March weather is a bit too chilly for me."

"Too chilly for what?" It was Dr. Lossing. "Finally, something my star patient can't endure?" She was in her surgical green scrubs and had my chart in her hand.

"Hi, Dr. Lossing! You remember my dad, Eddy? And this is his friend, Ginny," I introduced them. Then I added, "I hope you've got good news for me."

"Hello again, and nice to meet you, Ginny. And I do, indeed, have good news for you, Miss Ethel. You are free to go. I checked in with your therapist from this morning's workout. Their report shows that you are independently moving. Your strength is above 75 percent. You have just blown us away with how you've progressed. So you'll see me in a month. Call Dr. Simon to start back with your regular appointments for you and the baby, and a visiting nurse has been scheduled to check in with you for the first week or two. How does that sound?" she finished and gave me a big smile.

"I can go? Now? Whoopie! Oh, thank you, Dr. Lossing, so much! Thank you for all you've done!" I was so excited I looked from Daddy to Ginny, who both were grinning from ear to ear.

"Don't thank me, thank yourself, Ethel. You're the one who was determined from day 1 to get back on track and get out of here. I see no reason to expect any change in your condition that isn't constant improvement." She looked down at my chart and scribbled a signature. "I'll have your nurse come in and get your paperwork done. Now, any questions?"

"Daddy, do you have room in the truck for me?" I asked.

"Always have room for you, Ethel." He was smiling as he answered. Dr. Lossing shook hands with Daddy and left the room chuckling.

"Now, where's that suitcase?" I asked, and Ginny went to the room locker. "Charlie will be so surprised. I'll call him from home."

"Here it is. Let' get you packed," she answered and was happy to help get all my things put away. I heard footsteps and looked up.

147

It was Phyllis. She stood in the doorway with her hands on her hips. I smiled at her as she shook her head at me.

"You sure you're ready to take this ornery child back home?" she said to Daddy.

"I'd think you'd want her out of your hair by now," Daddy joked with her.

"This one I'll miss. Can't say why." She walked into the room and placed several papers on the tray table. "Okay, Ethel, I need your autograph on a few things, and then you'll be all set to go home." And she began to explain the discharge and give me the various instructions and follow-up appointments. I barely heard what she was explaining—my need to be outside was so great. With Ginny's help, I was all packed up and ready to go. Phyllis got up to leave and turned and put her arms around me. "You take care of yourself and that baby. The Lord's given you another way to look at things. Do Him justice." She looked into my eyes. Hers were glistening with tears that were about to cascade down her shiny brown cheeks.

"I will. I won't disappoint you," I said in a whisper.

CHAPTER 21

Almost home. As Daddy drove along the road to my house, I realized a new era had begun. Ginny sitting next to Daddy seemed like the most natural thing for the three of us to do. Ginny kept asking if I was all right and that maybe Daddy should go easier over the bumps. Daddy, of course, told her I was almost born in a truck and that I'd be fine. The ease of conversation and the light-hearted joking between the two of them made me so happy.

I was acutely aware of the approach of spring, as all around me there were full buds on the trees and hints of green here and there among the brown scales that winter was trying to shed. The river rushed along, fueled by the melting waters to the north of us. Even though the day was breezy and cold, the sun was bright and felt warm through the windshield. I realized how long I'd been in the hospital as I squinted and wished for my sunglasses. When my house came into view, I began to have a funny feeling. My breathing was a little shallower, and I stiffened my body.

"Ethel, are you okay? You look a little worried," Ginny asked, and I saw her glance at Daddy.

"Almost home, sport. Look, I think I can see the dogs," Daddy said, trying to focus my attention elsewhere.

"Daddy, stop the truck. This is where it happened, isn't it?" I said quietly, and Daddy stopped. I looked at each side of the road. There was the river whooshing along on one side, and on the other was a stand of birch and maple trees. Some of the young birches had been snapped at their bases. Close to the center of the trees was a huge maple. There was a deep gash in the bark showing the pale whitish yellow of the wood. "I want to get out."

"Ethel, I don't think it's a good idea. Maybe you should wait for Charlie," Daddy said.

"No, I want to deal with this now and get it over with." I was adamant. "I'm getting out."

"Ethel, you don't have a coat. It's still so chilly," Ginny pleaded and looked at Daddy for direction.

"I need to do this. Daddy, can I have your vest?" I asked quietly.

"All right, let's get this over with. I'll go with you." He took off his vest, and Ginny helped me into it. He came around and opened my door, and I got out.

The wind whipped across my face, chilling me. I gripped the vest around me as I walked toward the tree. Daddy put his arm around me, but I gently pushed it away. The ground was partially frozen, and I looked for rocks to step on to keep from getting my sneakers wet. My balance was good, but my baby was making me work harder to keep it that way with each step I took. Daddy walked beside me in silence.

When I reached the maple tree, my heart continued to race. I put my hand on the gash in the tree's bark. It was hard to describe what was going on inside of me. It was a subtle sensation, one that made me open my eyes wider, but then it made me slam them shut. I was suddenly aware of the beginning of the crash. It was as if I was watching it on television with the sound turned off. I could see Charlie, EC, and me, our mouths open. EC was crying. Charlie and I were screaming. When the Jeep finally hit the tree, I jerked to attention. And then it was gone. I opened my eyes and saw only my hand on the tree. The feelings were gone. The sounds of a black-capped chickadee and the rush of the river broke the silence.

"You okay, Ethel?" Daddy asked as he held out his hand. This time, I took it.

"I'm fine now, Daddy, thanks." I grabbed that strong hand that so many times had steadied me in my life. A feeling of acute exhaustion came over me. "Now, I'd love to race this old truck home, but Minnow and I'd really appreciate the ride," I joked with him, and he grabbed me into the biggest hug.

"Ginny, let's get this girl home." The smile on his face said all that needed to be said, and we got back into the truck.

As we pulled into the yard, I heard the dogs barking their greeting for Daddy. I didn't say a word as we walked up onto the porch. I moved to the side, away from the dogs' view, and waited. As Daddy opened the kitchen door, Mutt and Jeff came out with their soft, friendly woofing and snuffling at him and his pockets. It was Mutt who first spotted me, and then Jeff. I have never seen two dogs try to turn themselves absolutely inside out with joy. They were doing half-jumps, woofing and nuzzling every part of me. I sat down on the bench and let myself be buried by their furry golden embraces. My face was licked more times than I could count. I stood up finally and was escorted into the house with their gentle bumping as they guided me through the door. They took a seat by their bowls and waited patiently. Ginny and Daddy chuckled at the sight.

"My furry boys," I said and went to fill their bowls. "Back to normal. This is what I missed."

"How about I make supper for all of us?" Ginny said. "What would you like?"

Thinking for moment, I finally said, "I would love a juicy cheeseburger and mashed potatoes. The box potatoes and those gray-beige meat patties at the hospital were awful. But I don't know what's in the fridge," I said, aware that I had no idea what was available to cook with.

"That's okay. Eddy can go over to Pappy's. Ruthie told me that he's starting to stock some of McCreery's beef and pork in the store." Ginny had sprung into action, opening the fridge and inspecting the contents. "I think we'll need a few more things, by the looks of it." And I peeked around the door and found that outside of milk, juice, and some condiments; there wasn't much else left.

"You make a list and I'll be on my way," Daddy said. "I'll stop by Ruthie's too."

"What have Charlie and EC been eating? My god, there's nothing in here!" I was astonished at the barren wasteland. I opened the freezer and found frozen waffles, ice cubes, and ice cream that I'd bought at Christmas.

"We'll get you back on track. Now, let's make a list." Ginny and I quickly put one together after opening and closing cupboards. Daddy took it and was off to town.

After doing a quick check on the rest of the house and deeming it still livable, I made a fire in the fireplace, while Ginny made some tea.

"I'm bushed," I said. "But I don't know why." I had collapsed into my chair, and the dogs couldn't get close enough as they lay down beside me. They both took a deep sigh as the warmth of the fire started to permeate the room.

"Ethel, you've been through an awful lot. And coming to grips with where the accident happened, why, you're emotionally drained," she summarized. She brought over the cups of tea and sat on the couch.

"Oh, how I've missed this," I said and blew on the hot tea. I warmed my hands as they encircled the mug.

"Simple pleasures can never be replaced," Ginny stated.

"That's for sure," I said and hesitated before I spoke again. "Ginny, I have to ask you something."

"Anything, Ethel. What is it?" she said and waited.

"How's my dad? I mean, has he followed up with the doctors the way he was supposed to? And how are you two?" I realized I didn't know if Daddy had ever followed up with Doc. And of course, with seeing them together today, the way they acted was very telling as to how close they had become.

"Where to begin…" She smiled at me and spoke. "You probably don't remember, but the night of your accident, Eddy had come up to take me to dinner. When he got there, the snow was really coming down, so we decided to stay right where we were. I made, oh, gee, I think it was meatloaf and mashed potatoes. Which I now realize is one of his favorite meals. I put a few LPs on the stereo, and we had one of the best nights that I'd had in a long time. He said so too. We talked about a lot of things. My Abe, your mother, and you. And then we talked about our hopes and fears. I tell you, I never thought I'd get through that hard crust of his, but that night I did. The weather wasn't getting any better, so he stayed the night." Ginny blushed a little at this point, and my heart swelled to know that happiness had found them in a snowstorm.

"That is so sweet," I said as my grin went from ear to ear.

"We didn't know anything about your accident until the next morning when he got home. He called me, and I swear we both wept. During these past two months, we've grown closer than I'd ever thought possible for a couple of old fuddy-duddies like us. He kept his follow-up appointment with Doc McAllister, who said, from all the reports that have come back, that it probably just was a lack of eating regularly that day. Seeing you in the hospital, well, that really set him back on his heels. We'd visit and he'd sit there and tell you all about where he was going to take Minnow and EC fishing when the weather got better. The day you woke up, he called me from the hospital lobby, and I could tell how happy he was. So I guess that's a long way of saying that he's good, and so are we," she finished and beamed at me.

"Oh, Ginny, I am truly so very happy for the two of you! From the first time we met, I felt that there was something about you," I said. The phone rang, and Ginny got up to answer it.

"Hello! Why, hi, Charlie. Yes, she is, just a minute." I got up as Ginny handed the phone to me.

"Hi, honey. Surprise!" I said into the receiver as I held back my tears. "I'm home."

"So I just heard. Good thing I saw your dad. Otherwise, EC and I were on our way to the hospital. Pappy let me use his phone to call," Charlie gently scolded me.

"I'm sorry, but the doctor came in and said I could go, so I hopped in the truck with Daddy and Ginny, and here I am. Ginny's going to make supper once Daddy gets home with a few things," I replied.

"Ah, about the house. I'm sorry, we really have been eating well, just not at home. And Minnie has been swell about having things for EC to eat. Oh, I'm so happy you're home! I love you!" I could tell he was choking back tears.

"That's okay, honey, just come on home," I said. "Love you too." And we hung up.

When they arrived home, EC was so happy to see me he ran to me and hugged and kissed me. He was also very aware of Mommy's belly and why he couldn't sit any closer. He lifted my sweatshirt to see if he could find the "ball." There would be time enough to explain how he was going to be a big brother. I could envision the two of them—EC holding Minnow's hand and helping her along the way.

Daddy arrived with the groceries, and Ginny put together the burgers for Charlie to cook on the grill. And her mashed potatoes were just about as good as Mrs. F's at the Inn. She'd even made a spinach-and-strawberry salad with a homemade dressing. It was good to eat using my own dishes, in my own house, with my family. Over dinner, we exchanged conversations about hospital food and spring and fishing and everything in between. Noticeably absent was any conversation about Sophie. I knew I would get back to that, but just not tonight.

Daddy and Ginny left, and Charlie and I put EC to bed. Kissing my little boy good night gave me an appreciation for things that were pure and simple. We went downstairs and cuddled on the couch and watched the fire as it slowly dwindled to amber and scarlet embers.

"It's good to have you home," Charlie said and drew me into his arms. He gave me the softest, most meaningful kisses. The message that passed between us as we looked into each other's eyes was so strong that no other words were needed.

Yes, I was home. *Home* is a word that has one meaning. Yes, the house is the dwelling, but the home is the spirit that rounds out the rough edges and angles of the structure. A house can be huge or humble, but a home is more precious to its family than anyone could ever place a value on. A home will dwarf the grandest of houses or create a palace out of a hovel. Yes, today I was home, and I was never going to forget this feeling.

CHAPTER 22

THE NEXT FEW WEEKS WERE frustrating, as I wanted to—no, I needed to—get going. Now that I wasn't confined to the hospital, I definitely didn't want to be confined to the house. But there were visiting nurses and home physical therapists who were incessantly visiting and checking and poking. If the therapist said to do five reps of each exercise twice a day, I doubled that. The nurses were happy to have a compliant patient and signed off on my care after the second week but cautioned that I keep my appointments to keep a check on the baby. The therapists deemed my case closed after the third week but made me promise to keep up with the tennis ball for my fingers. They had healed well but still were not as fluid in their movements as they would have liked. Tennis—I was beginning to despise the game.

Jackie had come by a couple of times and helped me get the house back in shape. It wasn't that Charlie hadn't cleaned the house; it was just that he was still a guy and a dad. And what with taking care of EC and coming to visit me at the hospital every day, well, there hadn't been much time for being tidy. And with two golden retrievers, let's just say the dust bunnies seemed to be in their second generations.

I also needed to go shopping for maternity clothes. In the meantime, I had gotten some catalogs and leafed through the pages of necessary evil. In under two years, it was amazing how maternity fashion was changing. I was thankful that the big blousy tops had been replaced with ones that looked like regular clothes with just a bit more room. Pants were still lacking style—that stretchy panel made me feel dowdy—but I consoled myself that I had only a few months to be in them and that I might actually switch to some type of flowy dress as the weather warmed.

Lots of friends and relatives had come by to visit and drop off casseroles and express how glad they were that I was home and how pleased they were for us with our second child on the way. I frequently invited Daddy over to eat supper with us—we had such a bounty. And he was more than willing to help out, devouring the meals and having the opportunity to sit with his EC. I busied myself cataloging the dishes and writing thank-you notes to go with each one. Daddy then delivered the empty dishes and notes back to the givers for me, sometimes resulting in yet another plate of someone's delicious intentions.

One urgent need was to get a new vehicle for me. The Jeep had been totaled. And understandably, Charlie was hesitant to look for a new vehicle without knowing when or if I would recover. He and EC had been managing very well in Charlie's pickup, but now we needed to find something. I was happy to have a Jeep again, but Daddy was worried. The state trooper had determined there wasn't a vehicle made that would have prevented our accident, but Daddy insisted on something safer. Uncle Ellsworth had bought a 1979 Volvo station wagon, and he assured Charlie and me that it was almost brand-new and it had a tremendous safety rating. When we saw it, I was sold. It was white, impeccably clean leather interior, room for two car seats, and a roomy hatchback to carry the dogs. It also got better mileage than the Jeep. In the end, we bought it and promised ourselves that we'd never drive in a snowstorm again.

The dream I had of Sophie and Momma kept replaying in my mind. "The answer is right in front of you," Momma had said. This morning, I spread the contents of the box on the table to determine what that answer might be.

The letters from Joseph and Daddy, the coin, the diary, and two of the three pictures all had an explanation. The relevant part of the diary appeared to be two pages with words that were explained by dates, the end of World War II.

I took out the letters from Daddy. Untying the pale-blue ribbon, I checked those dates. They were the last ones he had sent prior to returning home. When I had initially opened the box, I'd hastily read his letters. At that time, I was focused more on finding Joseph. Now, as I really read these letters, I saw yet another side of my father and how sincere he was. His love grew as he got closer to coming back to the love of his life. In his last one, he wrote of how much he missed her and proposed to her in the way only Daddy could.

Dear Stephanie,

I'm counting the days until I return. Your picture is in my pocket, close to my heart, and that is where I want you to be. I think of your smile, and it makes me smile. I know we talked a little about what would happen when or if I got to come home. Well, I'm coming home, and I want to make sure you know how much I love you and how much I want to be married to you.

Love,
Your Eddy

Those were sweet yet simple words about a love that was only strengthened by being oceans apart. I remembered the picture that Daddy had on his mantel of him and his buddies in the service. Handsome young flyboys with that roguish attitude. Their leather bomber jackets over their crisp uniforms. They were invincible. Out of those five young men, Daddy had been the only one who had returned. The others were shot down in combat. I thought how they, too, must have had someone waiting, hoping for the love of their life to return. How lucky for Momma that Daddy had returned to give her that love she so wanted and deserved.

The only thing left unexplained in the box was the one picture of Momma and another girl. They were smiling, that college coed glow on their faces. But what was behind that smile could fill volumes. Clad in their plaid skirts, bobby socks, and loafers, they appeared to be at what I surmised was most likely the Keene State campus. On the back of the photo had been written "Chums." I had chalked the word *chums* up to meaning "friends." Was this the answer that was right in front of me?

Going to Keene State was an option, but what would I get out of that trip? I could find the building and ascertain that yes, it was indeed Keene State. That would only prove that it was the campus and nothing more. No. Finding this girl was the answer. The only way I could think of discovering who she was might be their college yearbook. And hopefully, Momma's friend had graduated with her. And just maybe, she would know what had happened to Sophie.

I knew it was a long shot. *Well, get to it, Ethel,* I thought. I picked up the phone and dialed Information.

"Information. What state and city, please?" The voice sounded like comedian Lily Tomlin's character Ernestine, whom I had enjoyed watching on the television show *Laugh-In.* I smiled to myself as I pictured the updo of her dark hair and those huge round earrings.

"Yes, operator. Keene, New Hampshire. The number for Keene State College, please," I answered and waited.

"One minute, please," Ernestine said, and then there was a click. "There are several numbers. What department are you looking for?"

I thought quickly and responded, "Alumni Services. Is there any listing for that?" I hoped I'd chosen correctly.

"Yes, there is. Would you like me to dial that for you? While you think about that, the number is…" And she read the number to me twice. I thanked her and said I would dial myself, hung up, and without hesitation, dialed.

"Alumni Services, Keene State, this is Amy. How can I help you?" the young voice said. She sounded like a perky undergrad who was working a part-time job. I remembered those days when I had a job at the college paper. You were ecstatic when the phone rang, hoping for something that would take you away from some mundane task.

"Hi, Amy. I'm looking for a yearbook from a certain year. I was wondering if you could help me?" I asked as cheerily as she sounded.

"Sure, what year?" Amy responded.

"Ah, 1945," I stated.

"Wow, that's a long time ago, but I'm sure I can find it. We have a Kronicle for each year right here in our foyer library. Let me put you on hold." And the phone clicked. A nondescript music track played for about two or three minutes, and then a click, and Amy was back. "Okay, I found it. Are you looking for someone or something in particular?"

"I am looking for my mother. Her name was Stephanie LaChance," I said. "Can you find her name?"

"Wow, that's cool. Hang on, let me see. Yes, I got it right here. Stephanie M. LaChance, early childhood education. Now what?" she asked. Now what, indeed. *Think fast, Ethel.*

"Would I be able to borrow the yearbook?" I said, thinking that might be a possibility.

"Oh, no, ma'am, we can't do that. You could stop by and look at it any time Monday through Friday, between the hours of nine in the morning and four in the afternoon." Her enthusiasm was very punctuated by her sense of right and wrong.

"I really can't do that, Amy. You see, I'm pregnant and due anytime now. My doctor would never let me make that long of a trip. Is there any other way?" I asked, telling a little white lie.

"Well, I see. I could fax whatever you'd like. How would that be?" Gosh, I loved this kid.

"That would be super. Could you fax me the pictures of all the graduates? Would that be possible?" I had my fingers crossed at this point.

"Sure, let's see, that's about fifteen pages. Make sure you have enough toner in your machine, and I'll start. I'm going to copy them first so they'll fax better. I'll start in about fifteen minutes. Is that okay, ma'am?" I could see her, dressed in her Keene State sweatshirt, happy to be helpful.

"Yes, that will be fine. Here's the number, Amy, and give me twenty. How's that?" I said as I gave her the number for *The Bugle* and started to put my shoes on and find my vest and keys.

"You got it. Thanks for calling Keene State. And go Owls! Whoo, whoo!" she continued, and I was out the door as she was probably singing the Keene State fight song to end the conversation.

Getting into the car, I realized that this was the first time I had driven since before the accident. I pushed the momentary insecure thought out of my head and turned the key. I adjusted the seat and the mirrors and put it in gear. The ride was smooth, and it took no time to arrive at the office. I waved at a few folks as I bounded up the steps of *The Bugle*. Well, not really *bounded*. My five-month baby belly was slowing me down just a bit.

"And good day to you too. What's the hurry?" Caleb asked as I headed straight to the fax machine to check it for paper and toner. "Good thing you showed up. I was about to advertise for an assistant editor."

"I've got it figured out, Caleb," I said, ignoring his comment as I tapped my finger and stared at the machine, willing it to start. Why hadn't I told her fifteen? I glanced at my watch and saw I had a least ten more minutes to wait.

"Figured what out?" he said.

"The answer to who can help me find Sophie," I said.

"Back up a minute. And sit down. If there's a fax coming in, we'll know by all the racket it'll make." And Caleb steered me to my desk.

It was then that I noticed a bouquet of crocus in a tiny vase on my desk, with a note that said, "Welcome back." I immediately felt horrible at rushing in and focusing on only one thing.

"I started out with snowdrops. I change the flowers about every third day, hoping you'd come walking through that door," he said, and I was touched by his sentiment. "I keep the water hot for your tea too."

"Caleb, that's so sweet. I'm so sorry for busting through the door. Thank you," I said and got up to give him a hug.

"It's okay. I'm glad to have you back. I've missed my sparring partner," he said as he patted my back. "Now go get yourself a cup of tea. When the fax comes, it comes." I took my mug and went into the back room to make my tea.

"So what's been happening? I know you've said it's been status quo, but really, what's been going on?" I asked.

"Big story is the assassination attempt on Reagan. What a shock that was. Poor Brady got the worst of it. It's still touch-and-go from what's coming out of Washington. Bush was on TV a couple of times, but old Ronnie was quick to put in an appearance," Caleb began.

"It's unbelievable. With all the Secret Service around, you'd think something like this could never happen," I replied. "And what's going on in town?"

"Russell and Robert come up about every other weekend now to finalize getting the Emporium ready. The opening is just a little over a week away. Sadie's been busy with inventory and decorating," he began.

"She must be having a ball," I commented as I came back with my cup, dunking my tea bag.

"She is. It keeps her occupied, so she's not experimenting with her culinary delights, if you catch my drift," he answered. At that comment, the door opened and Sadie walked in, full of smiles. She wore a bright-blue cardigan over a perfectly starched white blouse. Her blue jeans gave her a youthful look and ended in her red sneakers. Her well-fitting clothes over her trim figure made me jealous. I'd thrown one of Charlie's hooded sweatshirts over my T-shirt, hoping it would hide my ill-fitting, stretchy bottoms. I'd been so intent on the incoming fax I really hadn't thought about how I looked when I'd left the house.

"Who's catching your drift now, dear?" she commented as she gave Caleb a quick peck on the cheek. "Ethel, I saw you through the window, and I had to come right over." She gave me a big hug and then stood back. "You look terrific."

"Thanks. I feel good too. And you look like the Emporium is agreeing with you," I noted.

"It is. I'm having a splendid time," she said as she straightened the newspapers on the table and then announced, "Well, I'm off to work. Lots to do, lots to do. Why don't you two come over for lunch and Ethel can see what's been going on?"

"Sure, I'd love to," again realizing I'd been away for much of the hubbub of Piney Bluffs's newest business. Then the door closed as quickly as it had opened, with Sadie waving goodbye.

"And that would be what she does every day now," Caleb chuckled as he took a sip of his coffee. "She breezes in and she breezes out. God, I love her."

"You'd better," I answered. "Nothing else?"

"Everything is very calm. A few things keep it interesting. We'll have the Emporium opening to coincide with first day of fishing season. Tubby, Ruthie, and the Brownings are organizing a weigh-in in conjunction with the ribbon cutting. Beulah's having her first class of young ladies graduating from her fishing school give demonstrations on fly-tying and casting at the New England Fishing Expo in Portland next week. They're pretty enthused. I'm going to let Jimmy take my camera and be our roving reporter to tag along with them," Caleb said, but he seemed a little evasive.

"That sounds like a great idea. Jimmy must be excited about that. After we get back from lunch, I'll do a story on the Emporium. Bring that camera along," I commented. I looked over at the fax. Still nothing.

"Why do I think there's still something you need to tell me?" I said and waited.

"You're pretty good at this, you know. There is one thing that I know you'll just love," he said and looked very proud.

"And that would be?" I asked.

"Becoming a small printer for local authors or whoever needs to have a book printed. Like Ruthie, for instance. I know Russell and Robert were going to take care of her. But I looked into the process, and I think this might be our next best venture," Caleb finished. "Right now, I'm subcontracting the presses up at your old alma mater, University of Maine. But within the year, we'll have all our own equipment."

"Caleb, that's a wonderful idea! This is a great opportunity, and think of the new folks that this will bring into town. Why, with the Emporium and the press...this is great! Have you thought of a name?" I commented, ecstatic with his news.

"I have. PB Press, you know, for Piney Bluffs. Short and sweet," he said.

"I like it, and I can hardly wait to see Ruthie's cookbook," I added.

"It came out good, if I do say so myself." Caleb looked quite pleased with himself. I looked over to the fax—still nothing.

"Ethel, stop it. It's like watching a pot and waiting for it to boil," Caleb chided me.

"Well, let's see if my fingers remember what to do." I removed the cover from my typewriter and rolled in a fresh piece of paper. I stretched my fingers and typed that exercise from my high school typing class: "Now is the time for every good man to come to the aid of his party."

"And…?" Caleb asked as he watched me.

"The ring finger's a little achy, but if that's the only residual from the accident, then I've got nothing to complain about," I continued and repeated typing that sentence a few more times.

"How about the baby? Is she going to be all right." Caleb had a serious tone, and I turned my chair to face him.

"The doctors told me everything is fine. She's a little small, but with me being out for almost two months, I guess that was to be expected. While they don't say it, I know until she's born, we won't truly know how she is. But I have great faith that she's a little fighter. I have an appointment with Dr. Simon. I think it's next week. Wait. What day is it?" I asked as it finally hit me.

"It's Thursday, April 2," he responded.

"Oh, no, it's tomorrow. Oh, gee, Caleb, I know I was going to start back tomorrow," I said sheepishly and gave him a little smile.

"Ethel, one more day isn't going to make a difference. Start fresh on Monday morning. You best keep that appointment," he lightly scolded me.

"I fully intend to. It's just my mind lately, it just prioritizes differently," I said, annoyed with myself. I got up and went to the fax machine again, and miraculously, it sprang to life with those ear-piercing tones. "Yes, finally."

Amy had thoughtfully sent Momma's page first. Her picture, her name, Stephanie M. Lachance, Early Childhood Education. It was like looking in the mirror. Her hair was long and fell around her shoulders. Head tilted to one side, her smile and mine the same. Would my little girl look like me too? The next pages started alphabetically, As, Bs, and then there it was.

"Here she is, last one on the page. Madeline H. Chumerford, Early Childhood Education." I wished I'd brought the photo of Momma and her friend with me, but I was 100 percent sure that Madeline was the one. I took the next page to put behind it but then saw the name of the first person. This was definitely something I wasn't counting on. "Oh no, Martha H. Chumerford, Early Childhood Education too. Identical twins?" Their pictures were the typical college head shots, but there wasn't a thing to distinguish one from the other.

"And they would be?" Caleb asked.

"The answer that Momma told me about," I said and looked at the pictures like it was the Holy Grail. "But this just got very complicated."

"Who are they? And why is it complicated? And *when* did your mother tell you about them?" Caleb's face showed he was a little concerned.

"Let me explain. Right before I came to, I had two dreams. In one, I was with Sophie in the snow. She wanted me to come sliding with her on *the* sled. She said that Momma wanted us to share it. And the second one was Momma herself telling me that I had lots to do and that the answer was right in front of me," I said as the details came spilling out. When I'd finished, I took a sip of my tea.

"Really," he commented but still looked a little skeptical.

"I know it sounds crazy, but yes, really. I never saw either of their faces, but oh, they were so real, Caleb, just out of my reach," I said softly. I closed my eyes and took a moment. I could still see the image of Sophie and thought I could feel Momma's touch. And then it was gone.

"So Madeline and Martha, they're your answer?" Caleb asked.

"No, only one of them is, or that's what I thought a moment ago. The picture of my mother and one of these two women is the only thing in that box that hasn't been explained. You see, on the back of the picture, it said 'Chums.' I've thought that meant 'friends.'

But now I know it must have been a nickname for either Madeline or Martha. If I can find the right one, maybe she knows what happened to Sophie," I said excitedly. I could feel that finally I was on the right path, save for the twin fork in the road.

"And how do you expect to find them?" Caleb asked.

"The only one that I can think of to help me would be Frank. Do you think he would do it?" I said with a sheepish grin.

"I'm sure he would. He's called several times since your accident, wanting to know what he could do to help. So yes, I'm sure he would. He told me a couple of weeks ago how their files are beginning to be loaded into a big computer," Caleb added. "Searching and discovering information is about to get faster. He said that in less than ten years, everyone will have one."

"I can't imagine having that kind of information at my fingertips," I said as I continued to look from picture to picture. What I really couldn't imagine was talking to a person who had been my mother's friend. *So now, which one are you? Madeline or Martha?*

CHAPTER 23

AFTER CALLING AND FINDING THAT Frank wasn't in the office today, I left a message for him. It was just about eleven thirty, so Caleb and I walked over to the Emporium to meet Sadie. Charlie had painted it white to the specifications of the Brownings. The black shutters were offset by the sunny yellow double doors. The building had such an inviting look. It had large paned windows and a wraparound porch, which seamlessly connected it to Ruthie's. A canvass drape covered what must be the Emporium's sign, no doubt waiting for opening day. I pulled up a corner to get just a peak and saw a richly carved sign in black and dark red with gilt filled lettering. I tucked the covering back in and continued to explore the new life that this building was giving to our town.

There were several rocking chairs on the porch, where patrons would be able to gather with their new book or a delicious baked good from Ruthie's bakery. With their natural finish and slat backs and wide arms, the chairs reminded me of the one that my grandfather had made.

"Come on in," Sadie announced as she opened the double doors for us. My eyes traveled from the racks of books to the rich tones of the braided rugs to a gift area. It felt open and airy, with the rough-cut wood providing another layer of brightness. Skylights on the sunny side of the roof let in more natural light. Even on this cloudy March day, the interior had a golden glow without glaring light fixtures. "What do you think?"

"This is wonderful. It's like being inside a log cabin library. I love how it's not too big and not too small. It's just perfect," I replied and continued to notice little details here and there that gave it just

166

the right touch. A display with all types of bookmarks, teeny book lights, and wooden book stands for cookbooks. An Emporium mug had been designed in bright yellow to match the front doors and with the word Emporium in much the same style as the sign. There was a special section devoted to Maine and the fish and game industry, showcasing Beulah and her story. On another endcap was a picture of Ruthie standing in her bakery and stacks of her cookbook on display. I picked up one of them and smiled as I thumbed through the book and saw the recipe for Surprise Muffins, one of her daily mainstays. Caleb had taken the pictures, giving thought to the colors of the food and plates and tableware. Each dish looked more delicious than the next. And there it was on the back, in an oval, PB Press. Very nice indeed.

"Between Sadie, Charlie, and the boys, this has turned out quite nice," Caleb commented. He was starting to take some pictures of the books, displays, and Sadie standing at the counter.

"I'll say! Every place you look, there's another detail for the booklover. Okay, I'll be right here if anyone is looking for me," I said as I walked over to one of the Bean leather chairs and sunk into it. "These are just the right firmness. Not too squishy to make you want to stay all day and not too firm that would make you jump out of them." I put my feet up on the ottoman and closed my eyes for a moment.

"Is that my Ethel?" It was Ruthie I heard. "You look so good! How's the baby?"

"Oh, Ruthie, I'm good, and so is she," I said and got up to greet her. As I hugged her, I caught the aroma of chocolate. "Yum. What kind of chocolate-something are you making?"

"Good nose, my dear. Years of my intensive training, no doubt." And she laughed. "Brownies."

"Do you have any extras, Ruthie? I'll need a pick-me-up by the afternoon. You know, the days have been kind of long since some-one's been slacking." Caleb threw a jab my way.

"Boy, you're tough. Good thing I'm coming back. You'd never find anyone to put up with your taskmaster ways!" I returned the jest. Gosh, it was good to be back with these people.

"Now, let's get you some lunch. What have you got today, Ruthie?" Sadie said. We walked through the covered porch into the bakery. It was a gallery of sorts. Caleb had taken pictures around town, and the black-and-whites gave patrons another view of Piney Bluffs through his talented eye. They were terrific shots.

"You're doing lunch now, Ruthie?" I asked.

"Only a sandwich and a soup. I didn't want to infringe on Andy's business. So today we've got chicken salad with apples and walnuts on a raisin bread. And soup is a chicken barley with rosemary," Ruthie said and waited by the counter as we found a seat in the bakery. It looked like a few more tables had been added, and they were almost full as patrons sipped coffee and munched on the bakery's best. I noticed that the Polomski twins were waiting tables. Vicky and Violet had graduated from high school last spring, and from what I remembered, they had wanted to enlist together in the Air Force.

"Hi, everyone. Good to see you, Ethel," Vicky said as she came over to our table and placed a glass of water in front of each of us. "What can I get you?" Her short raven hair was stuffed under a Piney Bluffs High School ball cap, while her sister let her long dark braid fall almost to her waist. The girls wore white T-shirts and jeans for a casual look.

"Vicky, it's good to see you. Are you and Violet still planning on a military career?" I asked.

"Yes. Good memory. Going in May, so another few months, and then Colorado Springs here we come," she replied. "Your dad's taken us up in the planes over at the airstrip a few times. It's been a blast having him show us around those little planes. But we've got our eyes set on the big jets." Her eyes shone bright with the excitement of youthful dreams.

"Well, congratulations. Let's see, I'll have today's soup and sandwich," I added.

"Me too," said Caleb. "Sadie?"

"Just the soup for me, please, but I will have a nice slice of sourdough, toasted with butter," she answered.

"You got it." And with a turn of her heel, Vicky was off to the kitchen.

"When will Russell and Robert be back next?" I asked. "They must be getting excited."

"They're due in Friday. They have a few more surprises that they're planning for the opening. But they've been very tight-lipped about the whole thing. I never know with those two," Sadie answered. "So, Ethel, I assume you'll be letting this search for your sister go by the wayside until you recover and get settled with your health and the new baby."

"Not really, Sadie. In fact, today I got a copy of the pictures of my mom's college graduation class. I think I know how to find the answer," I replied.

"Oh, Ethel! Pictures?" Sadie asked and looked disappointed as her brows knit together.

"Yes. The only thing left unexplained in Momma's box is the one picture of her and a classmate. And that's where my focus is going to be," I explained.

"Ethel, you're amazing. You're not going to let this rest, are you?" Sadie said and shook her head.

"I can't, Sadie. Like I told Caleb, I had a dream right before I came to. And now I know I'm on the right path," I said and smiled at her.

"Here we go, folks. Lunch is served." And with that, Vicky began to place mugs of soup and sandwich plates in front of us. Steam rose from the chunky soup, bringing the aroma of the rosemary to my nose. The sandwiches were stuffed with the chicken salad, and bright spots of apple peel peaked out through the mayonnaise. The raisin bread was a sturdy grain, with a nice green leafy lettuce between the bread and the chicken salad. It was a sweet and yummy treat.

Lunch gave us time to catch up on things around town and saying hello to those who came and went in the bakery today. Ruthie waved to us from the kitchen, and we gave her a thumbs-up for the tasty lunch. She was proud to have made the investment in the Emporium. While her air of confidence had never been lacking, her smile showed that she had new vigor.

Piney Bluffs was growing bit by bit and in the way it wanted to grow. Those who had found our town enjoyed and respected it for what it was and not necessarily for what they had hoped it would be. That was what made it so real for all of us. We were what we needed to be and not what someone wanted us to be. We were enough.

CHAPTER 24

W E RETURNED TO THE OFFICE after lunch at Ruthie's. It had been good to sit and talk about everyday things with Caleb and Sadie. Caleb was pleased with me being back. Sadie said he hadn't been the same, what with worrying about me. Sadie was very committed to making the Emporium the best it could be. Her enthusiasm was infectious, and I found renewed energy as I sat back at my desk. Caleb and I had started to plan for the next week when the phone rang.

"*Daily Bugle*, this is Ethel. How can I help you?" I said as I picked up the receiver.

"Well, it certainly is good to hear you," Frank's familiar voice responded. "It's been painful listening to him for the past two months."

"And nice to be heard, Frank. Thanks for calling back." I smiled at his comment. "Caleb tells me that there's a new super-duper information system that you put in just to help me. How's that going?"

"I don't really have too much time today to get into it, what with the attempted assassination business. But yes, with all your mystery hunts we've been on, I had to do something," he joked. "All kidding aside, the future is going to be amazing. It will be faster for us to get right to any piece of information that we need. It will shorten the time frame of, well, everything. Now, what can I do for you? Is there another bad guy that you're chasing, my dear lady?" he asked.

"No bad guy this time, thankfully. I hope the bad guys in my life are long gone. I'm looking for a classmate of my mother's. However, she's a twin, so I'm not sure which twin is the right twin," I explained.

"Okay, bad guys off the list. Coeds are on. What are the names I'm looking for?" he asked.

"Madeline H. and Martha H. Chumerford. They were both Early Childhood Education majors at Keene State in New Hampshire with my mom. I have their pictures from the yearbook. Want me to fax them?" I asked.

"Sure, that would be good. At least I can have a comparison if I find something. And when did they graduate?" Frank noted.

"Ah, 1945," I said, and he let out a low whistle.

"Wow! Well, I've got my work cut out for me this time, don't I?" he said. "What's so special about these two?"

"I'm sure that one of these women has the answer that will end the search for my half sister, Sophie. The picture of one of them and my mother is the last unexplained thing of my mother's that I have. The timing of her going to Keene State and the birth of Sophie coincide. And my hope is that one of them knows something about all that," I explained.

"You're always looking for that needle in the haystack," he commented.

"It does seem that way, doesn't it?" I replied.

"And I have to hand it to, you always seem to find it too," he added.

"This needle is probably the most important thing that I've ever looked for, Frank. I only hope that when I do find her, she can lead me to Sophie," I said and let out a sigh.

"Ethel, I'll try my best. Have you got any other ideas? Seems like there's always another something in your back pocket," Frank asked.

"I do have the address of a doctor that I found on an old envelope flap in one of my grandmother's cookbook. Its location is so close to Keene State that I know it has some importance. I have no idea of the time frame, but it seems that it might have been a doctor my mother sought out, away from the eyes of those at college. So I'm going to take a ride out to Westmoreland Depot in a few days," I answered. Stating that I was going to New Hampshire surprised me, and I saw Caleb raise his eyebrows as well.

"I've got to go now. I'll add that town to the information. Well, good luck, and I'll get back to you when this big stuff quiets down," Frank said.

"Thanks, Frank, and I completely understand. National security is more important," I said and ended the conversation.

"I hear a road trip is in your future. And not to mention the doctor appointment," Caleb noted and waited.

"I've got to do this, Caleb. Before my accident, I didn't know what direction to go in. I would sit and stare at the pictures of *Sophie's Sled* and wonder about the address on the envelope. But now I know I've got to go and find this doctor. I know there's a reason that envelope was left. It's like my grandmother was reaching out to guide someone. And that someone's going to be me," I replied. I felt an exhilaration about my decision.

"That's a pretty decent ride over there, almost three hours. Charlie should drive you," Caleb commented with the concern of a friend.

"I'd like to do this on my own. And I know it will be a long day, but if I leave early, I'll be back before supper," I answered. And then I felt it. A little kick. I put my hand on my side. "Oh, wow, Minnow's up!"

"Really?" Caleb chuckled. "She's going to keep you in line, Mommy. You think maybe she's telling you to take Daddy along?"

"I'm not fragile, I'm just pregnant. But thank you," I said.

"Don't thank me, you've still got to sell this idea to Charlie first," Caleb cautioned. "Now, let's get to planning for opening day of fishing and the Emporium."

"Anything special for opening day at Tubby's?" I asked.

"He's got a couple of tackle companies coming in with giveaways. Tubby will announce the weigh-in at noon for the Emporium opening's weigh-in contest. The companies are giving two pretty nice prize packages to include equipment, a guide, and a two-night stay at a premier fishing lodge in Canada. That will take place right before the ribbon cutting. And then there'll be a local author or two, one of which will be Ruthie. They'll talk about their books and do readings and signings. And that will be that," Caleb said as he ticked off the items on his mental list.

"Sounds good. Maybe Beulah can have her first class do a fly-tying demonstration at Tubby's. That would be great for the folks in town to see how Beulah delivered on her promise to teach young women an appreciation for our natural resources," I added. "I'll give her a call." I picked up the phone and dialed Beulah.

And so I settled back into work. The work that I loved. Reporting the stories of the people I loved, our local heroes and heroines. We were far away from the harsh reality of the nation's and the world's daily tragic stories. Everyone had a story, even those who weren't here to tell it. Like Momma. And I was going to make sure that her story was finally told.

CHAPTER 25

I STOPPED AT MINNIE'S AND FOUND Charlie had picked EC up about a half hour ago. I glanced at my watch and realized it was almost five thirty. Charlie must be wondering what happened to me. He'd taken EC to Minnie's this morning so I could rest before I went back to work. But that had gone out the window when the yearbook fax proved to be more urgent than any rest that I planned.

Pulling into the driveway, I saw that Daddy's truck was parked next to Charlie's. The dogs were outside and began barking to welcome me.

"There, there, good boys," I said to them as they about spun themselves inside out, waiting for me to pet each of them. They led the way as I opened the door to the kitchen.

"Are you okay? I called the office, but there was no answer." Charlie came over and gave me a big hug. "The house looked like you'd left in a hurry. I wasn't sure if you'd driven yourself to the doctor or what." The worry in his eyes showed the depth of his love for me. "I called Eddy to come and watch EC. I was just about to head out and try to find you."

"Oh, Charlie. I'm fine, and I'm so sorry. I ran out to the office to get a fax." I realized I had three sets of male eyes that were relieved to see me. Charlie reached out to hug me and let out a relieved sigh.

"I told you she was fine. But I have to admit, I was a little worried too," Daddy said. He was sitting on the couch, playing with EC, who was quite content with Grampa. EC looked at me and then slid down from Daddy to come over to me. I gathered him up in my arms.

"Somebody's getting so big," I said and hugged my little boy. "Whew, Mommy needs to sit down for a minute." I realized that the half-day I had spent at the office had made me a little more tired than I'd expected.

"Here, let me take him back. Come on, Junior, come back to Grampa," Daddy said as he got up to take EC back with him.

"So what happened? Why were you chasing a fax? Or do I have to ask?" Charlie asked, although he looked like he knew.

"I found the last 'unknown' thing from the box," I said quietly.

"What last thing? That damned box, I never should have given that thing to you. Been nothing but trouble," Daddy remarked, and then he said to EC, "See that Mommy? She's a darn silly girl running around, looking for trouble."

"The girl in the picture with Momma," I answered. "She's the only one who couldn't be explained. But I think I finally found out who she is."

"Ethel, you promised me that there'd be no more of this until after the baby was born." Charlie was exasperated as he ran his hands through his wavy brown hair.

"I know, I'm sorry, but I have to. You both know I have to do this. It's only this one more thing," I pleaded as I looked at the two most important people in my life. Daddy shook his head and focused on EC. Charlie stared at me and shook his head, knowing he was giving in.

"All right, but this better not go sideways like the last two 'oh, what could go wrong' adventures with you," Charlie said. He came to hug me, and I heard his stomach growl.

"Somebody sounds hungry." I looked into his beautiful eyes and smiled. "Gee, I sure wish there were someone's casserole left in the refrigerator."

"You may have to start cooking again there, missy. Do you remember how that stove works?" Daddy joked with me.

"I think you'll have to show me. It might take me a while before that part of my memory returns." I gave it right back to him.

"There must be something in here," Charlie said as he stood gazing into the refrigerator. "We've got eggs, an entire chocolate cream pie, and milk. Let's see, there's a few slices of cheese and an apple. How's that?"

"I could make an omelet, oh, nuts, no bread for toast. I really have to get back on a grocery schedule," I answered. I looked in the pantry too: not much in there either. I was thinking for a moment about trying to invent something from nothing when the phone rang. Charlie went to answer it.

"Hello," Charlie said. "Hang on, here she is." And Charlie handed the phone to me.

"Ethel? Listen, this is Aunt Ellie. I don't know if you all have eaten yet, but I made a big batch of spaghetti sauce and meatballs. And if you don't mind, Ellsworth and I will bring it over for your supper." Her voice made me happy. Not because she had solved my immediate problem of what to have for supper, but she knew that one of my all-time favorite meals growing up was her spaghetti and meatballs.

"Oh, Aunt Ellie, that's great! Do you have enough for Daddy too? He's here visiting," I asked, knowing full well I really didn't have to worry. When Aunt Ellie cooked sauce and meatballs, she could feed a sold-out church supper without batting an eye.

"Of course, I do. Now put on a pot of water, and by the time we get there, the water should be boiling." And with that, the phone went click.

"Well, gentlemen, we've been saved. Aunt Ellie is bringing over spaghetti sauce and meatballs," I said, relieved that for one more night, I wouldn't need to worry.

I put the big pot of water on the stove, while Charlie set the table. I found some refrigerator rolls and got them ready for the oven. EC was busy showing Daddy his new truck. He pushed the big yellow Tonka dump truck all around in front of Daddy's feet, making the appropriate truck noises and giggling all the way.

True to her timing, Aunt Ellie and Uncle Ellsworth were there when the pot was coming to a rolling boil. Uncle Ellsworth came through the door first, carrying the big pot of sauce and meatballs. Aunt Ellie was right behind him with a bag that seemed to be brimming with the rest of the meal.

"Coming through, hot stuff!" Uncle Ellsworth announced as he set the pot on the stove.

"Aunt Ellie, thank you so much." I hugged her and took the bag. She had brought two boxes of spaghetti, a loaf of Italian bread from Ruthie's, and a salad.

"Oh, wasn't nothing to put this together. Besides, I haven't seen you too much since you've been home. Now, let's get supper on for these hungry guys." We went straight to work getting the pasta in the pot. I cut the bread and put it in a basket along with my hot refrigerator rolls and then dressed the salad with a little bit of oil and vinegar. I found a lemon, too, and gave the salad a squirt for good measure. A little salt and pepper, and we were ready.

"Good thing you called, Ellie. We were sure to have starved," Daddy kidded as he heaped his plate. EC's little head barely crested the table as his hand reached up to Daddy's plate and he grabbed a meatball.

"Okay, there, big guy, let's sit you up here with your own plate, put your bib on, and we can let you go to town," Charlie said and picked up EC. Bib on, EC was ready to eat as Charlie placed him in his high chair. Happy he could see us now, he continued gnawing the meatball and then just pushed it all into his mouth. This sight brought us all to laughter.

"I think it'll be a cold day when you almost starve, brother," Uncle Ellsworth said to Daddy.

"Enough, you two. Now, how're you feeling, Ethel?" said Aunt Ellie, nipping the brotherly love in the bud.

"I'm fine, a little tired. I plan to start back to work tomorrow, but I went in for a little while today. Following up on a lead," I replied.

"Oh? What lead would that be? Got a new story you're working on?" she asked.

"No, nothing like that. It's more information about finding Sophie," I replied.

"Oh, that's right. I remember you telling me about her when we were in the hospital, waiting for your dad," she said. "You think you know where she is?"

"Not really. I just have a picture of Momma with a girl that she graduated from college with. I'm hoping if I can find her, she might have known something about Momma's secret," I answered.

"Foolishness, pure and simple. She will not let this thing alone," Daddy stated, and he looked perturbed.

"Now, Eddy, you know your daughter. She's got to do this. You taught her to finish what she started, so don't be complaining now." This time, it was Uncle Ellsworth who came to my defense.

"Thank you, Uncle Ellsworth. You all have to understand that there's a person out there who has no idea how wonderful Aunt Ellie's spaghetti and meatballs are," I said with a smile. "And how's Ginny doing, Daddy?" Changing the subject made Daddy squirm in his seat a bit.

"She's okay. Why do you ask?" he spoke into his plate of spaghetti, avoiding eye contact.

"I haven't seen her since you picked me up from the hospital," I said, and I waited.

"I'll see her Friday. She's got this place she likes to go to for fish and chips. Beats eating alone," he answered in a deadpan fashion.

"That's not what you told me, brother," Uncle Ellsworth piped up and grinned. "Your daddy said she was a fine woman."

"Aren't you the big blabbermouth!" Daddy said and pointed his fork at his brother. "That's the last time I tell you anything. And you wonder why I never tell you about any of my secret fishing spots."

"There are no damned secret spots, you fool. We've lived in this town since dirt was stones. You don't think I know where you go?" Uncle Ellsworth waggled his finger at Daddy.

"Okay, you two. Now, who wants chocolate cream pie?" I decided to end the discussion that more than likely would bear only ill feelings if it continued. The pie was the perfect way to end on a sweet note and get the grumpiness out of Daddy's craw. Aunt Ellie helped me with the dishes, and the guys went out on the porch. March had turned into a beautiful April, and tonight had just enough warmth in it to enjoy the outside with a light coat.

"Aunt Ellie, I know I've asked you this before, but are you sure my mother never hinted at anything of her life before she met Daddy?" I asked as I dried the big serving bowl.

"Ethel, honey, I wish more than life itself that I could give you something, anything that could help you find Sophie. But honestly, she never said one word. We were all raising our kids and were so happy when Eddy found her. Then he went off to war and we prayed to have him come back to us. They got married as soon as he came back, and then, well, you know the rest. She was smart, pretty, and loved your daddy to pieces." Aunt Ellie had told this story to me so many times, and sadly, it never changed. There was never an "Oh, but she did say this…" Never anything that Momma had said that would have tipped her hand to her past.

"Thank you, Aunt Ellie. I appreciate you tolerating my relentless questions," I said and put my arm around her sturdy shoulders. She'd given up her housedresses long ago and now wore khaki pants—not jeans, they were for the youngsters—and a cardigan sweatshirt with a polo shirt underneath. On her feet were her sneakers that always had a splash on them from whatever she'd been making. I looked down, and sure enough, there was a spot of spaghetti sauce on the toe of her left one.

"Well, I better get Ellsworth off the porch, or you kids won't get to sleep before midnight," she said as she went to open the porch door. "Ellsworth! Come on now, these kids need to get that baby to bed."

"Oh, all right. I was telling Charlie how not to believe all that Eddy says when it comes to fishing," Uncle Ellsworth said. "Now, if you want to, Charlie, I can really show you where the big ones are."

"You're just a fool, you know that, Ellsworth? A dang fool. Charlie's got more sense than to go fishing with you," Daddy said and shook his brother's hand goodbye. "Go home, I'll be right behind you."

"I don't know, Ellsworth. I might take you up on the offer. Then I could compare and see who really is the best," Charlie said, knowing that comment would get a rise out of Daddy.

"Ethel, you better talk some sense into this husband of yours. He could be making the mistake of his life," Daddy warned me with a little wink.

"Okay, now, truce, all of you. Thank you so much for coming over tonight. Love you all," I said as we gave hugs all around. I watched as the taillights from their vehicles bumped down the drive-way and then vanished as they turned onto the road.

I walked out onto the porch and breathed in the night air. Spring wanted to come out, that was for sure. I could hear the peep frogs now. And the moon was but a sliver as I looked out over the fields toward the river. A peaceful feeling came over me. I knew what I was doing was right. I only hoped that the Chumerford sisters would feel the same way.

CHAPTER 26

IT WAS A BEAUTIFUL MORNING when Charlie and I dropped EC off at Minnie's. How different it was now: EC barely waved goodbye, happy to spend time with his friends. We helped him off with his coat, and away he went to find a book and "read" to anyone who would listen to his babbling. Minnie waved from the other side of the room and shook her head and smiled. What a difference a few months had made.

And now on to Portland for our eleven thirty appointment at Dr. Simon's office. But first, we were going to stop at the mall. New maternity clothes were a necessity. I'd felt a little embarrassed yesterday wearing the stretched-out maternity pants from two years ago and Charlie's hooded sweatshirt. Today's outfit was not much better. I'd found some pants that fit snugly and a blousy top to hide the waistline. I gave up trying to find a coat and settled on a scarf around my shoulders.

The Mother-to-Be shop had a variety of clothes for those who worked in the corporate world as well as for those who needed less-structured clothing in their lives. Thankfully, I was in the latter. But as I felt the crisp material in the mommy business suits, I was a little envious, if only for a moment. Where would I have been if, eight years ago, I'd made a different decision? Making my home in Boston and working like a madwoman to meet the deadlines? I looked over at Charlie, who was going through a rack of tops and picking up ones he thought I might like. I smiled as he looked up and gave me his grin. No, there was no doubt in my mind: this was where I was meant to be.

"Do you like this blue one? It's kind of like the shirts you wore when I first met you." Charlie held up a peasant-type blouse in a blue-and-white paisley design.

"You know, I do like that. And it's getting warmer, so that type of shirt will be great," I said. The saleslady, who herself was pregnant, took the shirt to the dressing room for me.

"I love this top. We've got some in that same style, but different colors and sleeve lengths. I'll put some of those in for you too," she commented and waddled away.

"How far along are you?" I asked. From my estimation, she looked like she was way overdue.

"Oh, I'm due in a few weeks," her face was red, and her feet swelled out of the tops of her shoes. Her black hair was pulled up into a bun on the top of her head, which made her face seem all the rounder. She wore a maternity dress that fit snugly around her belly.

"Wow, and you're still working," I said.

"Yeah. I still feel fine. I'm expecting twins, so that's why I look like I'm twelve months along." And she laughed.

"Twins? Do you know what you're having?" I asked this woman, who appeared to be about my age.

"Both boys. Thankfully. I've got two girls at home. From what everyone says, boys are much easier to take care of. I really don't care if I never see another pink dress in my life. Don't get me wrong, I love Kellie and Kathy. I'm just ready for pants and T-shirts," she said and rested her arm on the top of a rack of pants.

"Well, it sounds like your world will be complete with the boys," Charlie commented. He had taken a seat, having completed his shopping experience.

"Oh, it will be. Kenny had a vasectomy after we learned I was having twins," she said, and I could see Charlie wince a bit, thinking about Kenny. "You might like these pants. They don't look so balloon-like." She held up pairs of black, tan, and denim ones.

"They do look nice," I said and felt the material. They were a good quality and didn't seem like they would stretch out. She helped me find my size, and I went to work, giving Charlie a mini fashion show. Being five months or more along, I didn't need to have too many things. I'd also found some capris and shorts, soft T-shirts, a long skirt, and a few underthings. I chose a pair of the denim pants and the shirt Charlie had first chosen and asked the salesgirl to clip the tags so I could wear them now. Looking in the mirror, I felt much better about my reflection.

"Mrs. O'Connor, you happen to be the most beautiful mother-to-be that I've ever seen," Charlie said as he paid for my final selections.

"You keep talking like that, Mr. O'Connor, and we might have to have a third child," I said as we walked away. He grinned back at me as he gathered up the shopping bags. We stopped at a hot dog cart before we left the mall for a bite to help my gnawing stomach. The hot dogs were big, juicy, and exactly what I needed. We ate quickly and then headed to the car.

Dr. Simon's office was a short drive away. Checking my watch, I realized we were arriving just in time for the appointment. Susanne, the nurse, was sitting at the check-in window.

"Hi, Ethel, Charlie. It is so good to see you," she said and came out to give me a hug. "When Doc told me what had happened to the two of you, well, I couldn't believe it. You look great."

"Thanks, Susanne. I'm feeling great, a little tired, but all in all, good," I answered.

"Come right in, and we'll get started." She opened the door to the exam area. We left Charlie in the waiting room to read from the well-worn *Parents* magazines. She walked me into the room and pointed to the gown. "Here's your gown, and if you can, pee in the cup, please."

"Are you kidding? If I can? I've had to pee ever since we left the house. I swear this child is jumping up and down on my bladder constantly," I said and went immediately to the bathroom. I hung up my clothes and put on my paper gown. A gown. When did someone decide to call this flimsy piece of paper a gown? Whenever I was in a doctor's exam room, I always thought how absurd we looked, wearing a piece of paper and our socks. I chuckled to myself and felt a kick at the same time. "You think that's funny too, do you?" I took a seat on the table to wait.

As in the other rooms, the walls contained pictures of families and babies. There was one with a family of four, with a boy and girl in between the mom and dad. They were walking in the woods on a snowy day. The dad was pulling a toboggan. A snapshot of winter family fun. I knew that Charlie and I would look the same way with our two. I wondered about Sophie and her family. How many children did she have now? Or did she have any children at all? My reverie was broken as the door opened and Dr. Simon walked in. He was followed by Susanne, who brought the ultrasound machine with her.

"Ethel, so good to see you." He reached out to take my hand in both of his. "You look wonderful. How are you feeling?"

"No complaints. I'm tired at the end of the day, but it's EC, he keeps us pretty busy," I said and waited for the poking and prodding to begin. Susanne weighed me first and then did vitals as Dr. Simon transcribed the results into my chart. She also drew out a couple of vials of blood. He then did his exam, poking, prodding, and listening to both me and Minnow.

"Let's see. You've gained about ten pounds, and that's fine. Both your and the baby's heartbeats are strong. The blood will go out for genetic testing, but I suspect that will be normal. I want to do another ultrasound today to see how big your girl is getting to be," he said and put his stethoscope back around his neck.

"Can Charlie come in for this?" I asked.

"Certainly, he can," Dr. Simon said and went to open the door and called to Charlie. With all of us in the room, Susanne prepped me with the cold gel and began the scanning.

"I see her hands. And look at her head! It looks huge. Is that normal? I can't remember EC's looking that big," I said, thinking that this was an awful sight.

"She's fine. Heads are always a little bigger at this point. She's a little small, but everything's in the right places," Dr. Simon assured us.

"She's really active. Look at her—she's doing a somersault!" Charlie said.

"You ought to feel what I'm feeling with that. Whew. Maybe she'll be another Nadia Comaneci," I added. "So, Dr. Simon, what do you see?"

"I see a very healthy six-month-old fetus," he stated. "And as I said, I'm sure the blood tests will show that as well."

"And no injury from the accident?" I asked. Even though I felt fine, the worry never went away.

"I know how worried you both must be. But from what I'm looking at, you two, or should I say three, have nothing to be alarmed about," Dr. Simon said.

"That's wonderful news, sir," Charlie said and held my hand.

"I'll see you two in my office when you're dressed, Ethel." And Dr. Simon adjourned to his office.

"Okay, I'll be ready in a jiffy," I said, and both Charlie and Susanne left the room.

Alone, I sat for a moment, wiping off the gel with my paper drape. I felt another kick. *Hello, Minnow. Yes, honey, Mommy knows you're there. And I can't wait to tell you all the wonderful things about you and what your life is going to be. It will be one of the best, you can count on it.* I'd made a promise to Phyllis, and I intend to keep it.

CHAPTER 27

"WE NEED TO DECIDE ON a name, wouldn't you say?" Charlie asked as we drove home.

"What? You don't think Minnow would work?" I laughed. "Minnow Charlotte O'Connor has a nice ring."

"Ethel, really. And where did the Charlotte come from?" Charlie wrinkled his face, showing his disapproval.

"From your name, silly. We can skip right over the Minnow part and call her Charlie," I answered.

"I think you really hit your head much harder than the doctors are telling us," he said and reached out to take my hand. "Doc says you're doing fine. You are, aren't you?"

"I certainly feel fine. I still won't be sure until I see all her fingers and toes, though. But that big head! I can't believe her head is that big!" I said again.

"The doctor said don't worry, so don't worry. Now, back to the name, how about Catherine Stephanie? That's Catherine with a *C*. Catherine was the name of one of my grandmothers. We can call her Cate, and then we get your mom in there, too," Charlie said as he brought my hand up and gave it a kiss.

"You know, I like it. But Daddy will still call her Minnow," I agreed and smiled at my thoughtful husband.

"No doubt there. Why don't we stop by and take him to the Diner?" Charlie asked.

"Good thought, but it's Friday, remember? Every Friday night, he goes up to Oxford to take Ginny out for fish and chips," I replied.

"He was so funny when Uncle Ellsworth was spilling the beans on him," Charlie said.

"Daddy doesn't want to admit anything about Ginny. I'm only hoping they have a good time together. Both of them have been alone for so long. It only seems right for them to enjoy their lives," I replied.

"Well, then, let's get EC and the three of us can go to Andy's," Charlie said. In about twenty minutes, we arrived at Minnie's. When we walked in, we saw that EC was curled up on one of the cots. I shot Minnie a surprised look, hoping that he wasn't ill.

"He fell asleep not fifteen minutes ago. He was going and going all day. With the nice weather today, I had them all out on the pedal cars and running around," Minnie explained.

"I think he's going through a growth spurt too. He didn't sleep well last night, hence the instant nap," I offered.

"How are you doing, Ethel?" Minnie asked, although I felt I should be the one asking her the question. She did have two helpers, but by the end of the day, ten toddlers and an infant showed the toll they took on her.

"I'm doing well. I'd say I'm tired, but I'd be preaching to the choir," I observed.

"Oh, this is fine. It's a good tired. And at the end of the day, I go home to Bob, the dogs, and a glass of wine," Minnie said, and the three of us laughed. Hearing our laughter, EC woke up. He rubbed his eyes and then ran over for his hugs.

"Mma, pee," he said, or did he? I looked at Minnie for confirmation.

"Yes, he did. Freddy's two and half years now, and he's EC's mentor, so to speak. I'm trying to enforce potty-training him, and EC is copying the behavior." Minnie showed me where the bathroom was, and sure enough, after getting his diaper off, EC got on the potty seat and peed.

"Holy cow, what a savings on diapers if he can do this!" I was overjoyed that my toddler, who I thought was never going to walk, was peeing before most boys older than him. My life was almost complete!

"You're not kidding. If he keeps this up, he'll be asking for the car keys next month." We both laughed at that and left the bathroom with my big boy.

"Did he?" Charlie asked in disbelief.

"He most certainly did. Although he's not ready for target practice yet," Minnie said. Charlie looked baffled for a minute, and then it sunk in. He grinned a little sheepishly at missing the metaphor. "You can get some training diapers now that he's thinking about it. That should make it easier to get the diaper off, and then who knows when it will be time for target practice?"

"Thanks, Minnie. Have a good weekend. See you bright and early Monday morning," I said and headed out the door.

"Now let's celebrate with a hot dog," Charlie said. Our boy was all smiles at the mention of *hot dog*. EC's little hand disappeared into Charlie's as they walked to the car.

"Ooh, not for me. That one I had for lunch didn't settle well. Maybe some toast or soup," I said. In no more than five minutes, we were at Andy's Diner. It was almost six o'clock, and there was only one booth left. From the window I saw Dottie and Charlotte sharing a dessert and coffee. Doc McAllister and his wife, Nancy, were sitting at a table in the back. Folks were crowded in at the counter, no one looking particularly familiar, but then all I could really see were their backs.

"Hi, folks!" Judy greeted us as we came through the door. We grabbed a booster seat for EC and took the booth that was across from the grill. We saw Andy Jr. was cooking tonight.

"Hi, Judy. And who's that manning the grill? I don't know, honey, we may have to go elsewhere," Charlie kidded to Andy.

"And for that, whatever you want, we're out of. For Ethel and the little guy, I've got everything," Andy said back and pointed his spatula at his friend.

"Do you have something light for my stomach, Andy?" I asked and held back a burp. Damn that hot dog I'd grabbed at the mall. Well, they were off my list for a while, at least until the end of the pregnancy.

"I can broil a nice piece of cod for you. And I've got some fresh asparagus. McCreery brought in his first cutting today. I can steam that too. How's that sound?" Andy offered as he stood with his hands on the counter. I nodded in agreement with his choice for me. "I know the little guy wants a hot dog. And you, big guy?" He smiled at Charlie.

"I'd love a cheeseburger, rare, some fries, and how about some coleslaw?" Charlie said, and I immediately wanted to have what he ordered as well as my fish. I was so hungry again, or was it still?

"Let's see, chocolate milk for EC, for Ethel water with lemon, and, Charlie?" Judy asked as she filled glasses at the fountain.

"Ginger ale is fine, Judy, thanks," Charlie said.

"Here we go. A beer for Daddy, a white wine for Mommy, and chocolate milk and some oyster crackers for the soon-to-be big brother." Judy chuckled as she put our drinks in front of us. She had put EC's milk in a cup with a cover and a short straw. He had finally gotten the hang of using a straw. I opened the bag of crackers, and EC's little fingers selected two and popped them in his mouth.

"Don't we wish," Charlie said. "Andy, when's your dad going to get a liquor license in here?"

"Aw, I don't think that'll happen. You know, he doesn't want to compete with the Inn. And besides, not that people would abuse it, it's best to keep to what we're good at, home cooking," Andy replied.

"You're right, Andy. I think you could apply that thought to lots of things in life. If every place sells it, or does it, then it doesn't make the 'it' as special as 'it' once was," I said and reflected on the uniqueness of each business in Piney Bluffs.

"Caleb must be paying you a lot of money to come up with philosophical crap like that," a familiar Boston brogue said. A man at the counter turned around, and it was Mike O'Brien. The graying reddish hair and smirky smile were waiting for my response. Mike had almost been my boss. The decision to stay in Piney Bluffs and not take the job at the *Boston Herald* came into my mind every once in a while. Like today, at the Mother-to-Be store, when I was fingering the material in the suits. While never focusing on it for very long, I was always certain my choice to stay here had made all the difference in my world.

"Mike? What are you doing here unannounced? You know I like at least a week's notice to get ready for you," I quipped back at him. He'd come over to the table with his coffee and gave me a hug. Then he took a step back to look at me.

"Holy mother, are you pregnant again? You know you don't have to keep up with me. I tell you, it's not all roses and fairy dust," he said and laughed and postponed answering my question.

"Hey, Mike, we could never keep up with you. Why don't you have a seat?" Charlie said and reached over to shake his hand.

"Now, really, tell me why you're in town," I asked, my mind trying to come up with some kind of theory.

"Caleb asked me to come up and meet with Robert and Russell to get ready for the Emporium opening. He said he wasn't sure when you'd get back to work, slacker that you are," he said snidely.

"The Emporium opening? Really? Doesn't seem like that would be on the *Herald*'s radar. Or are you that desperate for news items in Boston?" I asked.

"It's not the Emporium, per se. It's the author who's going to be making an appearance," Mike said. "And I'm here for WBZ too."

"TV and newspaper, that seems like a lot of fanfare for Miss Ruthie," I said and waited. Now I knew there had to be something else.

"Ethel, really? I love Ruthie and her bakery. And I've seen her cookbook. She and Caleb did a swell job with it. No, this is big. This guy doesn't usually do appearances," he said and lowered his voice.

"So? Who is it?" I asked in a hushed tone. Charlie leaned in, waiting for Mike to reply.

"Lynwood Newcastle," Mike hissed in a whisper. "What do you think of that?"

"Jeepers, this is huge!" I said in hushed amazement. "Our very own famous Maine author. You know, he went to University of Maine too. He was a couple of years ahead of me."

"That's the guy who wrote the Sebago Lake Mystery, the series, right? They're making those into movies, too?" Charlie asked.

"Yes, indeed. It will either be movies or a TV series, and he'll be here for the ribbon cutting. He'll sign his books and do a reading. Rumor has it, he may also go fishing," Mike continued.

"Fishing—now there's a trip I'd like to be on," I said.

"You're pregnant, you can't go fishing," Mike noted.

"For crying out loud, I'm pregnant, not paralyzed!" I said in exasperation. "Have you forgotten how I was pregnant for the ice-fishing derby a few years ago? And that was below-zero weather. This would be a walk in the park."

"I'm not sure if Russell and Robert might want to go along too," Mike stated.

"Oh, that wouldn't work. They're wonderful guys, but no, I think he'd need someone like Daddy. Wouldn't they be a hoot together?" I said, more excited thinking about going fishing with Lynwood Newcastle.

"Easy, Ethel, let's just make sure he gets here and does the things we want for the opening. After that, whatever he has time for, he's all yours," Mike cautioned. "Now remember, Russell and Robert want to keep this hush-hush for another week or so while we get the final details worked out."

"Sure thing. And whatever help you need, you can count on me," I said.

"Here we go, folks, supper's ready," Judy announced and arrived with our plates.

"Mike, are you having supper?" I asked, hoping he could stay with us.

"No, thanks. I just came in for the caffeine. I'm meeting Russell and Robert at seven at the Inn," he answered and put his money on the counter. "I'll be leaving in the morning to go back home. The girls are having a sleepover tonight and then going to get prom dresses. I'm staying as far away from that as I can. See ya, little guy." Mike waved at EC, who had already grabbed onto his hot dog and waved back to Mike with his empty bun.

"Wow, what do you think of that?" I said to Charlie. "I can't believe the brothers got him."

"That certainly will be quite a day, to say the least," Charlie stated and began biting into his scrumptious-looking cheeseburger. "How's the fish?"

"Much better on my stomach than that hot dog I had for lunch," I replied. Andy had broiled the thick cod loin with a squeeze of lemon and some salt. It came apart in large tasty white flakes. Along with the asparagus, it was light and satisfying. Fingers crossed now as to how my stomach would handle it.

"Hot dog," EC said and held up his half-eaten dog.

"I know, honey. Is that hot dog good?" I said to EC, who smiled a toothy grin. "Pretty soon, we'll have one on each side, Daddy."

"I can't wait," Charlie said and turned to EC. "If your sister's half as cute as you, I'm going to have to teach you how to be a protective big brother." EC looked up at Charlie with the biggest smile. My two men. How they made my heart swell with love.

Today had me reflecting on choices and opportunities. I knew whether it had been to stay in Piney Bluffs, to talk to a stranger on the bus, or to delve into my mother's past, so far, they'd all proven to be the best ones that I could have made. Life is about choices and the fact that you have to decide on something. You live with your decisions and rejoice when it's the correct one. If at first it doesn't seem correct, you have an opportunity to make it so. Acknowledging opportunities is what makes life interesting, and so far, life had been quite the ride for me.

CHAPTER 28

SATURDAY MORNING, WE AWOKE TO the dogs barking and hearing knocking on our door. I looked at the clock and saw that it was just seven o'clock.

"Who in the heck could that be?" Charlie said and jumped out of bed, pulling his sweatshirt over his head.

"Who, indeed?" I said sleepily. I had finally found a comfortable spot about four o'clock. It seemed that Minnow now enjoyed a few hours of calisthenics from midnight to four in the morning. I tied my bathrobe as best I could around my pajamas. I shuffled into my slippers and went to EC's room to check on him. Sound asleep. *Good, let's give him as much time as he wants.* I quietly backed out of his room. I heard several voices as I neared the bottom of the stairs.

"Well, there's my sunshine," said Russell. He and Robert stood in the kitchen with Charlie. The brothers were armed with coffees and two boxes from Miss Ruthie's and appeared to be quite pleased with themselves.

"We're so sorry to come this early, but we're heading back to the city this morning and wanted to visit. We haven't seen you since the night of the accident, and we've been so worried," Robert explained and came to give me a hug. Since coming out of my coma, they had routinely sent me books and beautiful cards filled with their funny stories. "How are you and the baby feeling?" He put his hands on my shoulders and searched my eyes. Today the boys were in their spring attire, wearing variations of pale-green and light-blue shirts and pull-over sweaters with khaki slacks. With well-shined penny loafers and navy sport coats, their casual New York Saturday outfits were complete. I pulled my robe around me and felt the need to immediately iron it.

"It's so good to see the two of you as well. And I'm fine. Got a glowing report from my obstetrician yesterday, so now we just wait for the big day," I replied and returned their hugs. Charlie had taken the coffees out of the bag and handed one to me, and I took a sip, knowing I'd probably regret this later. "Please have a seat. Thanks for the coffee, but you didn't need to do this."

"Nonsense! We wanted to get your read on our big story. Mike said he let you in on it yesterday. So what do you think?" Russell all but gushed as he waited for my response. They sat down, and Robert opened the boxes and held up what looked to be an apple crumb muffin and took a bite.

"I think it's absolutely amazing! How in the world did you get Lynwood Newcastle?" I asked and looked in the box for my treat. I spied a piece of blueberry cake and claimed it. The first bite was bursting with plump blueberries and cinnamon, and of course, it was delicious.

"We've known Lynwood's agent since the first of his murder series came out. We get together from time to time, and it seemed like Lynwood wanted to do something close to home. And naturally, the Emporium was just the ticket," Russell explained.

"And he may even want to go fishing, with it being opening day," Robert added. "So we thought that, maybe, if he wasn't busy, we'd ask Eddy to take him. I mean, we could go with Lynnwood, but let's face it, we know our strengths, and fishing, as much as we love it, is not one of them."

"I thought about that too. That would be quite the twosome—Daddy and Lynwood Newcastle," I said and smiled. The dogs began to bark again. Looking out the window, I saw that it was Daddy pulling into the yard. "Well, looks like you'll be able to ask him for yourself." And moments later, Daddy walked through the door. The dogs sat patiently by the counter, waiting for their treats. Daddy rummaged through his pockets and found one for each of them. Satisfied with the offerings, the dogs returned to their beds, happily chewing.

"Good morning! Hope I'm not interrupting anything. Oh, boy, Ruthie's. Got an extra coffee there, Ethel?" Daddy asked as he came in and went straight for the boxes from Ruthie's. Daddy was dressed in stark contrast to the brother's well-selected apparel. He wore his spring white-and-black buffalo plaid overshirt, black T-shirt from Andy's Diner, and his green work pants, stuffed into the tops of his work boots. I noticed he had a new ball cap from Norway, Maine. *Hmm,* I thought as I smiled to myself. Ginny's hand was becoming evident.

"I'll put some on. Won't take but a few minutes," I answered and got the coffee out. It might have been the sound of Daddy's voice that finally woke him, but I heard EC call out. Charlie motioned that he'd go up and get him, and I continued making coffee. "Go ahead, Robert. Ask him."

"Ask me what?" Daddy said through a mouthful of muffin.

"To celebrate the Emporium's opening, we're having Lynwood Newcastle make a special appearance, signing his books. And after that, he may want to go fishing. And we were hoping that maybe you'd take him," Robert finished with a quick sigh of relief.

"Who's Lynwood Newcastle?" Daddy asked, still thoroughly enjoying his muffin. The brothers didn't quite know what to make of Daddy's indifference to the mention of their celebrity's name.

"Daddy, he's the most famous author from Maine. He's written the Sebago Lake Mystery series. They're going to make them into huge motion pictures or a television series. Sound familiar?" I asked, trying to jog his memory.

"Maybe. He writes that creepy stuff that makes the hair on the back of your neck stand up? That the guy?" Daddy questioned further. Charlie came into the kitchen, carrying EC, who immediately wanted Grampa.

"Who's creepy?" Charlie asked as he handed EC off to Daddy.

"It seems that Daddy is not too familiar with Lynwood Newcastle," I answered. The coffee had finished dripping, and I poured some for Daddy. He'd taken a seat at the table with EC on his lap and began to share his muffin with his grandson.

"Eddy, it doesn't matter if you know his work or not. The main thing is that while he's in town for the opening, and after he does a reading and signs some books, he may want to go fishing. And we thought that you'd be the best person to take him," Russell explained.

"On opening day, you want me to take a guy fishing who writes creepy stuff? Is that what I'm hearing?" Daddy summarized the simple facts and took a sip of his coffee.

"Yes, that's it exactly," Robert confirmed with a broad smile.

"Nope, not doing it," Daddy said and continued with his muffin. "I think Junior needs some juice over here, Mommy."

"Daddy! What do you mean *no*?" I asked and went for a cup of juice for EC. He was quite happy to sit with his grandpa and share a muffin. Daddy looked very absorbed with EC as well. But the brothers were almost apoplectic at Daddy's refusal.

"It's opening day. I don't take nobody with me on opening day. Period, end of story," Daddy said and focused his attention on EC.

"But by the time the Emporium has its ribbon cutting and Lynwood does readings and such, it will be the afternoon. You'll have your limit, before Sadie unlocks the door," I challenged Daddy.

"I know. Just not interested," Daddy continued with his protest.

"Mind telling me why?" I asked, almost incredulous at his objection.

"Look, I've brought a lot people fishing in my time. Celebrity this and governor of that. But if a guy writes creepy stuff, he's got to get his creepy ideas from someplace. And being alone in my secret fishing spots with a guy looking to write new creepy stuff, well, you think about it. I don't want to be the next creepy idea about how a fishing trip turned into a murder." And Daddy was done.

"Daddy! You're not serious?" I started to laugh. Russell and Robert did as well. Charlie tried to hide his amusement but chuckled along with us.

"Eddy, Lynwood Newcastle has so much creepy stuff going on in his brain that you don't have to worry about him looking for something new that includes fishing with you," Russell said.

"Well, maybe. But you can't be too careful. And especially if he knows his way around a fishing pole. Why, he'd probably come back and fish out my spots!" Daddy said, somewhat relenting to fishing with a celebrity but now inventing a new reason that he might not.

"Okay, then, we'll put you down as a definite maybe," Russell said and shook his head at Daddy.

"I think Daddy is more worried about losing his secret fishing spots than being the subject of a new novel," I commented.

"She forgets that those secret fishing spots put food on the table and shoes on her feet when she was growing up," Daddy stated with a little edge to his tone.

"Now, Daddy," I said. "How about we leave it up to you once you meet him? You'll be the sole decision maker whether you take him fishing or not."

"I'm sure Eddy will be able to size him up and decide on what kind of a fisherman he is. You did the same thing with me, if I remember correctly," Charlie commented, changing the conversation ever so slightly.

"You're right about that. I wasn't so sure about you, but you're coming around." Daddy chuckled.

"Well, we must be off. We have a flight out of Portland, and we don't want to be late," Russell said with a look of relief on his face. He gave me a big hug and whispered, "I don't know what we would have done if something had happened to you." And he held me for a moment longer. He wiped a tear from his round red cheek as he walked to the door.

"Yes, my gracious. Our flight leaves at noon, and this time we're driving ourselves to the airport. I hope we make it," Robert remarked. He mopped his brow with his monogrammed handkerchief. "Oh, Ethel, I need one more precious hug from you." Robert put his arm around me and then pressed an envelope into my hand. I looked at him with surprise. He put his finger to his lips to shush me.

"You've got plenty of time. Be careful of the moose, though. They like pale green this time of year," Daddy joked with them as they hurried to the door. They turned and gave Daddy an astonished look and then realized he was joking.

"Boys, you've got a little over an hour's ride ahead, you'll be fine," Charlie called out to them as they got into their rental Land Rover. He stood and watched as they drove off.

"Those two, I swear," Daddy said and continued eating with EC.

"Oh, my, what in the world!" I said. I had looked in the envelope. Robert had written "For your new little one" on it. I quickly opened it.

"What is it?" Charlie asked, stretching his neck to see.

"It's a check. And a sweet note," I said and started to read aloud. "Ethel and Charlie, we have come to realize how much you two and EC mean to us. You're that piece of family that everyone, especially the two of us, needs in their lives. We hope you have another beautiful baby. Love, Russell and Robert. PS: Maybe we could be uncles?"

"How much?" Daddy asked in his get-to-the-point fashion.

"It's for five hundred dollars," I said softly.

"Wow," Daddy said and then let out a low whistle. EC tried to mimic Daddy's whistle but only sprayed a mouthful of crumbs all over the table. He laughed at the mess he had made as Daddy gave him a stern look.

"Those two," Charlie said and took the note from my hands and shook his head.

"This will certainly help with the furniture that we need for her room, clothes, and well, everything girls like. I was looking through the Sears catalog the other day and saw the cutest bureau set." I had taken a seat and just stared at the check. "Some folks are very surprising."

"And I have another surprise," Charlie said with a little grin.

"Really? What now?" I asked and stared at him, waiting for what was next.

"Well, I was going to wait until we started really talking about the furniture, but..." And he stopped.

"But what? Come on, I'm a pregnant woman who needs a little more information," I implored him.

"My dad and brother have made a crib and bureau for Cate. My dad called me the other day. He said, after all we'd been through, they wanted to do something special," Charlie finished.

"Oh my, this is too much! They didn't need to do that," I said, and the tears began to fall. "I don't know what to say. First, the check from the brothers, and now the furniture from your family." I closed my eyes for a moment and then felt Charlie's strong hands on my shoulders.

"Ethel, you're very fortunate to have come through this whole thing without much of a scratch. You're an extraordinary person who's been put on God's great earth to do something special. I knew that when you were just a little girl," Daddy said thoughtfully.

EC had slid down from his lap and come over and climbed up on mine. He pointed to my belly and said, "Baby." Then he took his little hands and wiped my tears from my cheeks and blew me a fish-lips kiss. I wrapped my arms around this precious boy and hugged him.

"The two of you know I have to do this one last thing," I said and looked at Charlie and Daddy. "Sophie's out there, I know she is, and before this baby comes, I've got to go and find her."

"I wish you'd put this damn search away. It's like me going fishing day after day, trying to land that biggest trout. I've heard of it. And I think I'm the only one who can catch it. It'll drive you crazy if you let it." Daddy was still trying to dissuade me.

"Daddy, I'm not crazy. But this is the only thing that's left, to go to New Hampshire to find this doctor. He's probably been dead for twenty years, but I still have to try," I implored him. "Say, what're you doing today?"

"What? Me? Why, nothing! I was going to scope out a new fishing spot," Daddy answered.

"How about you take your grandson with you? Then Charlie and I could go to New Hampshire. It's only a couple of hours' drive, and we'd be back before supper. How about it?" I asked and hoped that he couldn't resist a day with EC.

"Well, I suppose he's old enough to go looking with me." Daddy was considering the offer. He looked down at EC, who in turn looked up at him. EC took his little hand and fished around in Daddy's shirt pocket and found a dog treat. EC was tickled that he'd found something.

"Daddy, I have to ask, Why did you come over this morning?" I questioned him.

"When I listened to you telling Uncle Ellsworth and Aunt Ellie the other night about what you wanted to do, I knew you'd be trying to figure out when you'd be going. I came to talk you out of it and let it be until after the baby. But I can see that's not happening." Daddy sat back, not entirely satisfied, but he knew the end of this was near.

"Oh, Daddy," I said and got up to give him a hug.

"Now don't go getting all mushy. Get this thing over with. That's all I want. Good, bad, or indifferent, I want this chasing ghosts of yours to stop. Now run along and get some fishing clothes for Junior. I think it's time he learned how to fish." Daddy returned my hug and then motioned for me to scoot.

"Fishing clothes?" I asked. "But, Daddy, he can barely hold a spoon, never mind a pole."

"No time like the present, then, is there?" Daddy smiled. "Too nice of a day to stay cooped up. I'll show him my secret spots. I won't have to worry about him telling anybody about them."

"I wouldn't be too sure about that. I think he has his own language with his buddies at Minnie's," Charlie said and laughed.

"Well, then, we'll have to have a little heart-to-heart talk about my fishing spots," Daddy said. "Now, go. It's almost eight, you won't be there till about eleven."

"Yes, sir," I said.

"I'll get the little guy straightened out." Charlie whisked EC upstairs, leaving Daddy and me alone.

"Thanks, Daddy," I said. I had taken my seat at the table for a moment. "I know this whole thing is not what any of us ever imagined."

"I know that, and I've made my peace with whatever happens from here on in, Ethel. I only want your mother's story to be finished. If I'd have never given you that box, you wouldn't have found the damn thing until after I was gone. By then you'd probably be so old you wouldn't care about a few old pictures and letters." Daddy chuckled but then got serious. "Remember, whatever you find today has got to be the end of it. We all need to get on with our lives, present and future, and stop looking back."

We sat quiet for a bit. I realized in that moment that without saying it, Daddy was ready to move on with his love. He had loved my mother so purely for more than thirty years. But now, with all that had transpired in the past few years, he was letting go.

I was ready to let go too. I thought about how a balloon is so pretty and then accidentally someone lets go of the string and it drifts up and up until it's out of sight. The beauty of it is still in your memory. I was almost ready to let the beauty of Momma's balloon go. Almost.

CHAPTER 29

"WE'RE MAKING GOOD TIME. I think it should only be a two-hour drive," Charlie said. "I know your dad said three, but I think I drive a little faster than him." Charlie had checked the map to see if we could take interstates, but no such luck. We'd made our way across Routes 202 and then 9. Daddy had been right; it was really a great day for a ride. No more snow to worry about, and April showers weren't due for another day or two.

"Here we are again. In the car, driving into who knows what," I said. I looked at the picturesque New Hampshire towns as we passed through the state. Today's trip would bring us almost to the Vermont border.

"At least it's not a state prison," Charlie stated. "I think that was the worst."

"I agree. Even going to the Knight's house where Joseph masqueraded as Father Bob wasn't as bad as that prison." I let out a little shudder at the thought of our visits to Maine State Prison and its assistant warden. "Osgood was a character straight out of a Lynwood Newcastle novel. What did you think of Daddy's comment about creepy Lynwood Newcastle?"

"Your dad is really funny. But I think he was pulling your leg. You know how your dad likes to be sweet-talked into things. I think if you'd have told him you were going to ask Uncle Ellsworth to take Newcastle fishing, why, your dad would have been asking what time we wanted him and where," Charlie commented.

"You know, I think you're right. How did I miss that?" I said, realizing Charlie had hit the nail on the head.

"Observation, my dear, observation," he finished and pointed to his eyes.

"What was it again that you did in the service?" I asked.

"My observation skills have nothing to do with my time in the service. It's one of my endearing qualities that attracted you to me. You need to sit back and look and listen," he explained.

"So then, you're saying that I'm too chatty?" I asked.

"Now, don't go putting words in my mouth. Let's focus on today," Charlie said and changed the subject. "What do you expect you'll learn?"

"Well, I'm hoping that the good doctor kept explicit records with dates, names, and addresses. Then we'll follow that address and find Sophie. She'll ask what took me so long, give me a hug and kiss, and we'll be home by dinnertime," I answered matter-of-factly.

"Really?" he said.

"No, not really. For all I know, the doctor passed away, the office burned down, and this will be a dead end. Period. End of story," I said, defeated. "I only hope we find something that lies in the middle of these two extremes."

"You've yet to be wrong about any of these rabbit holes that we've ventured down. I doubt that today will be any different." And with that, Charlie picked up my hand and gave it a kiss.

As we passed the Keene State campus, I kept thinking about the timeline of the events we knew about. Sophie had been born just prior to Momma enrolling in college. Henry had been no help at all in determining where Joseph's father had sent her to have the baby. He only knew it was someplace in New Hampshire. This address that we were looking for today, 10 Willow Lane, Westmoreland Depot, from my grandmother's cookbook, was my only hope.

I reached into my purse and took out the picture of Momma and her friend. That smile hid the circumstances that had turned her from what appeared to be a demure coed into a woman with a life filled with disappointment and sacrifices. She must have possessed incredible strength to close that first chapter of her life and start a new one. Minnow gave me a little kick, and I patted that spot. *Yes, I know you're there, my little one. I'll have so much to tell you about your*

204

grandmother. And as Momma passed her strength to me, I will pass it on to you.

"Here's the sign for Westmoreland Depot," Charlie noted as we wound our way closer to our journey's end. The town was about ten miles past the Keene State campus. It was similar to most New England towns, with the spire of its white clapboard church pointing toward the heavens. An old pickup truck went past us, and the driver waved. Small towns. I loved how people waved to everyone, not wanting to slight anyone.

"Now where to?" Charlie asked. We had pulled over near the fire department.

"Well, this looks like a good place to start. Let me see if anyone's around," I said and got out. Even though small towns had volunteer fire departments, there was usually one fellow at the station keeping watch over things. The garage door of the department was closed, so I went around to the side and found an older man standing outside, having a coffee.

"Can I help you, miss?" he asked. He had on a baseball cap embellished with WDFD. Red suspenders held his blue jeans up over his green flannel shirt. His black boots were unlaced, ready for action.

"Hi, there. I was wondering if you could help me. I'm looking for Willow Lane," I stated.

"Go right along straight in front of the firehouse for about a mile. Willow will be on your left. Who you looking for?" As he gave the information, he seemed to focus on my pregnant belly.

"Dr. Heard's office," I replied and thought his gaze really made me feel a little uneasy.

"Doc's office is down on the right. Big house. You can't miss it. Good luck to you," he said, and now his demeanor softened. What in the world was this all about? I wondered.

"Thanks a lot," I said and went back to the car.

"How'd you make out?" Charlie asked as I got in.

"The good news is that the doctor is still alive. But I got directions from an old guy who had a very odd reaction to my pregnancy," I said and directed Charlie to continue and make the turn.

"What do you mean?" Charlie asked. "Do I need to go and straighten him out?"

"Easy, my knight in shining armor. He was just an old guy at a firehouse. I was probably disturbing him from his quiet cup of coffee," I said and put the man's reaction off to just that.

In a few minutes, the house came into view. A massive Victorian, an aging painted lady.

The colors of the old girl were fading for sure. The shutters still held a bit of pink, while the main color, having once been yellow, now paled to a soft cream. Today, the sun helped to bring the colors to life. Charlie and I got out and walked up to the front porch.

The neatly painted sign to the left of the once-green door said "Dr. A. Heard." That, too, showed signs of aging. I imagined Dr. Heard as aged as his house. Soft white hair, balding in the front, smile on his face, bushy white eyebrows, and glasses resting on the tip of his nose. Wearing an old oxford cloth shirt, cuffs turned up to hide the frayed edges. Worn black trousers, with a shiny seat, and a back pocket that had been sewn numerous times at the corners to keep his wallet contained. He'd be a little stooped over from years of listening to his patients. And yes, he would still be seeing patients.

I thought how ironic it was that I was pregnant, standing, no doubt, where my mother had once stood. I was sure she must have been afraid. So young and having no choice as to what was happening to her life, her body, and her child. I could imagine Joseph's father standing here with her. And how unfeeling he would have been toward her as he lectured her on how dare she sully Joseph's reputation. I reached out for Charlie's hand.

We stood by the open screen door, and I turned the knob of an old doorbell. I heard a faint *brrrrinnnng* from inside. I waited a bit, and just as I was about to ring again, I heard footsteps. The door opened, and there stood a woman about forty years old, wiping her brow with a blue bandanna. Must be a housekeeper, I thought.

"Sorry to keep you. I was in the kitchen, mopping up. Damned icebox is leaking all over the floor," she said as she straightened her shirt. She was dressed in jeans, Keene State T-shirt, and flip-flops. It was funny to hear the term *icebox*. Aunt Eleanor still used that term to refer to her refrigerator. She wiped her hands on her jeans and held out her right hand. "I'm Abby." She looked me up and down, and then her eyes rested on my protruding belly. She next turned her attention to Charlie, a little puzzled, it seemed.

"Oh, I'm not here to see the doctor," I responded to her unasked question about my obvious pregnancy. "I'm Ethel O'Connor, and this is my husband, Charlie. Do you need some help?" I said and offered our combined services.

"I'm all set, really. But you're the ones who've come to my door. What can I help you with?" she said as she held the door open.

"I'm not sure, exactly," I started, and she looked at us rather quizzically.

"Well, if you don't know, then this will be quite a long afternoon." She laughed and waited.

"I'm sorry, that didn't come out quite right. I'm looking for my half sister. I only discovered her existence a few months ago. And I wasn't sure where to begin. My mother went to Keene State, and in looking through my grandmother's things, I found an old envelope with this location as the return address. I was hoping to speak with Dr. Heard. Is he in?" I hoped that was succinct enough to warrant some time with the doctor.

"Well, I'm Dr. Heard," she said and waited for my reaction.

"But you can't be. These letters are thirty-plus years old," I said, astonished at what I'd just heard. I looked at Charlie, who was equally baffled. Her face broke out into a wide grin as she shook her head.

"I'm sorry to tease you. I couldn't help myself. No one's come looking for my dad in quite a while. I hope you'll forgive me," she said. "Now, why don't you come out to the back porch and we can talk?"

"You're forgiven," I said, and we entered into another place in time.

The entry hallway held an old tapestry-upholstered settee and side table. An old service bell, like the kind used to ring at a hotel front desk, was the only adornment on the table. A mahogany staircase undulated its way to the second floor, the dark wood smooth from years of guiding hands up and down. The open hallway on that floor gave the appearance of a grand balcony with intricately turned spindles. The carpets were old Persian rugs, now almost threadbare. They softened our steps as we walked down a hallway darkened by old wood paneling. We passed through a room off to the side of the dining room that was once, no doubt, the domain of the wait-staff. Glass-front cabinets went from floor to ceiling. They must have stored the embroidered linens and fine china for the master's dining room. The kitchen had a huge stainless steel-topped center island with all types and sizes of pots and pans hanging on the ceiling rack overhead. I imagined the maids listening for the master's call and readying the next course. I was looking this way and that at all the details, with Charlie behind me doing the same, not noticing that our host had disappeared. It was then I realized that there were five doors in the kitchen. Where had she gone?

"Hello? Sorry, but we don't know where you went," I called out, and we stood and waited.

"Whoops, come this way." Abby poked her head in from door number three in my counting. We stepped around towels that had been laid on the floor in front of an aging Kelvinator. The water had soaked through most of them and was now starting to make a run for the center island.

"Do you want me to take a look at it?" Charlie asked, as he could see her predicament was worsening.

"No, damn it. I'm just going to have to get a new one. I was hoping that I could wait a bit." She took another towel from an open shelf above the counter and threw it down to stop the small river and motioned for us to follow her. We walked behind her, around the corner, to the dry pantry and finally found our way to a sunny back porch. A round wrought iron table with a glass top was tucked into the corner. There were four chairs of similar design with yellow pastel chair pads. On the top was a pink vase filled with daffodils and pussy willows. A double-tiered side cart held a selection of mismatched glasses and a heavy glass pitcher. She motioned for us to take a seat and poured a glass of water for each of us.

"This is a lovely spot," I said as we pulled out our chairs. It was a warm early-April day, and the sun felt good. The backyard had a series of gardens that were waiting for the next burst of spring warmth to bring them to life. A massive weeping willow stood in the middle of the largest garden as the protector for the smaller ones. Its branches swayed gracefully as they caught the afternoon breeze. I thought that this must have been the reason for the name Willow Lane.

"This is where I come to get away from the darkness of the house. Don't get me wrong, it's a beautiful place, but the first floor can be very stifling," she said as she took a sip and gazed out to the sprouting of spring.

"Those gardens are so intricate with all their winding paths. I'll bet this place just goes from one season to the next, blossoming all the time," I said as I admired the landscaping of the areas as they went from shade gardens to sunny spots. There was even a bridge with a small creek running under it. There was something very familiar about them. And then I saw it. The hill. The same hill that Momma had drawn in Sophie's Sled. I thought of the days that she was here, confined with her thoughts. Her only means of expression was her writing and sketches. This was where the story had begun.

"Oh, Charlie, this is it!" I exclaimed. "It's the same as in Momma's book."

"You're sure?" he asked.

"What is it?" Abby asked, no doubt wondering about my epiphany.

"In my mother's things, I found that she had started to write a children's book. She had several drawings, and I just realized that those drawings are here. This yard. That hill. The bench under the tree. It's all in her drawings." I was a bit overcome and took a long swallow of water. "She had to have been here. This can't be a coincidence."

"Wow, that's something. I would love to see them. The gardens were my mom's designs. They were beautiful when I was a child. But I'm afraid they're getting a little old. Just like everything else in this place. I try to tend to them the best I can. But other things take precedence. Like today, it's the icebox. Tomorrow, who knows what it'll be? And then there are my patients," she said.

"So you're a doctor too?" I asked, annoyed with myself for thinking that she was the housekeeper.

"I am. Followed in my dad's footsteps, graduated from Harvard. After my residency, I had plans to stay in Boston. But then Dad got sick and I came back home. I looked after his patients and him until he died a couple of years ago, and then I stayed," she answered and ended with a sigh. I knew that sigh. I'd had felt that way, too, when I gave up the *Herald* to remain in Piney Bluffs and work for Caleb at *The Bugle*.

"I know what you mean. Life happened to me about the same way. I was disappointed at first, but now I see that Piney Bluffs is where I'm supposed to be. It's where we've made a wonderful life." I reached out to hold Charlie's hand.

"Piney Bluffs? Where's that?" she asked.

"Maine, off the border of New Hampshire. Go to Fryeburg and keep on for another half hour or so," I answered.

"Holy cow, you've come a long way to look for an address!" she remarked.

"It has been quite the journey that's led me to you," I agreed.

"I really don't want to face the reality of that refrigerator. So why don't you tell me all about it?" she offered. And so I obliged.

Over the next half hour, I related the story of almost my entire life. Daddy, Charlie and EC, and *The Bugle*. The visits to prison with Andre and helping to get him released. The discovery of Momma's other life before Daddy. And finally, the last piece of my family puzzle, my half sister.

"Wow, you're like a female Geraldo Rivera," she commented when I finished.

"It's been one turn after another. But I have to keep going until I find her. That's why we took a two-hour drive to get here today. I was hoping that there was some reason my grandmother had this address in her cookbook," I said. I opened my purse and took out the triangle of paper. As I listened to myself, I realized how hopeless this all seemed. "And I also have a picture of my mother with a friend. It was taken when she was at Keene State. And here, too, are pictures from their yearbook."

"Let me see the pictures," she asked. I took them out and showed them to her.

"My mom's the one on the left. And here are the three girls from their college yearbook. One of the twins was my mom's friend."

"Pretty girls. Most of them were that came here," she said. "But I've got good news and bad news," Abby said.

"How do you mean?" I asked, trying to hide my excitement for the good news.

"My father, Dr. Anders Heard, started out as the family doctor, but he ended up being known to people in the area for helping girls who were in trouble. My mother helped him turn this house into a home for unwed mothers. She got tuberculosis and passed away when I was ten. I helped my dad after she left us. By the time I was in high school, no one came to the door anymore. So for the good news, it's most likely that your mother was here, given that you have that envelope," she stated.

"My word!" I said. "Did your father keep any records?"

"That's the bad news. Of course, Dad kept records on all of them, and he had a registry of sorts. He said it was to protect all of them and us. It had abbreviations of the name of the girl, but of course, that depended on if they wanted to give us their real name or not. It also included when they came in and when they left. The baby's sex and then sometimes where it went, if the child didn't go back with the mother. It goes back quite a few years," she offered. "What year are you looking for?"

"The birth certificate says March 20, 1941, but with the conniving ways of Joseph's father, there's no telling what he could have paid someone to write," I conceded.

"The books are by years, sometimes a few for each one. Come over to the office and let's see what we can find in the record room." She got up, and off we went back through the kitchen. The last towel she had laid out for the leak had contained the water, and she gave a little thumbs-up for that small victory.

I believed that I was about to find the information that was going to get me closer to Sophie. I said a silent prayer to Momma, hoping that this would be the day that I finally knew what had happened.

CHAPTER 30

W E FOLLOWED ABBY THROUGH THE kitchen and down a smaller hallway. Turning a corner, we were now in the doctor's waiting area. In sharp contrast to the front of the house, sun streamed through several large windows that were framed by pots of hanging ferns, vines, and cacti. There were chairs of varying size and styles in the room. A coffee table was laden with old issues of *National Geographic* and *Reader's Digest*. A gray tiger cat was curled up on one of the cushioned chairs and raised its head as we entered.

"That's Nurse Cherry," Abby said and stopped to rub the cat's chin. "You remember those books, don't you?" Nurse Cherry stretched her neck so Abby could reach all of it.

"I sure do. Nurse Cherry Ames. I think we all wanted to be a nurse like her. Either that or a detective like Nancy Drew. Weren't those simpler days?" I said and stopped to pet the cat, who was happy to have another hand giving her attention. "How many patients do you have now?"

"Oh, there's about a hundred or so. Families that Dad treated, the older ones come back. Their kids, the ones my age and younger, they go elsewhere, to the shinier office buildings. But when they have that emergency in the middle of the night, they always seem to find my number. And I go right out," she answered, contented.

"You make house calls?" Charlie asked, astounded.

"Yes. Funny, if I'd have stayed in Boston, there'd be none of that. Unless you wanted to pay for it." She chuckled. "No, this really gives me peace. With the exception of that damned ice box, life is grand." She opened a door to reveal the file room. Several old metal four-drawer cabinets were against one wall, and on the opposite wall were floor-to-ceiling, color-coded files. On closer examination, the drawers were labeled with years. Abby tugged open the squeaky metal drawer of one with dates of 1939 to 1944. "Here's the drawer you're looking for." Inside were blue-cloth-and-leather-covered ledgers. The drawer contained about ten of them. "Let's take them out to the waiting room. Better light out there." We each grabbed a few and went back to spread them out on the table.

"I see what you mean with the names. This one has three listings for Jane Doe. But then this one just has initials," I said and felt deflated. "Remember, Momma's initials were SML."

"What exactly are we looking for?" Charlie asked.

"Most likely, it would be the initials. You never know, we might get lucky," Abby said, and we continued to look. It was a bit confusing. Notations were made for a particular day on all the patients. But once I figured out the system, it was quite easy to follow. I showed Charlie, and he nodded his understanding. Each patient was given a number and initials, so the three Jane Does were easy to tell apart. Some stayed for several weeks, while others left as soon as the baby was born. Some left with the baby, and some without.

"What happened to the babies that were left behind?" I asked, feeling sad to think that a child could be left, not knowing who its mother was. I imagined that must have happened to Sophie.

"We had a nursery with lots of bassinets. There were a couple of ladies in town who would help us feed all of them. Dad said it was sad when the mothers made the choice to leave their babies behind. That was the harsh reality of all this. But he'd made some connections throughout New England, and it was never more than a week or two before a good family was found that truly wanted the baby. Not like it is today, with all the red tape and all the money that's needed. No, Dad made sure they were going to good homes. He had friends that would follow up to make sure the homes stayed good too. He was his own social service organization. He would've been in so much trouble today if this still happened." She smiled at what I thought was probably the happy memories of her dad.

"Country doctor and adoption agency all rolled into one," I said, thinking of where all these babies could have gone.

"It was certainly the times. Dad told me the years between 1940 and 1960 was the time period with the highest number of adoptions. Women had been left pregnant by the men, who had gone off to the different wars and never returned. The women wanted a new life, and barren couples wanted to belong to the baby boom. It seemed to be a win-win situation for everyone concerned," Abby explained.

"How did you feel about all this going on in your house?" I asked, picturing all these pregnant women showing up at all hours of the day and night and wandering about in labor. The sounds of babies crying in the night, needing the comfort of the mothers that had left them behind.

"The mothers were kind of like my big sisters. I would massage their feet or their backs and run and get them water and tea. And the stories they would tell me. Oh my! Some of them truly loved the guy that had gotten them pregnant. Others wanted to forget about everything. Being with and listening to all of them made me very aware of what not to do when and if I was ever in the 'love is blind' stage. I used to ask my dad why he helped them. And he would tell me that he took an oath to help people. Somehow, his world of a simple county doctor and their world of need and shame had collided. He said he was never sorry. He knew that he helped the mothers to have a healthy delivery and the babies could have a safe beginning. He died a happy man." She had a wistful smile as she ended.

"What about the folks in town? Were they…how should I say this?" I began, and she stopped me.

"There were two sides. The ones who were so above all this, until it happened to one of their daughters. Then they were damned glad of what my dad did. And then there were the ones who knew Dad first, before this started. They respected him for helping. Most folks don't say anything about it now. It was born out of need, and Dad filled it," she said as she continued to thumb through the pages of the ledgers.

"Then that explains the look I got from the fellow at the fire department. I stopped to get directions before finding you," I said, finally understanding the reason for his odd demeanor.

"Oh, you must have talked to Rusty. He's at the station all day, every day. Old guy with red suspenders and coffee cup in his hand?" Abby asked.

"Yes, that's him," I replied.

"His daughter had been one of the girls. She left her baby girl behind and took off for the bright lights of New York City. Sad to say, she never returned. Rusty wanted to find his granddaughter and bring her back here, but his wife died of pneumonia soon after his daughter left. He decided to leave well enough alone," Abby said, and I could tell how well she looked after all her patients and the people in town.

"Poor man, left to think about his family and what might have been. His granddaughter adopted and gone, perhaps very far away," I thought out loud.

"That was certainly the heartbreak of it all," she agreed. "I remember so many times the girls talking with one another about adoption. It wasn't an easy choice. Some who had come with the clear-cut notion that they were giving their baby up changed their tune once they saw their baby."

I couldn't imagine facing a decision like that. Alone, with no other option but to walk away. I instinctively put my hand on my belly. How my mother must have struggled with this decision.

"Wait, I think I have something." I had a volume that started in February of 1941. "'February 27, 1941, SML.' That's my mom's initials. There's no name, but it's got to be her. And look, there's lots of dollar signs and then a period and some more. What does that mean?"

"That meant someone paid Dad a lot of money at the door. Paid for care and silence. How many dollar signs?" Abby looked up, and Charlie came to read over my shoulder.

"Six, and then eight more after the period," I answered. "Does that mean..."

"Six hundred was paid at the door, and then eight more was for silence. Fourteen hundred dollars was a lot of money. Somebody sure must have wanted this one to stay quiet. What does the rest of the ledger say?" she explained and came to join me to review what I'd found. The next few pages followed Momma's care and the care of six other girls. The notes chronicled vital signs, examinations, and daily weights.

"That's got to be Momma. Joseph's father had a lot of money and, it seems, would stop at nothing to keep Joseph's connection to an illegitimate birth as far away as possible. The place of birth on the birth certificate was Portland, Maine. His father must have paid to have that falsified too." I shook my head and thought about the lengths this man had gone to in order to hide the birth of Sophie.

"We did have a lot of famous or noteworthy girls that 'spent some time in the mountains,' as it was put. The money that they paid helped to support the ones who showed up in the middle of the night. Most of those girls were too embarrassed to ring the front doorbell, so they came to the back door with nothing in their hands but a small satchel, a swollen belly, and tears in their eyes," Abby said.

As we continued to read the ledger, Abby interpreted the notes for Momma. One said, "Small for her stated months, underweight, but good VS," which Abby said meant *vital signs*. I reasoned that Momma had been in high school and trying to keep her pregnancy hidden, so she wouldn't have eaten very much. The next few entries made me feel better in that she had been eating more and gaining weight.

It was at that moment that I realized that my grandmother must have known about all this. What had this done to her? Her only child, pregnant. And knowing that they would be giving up their only grandchild. A punishing reality entered their world. What had my grandfather thought? He had been a man of strong convictions, from what I'd been told. This must have torn him apart. I was only four years old when my grandmother passed. The joy she must have finally realized when I was born, only to mourn the loss of her daughter. How cruel life had been to them all.

"Here, here's the entry of the birth. March 20, 1941, healthy female, six pounds, two ounces," Abby said excitedly, startling me from my daydream. "And here, they're doing well. Next, SML leaves on March 30, 1941."

"But what about the baby?" I asked, following along with her. I looked up at Charlie, and he could see the hope in my eyes.

"Let's see, BSML. Dad put a *B* in front of the mother's initials to know who the baby belonged to. Let's see. Nothing for a few days. Doing well, gaining weight. Here. Here it is. BSML and BMHC LWMHC. That's strange," Abby said as she continued to flip pages.

"What's strange?" I asked. "What do those letters mean?"

"The LW meant 'left with.' But the MHC, that's another patient's initials. That doesn't make sense that another patient would take another girl's baby plus her own." Abby went back and forth between the next few pages. "Very strange, indeed."

"What were those initials again?" I was dumbfounded at what I was hearing.

"MHC," Abby replied.

"Oh my. Now I understand," I said and pulled the book from her.

"*MHC* means something to you?" Abby asked.

"Yes, it's the initials of the girl in the picture with my mother. The picture that was taken at Keene State," I answered, almost on the verge of tears at this discovery.

"Finally," Charlie said and gave me a hug.

"Yes, indeed, finally," I said as the tears spilled from eyes.

"Oh, here. Don't cry," Abby said and held out a tissue.

"I just can't believe that I've found something. I mean, I was here on the thinnest of hopes that we'd be able to find something. And now the hard part," I said as I dabbed my eyes.

"The hard part?" Abby asked.

"Yes, which twin was it, and where is she now?" I said and closed the book and looked from Charlie to Abby and slowly shook my head.

CHAPTER 31

W E SAT IN SILENCE FOR a bit as this discovery sunk in. I was elated to have finally found where Momma and Sophie had been. We looked back through that book and found that MHC had come in the same day as Momma. So this was where the friendship had begun. I wondered what her story had been. And the fact that she, whether Martha or Madeline, had been able to graduate with Momma. From all I'd learned from Daddy, Momma had lived at college. If Chums had taken both babies, then where had they lived and who had taken care of their babies? Continuing through the ledgers, I saw that Momma and Chums had progressed about the same with their labor and had their babies born within an hour of each other. Sophie had been first, with Chum's baby coming next.

"Oh, look, she had a girl, too," I said. "What's this mean, 'Nevus, LT'?"

"She must have a mole. That's what a nevus is. And the LT would be somewhere on the left side. Nothing else. So it could be her arm or leg and anywhere on the left," Abby answered.

"Would they have been roommates?" I asked, thinking of two girls thrown together and sharing the secrets of a lifetime.

"*Roommates* was hardly the term. Dad had turned four of the five big bedrooms into four-bed wards. One of the four was the nursery," Abby answered.

"So you could've had a dozen girls here at any one time?" I asked and was amazed to think of a how all that had been managed.

"Yes, we could and did. During those days, they had a full-time cook and a housekeeper. The girls were expected to feed their babies and those of others who might have been too sick. They helped out with their laundry and worked in the kitchen too," Abby added. "As you can see by the number of ledgers, there were hundreds of babies born here. And then birth control methods graduated from the rhythm method to other manufactured ones. Religion changed people's views as well. Early abortion clinics came about. And then life slowly let Dad become a country doctor again."

"It just amazes me that places like this must have existed all over the country. People quietly going about the business of keeping secrets," I said.

"I asked my dad once about that very thing. I asked him if he knew of other doctors doing just what he'd done. He told me he hoped that there were. But he'd never found anyone who would admit it. He told me his intent was to make sure that the mothers were delivered safely and that these babies were given a chance at a good life. Even though he wished they could all have gone home with their mothers, he was a realist. He knew that some people weren't cut out for the job of raising children," she finished. Then she added, "I'm happy that we found what you were looking for."

"I am, too, but now I'm starting all over again. It seems that whenever I find what I'm looking for, it only sends me back to asking the 'Now what?' question," I said and drummed my fingers on the desk.

"Didn't you say you'd called Frank to check into the twins?" Charlie reminded me.

"Who's Frank?" Abby asked.

"Frank's a friend of Caleb, who's my editor at *The Bugle*. He works in Boston in a high-level government agency of some type. In all my efforts over the past few years, he's been able to provide me with information or an assurance that I'm headed in the right direction. But this time, I'm not so sure," I explained. "Say, could I use your telephone? I could give him a call. He might've found something."

"It's Saturday, honey," Charlie stated.

"Oh, crap, you're right. But he might be in," I said hopefully.

"The phone's over there on the desk. Go for it," Abby offered, and she pointed to an antique black desk phone with a cloth cord.

"It's long-distance. I'll leave you money," I said as I sat down and dialed Frank's number from memory. The dial gave a soft *rat-ta-ta* as I dialed each number. Abby motioned with her hand to forget it. The phone began to ring.

"Hello, who is this and how did you get this number?" I recognized Frank's voice, but not this stern tone.

"Frank, it's Ethel. Sorry to call on a Saturday. Is everything all right?" I asked.

"Ethel, what the heck are you calling for on a Saturday?" Frank asked. "Must be pretty important. Caleb doesn't have you working on a weekend, does he?"

"Not working for *The Bugle*. Actually, I'm in New Hampshire, following that address I told you about," I answered.

"Sorry, I haven't had time to check into those names you gave me. What with the attempted assassination of Reagan, we've been a little busy this past week," Frank stated. He was cordial, but I could tell I needed to cut this conversation short.

The previous week, on March 30, only sixty-nine days into office, President Reagan had an assassination attempt by John Hinkley Jr. The president and Secret Service agents had been slightly injured, but Jim Brady, the president's press secretary, was seriously injured after having been shot six times. I could very well understand that my request was not at the top of Frank's priorities.

"Frank, I completely understand. Thanks." And we quickly hung up.

"And…?" Abby asked, looking at me expectantly.

"He's been a little busy with the assassination attempt on President Reagan," I answered and felt deflated.

"He is high level if he's working on that," Abby said. "Now what?"

"Now what, indeed?" I repeated. I started to get up but sat right back down.

"Ethel, are you okay?" Charlie asked as he came over to me. "You look a little pale."

"I really need to pee, but I'm feeling funny," I answered.

"Here, let me help you to the bathroom, and then I'll take your blood pressure and do a quick once-over," Abby said as she got me into the lavatory off the waiting room. The bathroom was roomy, and she stayed with me.

"All set now," I said as I began to stand up. "Whoa, I feel light-headed." I grabbed for the sink to steady myself. I washed my hands and splashed some water on my face. I dried it with a paper towel.

"When was the last time you ate?" Abby had now switched to full doctor mode as she walked me out to the waiting room and helped me sit down.

"It was early, about seven thirty. I had a coffee and a couple of bites of blueberry cake," I answered. Abby had brought over the blood pressure cuff and was inflating it.

"Is she okay?" Charlie asked, the concern showing on his face.

"It may be low blood sugar, since she ate more than six hours ago. Do you have any allergies?" Abby asked as she removed the cuff and took my pulse.

"None that I know of," I answered. I wiped a little sweat from my forehead. "Is it hot in here, or is it me?"

"I'll be right back," she said and walked quickly through the hallway.

"Honey, what's the matter?" Charlie said as he sat next to me, holding my hand, the worry showing in his eyes.

"I'm fine. I think I just need a cracker or something. Didn't you promise me lunch?" I kidded with him and put a smile on my face. I put my other hand on my belly. No movement. *Come on, Minnow, stop making me think silly things about this. Now is not the time for you to take a nap. Move for Mommy.* And then there it was, a little kick. *There's my girl.*

"Here, have a little of this." Abby had returned with a glass of orange juice and peanut butter on a couple of saltines. She watched me intently as I ate.

"Oh, thanks. I think this is exactly what I needed," I said and immediately started to feel better.

"I'd like to do a quick exam, if you'd allow me. When's your due date?" Abby was opening the door to one of the exam rooms. She snapped down the table paper and motioned for me to come in.

"I'm due the middle of June. At least that's what it should work out to. But the accident may play a role on the exact date," I related.

"Accident? When was your accident? What happened?" Abby had helped me up onto the table and had me lie down.

"January. It was a snowy night, our car spun out of control, we hit a tree, and I ended up in a coma for two months. I came out of it about a month ago. Only broken bones were these two fingers. And I've had regular OB checkups. In fact, I just had one yesterday. Doctor said both the baby and I are fine," I told the brief story and watched her face as I held up my hand to show her the scars from the accident. She had placed her stethoscope on my abdomen and was now methodically working her way around and then poking here and there to see if I had any pain. She checked my eyes and pulses.

"Gee, but you're a lucky woman," Abby finally said after helping me sit up. "Baby's heartbeat is strong, yours is a little fast, but everything else checks out fine. How are you feeling now?"

"Better, thanks. But still a little hungry," I said and got down from the table. We walked back out to the waiting area. "I don't suppose you have any other information about the patients' destinations when they left here, do you?" Now that I was fine, I had to get the information I needed.

"You get right back to it, don't you? But no, not really. Sometimes Dad kept addresses of the girls who wanted to know where their baby had gone. However, there weren't many of those. Did you check with the college? Sometimes they keep in touch with their alumni for donations and such," she offered, a little hope to my dilemma.

"That's a good point. Now that I'm certain of who I'm looking for, I'll definitely do that. I wish it weren't a Saturday, or we could go over there now and check. I'm sure most of the campus offices are closed for the weekend," I said, frustrated with yet another delay.

"As a concerned doctor, I would advise that you take a break for the rest of today. Have a light lunch, nothing too saucy, creamy, or fried. Then get yourselves home and relax. You've had a lot of emotional input today. From being here and seeing the grounds, to realizing that your mother was here. Your subconscious is spinning, my friend." Dr. Abby was certainly spot-on with her comments. "And you can always call Keene State from home instead of taking another ride out here."

"I suppose, but I'm so close." I took in a deep breath and let it out. I felt so discouraged. She was right, of course. This was essentially a dead end until I could find out which one of the twins had taken Sophie. I'd have to ask Frank if he could find information on both of them. One would certainly know what had happened to the other. And then the next question would be, Where? She could be right under my nose, but she could also be on the other side of the country, or even the world.

"Ethel, come on. Let's find a place to have some lunch and then get you home," Charlie said and put his arm around my shoulders. "Abby, is there any place here in town to get a little something to eat?"

"Unless you want Rusty to fix you a coffee, I'm afraid not. If you drive a little farther to Chesterfield, there's a little café that makes great soup and sandwiches," she offered. "Stay on the main road and head south. The river will be on the right. When you get there, you'll see it. Only one place, you can't miss it. If you get to Vermont, you've gone too far."

"Chesterfield? That's where the postcard came from." Hearing that name, I had become instantly energized.

"What postcard?" Abby asked, looking puzzled.

"This one. It was in my grandmother's cookbook along with the envelope." I took the postcard from my purse and showed it to Abby.

"Say, this is an old one for sure," Abby said as she looked at both sides of the card. "Cryptic message at best, wouldn't you say?"

"Yes. 'Made it, all are well,' seems like it's saying a lot without saying anything," I agreed. I'd thought about that message over and over. Of course, my ideal thought was to have the message somehow connect to Sophie.

"Is the handwriting familiar?" she asked.

"No, it's not. I have several examples of my mother's, and that's nowhere close to it," I confirmed. "I've thought that maybe a friend of my grandmother's had gone on a little trip and wanted to let her know that they had arrived safely."

"We used to have quite a few girls come here after a visit to Chesterfield," Abby added.

"Really, from the picture, it seems like a quiet town, like here," I said.

"Oh, it wasn't in the early days. There was a woman by the name of Madame Sherri. Moved here from New York City. Her parties were notorious for any type of impropriety you could imagine and more. Her place burned down about twenty years ago. Only thing left is the staircase that led up to her bedroom," she said.

"That's right, Ginny said she remembered hearing about it. Ginny is my dad's, ah, well, I guess you could say girlfriend." It was funny; I'd never had to explain Ginny and Daddy's relationship.

"From the stories that Dad told me, things were winding down at the castle by the time I could understand what the word *impropriety* encompassed. Some of the ladies who helped feed the babies filled me in with tales of flamboyant parties with every kind of excess imaginable. They, in turn, had heard those details from some of the girls who'd come here after having gotten themselves into trouble," Abby said.

"Your dad was quite something for doing all this," I said, recognizing how this house had been a safe environment with caring people.

"He was. And my mother was just as committed to helping him with this. She'd graduated from Keene with a degree in sociology, so in a way this was like a lifetime internship for her. She could've gotten her doctorate in public health before social service was an actuality," she added and set her chin with a little nod. "I admire my parents for providing health care and loving support to women who might have looked elsewhere in less-than-desirable conditions. By continuing this practice and caring for my patients, well, that's the best way I know to honor what they did for so many."

"Well, thanks for all your assistance today. This has been very helpful in understanding my mother's story," I said as we walked down the hallway.

"No problem. I'm happy that we were able to find what you needed to get you started again. Please stay in touch. I'd like to know how you make out with your baby and if you ever find your Sophie." Abby gave each of us a hug as we said our goodbyes at the door. "And, Charlie, you make sure she doesn't get into any more trouble today."

"I'll try, but I never promise." Charlie chuckled.

As we drove away, I turned back for one last look at 10 Willow Lane. I thought of them, those who had arrived as girls and left as women. Had they turned back this same way? How many of them had wanted to run back and take their child with them? Reality was a cruel mistress. Whether they were taking their baby with them or leaving their baby behind, this was the place that had changed their lives forever.

CHAPTER 32

"Wow, I don't believe what we just found. A home for unwed mothers and an adoption agency all in one," I commented as we drove away.

"I know. It was eye-opening, for sure."

Keeping the river to our right as Abby had instructed, we found Chesterfield to be no more than a fifteen-minute drive. The town's center was small, like that of Piney Bluffs. We drove slowly in search of the café. There was a town hall and a church. We passed by a huge stone monument, erected in memory of those who'd fought in both the Civil War and World War I. Daffodils were poking up around the base of the monument.

"That looks like it must be it," Charlie said. He pointed just past the center of town to a white house with a sizable addition. A wooden sign that said "Café Open 6 to 2" hung on a metal post. It was evident by the cars that were parked on each side of the road that this must be the place. We followed their lead, parked along the road, and got out.

Another sign on the other side of the house said, "Vintage yard sale today." A teenage boy was rearranging a few old chairs close to the road. I hesitated for a moment, looking at the chairs and a milk can displayed on the lawn.

"Charlie, look at this milk can. Wouldn't that look great on the porch?" I said as my eyes roamed across the eclectic group of items.

"This way, my dear. We can look after you eat. It's almost one thirty, and the signs says six to two," Charlie said in his best stern fashion and steered me toward the door. Before I even opened the door, I could smell the bacon and remembered how hungry I was. I also remembered that Abby had cautioned me to eat light. *Oh, well,* I thought, *at least I could indulge in the wonderful aroma of the bacon.*

As we entered, all conversation stopped for an instant as we were given the once-over. The faint music from a radio on the counter was the only noise for a moment. We each nodded a silent hello to the group. And then, satisfied with our acknowledgment, the diners went back to their meals.

The interior was small but held six tables for two and a counter with three stools. It reminded me of a miniature Ruthie's. There were red-and-white gingham curtains and tablecloths to match. The chairs were a mix of styles, but all had been painted white and had red seat cushions to pull the décor together. A blackboard over the counter listed the breakfast and lunch offerings for the day. The walls displayed a variety of exceptionally detailed sketches of typical New England landscapes: barns, churches, rolling hills, and mountains, each one very well done. While they looked to have been crafted by the same artist, no signature appeared on them. There was one table left by a window, and we took it.

"I see what I'm having," I said as I looked at the menu board. "Egg salad on white toast and chicken noodle soup."

"At least you're keeping to what Abby recommended," Charlie noted. "I think I'm going to have a cheeseburger and potato salad."

The same young man who'd been arranging the vintage items on the lawn approached our table, having now donned a red apron over his T-shirt and jeans.

"Hi, folks, I'm Matt! What'll you have?" he asked. He was a tall handsome kid with deep-brown eyes that matched his dark-brown hair.

"Hi, Matt. I'll have the egg salad on white toast, a glass of water, and a cup of chicken noodle soup," I answered. He nodded, not writing my order down.

"And I'll have the cheeseburger, medium, and potato salad, with a ginger ale," Charlie said.

"Okay, thanks, folks. I'll be right out with that soup." He walked away, picking up empty dishes from the other tables and talking with the other customers about their day.

"Nice kid," Charlie said.

"Yes. I wonder if he's going to cook too," I added. "I don't really see anyone else in the kitchen from where I'm sitting."

"Don't worry. His ma's in the back, cooking," a male voice answered from the table next to us. Looking over, I saw an older man smile. He and a woman of about the same age were getting up from their table. "You'll like the food too. Okay, Matt, see you next trip." He gave us a nod, let the woman go in front of him, and they made their way toward the door.

"See ya, Buzzy, Ms. Alice!" I heard Matt yell from the kitchen. And before we had a chance to comment, Matt had returned with my steaming cup of soup and set it in front of me. Its broth had a generous amount of fresh-chopped parsley on top. Dipping my spoon in, I brought up bite-size pieces of both light and chunks of chicken, carrots, and celery, along with wide ribbons of egg noodles. Each ingredient had been simmered to perfection.

"Oh my," I said as I finished my first bite. "This is about the best chicken noodle soup I've ever tasted!" And I closed my eyes to savor the flavorful broth and herbs. A smile came to my face.

"I've never known anyone who enjoys soup the way that you do," Charlie said and smiled back at me.

"And that is one of the endearing qualities that first attracted you to me," I said as I continued to eat my soup. I felt a little kick and thought Minnow was liking the soup too.

"I'm pretty sure that soup was not on the top of my list in the attraction department," Charlie said and winked at me.

"Why, Mr. O'Connor, such conversation is not appropriate for a public setting or for our unborn child's precious ears," I said in my best Scarlet O'Hara voice. Matt soon returned with our sandwiches and drinks.

"You folks enjoy," Matt said as he finished setting our food on the table.

"We'll finish up as quick as we can, so you can get out of here," Charlie remarked to Matt.

"Aw, that's okay, take your time. My mom and I live here. And I'll be out doing the yard sale for a while. So don't rush." Matt gave us a grin. "We got one piece of chocolate cake with icing left, if you want me to save it for you."

"Oh, boy, do I," I answered.

"It's yours," he answered and headed back into the kitchen.

The rest of our lunch was as well-prepared as the soup. My egg salad had some fresh herbs in with the mayo and celery. The toast, with its brilliant green leaf lettuce cradling the egg mixture, was from homemade white bread and had just the right crunch to it. Charlie's burger was served on what also looked like a homemade roll. It was juicy and had a thick cut of cheddar cheese melting and dripping down its sides. Lettuce, tomato, and onion topped it. There was homemade ketchup relish served alongside it. I took a bite of his burger and wished for my own. I tasted the potato salad too. It was perfectly seasoned and had a great balance of potatoes, hard-boiled eggs and celery, and well-seasoned dressing. Matt returned as we were finishing our sandwiches and placed a healthy-size square of chocolate cake with white buttercream icing between the two of us. I could smell the chocolate.

"Matt, this is some piece of cake. I think you could have put two pieces on the menu," I said as I acknowledged the size of the cake.

"That's okay. Mom saw that you were pregnant, and it looked like a nice, big piece of chocolate cake would be the right finish to your lunch. She makes one every day. It really is the best." Matt smiled and slipped the bill under the plate.

The place had quickly emptied, and Matt cleared the plates from the remaining tables. Charlie and I dived into the cake.

"This is…" And I stopped as I put another forkful of cake in my mouth. The cake was dark and moist, and the frosting was thick and creamy with a hint of vanilla.

"I know, one of the best things you've ever eaten." He grinned back at me. "Do you think maybe it's the fact that you're pregnant and love to eat?"

"Maybe a little, but this really is good," I said, and we finished our simple yet decadent dessert. I thought back to the recipe in Gammie's cookbook. The chocolate cake recipe that she had made a note on that had said, "Stephanie's favorite." I was really going to have to make that recipe soon. I hoped it would be as good as this. Charlie took out his wallet and paid, leaving a good tip for Matt.

"Bye, Matt, and Matt's mom!" I called out as we got up to leave.

"Thanks, come again!" a female voice said from behind the wall. "Just leave the bill on the counter. Matt's taking care of dishes right now."

"Okay," Charlie said, and we left the slip with the money on the counter.

We headed back outside. It was a great spring afternoon, and the sun felt warm on my face. I walked over to the side of the house with the yard sale. With my appetite satisfied, I was now free to concentrate on looking for something that might remind me of today. There was a wooden box filled with old photos that caught my attention.

"My mom calls this box instant relatives." And it was Matt, who had rejoined us.

"Oh, are they of your family?" I asked. Most of the pictures were old black-and-whites, and others were silhouettes.

"Not that I know of. She used to collect them, thought that she might decorate the café with them. But she put up her own sketches instead," he answered.

"Your mom's an excellent artist. Those pictures in the café have amazing detail," I said.

"She was going to school for art for a while," he responded.

"Matt, I got some more stuff." His mother's voice called him away from us. He left but soon returned with a wheelbarrow full of clay pots. Charlie was looking at a couple of small fishing poles.

"These might be EC's size. What do you think?" Charlie asked, and I went over to inspect them. They were small handmade rods, almost identical, just the right size for a child. The reels were missing, but we could easily get a couple at Tubby's.

"They are definitely child size. EC can have one, and Minnow can have the other," I said and held the small rods.

"Those belonged to my mom and my aunt." Matt had come over to us. "Uncle George loved to fish and taught them how."

"My dad and uncles took me fishing a lot too. Dad still does from time to time. Do you still fish, Matt?" I asked. He had sat down on one of the vintage chairs while Charlie and I perused.

"I used to. My uncle would take me. But he passed away when I was ten. I still go with my friends, but it's not the same. Uncle George would tell me all kinds of stories about the twins. Double trouble, he called them." Matt showed clear affection as he talked about his uncle.

"Your mom was a twin?" I asked as I continued to look. I had now gone to the wheelbarrow and selected a couple of flowerpots. They would be nice on the porch with some geraniums, I thought.

"Not the identical kind, but she was a twin, all right. Here, let me get them." Matt came over and picked the pots up and put them next to the milk can.

"Well, I'm done. How about you, Charlie?" I said as I wiped the dirt and dust from my hands.

"Sure, I'll take the poles too," he said. "What do we owe you, Matt?"

"Let's see…" And you could see Matt mulling over the potential sales while still trying to be a good salesman. "How about twenty-five dollars?" And he waited for Charlie's answer.

"How about twenty?" Charlie countered.

"I can do twenty-three," Matt came back.

"Okay, settled. Twenty-three, it is." Charlie laughed. "You drive a hard bargain, Matt."

"Thanks! I'm trying to save money for tuition. I've only got a few more years before college," he shared with us as he put the money in the pocket of his jeans.

"Where're you going to school?" I asked.

"I've got my heart set on Keene State, but I'll have to see how much I can save and if I get accepted. I may have to start out in junior college. I want to be a teacher." Matt had rolled out his life plan for us.

"Good for you, Matt. Well, it was nice to visit with you," I said, and we headed for the car.

"Matt, come get these things," his mom called to him again.

"Coming." And Matt waved goodbye to us.

Charlie secured the pots and the milk can in the back of the car, put the poles in carefully, and we got in. As Charlie was turning the car around to head back the way we came, Matt was coming back to the yard with more items. He put down a large object and then raised his hand and gave us another wave. I had turned my thoughts to heading home when it hit me.

"Charlie, turn this car around, right now," I said excitedly.

"Why? What is it? Are you okay?" he said, and I could see he was concerned.

"Oh, I'm about to be perfectly fine," I finished and started to smile.

"What is it?" Charlie asked again as he slowed and turned the car around. Matt stopped and came over to the car.

"Is everything okay?" he asked. He looked concerned at the speed with which Charlie had turned around again.

"Everything's fine, Matt," I said and walked over to the things he'd just put down. "Where did you get this sled?" The sled, while old, was still in great condition.

"In the shed. Why?" he answered.

"No. I mean, whom did the sled belong to?" I had taken the sled and stood it up. My hands were almost shaking as I touched it. I was so sure.

"It was my mom's and her sister's. Their aunt gave it to them when they were little, and my mom gave it to me. Do you want to buy it?" Matt asked, not sure of what to do with a pregnant woman who looked like she'd just discovered gold.

"I'd like to talk to your mom, if I could. Can you get her for me?" I asked. I began to prepare myself for what to say. I'd never thought that this conversation would take place today. Matt left us and went back inside, calling to his mom.

"Ethel, it's just a sled. Come on, you're scaring me a little. Are you sure you feel okay?" Charlie said and was looking at me with a worried look.

"Don't you see, Charlie? His mom is a twin, but not identical. This is *the* sled. If Martha or Madeline took both of the babies from Dr. Heard, they were raised to believe they were twins. This is where it gets solved. Today," I said softly. Out of the corner of my eye, I saw Matt and his mom walking toward us.

She wore her dark-brown hair in a ponytail under a ball cap. She was about my height, and with the exception of me being pregnant, we could have been body doubles. Her smile lit up her face. I looked at Charlie, and his look told me he saw the resemblance too.

"Hi! Matt said you wanted to speak with me?" she said, and her voice was almost identical to mine.

"Yes, thanks for coming out. That was a great lunch and cake," I said, making small talk, all the while looking at her and becoming more convinced I was right.

"That cake gets everyone. It was my aunt's recipe. It was one of her favorites," she answered. Then she added, "I've printed copies. So many folks want to know how to make it. But truthfully, they usually come back here to have mine."

"Well, I'd certainly like one too, if it's not too much trouble," I said, but I believed I knew where that cake recipe had come from.

"I'll get you one before you leave. Find any good bargains?" She had an easygoing way about her.

"We found a couple of things. The fishing poles will be great for my son and this one coming along. I do like that sled. It reminds me of one I saw in an old picture," I commented and held my breath for her response.

"That belonged to me and my sister. Our aunt gave it to us. No use for it now. Matt's a little too old for sliding, or so he tells me. It's still in good condition and would probably be great for your family," she said and smiled at me.

"It does look like it would take another ten years or so of sliding," I noted.

"I see you're from Maine. Taking a road trip today? It certainly is a nice day for it," she continued.

"Yes, we were out for a drive today, trying to track down some information. Might I ask your name, please?" I asked. *Please, God, just have her say the words that I want to hear.*

"Why, sure. I'm Sophie, Sophie Anne Blake. And you are?"

CHAPTER 33

How did I put this? *I'm about to tell you the real story of your life. I'm going to tell you that you're not a twin and that I'm your sister and we share the same mother? No, that's not quite the way I'd want to hear it.* I was somewhere between elation and vomiting. *Oh, gee, I really should've thought this out.* I stared at her for a moment. It was almost like looking in the mirror. We had the same hair color, same piercing dark eyes. Mouth and nose—those, too, were so very similar. She must see it too; she had to.

"I'm Ethel. Ethel Koontz O'Connor. This is my husband, Charlie. We're from Piney Bluffs, Maine," I replied.

"Never heard of that town. But then, with the café and all, I don't leave the area much," she said.

"It's a half hour or so past the New Hampshire and Maine state line," I added, still trying to figure out how to broach the looming subject.

"You said you were looking for information. What about, exactly?" she asked and folded her arms across her chest. She wore a denim shirt over a white T-shirt. Her jeans fit snugly against her trim figure. She waited.

"Yes, I am. You see, I've been searching for someone for a story," I said, hoping this would open the way.

"Searching for who? What's this all about? If you're selling something, I don't have time for this," Sophie answered, sounding a little defensive.

"No, I'm not selling anything. Please, can we sit for a moment?" I asked gently.

"Sure, over here on the porch. Matt, go back to the kitchen and clean the rest of the lunch dishes up. I'll keep an eye on the yard sale," she instructed her son. She led Charlie and me over to a small side porch that overlooked the front lawn. We sat in folding aluminum webbed chairs around a small wooden table.

"You're sure everything's okay?" Matt asked, concerned for his mother.

"I'll be fine. Now go do as you're told, honey," she answered. "So what's this story?" She turned her attention to me with a hard look.

"To begin, what's your mother's first name?" I asked.

"Martha," she answered. Finally, solved that small mystery. *Okay, let's go on.*

"So your aunt's name is Madeline and they were identical twins?" I continued.

"Not *were*, they *are*. They're both still alive. But how do you know that?" she asked.

"And you also have a sister, a twin, but not identical. Am I correct?" I stayed with the one-line statements, each one helping me plan the next one.

"Yes. Again, how do you know this?" She was curious, but not agitated.

"And your birthday is March 20, 1941?" I added, hoping I wouldn't lose my nerve.

"Okay, you're almost scaring me with this. Please, no more questions. Explain how you know these things," Sophie said and looked at me, narrowing her eyes.

Okay, I thought, *here goes.* My palms were starting to get sweaty, but I remained calm. At that moment, Minnow gave a little kick, as if to tell me to get to it. *Deep breath. Momma, don't fail me now.*

"My mother's name was Stephanie Lachance Koontz. She lived in Oxford, Maine, and her parents were from Canada. She died a few days after I was born. My father, Eddy, provided me with very little information about her. The first thing of hers that he gave me was a letter that she'd written right before she passed away, when I was only a few days old. He gave it to me as I was about to graduate from college. Her letter spoke to me about the choice she had made in wanting to have a child. And while the doctors had warned her that she might die, she took that chance," I started and let that sink in.

"I'm sorry to hear that about your mother," she said. She remained interested and not dismissive.

"A couple of years ago, my father gave me a box that had belonged to her. There were several pictures, some letters, and a few other things. I tried to understand who the people in the pictures were and to explain the letters. In doing so, these things led me to uncover two men. One was an older man who had been wrongly imprisoned for murdering a friend of my mother when she was a child. And the other was a younger man whose lies had led to the older man being in prison for more than forty years. This young man's father was a powerful man and one who stopped at nothing to protect his son's reputation and the family's name." I hesitated for a moment to see if she had a comment.

"Look, I don't know where this is going, but I don't like this story. I'd rather have you leave, if you would." Sophie's face showed her distaste.

"Please, I know this may sound a little scary, but hear me out," I persisted.

"Okay, but I still don't see how this tale of prison and murder makes you know all about me," Sophie stated and leaned back from the edge of the table.

"During the questioning of the younger man—the man who lied—he divulged how my mother had been his girlfriend when they were teenagers. He'd gotten her pregnant and his father sent her away to New Hampshire to have the child. The baby's birth certificate was falsified with another man's name listed as the father and the place of birth. The young man's father also paid for my mother's college education in exchange for her eternal silence." I stopped again.

"Wow, this is really some story," she said but was still not seeing any connection. "But where do you get to knowing about me?"

"Realizing that I had a half sister somewhere, I started looking for her. In my mother's things that I'd found were her journals and papers from college. In checking, I found that your mother and your aunt graduated in the same class at Keene as my mother. I have a picture of my mother when she was in college. She is with either your mother or your aunt. This was the last thing in that box that I couldn't explain. The last thing that could lead me to my sister. I'd like to show it to you," I said and reached into my purse and took out the picture. I placed the picture in front of Sophie and waited. My mother's face—*our* mother's face—was smiling out at her. She had to see it.

"Wow, your mom was pretty, like you. My mom was too," she answered and kept looking at it. *Like you too,* I shouted silently at her.

"As I looked into where my mother could have been sent to have this out-of-wedlock child, I found information that led me to Dr. Heard in Westmoreland Depot. That was where we were before we came here today. This doctor has since passed. But his daughter, who is a physician as well, helped us look through the ledgers to find the record of my mother and the birth of my half sister." My story was slowing down as I was nearing the end. Sophie made no comment but looked from me to the picture and back again.

"Dr. Heard was pretty well-known for doing what was right for a lot of poor girls," she said, showing her empathy.

"On the day my sister was born, there was another baby girl born. She has a mole somewhere on her left side. Both my sister and that girl were taken home by the same mother. Her initials were MHC." And I looked as Sophie's eyes widened. "Among my mother's things was the beginning of a children's story. A story that had beautiful sketches. The sketches showed the yard of Dr. Heard's home in great detail. The story was about a young girl and her sled. The girl had a friend, Annie, and the girl's name in the story was Sophie." I stopped. There, it was out. All of it out and about to blow away with the wind. *Please, reach out and grab it, please.*

"Well, that certainly is interesting," she said and cleared her throat.

"If you don't mind another question, what's your sister's name?" I asked.

"Finally, something you don't know the answer to," she commented almost snidely. But then she quietly answered, "Anne. My sister's name is Anne." She placed the picture back in front of me.

"Hey, Mom, all set with the kitchen. Everything okay out here?" Matt had come back to the porch, where we sat in silence. He looked at the serious faces on the three of us, not knowing what to do.

"I'm fine, Matt. Do go back inside now. I'll be in shortly," Sophie said, and Matt did as he was told. Sophie sat silently, her jaw set in a hard line.

"I'd like to know what you think," I asked, knowing that the worst was about to come. My stomach was turning, or was it Minnow?

"You want to know what I think? You come here with a story that seeks to blow my entire world apart and you want to know what I think? I think this is nothing but lies! I think that you're some type of nut who's coming here to destroy my life, my mother's life, my son's life, and my entire family! Who the hell do you think you are? Looking for the last piece of your puzzle, to add some grace to the fact that your mother had a child out of wedlock! And you want me to believe that I'm that child? That I'm your sister? You've got some nerve! Get out, get out, both of you! Get off my property now, and never, ever come back here!" Sophie was shaking. She stood at the table and pointed toward our car to emphasize that we should leave. Charlie and I quickly stood and left the porch.

"If I could only speak with your mother, with Martha, and show her the picture. Please, I'm asking for your help. You have to understand that I mean no harm," I pleaded with Sophie. She glowered at me from the porch.

"My mother? Well, according to you, *my* mother is dead. Or don't you remember your own story? You'll never speak to my mother or anyone else in this family. Do you hear me? You mean no harm? How did you expect to tell me this cockamamie story and think that it would do no harm?" Sophie was red-faced and gripped the railing of the porch as she spoke.

"I am sorry, so, so sorry," I said, and tears were stinging my eyes. "If you change your mind, here's my phone number and address." I hastily wrote down the information on a piece of paper from my purse. I held it out to her. She refused to take it.

"Change my mind? Get out of here before I call the constable. Go back to wherever the hell in Maine you came from!" And with that, she turned on her heel and walked into the house, slamming the door behind her. I stuck the paper with my name between two boards to keep it from blowing away. Maybe in a day or two? Oh, who was I kidding? Sophie was never going to make that call.

There was nothing to say as we walked to the car, our heads down. The tears streamed down my face as I silently wept. I had left it all, the ugly truth, on the table, and it had blown away. Into the wind of life. At least I'd tried. I understood completely how she felt. When Joseph had told us about how he had fathered Sophie, I called him a liar. Daddy's heart had been ripped from his chest. The woman that he had loved unconditionally had kept this horrible secret and taken it to her grave. I, like Momma had done before me, had taken this one chance to tell the truth to Sophie. The situation had been discussed, but never before had the words been uttered: "You are my sister." There had been so much silence surrounding the facts of Momma's life. And now, finally, the silence had ended.

CHAPTER 34

AS WE DROVE AWAY FROM Sophie and the café, the tears continued. My tears had left a painful lump in my throat. The pressure I'd placed on myself to find Sophie now punched at my heart. And the ache racked my body as I cried.

"Ethel, honey," Charlie said. He'd pulled over and stopped the car, pulling me into his arms. I stayed there until the tears were gone. Wiping my face dry with my hands, I let out a sigh and sat back.

"I guessed this might happen, but I just hoped it would have been different," I said quietly.

"I know you did, honey," Charlie said and held my hand as we began the drive home.

"I understand why Momma couldn't take Sophie home, but why didn't she tell Daddy? They could have gotten her. I know they wouldn't have said anything to Joseph or his family. We could have all been together," I said and looked out the window.

"Ethel, you know your mother made the best decision she could. And if it turns out that Martha and her family did raise both Sophie and Anne as sisters, well, it seems that might have been the best option for your mother. The babies were loved and kept together and not turned over to some other family. If it were like adoption is now, who knows where they would have ended up?" Charlie's voice was gentle and soothing as he spoke of the reality that I hated to hear.

"It makes me feel so sad. When I think about adoption and children that are left behind for whatever reason, I just want to go and give them all good homes," I replied.

"That's my Ethel, wanting to save the world," Charlie said, and I saw the smile light up his face.

"I know what I said is unrealistic, but maybe we could find some room in our lives for another child that got left behind. In another year or so, what do you think?" As Charlie said, I was trying to find a way to right the wrongs of the world.

"Maybe. We'll see how we do with child number 2. How about that?" he said.

"Okay, I've got your word," I said, and I could barely keep my eyes open. Total exhaustion overcame me, and I napped most of the way home, drifting in and out of daydreams. They were a jumbled assortment of the events of the past few years. Voices and places faded in and out. At one point, I felt like I was falling off the edge. Looking down, I saw outstretched arms and a pale light. A soft voice called out to me, and I strained to hear what it was saying. I felt hands touching me, pulling me. I could almost make out what was being said. *Who are you? Why can't I hear you?*

"Ethel. Ethel, honey. Wake up. We're here at your dad's," the soft voice said. "Honey, come on. You're having a dream. Wake up." And of course, the voice was Charlie's. I opened my eyes and saw him smiling back at me.

"Oh, Charlie. I must've been dreaming," I said and sat up for a moment, looking at him.

"You certainly were. Now, come on, let's get into the house. We've got to rescue your dad." He laughed, and instantly I remembered that EC had been with Daddy all day. Why did it seem that we'd been gone for longer than that? As we walked up to the door, we could hear singing and laughter from within.

"That's a good sign," I said and opened the door. As we continued into the house, strains of "Row, row, row your boat" were being sung by quite a range of voices. There was a wonderful aroma of... hmm, what was it? Maybe chocolate chip cookies?

"What's all the racket going on in here?" Charlie asked. There at the table were EC, Daddy, Aunt Ellie, and Uncle Ellsworth, all singing their own version of the song. Broad smiles were on their faces.

"Come on in and join the fun!" Aunt Ellie said. EC held his arms up for me as I came over to his chair. I needed this boy's hug in the worst way. I picked him up and let his little arms circle my neck as he tried to keep singing. The tears came. EC felt the wetness on his cheek and pulled back to look at me. He began to wipe away my tears with his hands.

"I'm not sure who's having more fun," I said as I tried to dry my face. On the table was the remains of a casserole of macaroni and cheese, a bowl of baked stewed tomatoes, as well as a plate of sliced apples, and yes, a big plate of chocolate chip cookies.

"Sit right down, and I'll get a couple more plates. We just finished up. The casserole's still warm," Daddy said. Seeing my tears, he knew and avoided the obvious question for the moment. We took our seats. It was good to sit with these smiling faces, with family.

"I can't tell you when I've had more fun," Aunt Ellie said. She, too, could see the look in my eyes. "This little one has certainly kept us going today."

"What's this 'us'? I thought you were taking EC out to teach him how to fish?" I questioned Daddy. "I thought you said you'd be able to handle him for the entire day?"

"Now hold your horses there, Missy. We did go out and check out the fishing holes. But I didn't have a pole that was small enough for him," Daddy said defensively.

"Problem solved," Charlie reported. "We picked up two child-size poles at a yard sale. Now we'll only need to go to Tubby's for a couple of reels."

"Oh, Aunt Ellie, this macaroni and cheese is so good," I remarked as I tasted my first forkful. The cheese was thick and creamy, with a crunchy buttered-bread topping. It was exactly what I wanted, the taste of comforting food and understanding family.

"It's the same recipe I made when you were little. I don't think there's been a kid in this family that hasn't liked it. And don't be too hard on Eddy. He was good with this little guy until about two," Aunt Ellie said. She patted Daddy on the shoulder as she got up to clear their dinner dishes.

"So what else did you do?" I asked Daddy as I spooned some tomatoes onto the top of my macaroni and cheese. The bits of tomato, celery, onion, and parsley flavored the mac and cheese and added to my contentment. Charlie hadn't wasted any time either and was thoroughly enjoying Aunt Eleanor's homemade cooking.

"Let's see. After swearing him to secrecy about my fishing spots, we took a ride over to Art McCreery's farm and saw some of the new calves and the baby chicks. He liked that. The calves came right up to him and licked his face. And Art let him hold a little chick in his hand. You should have heard him squeal," he said, smiling at the recollection. "Then it was time for lunch, so we went to Andy's for a hot dog. I tell you, he's got Judy charmed to death. I think she filled up his chocolate milk three times for free. After that, we went to Ruthie's for a cookie. Of course, she wouldn't let him go without a bagful of treats. We came back here for some changing and a little nap. And here we are." I could tell by the way Daddy gave me the rundown of their day's events that he'd had a great time.

"And now it's time for Ellie's cookies," Uncle Ellsworth said as he reached over and took one. Aunt Ellie always made the best chocolate chip cookies. They were crispy on the edge, and if they were warm enough, the chocolate was still a little melty. I watched as he took a bite. He closed his eyes. "Yup, I can't ever leave this woman. She cooks too darn good." And we all chuckled.

"Grampa!" EC asked Daddy as he reached toward the plate of cookies. Daddy was only too happy to oblige. He picked one and delivered it to EC's chubby hands. In moments, the chocolate was smeared on both sides of his face. He was a happy boy.

"Well, somebody ask the question," Aunt Ellie said after a thoughtful silence of digesting both food and anticipation. "Do you want to tell us what happened, honey?" I looked into the face of a woman who had come to my rescue countless times over the years, and now she saw what needed to be done.

"I suppose it's better to get it out now," I said and took a deep breath. "We found her. Charlie and I found Sophie."

"Oh, Ethel, Charlie, how in the world?" Aunt Ellie said and clasped her hands together in front of her mouth.

"The address for the doctor was his home. He's long since passed away, but his daughter took over the practice. During the time when Sophie was born, the doctor operated his house as a home for unwed mothers. His daughter still had the records from those days. You wouldn't believe the number of girls who went there. Hundreds of them. They were only listed by initials, but the dates and the other information made me sure it was her. Then there's the fact that another girl, with the same initials as the girl in the college picture with Momma, had taken both babies home. And the grounds of this doctor's home looked exactly like the sketches that Momma drew in her story," I said.

"But how did you find Sophie?" Daddy asked, rather wary of my findings.

"It was only by chance. We were looking for a place to eat, and Abby—that's current Dr. Heard—told us to go to a café in the next town over. It was the same town where the postcard, the one in Gammie's cookbook, had been sent from. We ate lunch, and before we left, we went to check on the things in their yard sale. That was where we found the fishing poles for EC and Minnow. The café owner's son told us the poles had belonged to his mom and that she was a twin, but not identical. Then he brought out some other things, and one of them was a sled. It was *the* sled from Momma's book, I just knew it. I asked him if I could speak to his mom. She came out and said her name was Sophie Anne Blake. The same name on the birth certificate that Henry gave me. She also said that her sister's name was Anne. And that was the name of the other girl in Momma's story." As I retold the information to Daddy and my aunt and uncle, it sounded almost unbelievable to me.

"Holy cow, does that sound like a long shot!" Uncle Ellsworth said. "I'm guessing Sophie didn't buy it?"

"Not at all. She was very angry and told us to leave," I said.

"I hate to say it…," Daddy started.

"I know, Daddy. You don't have to finish. I found what I needed to know and it's all done, for now, at least, until this baby is born." I stopped him before the "I told you so" came out. "I know exactly how she felt. I had the same reaction, too, when Joseph told us his story."

"Ethel, I thought you said no more?" Daddy's voice got sharp as he narrowed his eyes at me.

"Daddy, I know if I can take a little more time with Sophie, I'll get her to listen. Maybe I can even get in touch with Martha," I countered but continued to think about my next steps.

"Ethel! Whatever will we do with you? I guess I'm sorry that you didn't find the person that you thought you would," Daddy said with a slight edge to his voice. "But maybe I wish you hadn't found her at all."

"Daddy! I can't believe you said that," I said and let out another sigh as I shook my head in disbelief.

"Now, now, let's settle down here. Think about what's going to go on in that house now that you've been there. There'll be some stewing, that's for sure. And if things are as you say, then there's been a lot of secrets kept for a lot of years. It's not something that most people take kindly to," Aunt Ellie commented.

And with those insightful words, she brought me back to the time when I would run to her house crying because I didn't understand things. She pushed the plate of cookies toward me and smiled. The antidote for all the world's ills, a simple chocolate chip cookie.

CHAPTER 35

"I THOUGHT PREGNANT WOMEN WERE SUPPOSED to be tired all the time. What the heck are you doing in here at this hour?" Caleb said as he walked through the door and looked up at the clock. It read five forty-five. He put the daily editions of both the *Times* and *Herald* on the side table and hung up his jacket. He unbuttoned the cuffs of his white oxford shirt and rolled them up. Now he was all set.

"I couldn't sleep," I answered and took a sip of my tea. "Coffee's on, and there's a couple of muffins from Ruthie's that I thought you might like."

"Why, thank you. Still and all, don't you have a husband and son to say good morning to?" he asked as he headed into the back room. I could hear him pouring his coffee and rustling the bag to see which muffin he wanted.

"I do, and they sleep like logs. I left them a note telling them that I loved them but I'd joined the circus as the fat lady." I smirked at him as he came and sat down at his desk. He chose the apple cinnamon muffin. The aroma of the spice-rich muffin and the coffee was very satisfying to me, who could only have tea.

"Lots to do today. We should run a follow-up piece about Hinkley, don't you think?" Caleb asked.

"Indeed, we should. What a nut this guy is. Trying to impress Jody Foster? I talked with Frank. He said he's been pretty busy with it as well," I said and got up to check the *New York Times*.

"Frank? When did you talk to him? Last I knew, you went to the doctor on Friday. By the way, how did you make out? Are you okay? And how is the baby?" Caleb asked, his voice a little muffled. He was thoroughly enjoying his treat.

"First, I'm fine. She's a busy little girl. Still a little small, but catching up on the missed time during my nap," I answered. "And I called Frank on Saturday to see if he'd checked on the names of my mother's classmates."

"Saturday? I'm surprised you got him," Caleb said and added, "Did he have anything?"

"He was a busy with the assassination attempt," I said.

"I can only imagine. So okay, where were you on Saturday?" He'd put down his muffin and took a sip of his coffee.

"Robert and Russell were our alarm clocks that morning. They couldn't wait to get my reaction to Lynwood Newcastle. By the way, nice job of hiding that from me. I had to hear it from Mike when we were in the Diner Friday night for supper," I began and reprimanded him for not divulging the information.

"Sorry. Sadie swore me to secrecy," Caleb said, defending himself.

"Then Daddy came along. The brothers are trying to get him to take Lynwood fishing after he does the book signings. Jury's still out on that one," I continued.

"I knew that too," he said and held up his hands to ward off any would-be attacks.

"You're a real stinker, you know that?" I said, and he gave me a sheepish grin. "Daddy had come by to beg me to stop searching for Sophie. But after a little talk full of promises and coaxing, he offered to watch EC so we could go and see if we could find that doctor in New Hampshire. And that was what we did."

"And...?" Caleb motioned with his hands for me to proceed.

"And we found everything. The doctor, who has since passed away, had run a home for unwed mothers back in the day. His daughter, who is also a doctor, showed us the cryptic records. That is to say, he only used initials and not the names. The ledgers showed my mother's initials and details of the birth of a girl who was born on the same day as the birth certificate that I have from Henry. It also listed another girl who had a baby, with the same initials as Momma's friend. Both baby girls were born on the same day. The kicker is, that friend left with both babies." I recounted the story again. "Oh, and the grounds for this house—they're identical to Momma's sketches in her story of *Sophie's Sled.*"

"That was quite a stroke of luck," Caleb commented.

"Wait. You haven't heard the best," I replied. "The doctor recommended a sandwich shop in the next town over for lunch. Quaint place with some great sketches on the walls. The owner's son waited on us and was a chatty kid. He said that his mom was a twin, but not identical. As we were leaving, he was putting stuff out for their yard sale. One of the things was an old sled. That was it. I asked to speak to his mother. She came out, and it was almost like looking in the mirror."

"This is unbelievable," he said.

"I know. I'm not quite sure how all this is even possible," I concurred. "She told me that her name is Sophie Anne Blake. Again, the same name on the birth certificate from Henry. She said her twin sister's name is Anne. I then went on to explain in baby steps what led me to her door."

"Interesting. And her reaction?" Caleb asked.

"As you might expect. We were told in no uncertain terms to get out. And so we did," I finished and took the last sip of my tea.

"And you're certain that this Sophie is your Sophie? It's not conjectures on your part to believe that the initials represent who you want them to be?" he asked.

"I'd swear to it, Caleb. The sketches on display in the sandwich shop were done in the same style as my mother's. The sled, the names, the locations—there's no way to deny that she's not my Sophie," I replied. "But I'll never know now. I wish that her mother had been there. If only I could've talked to her and showed her the picture of the 'Chums.'" I let out a sigh and shook my head.

"You finally find her, the conclusion to your search, and you only end up with more questions," Caleb noted.

"I know. I promised Daddy and Charlie that whatever I found, good, bad, or indifferent, this would be it until after the baby comes along," I finished.

"And what happens if Frank comes up with something? Remember, you did have him checking on those names," Caleb reminded me.

"What else could he find? I know that Sophie's mother was Martha, so that won't be a big discovery. If he finds one or both of them, I realistically won't be able to do anything. Their family has held a big secret for thirty-plus years. Whether or not Sophie starts to question her mother or her aunt, well, that's her prerogative. And then it would depend on what type of answers they come up with in defense of the situation. These were things you didn't talk about. I'm realizing how different things were for women of my mother's generation. They didn't have a lot of options. Having a family or a career was a choice that most weren't given. I'm in awe of the courage that my mother had," I said.

"That's very true. Women have had to sweep a host of topics away from prying and judging eyes. Can you envision what would happen if Sophie does start to ask about the veracity of the claims from a pregnant woman from Maine?" Caleb stated. "'Hi, Mom, my half sister stopped by today to tell me you're not my mom. Can you please pass the carrots?' No, I don't think that would play too well at the dinner table."

"It's always about the why, isn't it? Daddy reminded me that people do what they have to do and not necessarily what they want to do. For whatever reason, Martha took both of those babies and raised them as her own. But why? And consider the fact that both she and her sister, not to mention my mother, all graduated. I can't begin to understand what they all must have been through," I said. Not knowing the reasons bothered the heck out of me.

"It wasn't that long ago that you were faced with similar unbelievable truths about your mother. Give Sophie time. You never know what people will do. She may come to a point in her life when she wants to know the answers to the questions you raised," Caleb responded with his wisdom that usually gave me a moment's pause to consider the different aspects of a situation.

"You're right, of course. I thought the same thing as I was telling the story to Sophie. I've gone about these things in my search for Momma's family, charging ahead in my desire to make things right. Never stopping to think that everyone won't see it my way. Daddy was painfully hurt to find the hidden truth about the love of his life.

And so was I when I realized the perfect portrait that I'd painted of my mother had some flaws. If I only had a little more time." I was conceding my defeat, although not willingly.

"You made your promise. Now you'll need to live with it, for a while, at least. But I know you. At some point you'll find a way. You always do," Caleb stated.

"I will. I just hate having loose ends. But at least I did what I set out to do, and that's more than most people can say," I said.

"And so, my dear assistant editor, it's time to kick our little town into high gear. We've got nine days until opening day for both fishing season and the Emporium—something that folks won't soon forget," Caleb said, giving me a pep talk.

"Aye, aye, sir!" I replied and gave him a salute. "T minus nine and counting!"

CHAPTER 36

F ROM *THE BUGLE*'s WINDOW I had a front-row seat to the building momentum in Piney Bluffs. Opening day of fishing season
always brought a jump-start to the community. But coupled with the
Book Emporium's opening, well, we were certainly alive and ready.
UPS came daily to the Emporium. Sadie looked like a traffic cop
directing delivery men here and her staff there. Her high school students were moving, sorting, and stacking books. An alcove housed
the gift shop, which was quickly filling up with wonderful items.
There were greeting cards, merchandise with the Emporium's logo,
and gifts to commemorate everything, from well-known authors to
items handcrafted in Maine.

Russell and Robert had sent all of Piney Bluffs's residents
an invitation to join them for the opening. They were sparing no
expense with commemorative T-shirts and coffee mugs, drawings for
special gift baskets filled with either books and gifts or baked goodies
from Miss Ruthie's. Sadie was eagerly awaiting the brothers' arrival
to show them just how well this was all coming together. She was
almost as proud of this accomplishment as Russell and Robert were.

The bait shop was having its fair share of commerce as well.
Tubby had partnered with Beulah and her first graduating class of
young women anglers. They were running exhibitions for novice
fishermen each afternoon and early evening on Friday, Saturday, and
Sunday. The back deck of Tubby's was the perfect spot for fly tying,
casting practice, and baiting demonstrations. Some of the seasoned
anglers, like Daddy, had offered to help out and support the young
women in any way that they could. But he admitted, after attending
a couple of sessions, they pretty much had it all covered. Of course,

there was still the strategy of fishing, and that was something only time could teach. Daddy was only too happy to provide his expertise in that area and shared his stories with the young ladies after their classes.

The Inn, Bob and Beulah's fishing camp, and the Spa were almost full for the weekend and into the next week. This wasn't that unusual, as most were returning fishermen and they liked to enjoy a full weekend when the season began. But there were some new guests that were coming to see their favorite author. From reports of the calls placed to different businesses in town, we estimated that there would be a good influx of day visitors for the Emporium's event.

I had begun to run stories about different female authors from Maine. I'd found Maine's first novelist, Sally Wood, often referred to as Madame Wood, wrote several books in the genre of Gothic fiction in her over nine-decade life. Another female author, Florence Brooks Whitehouse, had been a suffragist in addition to her writing. After waging the battle with state senators to win women's right to vote, she continued her quest and worked on the Equal Right's Amendment. And the last was Esther Woods, who was a teacher, journalist, and author. I felt a kindred spirit with her works and her professional life of writing, journalism, and telling the local stories of the people in Maine. I felt a little nudge from someplace deep inside. Whether it was Minnow or Momma, they were letting me know that I, too, had stories to tell.

"*Daily Bugle*, this is Ethel. How can I help you?" I answered the phone on Thursday. "Yes, that's correct, sir. Lynwood Newcastle will be here next Saturday. Yes, we're excited about it too. He's due here about eleven o'clock. Thank you for calling."

"He's really turning out to be quite the big draw," Caleb remarked.

"That's the tenth call I've had today. People wanting to make sure they've heard right. Even folks in town are getting into it. Elva over at the library said his books have been loaned out ever since the news broke," I said and smiled. "Daddy's really getting worried now."

"That's right, the fishing trip," Caleb remembered.

"Daddy is so worried that people will be following them to the fabled Koontz secret spots." I laughed.

"Only Eddy can bring you to the real heart of a situation." Caleb laughed too.

"What's the heart of the situation?" Sadie said and slipped in like the wind. Wearing a white cardigan sweater over her blue T-shirt from Tubby's, she still looked letter-perfect in her jeans and sneakers.

"How do you do that?" I asked. "I never even heard the door open."

"Years of training trying to sneak out of my parents' house when I was a teenager." Sadie smiled and quickly took a seat.

"What's up, my dear?" Caleb asked as he blew his wife a kiss.

"I need to catch my breath for a minute," she admitted as she folded her hands over her middle and closed her eyes. In less than ten seconds, they were open again. And she was sitting up, looking like she'd had a three-hour nap. "Okay, all set now. What's up with you two? What's at the heart of the situation?"

"And how do you do that? You must have one heck of a metabolism," I said. "I was just saying that with the excitement that's building over Lynwood Newcastle, Daddy thinks he's in danger of having his secret fishing spots exposed by Newcastle's faithful fans."

"Your father and his fishing. I don't think I've ever known a man more passionate about that," Sadie said.

"You do know the rest of his brothers, my uncles, don't you?" And I laughed. "I was born knowing that fishing was two things: something to be respected and something to excel in."

"And you're a better woman for it," she agreed.

"That I am. I wouldn't have traded any of it for the world. Daddy has a very special bond with his brothers, and fishing only makes it that much stronger," I added.

"Speaking of family, Caleb tells me that you found Sophie. How wonderful!" Sadie stated.

"It's true, I found her, but I'm not sure *wonderful* is the word I'd use," I said and frowned. "My idea of finding a long-lost sister and Sophie's conversation with some crazy pregnant lady claiming to be her sister and that her mother isn't really her mother, well, you can understand her reaction."

"Facing a possible reality that changes your entire life is indeed a hard pill that most people wouldn't want to swallow," Sadie said and nodded in agreement.

"So how's the Emporium?" I asked, changing the subject.

"Ready for business. I don't think we could fit anything else in there. It's perfectly laden with the best books and interesting gift items. The brothers will be so pleased when they see how it's all come together. And Charlie, why, he's been in every day, going through a punch list of minor things. He is such a perfectionist," Sadie said proudly.

"That's a good way to be," Caleb noted. "Speak of the devil, here he comes." I looked out the window and saw Charlie walking toward *The Bugle*. He always made me smile with his ruggedly good looks. Dressed in a chambray and jeans, he had a pencil tucked behind his ear and a clipboard in his hand. He saw me watching him, and he waved.

"You know, I can put an addition onto *The Bugle*, Caleb. It'll help give you a little more space for your visitors," Charlie joked as he came into the office.

"I may actually need a little more space when we get the PB Press up and running," Caleb said.

"PB Press? What's that? Surely, it's not something to do with peanut butter," Charlie said and laughed.

"Hardly. The PB Press, short for Piney Bluffs, will be a small shop production service for local authors or anyone who has things to be printed. A lot of universities have them. So what do you think?" Caleb asked.

"That's great news. I definitely can build that for you," said Charlie as he walked into the back area to get a sense of the proposed expansion. "Probably need to upgrade the electrical while we're at it." With that, Caleb got up and joined Charlie.

"Whatever we need to do, we'll do. Let's get together in a few weeks. By then, I'll have the complete information on the electrical and space requirements," Caleb said. The phone started to ring again. Sadie waved goodbye and headed out the door.

"Good afternoon. *Daily Bugle*, this is Ethel," I answered. Charlie was making his exit, too, and blew me a kiss as he followed Sadie's lead.

"Do you ever sound crabby?" And the always-annoyed Irish tones of Mike O'Brien came through the phone loud and clear.

"If you lived in Maine, you'd sound like this too," I kidded back to him. "But then, your family wouldn't know what to do with the likes of a happy Mike O'Brien."

"True. Being annoying does have its benefits. I don't get asked much for help by those bleeding-heart types. Which brings me to you, Ms. Bleeding Heart 1981." His salty tones were softening.

"And I'm on your to-do list because…?" I asked.

"Thought you'd like to know what we've done for your little piece of heaven," he offered.

"You should have told me the other day when you were here. So okay, let's hear it, the grand plan from the master," I replied.

"I told you, the boys had me by the, ah, just say I was sworn to secrecy, and I did tell you, just not as soon as I knew the news. So then. The *Herald's* going to run a feature piece on Russell and Robert and their story of the publishing world and how they'd found their way to Piney Bluffs. That's set to run this Sunday in the magazine section. We'll put a piece in on Friday for events in New England, including your openings up there. It's a new segment we're trying out. And the boys from WBZ and I'll be out the day of, for the ribbon cutting. Of course, we'll get the feature interview with Mr. Newcastle," he relayed.

"Thanks, Mike. All kidding aside, you know how much this means to us," I said.

"Holy mother, don't go getting all mushy on me. I don't know why I do this for you. You're more trouble than you're worth," he replied. "I'm only doing this so when St. Peter gets to checking on me, he can see that I was good for something."

"You have to admit, we caught you on your very first visit to Piney Bluffs," I reminded him.

"Yeah, you and the whole sappy lot of you. You got me, hook, line, and sinker," he joked and laughed.

"Mike! I swear, if you were here, I'd...," I scolded him.

"Now, don't go getting all up in arms. I don't want you to go into early labor. How're you doing, by the way?" Mike loved to kid but did have a soft spot for me and what Piney Bluffs was all about.

"Feeling good, thanks for asking. Counting the days to the middle of June. I can't remember if I told you we're having a girl." And now the sparring had ended and it was a conversation between old friends.

"Oh, God bless you, and double so if she's born a redhead. I could write a book about raising the likes of those girls. Let me know when you need help," he offered. "Mine'll be the death of me for sure."

"They're such lovely girls," I said. He and his wife were raising five redheaded, strong-willed Irish lasses. And they were, as he confessed, the root cause for his hair turning gray.

"Lovely, yes. You let me know when yours turns twelve going on twenty. Then you'll see. Well, you've wasted enough of my time. See you next week," Mike said.

"Thanks for the warning," I joked back at him. A click, and he was gone.

"Words of wisdom from Mike?" Caleb asked.

"None other," I answered. "There'll be a nice piece in Sunday's *Herald*, and BZ will be out the day of."

"You feeling okay?" Caleb asked, and I could see the look of concern on his face.

"I'm fine, a little more tired than usual, I guess," I replied. "Although it might be time for a trip to Ruthie's for a little afternoon snack."

"I think that's just what you need. While you're at it, find something for me. Don't let Sadie know. For some reason, she thinks I need to be on a diet," he said and rolled his eyes.

"Diet? Seriously? You look fit and trim," I stated and got up from my desk.

"It's not how much I eat, it's what I eat. She read some article about fats and how the body processes these things." He looked perturbed.

"Well, she is managing a bookstore, and I would think that there's a pretty fair number of books in the health and nutrition section," I reminded him.

"I know that, but I feel great. Even now, eight years after the heart attack, there's been nothing," Caleb replied.

"She only wants to keep you around for a long time. I'll get you something healthy," I offered and grabbed my sweater as I left the office. The day was pleasant, with the strong spring sun providing a nice warmth to the chilly edges of this April day. As I walked across to Ruthie's, I saw a few people standing on the porch of the Emporium, peeking in the windows. A good sign. Folks were eager to explore their new business.

Pappy Lewis had come out to sweep his porch and held up a hand to wave to me. The general store was great place for people to get all those extras that weren't available at Tubby's. From all the grocery essentials to household items, Pappy was constantly expanding his inventory to be responsive to the needs of the clientele. While it was true, we didn't have a chain grocery store or a shiny, new department store, we had what we needed. I waved back to acknowledge him.

The lights appeared to be out in Ruthie's. I checked my watch: three thirty. Maybe she was done for the day. I tried the door, and it was open. There was no one around, the tables had been cleared, and there wasn't a sign of any activity from the kitchen.

"Hello? Ruthie? It's Ethel. Are you there?" I called out and waited. Maybe she'd just forgotten to shut the light off and lock the door, I figured. And then I heard the sound of someone crying. "Ruthie? Is that you? Are you all right?" I quickly went into the back kitchen, and there sat Ruthie, the woman who'd been my rock for more times than I'd care to count, crying. She looked up when she heard me and smiled. Her cheeks were wet, and her eyes were red.

"Oh, Ethel," she said softly through little sobs. Sheets of baking powder biscuits lay waiting to be baked. She was sitting on a stool at her counter. Wisps of her thick gray hair were escaping from her bun, and she kept pushing them behind her pen, which was ever present in her top knot. An old cookbook lay open in front of her. It looked familiar. As I came to give her a hug, I saw that it was her mother's, the one she'd shown me a while back. It was open to the recipe for the biscuits, with the note from her mother on how to triple the recipe.

"What's all this about? Here, let's dry those tears before I have to learn how to bake bread," I said as I took one of the bread towels and dabbed at her face.

"I couldn't risk my reputation letting you bake bread." She sniffed back her runny nose and let out a little chuckle as she took the towel from me.

"Looks like we need to turn the ovens on for these biscuits. What temp for them? Is three hundred degrees about right?" I said, hoping I could break whatever moment she'd gotten herself into.

"Three hundred? My dear child, you cook these at three hundred and you'll be another day older by the time they're done. Four twenty-five. Here, let me do it or you'll burn yourself," she scolded me and got up to turn the ovens on. She pulled her apron straight and cleared her throat.

"So?" I asked as I pulled out another stool and took a seat. Ruthie moved the trays over to get them lined up for the oven.

"So what?" she replied, not looking up, and started to clean up the bowls.

"At least let me help wash," I said and went to the sink to start some water. "So what's with the tears and making, by the looks of it, a triple batch of biscuits?"

"Oh, an old woman's foolishness. The church ladies are having a lunch tomorrow and wanted to know if they could get my recipe. Well, I told them I'd make the biscuits. They only have that old Hotpoint, which is pretty much on its last leg," she explained as she fussed with baking sheets.

"And the answer to the tears?" I pushed. She had stopped crying now and was avoiding eye contact.

"I got a little sentimental, that's all. Thinking about what I'm doing with the boys, opening the Emporium. And publishing a cookbook—my cookbook, with some of my mother's recipes. Well, I started feeling a little sorry for myself and wished I had some family to share it with." She looked down as she picked at a nonexistent piece of something on her apron. When she picked her head up, tears had started again.

"Oh, Ruthie, we're all family here in Piney Bluffs. Remember, you told me that yourself. We're not the family that you might have planned for, but we're all yours. And we couldn't be prouder of all that you've done for us, for the town, and most importantly, for you. Within the walls of this bakery, you've created a family that shares coffee, the news, both happy and sad. The food that you bake gives everyone a sense that someone cares to bake the very best for them, as only a true family member would. Your mom would be so proud to know that her one recipe gave birth to all this," I said, pouring my heart out to one of the very best women in my life.

"Ethel, what would I do without you? Giving an old woman that kick in the pants when she needs it. Now, come here and I'll show you how to bake these so they're light and fluffy." And Ruthie was back to Ms. Ruthie: chief baker, mistress of her own ship, author, and entrepreneur.

I stayed with her for the next hour while we baked and talked back and forth about the similarities in our lives. The loss of mothers and the loss of siblings left us feeling incomplete. But with the help of each other and the friends from this town, we'd managed to fill that void.

I know that when each one of us is alone with our thoughts, tears will most certainly come, as they had today for my dear Ruthie. Tears help relieve that ache, even if only for a moment. The reason for the aches will never leave us. I think that every one of us in Piney Bluffs had that moment. It's what makes us human, to have that memory, good or bad. And consoling one another in those moments of tears, why, that's what makes us family.

CHAPTER 37

THE EARLY-MORNING SKIES ON OPENING day were ominous. The dark-gray clouds of night were not yielding to the brightening sky. Most fishermen would agree that a cool morning with a cloud-covered sky was near-perfect conditions for fishing. How fitting that our guest author also relished this environment for his tales of dark suspense.

I checked my watch. Four thirty. I was sipping my second cup of tea in the office. I'd never been able to sleep past three o'clock on opening day. It must be genetic, I told Charlie. I got ready and left the house as silently as possible so as not to disturb my men. Andy had opened the Diner at four and already had a full counter, with more folks wandering in. From *The Bugle*'s window, I saw Judy stifle a little yawn as she placed steaming cups of coffee in front of the early-rising diners. Andy's was famous for his opening day Twofer Special. Two cups of coffee, two eggs, two pieces of bacon, and two slices of toast for two dollars. The thought of a couple of soft-poached eggs and rye toast was making me hungry.

But I was more tempted by the piece of blueberry cake that I'd bought yesterday from Ruthie's. Knowing that the baked goods would be flying off the shelf today, I'd laid in an assortment for the office, just in case. The lights in the bakery dining area went on, and I saw Ruthie, hands on her hips, looking out over the green. She'd always started her baking at three in the morning. Turning on the lights in the front area signaled that the bakery was fully stocked and ready for business. She looked over toward *The Bugle*, noticing the light from my desk lamp. I saw her strain to see who was in our office. Succeeding in seeing me, she raised her hand and waved. I blew her a kiss, and thus our day could start.

About a half hour later, the car from the Inn pulled up in front of the Emporium, dropping off Russell and Robert. They quickly made their way up the steps. They were dressed in identical yellow sweaters, the signature color for the Book Emporium. They checked the podium that had been placed on the porch yesterday. Later on, Tubby would bring over the digital scale and weighing counter for the noontime contest weigh-in and winner announcement. They looked up at the placement of the sign. Charlie had mounted the sign in the center front of the roof. The tarp had been set to come down with a slight tug of the strings. Satisfied with the exterior, they unlocked the door and went in.

The lights flicked on and dimmed as they adjusted the lighting. I could see them flit from place to place within the shop like two brightly colored butterflies. They did a quick run-through of the shop, adjusting items to look just so. Taking seats, they tried out the overstuffed leather chairs. No sooner had they sat than up on their laps appeared the cats. Russell had wanted the Emporium to have two cats, and so Sadie had found Ricki and Roxie at McCreery's farm a few months ago. They'd had their visit to the vets to be fixed, have shots, and now were settling in, content and warm, away from the cold of the barn. Roxie was an orange tabby, like Mr. Striper, and Ricki was a gray tabby. Both were the sweetest cats and were happy to have the brothers give them their full attention.

Satisfied that the shop was in good order, they made their way to Ruthie's. I saw the embraces and handshakes between the partners. Then I saw Russell putting something in his mouth. *Those two!* I laughed to myself. I thought they wanted the partnership just for the goodies. I heard a noise at the door, and looking over, I saw Daddy.

"Good morning, Daddy. Are you ready for opening day?" I asked as I went to give him a kiss on the cheek.

"Well, of course. I couldn't sleep, so I figured I'd come have breakfast. Want some?" he replied. He was dressed in his heavy green cotton fishing pants, which he wore under his waders. His thermal shirt peeked out from under a red-and-black buffalo plaid shirt. I knew his fishing vest was in the truck, ready with whatever new fly he'd invented for today's unknowing opponents. Cocked to one side on his head was his porkpie hat, with his fishing license clipped to the side. He'd had that hat for as long as I could remember. It looked it, too, with stains from whatever fish or worm he'd caught or used. A good idea for a Father's Day present from EC, I thought.

"No, thanks. I've got a couple of things from Ruthie's that I'll have later on when my stomach is up to it," I said.

"You feeling all right? You're not keeping anything from me, are you?" He was looking straight into my eyes with the truth-seeking look only a father can give his daughter.

"I'm fine, Daddy. My stomach and this pregnancy are not the match made in heaven," I tried to reassure him. "Now, go have your breakfast and get ready for a good day of fishing. And remember, you have a special guest to take out this afternoon," I reminded him.

"Wait a minute, I never said that I was taking this guy out. I have to size him up first. I'll let you know," he said and gave me a shrug of his shoulders as he went out the door.

I went back to my desk and took yesterday's *Times* from the table. Still more stories about the crazy Hinckley. I yawned and took another sip of my tea. *If I could get a little nap before everything happens,* I thought. Wait, what was that noise? A gun? I jumped with a start at the noise.

"Ethel? Don't you have a home to sleep in?" And it was Caleb's gentle voice that brought me back from my daydream.

"What do you mean? I was just reading the paper," I answered, quite offended.

"Then you must've been reading by osmosis. You've got newsprint on your face." He let out a little chuckle.

"Wait, what time is it?" I asked as I got my mirror out of my desk. He was right; my left cheek clearly had *Times* on it from the ink transfer. I started to rub it off with a Kleenex, which was only making it smear, creating a black blob.

"It's six in the morning, just in case you've been here all night. And yes, the shotgun start at Tubby's just went off," Caleb replied with a worrisome look on his face.

"I got in a little before four. Couldn't sleep. Never can on opening day," I said as I got up and went to the back sink. Finally removing the newsprint, I came back to my desk. Morning had finally broken through the dark clouds, but the sun seemed hesitant to show. Fishermen were rapidly dispersing to their favorite spots now that the start was official. It was time for the second wave of activity to begin. The regular breakfast-goers that weren't fishermen were starting to filter into the Diner and Ruthie's.

"Here come Mike and the crew," Caleb said as the truck drove past the office and found a spot near the Emporium. Three men, one of whom was Mike, got out of the white box truck with WBZ emblazoned on the sides. They went right to work and started their routine. The antenna was raised, lights were tested on and off and on, and finally Mike did a test interview in front of the camera. Caleb and I watched for a half hour or better.

"It's amazing how technology is changing. They used to come in here with big rigs and all kinds of wires going every which way. Now they're pretty much self-contained," I noted. "Here he comes, get ready." The other two guys were going over to the Diner. They motioned for Mike to join them, but he pointed toward *The Bugle*, indicating he was coming here. Dressed today in a sport coat and jeans, he looked happy to be here. The door opened with his usual banter.

"This town gets any smaller, and I can bring the whole damned place to Boston in the back of the truck," Mike said as he shook Caleb's hand.

"And what an improvement for Boston it would be! How are you, Mike?" Caleb said and returned the handshake.

"Mean and miserable as always. And look at you, Ms. Ethel. When you stop having kids, you know there's still a spot for your spunky chat in Boston. BZ's always looking for a know-it-all like you," Mike said and gave me a hug.

"I've missed that miserable face. How're the girls? Couldn't get one of them to come along today even with our famous guest?" I said and smiled at him.

"For the love of everything that's holy, they are five of the most contrary women, not girls anymore," Mike answered. "I told them about Newcastle, but they've got some damn prom to get the youngest one ready for. I already had to go dress-shopping—what an ordeal that was. The five of them and I. They thought it was fun, while I needed a drink. I hate to think when one of them gets married. But my wife, bless her beautiful soul, has got tonight all on her own. But I'm hoping I might make it back in time to give her date-the-old-angry-Irish-father speech. I love to watch how they squirm."

"You are horrible. That poor boy," I said and shook my head.

"Poor boy, my sweet aunt Irene's heart. She so much as looks like he's laid a hand on those lovely red tresses, why, I swear, I'll…" Mike was getting fired up.

"How about a coffee and something from Ruthie's?" I asked, cutting into his line of steam.

"That sounds good to me. I hope you got high test," Mike replied, and it seemed his blood pressure was coming down a notch.

"That we do," I stated.

For the next few hours, we talked back and forth about Piney Bluffs, Boston, and everything in between. From the attempted assassination attempt on Reagan to the Boston Red Sox, we carried on like the three friends that we were. Around ten o'clock, an old black Buick pulled up in front of the office. A tall dark-haired man with thick aviator-style glasses got out and walked to the door. He was easily recognizable. He was dressed in a sport coat over a turtleneck. He wore jeans, sneakers, and his signature red ball cap that had SEBAGO LAKE embroidered in white on the front.

"Good morning," he said as he entered. "I'm Lynwood Newcastle, and I hear I've got an interview to do."

"Good morning, I'm so pleased to meet you. I'm Ethel O'Connor, assistant editor," I said as I got up. "Please have a seat. Can I get you a coffee?"

"That'd be great. Just black, please," he replied and took the other chair next to Mike.

"Mike O'Brien, from the *Herald* and WBZ. I'll be doing the interview. Nice to meet you," Mike said and reached out to shake his hand.

"I'm Caleb Johnson, editor of *The Bugle*," Caleb said. "Thanks for coming today. I can't tell you how much this means to have you with us." I brought out the coffee and refreshed the plate of Ruthie's baked goods.

"These look great," Newcastle said as he took a chocolate-dipped almond crescent.

"Baked right over there," I said and indicated Ruthie's. "She's unveiling her cookbook today as well."

"That's right. My agent told me that your Emporium is a partnership with the Browning Brothers and the lady who owns the bakery," he offered as he took a bite of my favorite cookie.

"That's exactly right. We're all very proud to see an idea come to reality," I replied.

"Wow, this almond cookie is great! And those boys are a hoot. I've met them when I go into the city. They really love what they've found out here. By the way, Ethel, we have the same alma mater, don't we?" Lynwood asked.

"That's right, you were a couple of years ahead of me," I stated, surprised at the homework he'd done. "Best education in journalism."

"You got that right. Now, my agent tells me that there's a fishing competition as well?" Newcastle continued. "Would I have time to get in on it?"

"I'm afraid you're a little late. They've been out since six. Weigh-in's at noon. Then we'll have the Emporium opening, and then you'll have an interview with Mike. After that, we'd like you to do a reading from whichever of your books you'd like. Sadie—she's the manager of the Emporium—has set up the area for book signing, and that should wrap it up," Caleb said as he went through the schedule.

"Okay, good schedule, I got it. But is there any time to do some fishing after? I hear you've got some great spots around the lake. I brought all my stuff," he asked.

"Well, of course. I've asked my dad to be your guide once he gets back, but...," I started.

"But what?" Lynwood asked.

"He's got to size you up first," I admitted with a chuckle.

"Wouldn't be a fisherman from Maine if he didn't." And with Newcastle's response, I knew that he and Daddy would be fine.

"Can I go see the Emporium now?" he asked. "I'd like to get to know my surroundings and the people. And maybe grab a box of these goodies from that bakery. My wife and kids would really like them."

"Sure can. Let me go over with you," Mike said, and he and Lynwood got up and left the office.

"Well, that was certainly a surprise," I said to Caleb. "Who would've thought that Lynwood Newcastle would drive himself to an event?"

"I think it's not that surprising. He seems like a pretty even-keeled guy, even if he does write creepy books," Caleb commented.

"And I think Daddy will love taking him fishing," I added.

"I think so too," Caleb said. "Remember what your dad's always been telling you about his philosophy of fishing? It's not so much the catching of fish that's important, it's everything that leads up to it. The waiting and watching and how you fill that time—that, some-times, is the most important. And I think the waiting time between the two of them would be some of the best conversation there is."

"You've really been listening to him, haven't you?" I said. "Daddy surprises me with the observations that he's made about life."

"Well, he's seen a lot of life. More than half of his life was before you arrived on the scene. Going through the loss of his mother and father, the realities of war, the death of your mother. You've probably been the easiest time in his life. Well, except for the past few years with all that you've dug into," Caleb noted and gave me a smile.

"I know. I sometimes forget all that he's gone through. But that's because he doesn't say much unless I really drag it out of him. I mean, for crying out loud, every bit of information about my mother has come from my insistence and not his offering," I said, somewhat defeated.

"Ethel, your dad falls into a category of people I've come to know as the observers. They take in all that's around them, care-fully processing the pros and cons of situations. They only offer their opinions when prodded. They are most times the wisest of people.

The others are those who would intend for us know everything they think about," Caleb stated.

"Charlie thinks that way too. He certainly is an observer. So how did you get so wise?" I asked, realizing how much my boss and mentor was truly a good friend that life had given me.

"Time. Time is what gives you the experiences to draw from, process, and decide," he replied.

"So you'll always be wiser than me," I stated.

"I have to. Otherwise, you'll take this whole damn thing over and leave me out in the cold. Now, let's get ready for the observations of the day," he said and laughed.

And thus today's lesson had ended.

CHAPTER 38

NOONTIME HAD ARRIVED, THE SUN finally won out, and the festivities were about to begin. A bright-yellow sash was strung across the front of the Book Emporium's double doors. Taking their place on the porch, Russell and Robert shook the hands of Ruthie, Lynwood, and Sadie. Caleb was nearby with his camera, ready to take pictures for *The Bugle*. Mike O'Brien's crew was standing by with their camera and microphones, waiting for broadcast time. Charlie had brought along EC, who was now perched on his daddy's shoulders to see the *pfsh*, as EC put it. Ginny had come down for the day and was standing with us. Daddy was over to the side with my uncles and his other fishing buddies. When he looked over at us, he gave us a wave, which I really thought was just for Ginny.

"This is so exciting," Ginny said. "I can hardly wait to see the shop. I even brought my books with me, so Mr. Newcastle can sign them."

"I know. The Emporium adds another great reason for people to love Piney Bluffs. There isn't another shop like this for miles around," I agreed. "And then there's the fishing competition."

"Don't I know it! Eddy's been talking about this all week. Yesterday we went for dinner early so he could come back and get his shut-eye," she said.

"That's Daddy," I added. "Did he say if he'll take Lynwood fishing?"

"He told me he wouldn't know until he meets him," she answered. I shook my head as the microphone came to life with a finger-tapping.

"Gather 'round, everyone. Good day to you all, and welcome to the grand opening of the Piney Bluffs Book Emporium. For those of you who don't know us, I'm Robert Browning, and this is my brother, Russell. I can't tell you how happy we are to have found our way to Piney Bluffs more than ten years ago. We thank you, especially Big Bob, for welcoming two bumbling fishermen into your community. We also want to thank Miss Ruthie for her vision and partnership," Robert began his remarks as the crowd assembled. The crowd applauded at the mention of Ruthie's name. From fishermen to town folks to visitors, there were about two hundred people that were here in Piney Bluffs for this event. Tubby and his crew had begun weigh-ins around eleven and continuously posted the results on their tote board. Tubby signaled to Russell that they were ready to announce a winner.

"I'd like to get to the first order of business, and that's the winner of the opening-day contest. We have two categories. One for the biggest fish and second for top total combined weight for three. Robert and I are happy to donate two one-hundred-dollar gift certificates to Tubby's, as well as two fifty-dollar gift certificates to the Emporium, one for each of the winners. And to top it off, as a courtesy from the fishing equipment distributors, both winners will receive a two-night, all-expenses-paid fishing trip to Canada, complete with guide. Now, are you ready, Tubby?" Russell asked. And with that, Tubby turned the tote board around to face the audience. Murmurs came from the fishermen that were crowded around the board. Russell handed the mike down to Tubby.

"For the biggest catch of the day, Ellsworth Koontz, with a nice brown trout weighing in at three and half pounds. And for the combined weight for three, a brookie and two browns, totaling eight pounds, four ounces, Linda Richards. Linda's a senior in high school and one of Beulah's first graduates. She's got her eyes set on following in Beulah's footsteps and becoming a Maine guide. Oh, I almost forgot. For anybody that wants to, Alice, up at the Inn, is willing to put on a personalized fish fry tonight with your catch from today's competition. Come over and see me for the details," Tubby announced. Hoots and cheers went up from the crowd as the two winners made their way to the porch. Beulah gave Linda a pat on the back as she passed by. I could see Daddy shaking his head but smiling at his brother. The winners stood with Russell, Robert, and Ruthie as Caleb snapped their pictures. As the winners left the podium, Mike ushered them over to the weigh-in area for a couple of quick sound bites. Daddy walked over to join us.

"Well, if it couldn't be me, I guess I'm happy it was my brother," Daddy said, shaking his head.

"You can't win all the time, Daddy," I reminded him. "Maybe if you're nice to him, he might take you to Canada."

"That's what I told him too. And be happy that one of Beulah's girls won. She's the future of fishing," Ginny added. "You're always saying that you have to teach the next generation to preserve what we have. Now stop being grumpy."

"Oh, I know, and I'm not grumpy. I had a really good one that slipped off right before I set the hook. Was more than Ellie's, that's for darn sure," Daddy admitted. "Now, what do I have to do with the creepy author?"

"Daddy, he's not creepy, he writes suspense novels," I scolded him. And the microphone came to life once more.

"And now for the unveiling and grand opening," Robert said as he stepped to the side. "We give you the Piney Bluffs Book Emporium!" He, Russell, and Ruthie took ahold of the tarp's strings. The tarp floated to one side, revealing the beautifully carved sign. Applause and cheers went up from the crowd. To continue the momentum, Robert followed up with the introductions.

"We have two Maine authors with us today. Our first is our very own Miss Ruthie O'Hara, who has published her first cookbook with the secret recipes for her delectable goodies," Robert said and stood aside for Ruthie. Ruthie was wearing black slacks today and a red shirt under her white chef coat. She had donned her chef hat to finish her outfit.

"Thank you, Robert and Russell, for helping me to realize my dreams, both with my cookbook and the Emporium. The best a person can do is to make improvements any way they can to the world around them. Well, Piney Bluffs, you are my world. And I hope that's what the Emporium does for my Piney Bluffs's family," Ruthie said and handed the mike back to Russell. Everyone applauded our hometown favorite. Ruthie put a hand up to her eye to wipe the tear away.

"And now, our special guest today is one of Maine's premier authors. And a heck of a fisherman, I'm told. He's a master of suspense, currently with two of his novels being made into a television show. I am proud to introduce, Mr. Lynwood Newcastle, creator of the Sebago Lake Mystery series. Lynwood…" And Robert held the mike out for Lynwood.

"Thank you, Robert, Russell, and Ruthie. By opening this book emporium, you've shown your commitment in preserving and making available one of the best forms for furthering education, providing entertainment and relaxation, known to man and womankind. The book. Next to fishing, that is," Lynwood said. And with the last reference to fishing, the crowd let out a chuckle. I looked at Daddy, and he was smiling at the comment. "I am honored to be your guest today. What you have done today should be a blueprint for all small towns. Congratulations!"

"And now before we invite you to step inside the Piney Bluffs Book Emporium, Sadie, do you have the scissors?" Russell said. Sadie handed the scissors over to Lynwood.

"Usually in my books, if someone has scissors in their hands, then there's probably a body lying around," Lynwood deadpanned and peered off to the side. The crowd hesitated a moment and then began to look around, as if they should be looking for a body. "Just kidding with you," Lynwood finished. The throng laughed again as he cut through the ribbon. As the bright-yellow sash fell away, another round of applause and cheers came up from the crowd. Sadie stood back and welcomed Lynwood inside first, to take his place for the reading. People filed in, "Oohing" and "Aahing" over the beautiful books and gifts.

Ruthie had taken her place as well at a table for signing her cookbook. Her customers clustered around her, picking up their copies and wanting to know which of the recipes of their favorite goodies had been included within the glossy pages. Ruthie was glowing from the attention.

The crowds gathered around to shake Lynwood's hand and ask questions about the television series. He graciously talked with each one. As the crowed quieted down, Lynwood began to read from *The Sinking of Even Keel*. It was the tale of Jack Hendricks, a disbarred attorney from Boston who'd taken the job as winter caretaker of the Lakeside Motel deep in the woods of Maine. Lynwood's deep voice was captivating, and the crowd was silent as he read from his favorite parts. When he was finished, they applauded and lined up to have their books signed.

"Well, Daddy, what do you think?" I asked.

"I can't tell too much from someone reading a story. I need to talk to him, you know, man-to-man," Daddy replied. "I'll wait until the line goes down. Hey, look, there's some free samples from Ruthie's." Daddy pointed to several trays that had been put out for the grand opening, and he took Ginny over to the counter.

"Ethel, so what's going on with your dad? Is he going to take Lynwood fishing?" Robert and Russell pulled me off to one side, away from Daddy's earshot.

"He's got to talk to him first, he said. But I think he's softening," I answered.

"Oh, I do hope so. This is going to be such a feather in our caps," Robert said. "Oh, look, there goes Eddy." Daddy had taken his place at the end of the line, with Ginny in front of him, to get her books signed. Finally standing in front of Lynwood, the two shook hands as introductions were made.

"Fingers crossed," I said as we three stood and waited. The conversation was low but ended with a laugh and both men looking at their watches. Daddy came back over to us.

"Nice guy," Daddy said, grabbing another cookie from the tray.

"You got 'nice guy' from a few words and a handshake?" I asked. Robert and Russell were all ears about the captivating three-minute encounter.

"Yup. That and a couple of questions," Daddy remarked through his chewing.

"What kind of questions?" Russell asked, hoping for the answer to life itself.

"Can't tell you. Only between him and me." Daddy smiled like a Cheshire cat and finished his cookie. "Well, got to get ready. We're leaving in fifteen minutes. I got a couple of spots to show him."

Daddy gave Ginny a little wink and left Russell, Robert, and me standing and wondering about what just happened. Mike and the crew had come in for Lynwood's interview with the Emporium interior as its backdrop. In about fifteen minutes, Lynwood said his goodbyes to all of us. We watched as he went to his car, tossed his sport coat into the back seat, and grabbed his fishing gear from the trunk. Daddy pulled up with his truck, and Lynwood got in. I shook my head as they drove away.

"I'd like to be a fly on the wall with those two," Mike said. "That would make for some interesting conversation."

"You know, I thought that, too, at first. But I think it'll be quiet time between two fishermen," I commented.

"You're probably right," Mike agreed. "Well, Ethel, we've got to get back to the city before you roll up the sidewalks."

"You'd better hurry, before we take away the roads too," Caleb joked. Mike said his goodbyes to Caleb and me, the crew packed up the remainder of their equipment, and they were gone.

We walked back into the Emporium, where Sadie and her staff were busy with customers. Russell, Robert, and I took seats in the chairs. Ricki and Roxie jumped up, only too happy to have laps to sit on as they purred under the attention. Armed with bags of books and gifts, people stopped to thank the brothers for all that they'd done. Ruthie was still signing books and giving hugs.

"Hey, sleepyhead," Charlie said to me.

"What do you mean?" I asked, blinking my eyes open.

"You've had your eyes closed for about three minutes. Let's take you home," he said, and EC climbed into my lap.

"Bbbyy," EC said and patted my belly.

"Yes, that's your baby sister in there," I told him. EC looked at me as only a toddler could and put his eyes on my belly, as if trying to see inside of me. Minnow gave a little kick at the slight pressure on her. We all laughed at this simplest of actions. Already a bond between brother and sister, I thought.

"But I want to talk to Daddy about his fishing," I protested.

"He'll let you know, I'm sure," Charlie said and held his hand out to help me up.

"Time to take her home," Caleb said. "We've had quite the successful day, I would say."

"Thank you, thank you, thank you ever so much, Charlie, for building this beautiful place," Russell gushed, with Robert nodding while sampling another cookie.

"Don't thank me, you all were the ones with the great idea," Charlie replied, downplaying his carpentry skills.

"I have to give you the biggest hug," Sadie said and did just that. "This is absolutely the best thing I could have wished for this town."

"Now get her home so she and that new baby-to-be can get some rest." And this time it was Ruthie who was chiming in, coming over to say goodbye. She gave me a hug.

"Oh, Ruthie, congratulations!" I said to my friend. Charlie took me by the hand, with EC in his arms, and we walked down the stairs. I got into the car and he into the truck. With EC serenading me all the way home, I focused now on him and Minnow—Cate, Catherine Stephanie O'Connor, whatever we would call her.

All the things that we'd done today—building a new business, forging new partnerships, sharing stories—were for you, my dear children. Improving our lives, moving forward without forgetting what has come before us. There will always be a good book to read and a story to tell. The people of Piney Bluffs had made sure of that.

CHAPTER 39

A s promised, we hosted a family get-together in May on Memorial Day. Aunt Eleanor and I hatched that plan when Daddy was in the hospital. And as she predicted, it was time for strawberry everything. Shortcakes and salads and pies, everything was delicious. Everyone enjoyed themselves so much we decided to make these gatherings a monthly event. That first one had been in the house, but we were rather cramped. We were happy when the summer months let us hold these events outside. But the confines of the porch and one picnic table just begged for a bigger area. Charlie got an idea to make a picnic area near the river. Within eyesight of the house, it was about a three-minute walk to what had become our new favorite place.

In the flattest spot, he'd brought in some crushed stone and built four large family-size picnic tables. We could fit almost thirty people at the tables, and a few more if we squeezed in. Over to the side, he constructed a covered area for our outside kitchen, with space for the grills, a counter to prepare food, and a sink that was supplied by buckets of river water. In the middle he'd built an area for bonfires, ringing it with river stones. He made long benches all around for sitting close enough to make s'mores or roast a hot dog. While the picnics had started out as family events, there were always a few added folks that we called *framily*, our friends that were as dear as family. Not everyone came every time, but we were finding that more often than not, people were making it a point to be here.

Today might be the last outside gathering for the year. It was a beautiful Labor Day. Just the right day for the family picnic. The bright sun was reminiscent of a midsummer day, but by evening's twilight, there would surely be enough of a chill to have a fire.

After the spring opening of the Emporium, I'd settled back into work and had gotten ready for Minnow. Charlie had painted her room a pale pink. His dad and brother brought over the new crib and dresser set, and it couldn't have been more special, knowing that loving hands had crafted it. Jackie and Ginny had thrown a surprise shower for me at the Inn, which filled Minnow's closet and dresser with everything a little baby could need. The closer I was to her birth, the farther away Sophie and my questions about her receded.

Frank called a couple of times to say that he'd found both Martha and Madeline Chumerford. They'd taught in the school systems of New Hampshire for about thirty years. And as far as records indicated, they'd moved away from New Hampshire about ten years ago and now lived together in St. Petersburg, Florida. Nothing too much had been out of the ordinary about them. For all intents and purposes, the two moved to Florida as spinster twins who'd retired from teaching. As he dug deeper, he found that Martha was on record as having given birth to Anne on the same day as Sophie, but no father's name was listed. Both Sophie and Anne carried the last name of Blake, which I was sure was to stop any questions that might have come up.

There was still so much of this story that was unexplained, but both Frank and I agreed that even though I was 100 percent sure that I'd found Sophie, it was, at best, circumstantial. And until someone in Sophie's family asked that first question—"Is this true?"—well, there was nothing that could be done to coerce the truth from whoever in the Chumerford family had been entrusted with the secret.

Minnow, a.k.a. Catherine Stephanie O'Connor, was born on Father's Day, June 21. Until I heard her first cry and could count her fingers and toes, the fears of repercussions from the accident lurked in the back of my mind. But there she was at ten fifteen in the morning. *Perfect.* And while she was a little small, eighteen inches long and weighing in at six pounds and four ounces, everything within her tiny frame had fully developed.

Of course, Charlie and Daddy were ecstatic with the best Father's Day present in the world. They both decreed that even though the dates of Father's Day changed every year, it would always be celebrated on her birthday. EC was curious about his baby sister and would reach out to hold her hand whenever he could. Then there were times when he ignored her completely, wanting only to play with his furry brothers, Mutt and Jeff. Such were the ways of a two-year-old who was now a big brother.

"Ethel, is there room in the fridge for this potato salad, or should I leave it in the cooler?" Ginny called out to me from the porch. She and Daddy were the first to arrive today with her now-famous potato salad. After bringing it to the inaugural picnic, it had been crowned as the only potato salad that would be served.

"Since you're first, there's plenty of room. But keep that cooler handy. I'm sure we'll run out of room," I answered and held the door open for her as she carried in her blue pottery bowl and set it on the counter. The salad was garnished with sliced hard-boiled eggs, sprigs of fresh green parsley, and a sprinkle of paprika.

"It smells great in here. What are you making today?" Ginny asked as she gave me a quick hug. She wore a white corduroy shirt over her navy turtleneck and jeans. She always looked radiant for a woman her age.

"I've got a ham from McCreery's. I thought that would be a nice change. There'll be hot dogs and burgers for the little ones, of course. And speaking of smelling great, what do you have on?" I answered, noticing Ginny's perfume.

"Oh, it's nothing fancy, just my lavender and lemon concoction. I'll bring you some next time." She smiled.

"What're you burning today there, missy?" Daddy asked as he came through the door.

"Burning? Well, if you think it's burnt, then you'll be eating dogs and burgers with the kids," I sassed back to him.

"Now, don't go getting all ruffled. Where's the most beautiful baby in the world?" he asked, redirecting our conversation.

"She's asleep. Now, don't go waking her. I just put her down about a half hour ago so she can have a nap and be a happy little girl for the rest of the afternoon," I scolded him.

"I'll just go take a peek. And if she gets cranky, my belly will always be there to get her back to sleep," he said, paying no mind to my instructions, and off he went up the stairs.

"Daddy!" I called after him.

"Shhhhh," he whispered loud enough for anyone who was within a mile to hear.

"Honestly, Eddy, leave the poor child asleep," Ginny said, hoping he would heed her pleas. "Need any help, Ethel?"

"Sure, there's the supply wagon that could go down, if you'd like," I answered. Charlie had designed a cart to hold paper goods, condiments, and cooking utensils. He'd thought about making storage cabinets at the picnic area but decided that we didn't want to attract any more wildlife with the promise of food. We'd already had something—most likely raccoons—take off with the spatulas that had been left behind from the last picnic.

"You tell that mommy that you're not sleeping." Daddy reappeared with Minnow in his arms. At three months old, she'd completely stolen his heart. She was old enough now to know him and cooed and smiled at his soft kisses.

"Eddy, what did you do?" Ginny gently scolded him. But she went quickly to his side to get in her little pecks on Cate's cheek.

"Smile for Gammie G," Daddy said. We'd started to call Ginny by her new official title of Gammie G, purely on the whim of a child. After EC had spent an afternoon with her and Daddy, they said he'd come up with the name all on his own. I loved how it was the same name I'd given to my grandmother. And so there they were Grampa and Gammie G, happy to have each other and this family.

More cars started to pull up in the driveway. The unofficial start time was one o'clock, and it was now about quarter to. Aunts, uncles, cousins, and family greeted each other as they unloaded their cars with plates and Crock-Pots. The dogs woofed happily and accompanied everyone down to the river. Charlie and his helper, EC, were already placing the logs for the bonfire. EC's job was gathering small sticks for the kindling. That he did with great joy, toddling around the trees and back to his daddy with one stick at a time.

"Let's go down to the river. The ham's ready, and now that the princess is awake, there's no need to stay in the house," I said and grabbed my sweatshirt. We put the food on the cart, bundled up Minnow, and walked down to the river.

"Going to be a little nip in the air later on," Uncle Eubie said. "Good thing that fire will be going." Since Aunt Alice had passed on, Uncle Eubie never missed a picnic. She'd lost her fight with the demons from alcohol during the spring. Their daughter, my cousin Eunice, lived in Portland, where she taught high school science. She loved coming back for the monthly picnics. Plus, it gave her an excuse to check in on her father. Uncle Eubie told Daddy he was doing all right. He said he could finally get a good night's sleep now, knowing that God was watching her.

Ruthie, Caleb, and Sadie had come today as well. Ruthie, as always, bringing wonderful baked treats. Today she'd brought three apple pies, much to the delight of Daddy and Caleb. And Sadie had brought another culinary attempt, this time a fall casserole of butternut squash, onions, and rosemary. She was getting better with the help of Ruthie. Caleb was actually eating some of the casserole today, much to Sadie's delight. The ham was a big hit, with Aunt Ellie calling dibs on the bone. She promised pea soup at her house on Friday for anyone caring to come. Plenty of hands went up as we laughed and enjoyed the warmth of the day and the feeling of being together.

We were about done eating when I noticed that EC's plate was empty and he'd slipped away from the table. I glanced over at Charlie and saw he was by the fire with some of my cousins. I looked at Daddy and Ginny at the other table, and they only had Minnow. EC wasn't with anyone.

"EC?" I called out. Sometimes he liked to hide under the tables or behind trees. As they heard me call out, all conversation stopped. "EC?" I called again, a level of fear rising in my voice. Everyone now got up from the table and fanned out in the low brush near the river. I noticed that the dogs were missing as well. "Mutt, Jeff! Here, boys!" And soon all three names were being called out.

"Ethel, there they are, by the house. And it looks like they found some new friends," Aunt Ellie called out and pointed toward the house.

I looked up and saw EC and the dogs walking toward us escorting two women and a young man. As they got closer, I knew who two of them were and only guessed at the third.

CHAPTER 40

"EC, I was so worried about you!" I said as I walked toward them. He ran to me, and I picked him up in a big hug. The dogs stayed with the trio, wagging their tails and barking as they all made their way to where I was standing.

"Okay, boys, quiet down," I said, and the dogs silenced but continued sniffing the visitors.

"EC, come to Daddy," I heard Charlie call out, and off my son went as I set him on his feet. I turned to make sure he went to Charlie. I saw the questioning looks on the family behind me. Charlie looked at me and nodded that he knew.

"Hi, Sophie, Matt," I said and held out my hand. Both returned the handshake but looked like they were somewhere between running away and crying. "And you are...?"

"I'm Anne, but I think you probably guessed that. Nice to meet you," she said and extended her hand. Anne had long blond hair and sparkling blue eyes. Quite the contrast to her twin sister.

"We shouldn't have come. It looks like we've made a mistake barging in on you," Sophie said and took Matt by the shoulder and started to turn away.

"Nonsense! You'll do no such thing. It's our monthly picnic with family and friends," I said. "Have you eaten? I know you've come a long way. How about it? We've got plenty." And I extended my hand and walked them closer to the tables. Ginny started to clear one side of a table and set it with clean plates and napkins.

"I'm hungry, Mom. Can we stay?" Matt asked, and I could see him surveying the tables, picking out what his teenager's stomach might want if he was allowed to stay.

"Just for a moment, then. I really don't know what to say," Sophie replied. She looked lost as her gaze went from person to person. Each one smiling back at her but wondering who she was.

"Just eat first. Conversation will come," I said softly. As they took their places, bowls of food were passed, encouraged by aunts, cousins, and friends. Charlie started the fire, which helped gather everyone away from our visitors. That left me alone with them. Before any of us could speak, I heard Minnow begin to cry. Daddy had taken her when I'd gone to meet my sisters, but now he brought her back to me.

"I think Minnow needs a bottle, Mommy," Daddy said as he handed my little pink bundle off to me. I took a bottle from her thermal bag, tested it, and started to feed her. As I held her in my arms, I looked up at them.

"Sophie, Anne, Matt, this is Eddy, my father," I said and let them process what that meant. I could see the wheels turning, as even Daddy began to realize who they were to one another. It was Daddy who spoke first.

"Sophie, glad to finally meet you. I guess I'm your stepdad," Daddy said to my surprise. At that invitation, Sophie got up and held out her hand.

"I'm so happy to meet you," she said, and tears began to stream down her cheeks.

"Now, now, no need for waterworks. Don't be too happy. I'm pretty grumpy, from what Ethel tells me. You might not like me," he said, and that brought laughter through the tears.

"Well, then, I'll reserve my opinion for a later time," Sophie said and wiped the tears from her cheeks. "And this is my son, Matt, and my sister, Anne."

"Nice to meet you, sir," Matt said with a grin, and he, too, held out his hand.

"Matt, Anne, welcome to Piney Bluffs," Daddy replied. "Say, Matt, why don't you bring your plate over to the fire and I'll introduce you to everyone? We'll let these three gals get acquainted."

"Mom, can I?" Matt asked, getting up.

"Sure, honey," Sophie said, and we watched as the two went over and spoke to Charlie first. Charlie gave him a pat on the back, and then Matt met the rest of the folks. "She's a beautiful baby. What's her name?"

"If you ask Daddy, it's Minnow, but her name is Catherine Stephanie. Cate for short," I answered and smiled. Almost done with her bottle, Minnow was falling asleep in my arms.

"I have to apologize for the way I spoke to you," Sophie started.

"I would've done the same thing in your circumstance," I offered.

"That day, what you said, I tried to put it out of my mind. But it kept bugging me. A month later, I finally worked up enough courage to call my mom in Florida. I expected that she'd tell me it was nonsense," Sophie began after a sip of ice tea.

"But she didn't?" I asked.

"No, she didn't. I think that was the hardest conversation we've ever had. She'd always told Annie and me that she'd met and fell in love with our dad, Henry, right before he shipped out to join the Navy. He died six months later during the battle of Pearl Harbor. They'd never married, so she kept the name Chumerford, but we went by his name, Blake. And that was all we knew. We were told there were no relatives on Dad's side, that he'd been an only child and his folks had passed away before they'd met. So our uncle George, mom's brother, took the place of our father. He'd graduated from Keene a few years before Mom and Aunt Maddie and then went on to become a lawyer. He never married and lived just a few miles away in Brattleboro, Vermont. We had wonderful times together, just the five of us. It was the most normal life that we could have asked for." She stopped for a moment and looked down at her plate. Anne put her hand on her sister's arm, urging her to go on.

"You have to understand that this has turned our world upside down," Anne said and looked like she might cry.

"I do understand. You see, on my way to finding you, something similar happened to me," I said, and with Cate asleep in my arms, I told them the rest of my story. I touched on some of it the day that I first met Sophie, but now I went into more of the details of the evil of Joseph's father. When I'd finished, Sophie shook her head, tears in her eyes.

"They definitely were incredible women, doing what they had to do to survive. My mother told me how she'd met, oh, this is awkward, your mother?" And she let out a little chuckle.

"Why don't we call them by their first names for a bit? That might help," I offered as all three of us laughed through our tears.

"Okay, that'll work. Martha told me she'd gotten into trouble at one of Madame Sherri's parties," Sophie began again.

"Ah, the infamous madame's parties," I acknowledged.

"Yes, the very one. Martha said he was very handsome, older, and it was the thrill of the moment. And that ended with…," Sophie agreed and continued.

"With me," Anne said and held up her hand. It was then I noticed the mole on inside of her left wrist. There it was, that small mark, further cementing the truth.

"Of course, the pregnancy was in Martha's senior year of high school, and she and Aunt Maddie had already been accepted at Keene. My grandmother and grandfather were very unhappy and disappointed by the situation. But there weren't many solutions in those days. Dr. Heard was well-known, being just the next town over, and so it was decided that Martha would go there. Then after the baby was born, she would come back home and would be cared for by my grandmother while Martha and Maddie went to college. During Martha's stay at Dr. Heard's, she met Stephanie. Martha felt so bad for Stephanie and told our grandmother. After the babies, Anne and I, were born, my grandmother offered to take and raise the both of us as twins. While they all were in college, Stephanie came and stayed with us quite often. We called her Aunt Stef. I have this picture that was taken of the three of us." Sophie took a small black-and-white photo from her jacket pocket. "I have another one almost like this. You can keep it if you want."

"Oh, I'd love to. Are you sure?" I asked and held the picture in my hand. On the back was written, "Aunt Stef and the twins." There was Momma seated with Sophie, and Anne on her lap. While there weren't many pictures of me from when I was younger, the resemblance between Sophie and me was remarkable. Momma looked beautiful, smiling and full of joy. Joy that could only be shared with very few.

"Knowing now that she was my mother, I can certainly see the likeness between us," Sophie said with a sigh, surrendering to the truth of the matter.

"What was she like?" I asked, looking down at the picture and then up at them.

"She was always so sweet to us. Each time, before she left, she'd read us a story. Oh, she would act out the characters' voices. It was almost like a little play for us, and she played all the characters," Anne said, and her face lit up with the remembrances.

"The Christmas before they graduated from college, Aunt Stephanie gave Annie and me a sled. That was the sled that you saw at the yard sale. Which, by the way, I still have. Knowing the story behind it now, why, I'll never part with it," Sophie explained, the mystery of the sled now settled. "Their last summer, before they graduated from Keene, Martha told me that Stephanie had come to see her soon after she'd met your father. She finally met the love of her life. While he was in the service, she came by every once in a while. But she always sent birthday and Christmas presents. Martha and Maddie knew Stephanie was going to get married, but they stayed away from the small ceremony to not cause any questions. They didn't see her much after that. A phone call here and there. Martha told me that she learned about Stephanie's death from your grandmother in Oxford. Martha sent a birthday card to Stephanie, as she did every year. Your grandmother returned the card with a note explaining how Stephanie passed away shortly after you were born."

"But after they graduated from college, it must have been a hard decision as to the 'now what' of the situation," I said, thinking that Momma must have been torn about leaving Sophie behind.

"Martha told me that they all decided it was best to leave Annie and me as we were: fraternal twins with a father who perished in service to his country. It was like a story out of a romance novel," Sophie concluded. "And how could they tear us apart at that point and tell us we weren't sisters?"

"This is so wonderful, to finally understand what happened between Martha and Stephanie," I said. My mind was whirling now with so many more questions of when and who.

"How was Martha after she explained all this? I can't imagine it was easy."

"Mom admitted that she and Aunt Maddie were relieved in a way. They'd always wondered if there would ever come a time when someone might find a reason to ask the question. They knew that Stephanie hadn't told your father. She visited with Mom and Aunt Maddie, her Chums, as she called them. They said Stephanie tried at one point to figure out how to tell your father about what happened to her. She was so afraid of what he would think. He loved her so. She felt he would end up hating her. So she kept quiet. They knew about you, Ethel, but Stephanie begged them not to ever tell us about you. And so they remained out of your life," Anne said, adding some of the details.

"I have to ask, though, How did you ever find us?" Sophie asked.

"It was a mere stroke of luck, if that is even a way to describe it," I answered. "When we found that my mom's house was still almost untouched from when my grandmother had passed, there were a few things that I took from there. A cookbook of hers with two ragged bookmarks. One was the address for Dr. Heard, and the other was a postcard from Westmoreland Depot. Charlie and I went to the doctor's address that day that we came to your café. If the doctor's daughter hadn't become a doctor and decided to stay and practice in a small town, and if she hadn't suggested that we have lunch in the next town over…well, you can see how bizarre it becomes. I know this sounds silly, but I've always thought that there was some unknown force, that little voice inside of me, that's kept pushing me to find you, to figure this whole thing out," I explained.

"Well, I, for one, am glad you kept at it," Anne said. "I know for myself my history is a dead end. Martha told me she was sorry and embarrassed at what she'd done. But she was never sorry that she had me and that she'd kept Sophie and me together." She reached out and held on to Sophie's hand.

"Thank you, Ethel, for that little voice," Sophie said.

"I've found over the past few years that family is defined not as much for the blood that you share as it is for the love that you share. These people that are here today are my family, your family. So how about coming over to the fire and meeting everyone?" I said. With Minnow in my arms, I walked with my two sisters over to the fire. Hugs were exchanged along with introductions to the newest members of the family. We all settled around the fire and told stories and watched the golden embers reflect on the faces of one another. Faces that were happy to have our circle growing yet again.

EPILOGUE

"HEY, LADIES, LOOK THIS WAY," Caleb asked. The flash from the camera left a mark in my vision. "Now, each of you hold up a book. I'm sending these pictures up to the *Herald* for their Sunday magazine section."

"Christmas sales will be through the roof." Sadie gave us each a book as we smiled back at Caleb. We were dressed in red down jackets, black ski pants, and black boots. We stood on the front porch of the Emporium. "How about over here near the snow? Bring the sled too." And we moved from the porch to the garden area for more photos. Charlie had landscaped the left side of the Emporium with a circular path and stone benches to sit on. In the center was a six-foot-high blue spruce now covered with a light dusting of snow. The late-October snowfall provided the perfect backdrop for our picture. We propped the sled up against the tree. Readjusting its big red bow, we stood to the side. It was the perfect shot. Caleb was sending the pictures up to Mike, who, in turn, was putting in the weekend section of the *Herald*.

"Now come on back inside. There's lots of people waiting to get their copy," Sadie said and gathered us like a mother hen.

"I can't believe we did it," Anne said, reading to us as we walked back inside. "Originally published by PB Press, September 1982. Copyright Stephanie L. Koontz, Sophie A. Blake, Anne C. Blake, and Ethel K. O'Connor. All rights reserved. First print edition."

"I know. Pinch me," Sophie agreed. "Ethel, how can we thank you?"

"Don't thank me. This was a group effort," I answered.

"If you hadn't found those few pages…," Anne began.

"And if you hadn't inherited your mother's artistic abilities…," I said, directing my comments to Sophie.

"You two got all the talent in this family," Anne said, feigning sadness.

"Hey, it was your idea to finish the story, Anne," Sophie said, pointing at her sister.

"Come on, ladies, we have a line, and lots of fans have been very patient," Sadie reminded us. We obliged and sat down at the table and happily started to sign the copies of *Sophie's Sled*.

In the year that had passed since Anne and Sophie had come to the picnic, we'd formed an unexplainably deep bond. Outside of the monthly family picnics, we would visit each other at least once more between the outings. During the first visit, I'd shown them Momma's drawings and the story of *Sophie's Sled*.

As we looked at the drawings and read the very simple words, we realized how this was so much more than a child's story. It was our story. From that moment on, we decided that we would finish what Momma had begun. Sophie's style of sketching was almost identical to Momma's, as she recreated the first pictures that Momma had drawn. Anne and I found that we had the flair for telling the story, especially since she was a second-grade teacher. And of course, Caleb and the new PB Press were more than willing to help out fledgling authors such as ourselves.

Anne used her connections with the schoolbook associations to secure the appropriate language configuration for children's books. After that, we were ready to roll. Educators and illustrators alike loved the book and its story about sharing a sled. We'd even been nominated for an award from the Children's Book Council. Russell and Robert were so excited that we'd written the book that they'd reserved a date for us to come to New York for a signing prior to Christmas.

"Don't forget to put your tickets in the jar for your chance to win a new sled," Sadie reminded those who were purchasing a book. We'd bought a new Flexible Flyer to raffle at our signing, with the drawing to be held the week before Christmas. Ruthie had a custom cookie cutter made so she could bake sled-shaped cookies. The children were only too happy to put the red-and-white-iced cookies in their mouths.

After two hours passed, I finally looked up to see the end of the line. Daddy, Ginny, and Charlie stood in there, Daddy with EC and Ginny, Gamma G with Minnow. EC was waving and broke free of Daddy's hand to sit in my lap. He was all too willing to help me sign my name. So we let him and made the book out to Minnow. As the last of customers made their way through the store and congratulated us, it was time for the Emporium to close.

"I am so proud of you, ladies. You sold fifty copies today!" Sadie said excitedly. "Now, we're going to make plans for one signing each Saturday after Thanksgiving until Christmas. How does that sound?"

"Wonderful!" we said in unison and chuckled at Sadie's enthusiasm.

"Make that fifty-one. I want my copy. I need one at my house when these two beautiful bundles come to visit," Ginny said as she beamed at Cate.

"All right, then, fifty-one," Sadie noted. We each signed the book for Ginny. I wrote a little note, thanking her for becoming so special to all of lives.

"Ethel, you and your sisters are very remarkable women. You do understand that, don't you?" Ginny said, as she looked up from reading our notes to her. Her eyes glistened as she spoke.

"And you're pretty remarkable too, for all that you helped make Daddy a very happy man," I answered. "Say, why don't we all go over to the Inn and celebrate?" I asked as I reached out to hold on to each of my sisters' hands.

"Not this time, Ethel. Matt's got a basketball game tonight. He's been bragging to us that he's one of the best guards around. So I've got to be there to make sure he's telling me the truth. I told him we'd be home by five, and it's three now, so we'll have to rush. We'll come back soon, promise," she said and gave me a hug.

"Why don't you and Charlie and the kids come out for our Halloween party next week? Bring Grampa and Gammie too. We have a trick-or-treat dinner and big costume party starting at four at the café. Well, big by our town's standards, anyway." Anne laughed, and she gave me a hug as well and quickly got into the car.

"We'd love to. Bye! Love you!" I said. I picked up my hand and waved as their car sped off.

"Well, you did it," Daddy said as he came to stand beside me. He, Ginny, and Charlie had come out together with the kids, with Ginny on Daddy's arm. I linked arms with Daddy and Charlie and pulled them into me.

"I know people had doubts at times. Even I did. But I know this: I couldn't have done it without the two of you," I replied and squeezed their arms.

"I don't think anyone will ever underestimate you, honey," Charlie said. Minnow let me know she was there with a "Mama." She was all bundled up in his arms with her soft pink snowsuit. I pulled her hood snugly around her face. Her cheeks were rosy, and her smile at that moment was only for me.

"And now all this is finally over. All the questions are answered. No more chasing ghosts, or stories, or any more maybes," Daddy said. "You finally got what you were looking for."

"I know what I found wasn't always what any of us wanted. I guess that's what truth is," I said, almost thinking out loud.

"But look at all the other people you've found along the way. Andre, me, your two sisters. You never would have found us if you hadn't pushed for that truth," Ginny said and hugged Daddy's other arm tighter.

"Now let's go celebrate," Charlie said as he gave me a peck on the cheek.

"Cebrat," EC squealed, trying to imitate his father. We laughed at our little man and put the kids in their car seats.

"We'll see you there. Drive carefully," Daddy said as he and Ginny got into his truck.

As we drove over to the Inn, I thought about what Momma had said in her letter.

> *My wish and dream for you is to be the kind of woman that will make you proud of you. Life changes every day, and you will never be sure of your decisions until the end.*

While I was nowhere near the end of my ever-changing life, I'd reached the end of this story. I was proud of what I'd uncovered. I was proud, too, of the voice I'd given to the many silences in my life and the lives of others. The truth wasn't easy to face for anyone, especially when love was involved. And the truest form of love I'd found through all this was the act of forgiveness.

A TASTE OF PINEY BLUFFS

WHEN I WAS SPEAKING WITH readers at the various venues about the Gone Fishing trilogy, many have requested recipes of some of the delicious foods that were eaten by my characters.

I have included just a few here. Should those whet your appetite for more, please e-mail me at janeherr51@att.net, and I will include them in my blog at See Jane, See Jane Write.

Miss Ruthie's Blueberry Cake

Ingredients
  4 tbsp softened butter
  3/4 cup white sugar
  1 egg
  1 1/2 cup flour
  2 tsp baking powder
  1/2 tsp ground cinnamon
  1/2 tsp salt
  1/2 cup milk
  2 cups fresh blueberries (or thawed and drained)

Topping
  1/2 cup white sugar
  1/3 cup flour
  1/2 tsp ground cinnamon
  1/2 stick butter, cut up

Instructions

Preheat oven to 375 degrees Fahrenheit. Grease and flour and 8-inch square pan. In a large bowl, cream butter and sugar until fluffy. Blend egg into creamed mixture. In another bowl, whisk together flour, salt, and baking powder. Add the flour mixture, alternating with the mild to the sugar mixture. Beat well after each addition. Gently fold the blueberries into the batter. Pour batter into the prepared pan. Blend all topping ingredients together until it resembles a coarse meal. Sprinkle the crumb topping on the batter. Bake at 375 degrees Fahrenheit for 40-45 minutes (until a toothpick comes out clean); may take 50-55 minutes. Don't eat until someone catches a fish!

Miss Ruthie's Fish Sugar Cookies

Ingredients

    1 cup (2 sticks) butter, softened
    3/4 cup sugar
    1 egg
    1/2 tsp vanilla extract
    1/2 tsp almond extract
    2 cups of flour
    1 tsp baking powder
    1/4 tsp salt
    1/4 tsp ground cinnamon

Instructions

Beat the butter and sugar until creamy. Add egg and vanilla. Beat until fluffy. Stir in dry ingredients and mix until well blended. Divide dough in two. Form into balls, wrap in wax or plastic wrap, and flatten. Refrigerate about 2 hours or until firm. Roll out half the dough to 1/4 inch on a floured surface with lightly floured rolling pin. Cut dough with cutter and place on ungreased or parchment-covered cookie sheet. Refrigerate again for 30 minutes. Bake 7-9 minutes in a preheated 350-degree-Fahrenheit oven until lightly browned. Let stand 1 minute. Remove and cool. Mix confectioner's sugar, milk, and blue food coloring to consistency for frosting. Get ready for smile with blue lips!

Ethel's Favorite Almond Crescent Cookies

Ingredients
> 2 cups softened butter
> 1 cup powdered sugar
> 1 cup ground almonds
> 2 tsp almond extract
> 4 cups flour
> 4 oz semi-sweet baking chocolate
> ½ cup finely chopped almonds

Preheat oven to 350 degrees Fahrenheit

Mix butter and sugar until well creamed. Add almond extract. Add flour a little at a time to blend well.

Stir in the ground almonds. Using approximately 2 tablespoons of dough, shape into crescents and place two inches apart on parchment covered cookie sheets. Bake at 350 degrees Fahrenheit 12-15 minutes. Cool on wire racks.

Melt chocolate as directed on the package. Dip one end of the cookie into melted chocolate. Sprinkle dipped end with chopped almonds and place on wax paper to set. Makes approximately 4 dozen cookies.

Enjoy with a coffee and friends!

ABOUT THE AUTHOR

Jane Herr Desrosiers is thrilled to deliver to her readers the final installment in the *Gone Fishing trilogy, Gone Fishing:* The Sinker. The response that she has received from her readers has reinforced her passion for writing. Her sense of humor and plot-turning make this a book series that will make you feel good about life again. From her early days growing up in Canterbury, Connecticut, to her residence now in Baltic, Connecticut, her background provides the souls of her down-home characters. Retired from forty-five years in health-care information and risk management, she enjoys life with her husband, Eddy, and their family and her two cats, Ozzie and Harriet. Jane is also working on other novels, a collection of short stories, and poems. For more information, you can visit www.jane-herrdesrosiers.com as well as Facebook.com/JaneHerrDesrosiers, or e-mail at janeherr51@att.net.

CPSIA information can be obtained
at www.ICGtesting.com
Printed in the USA
FFHW022223100919
54914036-60612FF

9 781633 388741